UINTAH MOUNTAINS

UINTAH

ASHLEY CREEK

ROCK CREEK

NORTH FORK UINTAH RIVER

ASHLEY
VERNAL

Ft. UINTAH

EAST - CENTRAL
UTAH
1889

UINTAH
OR
DUCHESNE RIVER

Ft. ROBEDEAUX

"RHOADES
BURDER"

GREEN RIVER

WHITE RIVER

SHADOW LAKE

WEST FORK ROCK CREEK

MOHAWK LAKE

BETSY LAKE

LODGEPOLE LAKE

WEST GRANDADDY MOUNTAIN

GRANDADDY LAKE

HEART LAKE

HADES PASS

HADES CANYON

EAST GRANDADDY MOUNTAIN

2.

M. Yorgason '84

Brother Brigham's Gold

Christmas
1984

from Zella Kee

Books by Blaine M. Yorgason and/or Brenton G. Yorgason

Brother Brigham's Gold
Ride the Laughing Wind
The Miracle
Chester, I Love You
Double Exposure
Seeker of the Gentle Heart
The Krystal Promise
A Town Called Charity and Other Stories about Decisions
The Bishop's Horse Race
The Courage Covenant (Massacre at Salt Creek)
Windwalker (movie version)
The Windwalker
Others
Charlie's Monument
From First Date to Chosen Mate
Tall Timber (out of print)
Miracles and the Latter-day Saint Teenager (out of print)
*From Two to One**
*From This Day Forth**
Creating a Celestial Marriage (textbook)*
Marriage and Family Stewardships (textbook)*
Caring and Sharing (Blaine M. Yorgason—two taped talks)
Things Most Plain and Precious (Brenton G. Yorgason—two taped talks)
The Joyous Way (Blaine and Brenton Yorgason—two taped talks)
The Miracle (dramatized tape of book)
The Bishop's Horse Race (taped reading of book)

*Coauthored with Wesley R. Burr and Terry R. Baker

Brother Brigham's Gold

Blaine M. Yorgason
Brenton G. Yorgason

Deseret Book Company
Salt Lake City, Utah

ISBN 0-87747-633-0
Library of Congress Catalog Card Number 84-72515

First Printing October 1984

For Mont and Afton Wagstaff and Alta and Huish Yates.
Thank you for your terrific daughters.
We love them dearly.

To my Sweetheart of nyen
sixty one years— years
of love, devotion and tolerance
for which I am thankful.

aryyn.

Contents

Acknowledgments

The authors express appreciation to our rather extended family, who, without much complaint, have allowed us to fictionalize to a remarkable degree the lives of our good ancestors. We also express appreciation to those same ancestors, for we are certain that they would have squirmed with mighty discomfort had they been given any idea of the strange and wild experiences we would one day claim for them.

Introduction

Occasionally it's interesting to consider where our ideas get their birthings and their growth pains. Some, we'll scratch at for months and never even raise a blister, let alone a good story. Others, like this one, spring right out of the woodwork when they're least expected, and they appear full bloom when they do.

Now we don't want you to think that this story is a brand-new idea, for it isn't. We've been pounding folks's eardrums about *Brother Brigham's Gold* for at least four years—ever since we finished *The Bishop's Horse Race*. Furthermore, the story's been in existence for at least two generations before that. We just didn't know of it. But now we do, and we thought it only right to describe the hole in the lattice-work whence it sprang.

Some time ago we went to visit one of our elderly relatives, whose name, for obvious reasons, shall remain anonymous. She lived alone—had done for years—and most folks who knew her considered her somewhat teched. Because of this, we approached her doorstep with great concern.

"You knock," said one of us, being the elder. "Folks say this old bat's crazy."

"No," said the other, having more authority, "she's just eccentric. Besides, she's our relative. You knock!"

"It's your door," responded the first. "I took the last one, two years ago. Remember?"

"That's a joke," the ecclesiastically powerful younger of us replied. "In July this past summer I knocked on a door getting ready for the family reunion. You weren't even there, and I had to carry the burden alone. Now hurry up and knock."

Conversation ended. The elder timidly rapped on the door.

"Well?" someone croaked from within.

"Uh . . . anybody home?" we asked, and gulped, fearing the answer but fairly certain, nevertheless, that someone was.

"Durn fool pesky relatives," the old lady sputtered. "I saw you through the window. 'Course I'm to home. Where else'd I be, stove up as I am? Now come on in and put a cork in the door before the draft shortens my life by another week."

We looked at each other, and one of us, being the elder, graciously opened the door and held it so that the younger could go in first. The younger gave the other a look that would have made an icicle feel feverish, and both of us passed from the view of normal mortality.

Happily, we found our dear old relative relatively pleasant and hardly teched at all, and her disposition was as bright as morning light on a mountain meadow (well, almost that bright, anyway).

"My word and deed," she declared, sizing us up and down through her magnifying glass. "When'd the circus come to town?"

"Circus?" we both responded blankly.

"Must be—I got the two fat men from the sideshow standing in my living room. In fact, I'd lay odds that you two are big enough to be the main attraction. Don't our family ever come small?"

We both attempted a chuckle; she didn't respond, and so without further ado we sat down.

"Have a seat," she said as she watched her sofa sink toward the floor. "Make yourselves to home."

We did, there was a bit more minor chit-chat and good-humored insulting (which seems to be common in our family), and finally the three of us got down to serious visiting. We talked for an hour, sharing tales about the old days when folks still sewed themselves into red long johns come September and when most of them took a bath twice a year whether they needed one or not.

By the end of the hour the old woman was tired and we could see it. As we stood to leave, she raised her hand and stopped us. Then, struggling from her bed and coughing mightily, she hobbled into the only other room in her tiny frame cottage.

"What's going on?" the younger of us whispered.

"Just a minute and I'll pull out my crystal ball and tell you," the elder of us responded. "You've got to learn to be more patient, little brother. These things always come out in the wash."

"That's what I'm afraid of, " the younger of us retorted. "Probably all shrunk up and useless, too!"

As we listened, we heard the sound of metal scraping, the screech of old and rusted hinges, and the rustling of some sort of fabric. Moments later our extremely elderly relative was back with a little bundle of yellowed papers clutched in her hands. These she feebly handed to us.

"You boys want a story?" she asked, grabbing onto the arm of the younger of us for support. "Here's a whole handful of one. For years I've kept it secret, doing my best to protect . . . well, who knows what I've been trying to protect! But it's off my shoulders now, onto yours. I've tried once or twice before to shift it, long ago, but it wouldn't go. Too soon, I figured then. Folks just called me crazy. Thing of it is, they still do."

We each looked at the other, and a look of guilt spread across both our faces. Her insanity seemed to be a familiar topic. Fortunately, our antiquated relative seemed to be unaware of our discomfort, for she kept right on speaking.

"Stories, lies or not, die hard. You boys read them papers and then ask folks hereabout what they think of what you've read; most of 'em will tell you everything there is lies. I don't blame them, neither. It's easier to believe it that way. Trouble is, they're right as skunks smell sweet. What you read, boys, is the sum-total truth of the matter. Period.

"I'm thankful that's over with," she concluded as she sank exhausted to her bed. "Fool tale's off my shoulders for good. Now I can do what I been aching to do for some time."

"What's that?"

"Boys, I'm aimin' to pass away!"

"No," the elder of us argued. "You've got too much spunk in you to die."

"I always thought so myownself," she mused. "But I can feel the cold in my bones, just like that old buzzard who was your great-grandpa did before he died. Now take this story and do something with it."

We looked again at each other, not sure whether to be grateful or not for this small yellowed-paper favor.

"Uh . . ." the oldest of us said, hesitating, "we don't normally write other folks's stories. We've got too many of our own to do, and—"

"Just like your great-grandpa, the old goat. You want to be coaxed. I declare, don't families *ever* change?"

"Coaxing's got nothing to do with it," the younger of us retorted. "It's just that because of contracts and projects and syndications, the parameters of our available time frame and the marketability of certain projects have been narrowed somewhat, and would possibly indicate to the more astute observer—"

"No change so's a body would notice," the old woman interrupted, shaking her head. Then, looking at the elder of us, she asked, "Does this flannel-mouth always rattle on like that?"

"Only at certain altitudes," the elder of us responded, giving the younger of us a narrow look, "and when the moon is right. Still, we really shouldn't take these—"

"All right! All right! Two against one ain't fair, but you win! I'll coax. Here, rattle-mouth, take this."

Finally silent, the younger of us reached out and took from the old woman's two quivering hands a heavy, fist-sized rock. "Pyrite," he said after a brief examination, handing the rock to the elder of us. "Lots of iron pyrite."

"Har-de-har-har," the old woman cackled. "I take it all back. Families *do* change. They get dumber. That old crow-bait of a great-grandpa of yours would never have made that mistake. Nor would've your Grandpa Hyrum, who was given that rock by Tabby himself. That there's gold, boys, the genuine article."

Now both of us stared at the bright glint of the metal in the stone.

"But . . . but how . . . where . . . why . . ."

"The answers are in them papers, you chuckle-headed examples of poor posterity. Them and that chunk of gold are the entire shooting match, and they go together. Now, do you want them or not?"

Well, we looked at each other, and it was obvious to us that we were both wavering. The old woman saw that, and being altogether smarter than we'd given her credit for, she grinned and spoke again, and, dagnab it, what she said clinched it for us.

"Boys," she concluded, "I'd like you to write that account out as a book. 'Course I know you ain't the *best* writers around, but right now you're the *onliest* ones this family has. So get after it and do what you can. If the stars are lined right, if you're luckier'n our family normally is, and if the good Lord blesses you more'n He probably ought to, you might get it done. I hope you do, for your Grandpa Hyrum surely wanted it told.

"Now run along before I have to fix you dinner. You look as gaunted up as two stuffed turkeys, and I don't even have enough food around here to keep the mice happy."

Well, we grinned, thanked her for a wonderful time, said good-bye, and, as per her instructions, ran along with her papers. What follows, for what it is worth, is the story those papers contained.

And the fist-sized rock of gold? Well, forget we even mentioned that. We won't guarantee that it even existed, and besides, it wasn't worth much anyway.

1

September 1884

Confluence of Red
and Currant Creeks,
Utah Territory

Nervously Enock Rhoades stared out into the darkness. He had heard something—he *knew* he had heard some sort of movement. The old tent fluttered in the night wind, the sighing in the pines grew momentarily louder, and painfully he edged himself closer to the door-flaps.

Above him the stars hung like lanterns in the blackness, giving very little light. Down near Currant Creek a night bird called, and from above him on the mountain a coyote sent out an exploratory cry, a lonely wail that served only to emphasize the silence of the mountain night. Enock Rhoades shivered and wished that he had a fire, thought for a moment, and then wished even more that he had never been so foolish as to come alone after the gold.

Gold. Even the thought of it made men do crazy things. And the sight of it, especially in great quantities that were simply there for the taking, well, life itself seemed to mean nothing in the face of such treasure.

Enock thought of himself then, thought of his brother Caleb's reluctance to reveal the location of the gold, thought of his own stubborn insistence, and then wished again that he had never come. It had surely been a crazy thing to do.

The arrow wounds in his side and left leg pained fearfully, he was dizzy and weak from the loss of blood, and deep within him was the fear that he would never make it home alive.

He worried about that, and worse, he worried about the girl who waited for his return, the girl he intended to take to the temple and marry. That was why he had come alone; that was why he had insisted, even when Caleb had pled otherwise, that he be told the location of the gold. With a good poke of that gold, he and she would have the funds to begin a fine life together.

Of course there was also the meetinghouse that needed funding, and with Caleb laid up with a bad leg, he'd been able to use what the Church needed as leverage. But deep down, Enock knew, the real reason why he had wanted to come had been his intense desire to see the gold and to put a poke of it away for himself and his sweetheart.

Well, at least he had found the gold and had mined a small amount, and the leather bag was securely hidden for when he would have the strength to return for it. Only—

Again the wind picked up, two pines rubbed together with a wild screeching, and Enock stared fearfully out into the darkness. Were they there? Had the Utes, who for some reason considered *all* the gold in the Uintahs sacred, tracked him down? Somehow they had trailed him to the mine, and when he had come out with his small poke, well—

As he stared into the constantly moving night, doing his best to keep away the blackness of unconsciousness, Enock thought again of the piece of gold ore he had found in the Narrows the day before and of the excitement he had felt. Pushing forward as Caleb had directed, he had followed Currant Creek to its junction with Red Ledge Creek. He had then pushed his animals up the steep slope, over the ridge, and down Red Ledge Hollow and into Bear Hole Hollow. And there, just as Caleb had described, was the hidden entrance to the old Spanish mine.

As he anxiously prepared to light the candle, he had suddenly been gripped with fear. What if there was nothing there? What if, after all his efforts, this was simply a hole in the rock? No, it couldn't be! Not after what Caleb had told him.

Shaking uncontrollably, he had lifted the stub of candle into the air, stepped forward, and stopped dead, thunderstruck!

He had not been able to breathe! He had not even been able to think. The enormity, the magnitude, of what he had beheld had been beyond his ability to comprehend. Everywhere, above him, beside him, beneath him, gold had glinted in the flickering candlelight.

Slowly he had let out his breath and had stepped forward, reaching out to feel the dancing rock. As Caleb had promised, the basic formation was quartz, rotten and soft, and everywhere it was laced, honeycombed, Caleb had called it, with wire gold. The yellow metal was totally pure, and the long strands were frequently as thick as an eighth of an inch.

With prying fingers he had pulled a chunk of rock loose from the wall. Holding the candle close he had examined it, his heart racing faster. It was even more than Caleb had said!

Setting the candle down, he had feverishly torn the rotten quartz apart, picking out the strips and strands of gold as he did so. Quickly he had pulled another chunk of ore from the tunnel wall, broken it down, and had piled more gold onto his small but growing mound.

For an hour Enock had worked without stopping, burning through three candles, ignoring the dripping sweat that soaked his shirt and blinded his eyes. He had never *seen* so much wealth! Never in all his twenty-four years had he even imagined such a thing. Of course, he had known about the mines, both from Caleb and from his father, John, but still, it was so much more than words could possibly convey.

Enock had paused then and wiped his brow, his eyes never leaving the small pile of gold he had accumulated. He *had* to stop for a few moments. He needed water, and he needed as well the equipment that was on his mules. Then he could begin mining in earnest.

From his pocket he had withdrawn a small leather pouch, upon which he had branded his initials. Opening it, he had stuffed his mound of gold inside. A thousand dollars, he had thought as he had lifted the bag. There had to be at least a thousand dollars worth of gold in his poke!

Stuffing the bag beneath his vest, Enock had turned and made his way toward the entrance of the mine. There had been several hours of daylight left, and in that time he had felt he could fill the packs of both mules quite easily. That would have left him free to travel at night, and the Indians would never even have known he had been there.

At the entrance, he had paused to allow his eyes to adjust to the brightness of the September day. His animals were down the slope in a small copse of aspen, and within minutes he had descended to them.

"Well, gals," he had said quietly as he had carefully packed his poke of gold into his saddlebags, "we've done'er. 'Course you'll have a heavy load going down through Park City and into Salt Lake, but I'll make it worth your trouble, and that's a promise.

"Now stand easy, girl, while I get this cinch loosened. I don't . . ."

Suddenly he had spun around, fear gripping him tightly. He had heard something, some sound that had been foreign to the noisy still-

ness of the mountain. From the shade of the aspens he had stared outward, examining everything—every rock, every clump of brush. But
there had been nothing, nothing but the intense stillness of the afternoon.

Stillness . . .

There had been no birds singing! The squirrel down the slope had
stopped chattering, and Enock had chilled with the knowledge that he
was being watched! Caleb had warned him of the Indians. Still, until
that moment Enock had felt confident he could come and go without
detection. At that moment, however, he had wondered if they had
somehow discovered him, and—

Whoosh!

Spinning to the sound, he had been knocked forward by the shock
of the arrow, which had struck him low in his side. Strangely, there
had been no immediate sensation of pain, but the stickiness of blood
had been instant, and Enock had known he had been hard hit.

Dragging himself around, he had pulled the old Walker Colt from
his pocket, aimed at a likely clump of brush, and fired.

Nothing had happened, but as the echoes had bounced back and
forth among the peaks, two more arrows had whispered their fearful
way through the aspen grove. Tugging at the shaft buried in his side,
Enock had jerked it free. Then, staggering, he had freed the two jennies and had dragged himself into the saddle of his horse.

With a wild shout, he had plunged out of the aspen and up along
his back trail. Another arrow had buried itself in his thigh as he urged
the horse forward, and a third had barely missed his head as it whistled angrily past. Then he had been free, the horse had been running
full out, and Enock, the pain suddenly hitting him, had grabbed hold
of his saddle horn, started to tie his wrist to it, blindly given the horse
its head, and known no more.

It had been late afternoon of what he thought was the next day
when Enock had again opened his eyes, and immediately he had
known where he was. Off to the south had loomed Currant Creek
Mountain, and so he had not been far from the confluence of Currant
and Red Creeks. That had startled him for he had come much farther
than he had expected. Still, it would be at least a two-day ride before
he could get back to Caleb, and he was in no condition to travel.

He had also been startled by something else, something that
might very well mean his escape could be successful.

His mules, and thus his supplies, had followed him!

Grimacing with pain, Enock Rhoades had rolled over and stared

upward. Food and shelter had been taken care of, but he also had
another problem. What if the Indians had followed his two jennies?

Quietly he had called his horse, thankful that he had trained it to
come in that manner. When it did, he had taken up the lead ropes of
the jennies, dragged himself up to the saddle, and tried to mount.

He had not been able to do it, but he had managed, finally, to drag
himself up and drape his body over the horse like a corpse. Calling
quietly to the jennies, he had urged his horse forward, and with the
pack animals trailing behind, he had ridden the horse down into the
water.

Until long after dark he had let the horse carry him, leading the
mules, and by then he had been certain that he was nearly dead. His
side felt as though it were about to burst open, and he had known he
had to stop. Reaching out he had caught the reins and pulled his horse
off onto the north bank of the stream.

In the starlight he had realized that he was on a large horsehoe
bend in the creek, and once again he had recognized the location.

Without hesitation he had urged the horse up the steep bank,
across a grassy plain that was narrow and flat, and up into more
timber. For perhaps thirty yards the horse had climbed, and suddenly
he had come out in a small swale, out of which a tiny spring flowed.
The swale was surrounded by timber, plenty of dry wood was close,
and Enock Rhoades had felt certain that here he would be safe.

With difficulty he had dragged himself from the saddle, fallen,
and lain still, trying to stop his head from swirling. At last, with
energy he dragged forth from who knew where, he had removed the
tent from the mule and had set it up. He had thought of a fire and had
not lit one because he had been so tired. He had, however, pulled out
his bedroll, and that, finally, along with his saddlebags, he had worried into the tent.

At last, exhausted, he had dragged himself onto the bedroll and
closed his eyes, ready to . . .

The gold!

Amazed that he had not thought of it already, Enock had pushed
his hand into the saddlebags. It had been there, still in the little
leather bag where he had placed it. At least, he had thought, the trip
had not been totally useless. At least there was still the gold for his
wedding.

Suddenly he had had an idea. He could rest in this place. Here he
would be safe from everyone but the Indians. And they would likely
come. He knew that.

Only they would be after a man who had taken gold from their lands. If he had no gold, then there would be no reason for them to be after him. He would simply be an innocent passer-by, and he would prove it by letting them search his camp. Of course, there were his wounds, but if he told them he had fallen from his horse and had been stabbed by dead tree limbs during his fall, that would explain everything.

It had all seemed so simple, so foolproof. Only—

In the darkness Enock had pushed the gold back inside his shirt and vest, dragged himself from the tent, looked around, finally seen a fallen tree, and crawled toward it. If it was old and rotted, then perhaps it would provide what he needed.

There was another gust of wind, the two pines screeched together again, and Enock Rhoades gasped with fear and pain. His eyes wide, he stared into the darkness, his Walker Colt at the ready. But there was nothing, nothing but the wind and the grass and the trees and the stars. Slowly he lowered the huge pistol, dropped his head onto his arms to try and stop the dizziness, and suddenly, inches from his head, a tiny twig snapped.

With his breath stopped and his eyes wide with a terrible understanding, Enock Rhoades jerked his head erect, stared into the darkness, saw that the stars before him had vanished, realized that something—no, *someone* very tall—was blocking his view, and with desperate energy he leaped to his feet.

Somehow he had dropped the Big Walker Colt, but his knife was close at hand, and so with one sweeping motion he brought it forward, felt it strike flesh and bone, realized that he was too high, and realized also that he could do nothing else.

For a fraction of an instant time held still while he thought of his death and sorrowed over it and over his loss of the girl who waited. Then, in that slow way that is sometimes given to man as the end appears, he saw a sudden blinding explosion that seemed to fill all the earth with a numbing power. There were flashes of light then, no pain, but lights and a tremendous rushing noise as he was catapulted up and backward through the darkness of a tunnel. Then he saw a light, distant yet bright, and he was moving toward it and suddenly his soul felt peace. Slowly his eyes glazed over, and that light was the last thing the mortal Enock Rhoades ever saw.

The Utes had come again.

2

June 1889

Strawberry Flats,
Utah Territory

When I squatted across the fire from Zenos Hill that morning, gold was the furthest thing from my mind. It was frosty cold despite the month, our breath hung misty in the air, and I wanted to get warm. Besides that, the mules had strayed.

"They're plumb gone," I said disgustedly as I shifted to get out of the smoke from the sagebrush fire.

"Umph," grunted Zene, exhibiting his usual way with words. Zene was about the darkest-skinned Lamanitish Indian Mormon I'd ever seen. He'd been baptized at age eight and promised that he'd become fair and delightsome, but it must've taken only on the inside. Outside he was still regular dark Indian brown.

Zene was twice my age or thereabouts, and the way I heard it, Zene's Mormon pa and his wife had come upon Zene down by Ephraim when he was real young. Zene's Indian ma had died, his Indian pa was away on a hunt, Zene had been crying, and the tribe of Utes, not liking all that noise, had tied him to a tree, piled brush about him, and set it on fire. That's when the Hills rattled up in their wagon.

Well, the fire was scattered pronto, and when the deal was done, Old Man Hill had bought that little Indian kid for something like an old cow, a broken pistol, and two bags of flour. The Hills adopted Zene as one of their own, and he was raised pure white and pure Mormon. And he was, too, on the inside. But like I said, he could mask it pretty easily with his outside, and ofttimes he seemed to take real delight in doing so, that morning being a prime example.

"You reckon them mules went back to Aspen Wells?" I asked, still pushing to get a discussion going.

"Umph," he grunted again, and I could see I wasn't getting much enlightenment. Talking things over with Zene was pretty much like having a conversation with myself. Still, I liked Zene, I liked him a lot. I reckon that was because I knew he liked me. He never bothered me about my gimped-up foot, he never teased me about Ida Mae Sorenson, and he never took pity on me, like some folks did. He treated me like a regular fellow, made me work hard as he did, and I appreciated that a whole lot.

Zene had married a white girl named Amelia Hicks, who folks said was a mighty fine woman, and it seemed like he and she were set on raising a whole tribe of their own. They had six little boys, whose names made a rhyme when they were said fast: Nick, Nuck, and Chuck; Daver, Deve, and Dal. They also had two fine-looking little girls, but I never could tie no rhymes to them, so I don't remember only the name of one, which was Emma.

"I reckon one of us'll have to go back for those mules," I ventured, hoping he'd send me. We were both herding sheep for old Andrew Aagard, but Zene was the herder and I was just the camp tender. Still, with Pa in prison for polygamy, our family had fallen on some hard times. All of us kids had dropped out of school to go to work, and all of us were thankful for anything we could get. That meant Lyman and Jim were out on the west desert, Johnny had found work herding horses for Scott Cook down in the San Rafael area along the Green River, and Ernest, who was still too young to get a real job, was being paid a few pennies a day to read to Deaf Man Hibbard, down in Aspen Wells, which folks were now calling Fountain Green. I reckon I should call it that myownself, the town, I mean, so from here on I will. Anyway, my sisters Mary, Elinor, and Laura had even found work, either working at the Co-op, clerking for A. E. Christensen at his general store, or working as hired girls for some of the richer folks up north in Provo. All the little kids, of course, were still at home.

And, naturally, working kids also included me being chief cook and bottle washer to a Mormon Indian sheepherder, which was awful unlikely employment, and not too gainful either, for that matter.

I'll admit, though, that I really liked the job. In some ways, of course, it was boring. I mean, watching those woollies wrap themselves around acres of high-country grass was about as exciting as watching the first 4,300 heats of the national desert tortoise races, out to Ely, Nevada. On the other hand, that very propensity of the sheep gave me a great deal of free time, and I used every minute of it that I could.

My Pa was an educated man, though unschooled as far as formal education went. Still, he had a mind that was respected by folks far and near. He was intelligent and observant and was quick to lend either a strong back or his amazing wisdom to whomever might be in need, and I longed to be as wise and to be thought of with the same respect.

"The best of all things is to learn," Pa had said to me one day as we rode toward his dairy in the Big Meadow down south of Fountain Green. "Money can be lost or stolen, health or strength may fail, but what you have committed to your mind is yours forever."

I believed that, for I had seen how he had grown, and I could see within myself the beginnings of such a change as well. So I was doing all I could to learn more. I was on my third reading of the *Book of Mormon,* my second reading of Frederick Farrar's *The Life of Christ,* and my first reading of the writings of Tacitus and Blackstone's *Laws,* and I couldn't wait for a chance to get back to Fountain Green and pick up some new books. Then, too, there were my family and Ida Mae Sorenson, and I was tolerable anxious to see them as well.

Trouble was, Zene knew that, and he enjoyed watching me squirm.

"Well," I ventured, stretching up to my feet and looking down across the sagebrush-covered flat toward the Strawberry River, "reckon I'd best get moving, providing I aim to catch those ornery mules this side of Fountain Green. Hope that's the way they went. I'm not hankering to tangle with your people over on the reservation. Sure as bear sign smells bad, that's the truth."

Zene looked up at me with an expression I'd never seen before, and right off I knew I'd said something wrong.

"My people are Mormon," Zene stated softly, in one of the longest speeches I'd ever heard him make. "But those are Ute mules, and that's where they'll be."

"Zene, you're an Indian and you know it," I stated, not even thinking about what he'd said concerning the mules. "You'd ought to own up to it and be proud of it."

Zene looked at me again, his black eyes like burning coals.

"How'd the marshals catch your pa?"

"What?"

"The marshals," he repeated. "Tell me how they caught your pa."

Slowly I shifted until I was out of the smoke. "What for?"

Zene looked up from his steaming cup of scorched water and glared at me. "Mules'n polygamists are about alike," he muttered. "Least I'd bet they are. You want to find those mules, then talk."

I'd never seen Zene look as he did then, nor had I ever heard his voice go so low and gravelly. "Shucks," I said nervously as I hunkered back down, "I hate to do that. Too embarrassing."

"Umph," Zene grunted unsympathetically.

"He . . . he's not only my pa, Zene, but he's the bishop, and that office ought to be respected. I hate to drag his name around any more'n I have to."

Zene took a sip from his tin cup in response. Finally, seeing he wasn't going to let up, I plunged ahead.

"Those dirty marshals took advantage of him!" I growled angrily. "Dressed up as women, they did. Clawson and that other one from up to Salt Lake—Dyer, I think. How Pa ever thought Old Clawson looked feminine beats me, but he did.

"The marshals wave to him down in town, he waves back, grins with all his masculine charm before those genuine beauties, and sashays right on over to make their acquaintance.

"Well, simple as that, they had him. Had a regular arsenal hidden up under their skirts. They threw down on Pa, he jerked his hands up into the air mighty pronto, and those two legal Lily Langtrees had the last horselaugh, I'll tell you that.

"First we knowed of it was when Old Hans Tinker brought Ma the word. The marshals were already on their way to Provo by then. Pa's still in jail, too. Him and his third wife and their new baby, who they're going to use as witnesses against him. And they'll all three rot there unless one of us can spring Pa's bail, which doesn't look any too likely.

"Now, what's all that got to do with mules?"

"Mules and cohabs," Zene repeated. "Predictable as thunder follows lightning."

"What's that mean?"

"Cohabs are drawn to women," Zene explained, waxing truly eloquent, "and mules are drawn to home."

Well, I shifted to get out of the smoke again and took another long look at the Indian herder.

"That's what I said," I declared. "So if you've chomped this around long enough, then I'll be on my way back toward Fountain Green after them—"

"Ute mules aren't home in Fountain Green."

"Those are. They're Old Man Aagard's and his home is—"

"Brother Aagard bought them from the Utes out in the Basin," Zene declared. "Home's there."

The Basin, I thought. *That's the reservation. I wouldn't go out there for—*

"You'd better hurry," Zene said quietly. "Currant Creek, Red Creek, somewhere along there you'll find the mules."

"Now see here," I declared. "I don't care if you are the herder. I ain't going onto that reservation. Right now them Utes are thicker'n bottle flies at a buffalo shoot, and the way the government's been running 'em around with new reservation boundaries every month and such truck as that, they're a mite stirred up, too. The way I've heard it, they've got every trail into that reservation sealed off tighter'n a sun-shrunk cowhide. I heard that just last month they found two arrow-shot fellers up there, so full of feathers they'd have flown, happen they'd been launched.

"No sir, Mr. Hill, you're the Lamanite amongst us, not me. I'll leave traveling among your heathen kinfolk to you."

Zene looked up at me, his dark eyes burning, took a last gulp from his tin cup, and rose fluidlike to his feet.

"Maybeso whiteskinned pup wantum smashed head," he said quietly, slipping suddenly into the Indian lingo used by all the Utes from out on the reservation.

I stared at him, surprised. From him I'd never heard that kind of talk, and abruptly it dawned on me that I'd offended him, twice.

"Zene," I said, "I'm sorry. I—"

"Heap long day," he grunted. "White pup go, findum mules all same don't. Come back withoutum maybeso getum bashed head anyway. Me decide later. White pup all the same dumb bishop. Predictable. Like mules."

Scornfully he turned away, and I stared after him wondering if murdering an Indian came under the same statute as doing-in a regular human being. Probably get me six months, I decided, if I did it the cold-blooded way I had in mind. Accordingly I dropped the plan and went to saddle the swaybacked, crow-bait cayuse Old Man Aagard had given me for a horse.

That done, I swung up and pulled the animal around so I could see Zene. He was intently studying the far horizon, so I angrily pounded my spurs into the horse, and me and that animal took off for the eastern borders of the land of the Lamanites.

And I'll say this much more, and then be done with it. I decided that morning that there's nothing so useless as a splendid education squandered on a dumb-tongue Indian sheepherder who is stupid enough to go back to being something he never even was! Unless it was, as the old saying went, teats on a boar pig. Wings on a garden mole. Buttons on a pocket gopher. Or maybe, I thought grinning, hobbles on a dead horse.

No sir, as far as I was concerned, Mr. Zenos Hill could take a long flying leap, and I'd not care at all. I was done with being his tender, for good! I'd get those mules, and then I'd be gone.

For an hour I rode as hard as I could, and that animal was about the roughest running cayuse I ever sat astride. It was gaited like a hybrid buffalo and was thinner than the running gears of a desert grasshopper. Every time its hooves plunked down it felt like my eyeballs had impaled themselves on the roots of my upper molars and my vertebrae had all compressed down toward the saddle. I'll bet I lost a good four inches in height during that hour. It was, in short, one rough ride.

Blast! Why couldn't Old Man Aagard at least give me a decent horse? It wasn't because he was broke, I knew that. I'd once heard Pa tell Ma that before Mr. Aagard came over from the Old Country, he'd talked some elderly sister into sewing his underwear full of five- and ten-dollar gold pieces. Once here he'd played broke and picked up houses and stock and things for a nickle and a song. It wasn't long before he had played himself into being one of the wealthiest men in the county.

In spite of all that wealth, I had the worst horse in maybe *three* counties to ride, and it made me mad. I'd spoken to him about it once, asking for a better mount, but he'd yelped like a young stud whickering over a bellyful of sour oats, so I dropped it and only cussed him every time I climbed aboard the quarterdeck of that mangy creature.

Of course, I was in a pretty ornery mood that morning, I'll admit it, and that made things seem worse. Normally I don't begrudge folks their good fortune, for I've had considerable of my own—not money-wise, but good fortune, nevertheless. In fact, Pa's arrest was the first setback any of us Soderbergs had had since the great horse race of the year before. I'd been getting on fine with Ida Mae, I hadn't worried any more than a little about being crippled, and things just seemed to be going good. I'd even got the job tending camp for Zene when I needed it.

Still, now I was headed smack into the middle of the Ute reservation, and deep down I had a bad feeling about it. In fact, the farther I rode the worse it got, and it come to me that I was heading for a setback like nothing since old Brother Brigham's seagulls had sailed into those anti-Mormon crickets back in '48.

All morning I rode, following the Strawberry eastward until I came to Stinking Springs. From there I cut northeast up Pine Hollow, crossed the top, and worked my way down Wildcat and into Deep Creek Canyon, still going east. That country across the top was rough and rumpled as a messed bed. It was cut by a thousand nameless draws, crossed by another unmapped thousand gulches and arroyos. And up there it was dry. It was scant of water as whiskey was scarce at a Shouting Baptist prayer meeting. It was badlands, getting worse. And still I rode on, following those mules and cussing them every inch of the way.

Course, it was my fault they were gone, for I'd staked them out the night before and had been too lazy to put the hobbles on. I'd learn, but often that day I found myself wondering when. Besides, who'd ever have thought those two stubborn critters'd make such long-legged tracks for their reservation home?

I was feeling bad, too, about what I'd said to Zene. He was a good man, and one of the best friends I had in all the world. Being away from Ma and my little sisters and having my pa in jail and my brothers scattered over half of creation was bad enough, but now I'd gone and alienated myself from Zene as well, and I truly did feel lonely.

What it came down to, I suppose, is that I was out and out homesick. I truly did miss my family. Pa says that a child is given a family as a point of reference. What I think he means is that this is an awful big world, filled with all sorts of folks with problems. It's pretty difficult trusting *any* of them completely. With a family, however, it ought to be different. In a family everybody loves everybody, so everybody can be completely trusted. When a kid grows up in a good family, no matter how bad his troubles are, he can always turn back to his family for love and trust. That's what things are like in my family, and that's what Pa means by a point of reference.

For instance, my family is tolerably large and, what with Pa's three wives and three houses, it is sort of spread out. Still, us youngsters, no matter which of Pa's wives is our mother, all call each other brother or sister, and the other mothers are simply Aunt so-and-so. We think of each other as a family, too. If one has a problem and the others hear about it, why, we all just naturally come a-running.

Pa says the bunch of us are especially handy to him. If one of us sees or hears that the federal marshals are making a raid to catch themselves a certain plurally married bishop (which same plural marriage became truly illegal two years ago when Congress stuck their pious and interfering noses into the practice of religion and passed the infamous Edmunds-Tucker Act), why then Pa just naturally gets a prompt and fair warning that the minions of the law are coming. With that in mind, it's easy to see why Pa makes the unlikely brag that the more wives and children he has, the safer from the marshals he is.

So as a family we're close, mighty close. It gives a body a good feeling just knowing there are a few folks out there who love him and can be depended upon. As far as I've been able to tell, there isn't any trouble too big that a few of us Soderbergs can't handle it.

That's why I was crossing that mountain in pursuit of Andrew Aagard's mules, that's why my brothers and sisters had all gone to work, and it was also why I was feeling so lonesome and homesick. I surely did miss that bunch of Soderbergs who were my family, and I could see no end to my separation from them.

It was coming onto dark when I finally spotted our pack animals. They were both grazing peacefully on some lush grass down on what I figured to be Currant Creek. I rode up slow-like, expecting trouble and wishing my younger brother Ernest was with me, for he's better at sneaking up on ornery critters than any other two-legged human being I've ever met. He is also pretty good at imitating animal sounds; sometimes he even does better than the animals themselves. Fact is, under certain conditions I can sound like a few critters my-ownself. However, when it comes down to scary or tight situations, Ernest either has more innards than a cornered bobcat or he isn't quite bright. Whichever, he's a handy kid to have around, and I suppose that of all my brothers, it was Ernest and his sunny-bright disposition that I missed the most.

Anyway, I rode carefully up to those mules expecting all sorts of trouble, and I was almost mad when they acted joyful about seeing me.

"Dad-gum it," I growled as I threw my rope over the head of the one I called Lizzard on account of her being so sneaky-like and mean-quick about things, "why didn't you miss me at six-thirty this morning instead of now? And you, Aristotle, why'd you have to follow this slimy critter Lizzard. I've told you plenty how she'd just get you in trouble. Now see, I was right. It's coming on dark, and here we are smack-dab in the middle of the reservation. I'm nervous, and you two ought to be. I hear tell Indians love mule meat more than about anything else."

Well, I snubbed them up and reined around to start back, and suddenly I had this powerful feeling I was being watched. The skin on the back of my neck started crawling, my hair stood straight up, and, I'll tell you, I was worried as a snow-bound buffalo bull in wolf country.

Up on the ridge a coyote yipped at the first stars, and a bat dove through the twilight above me after some fleeing insect. Somewhere down the creek a nighthawk called out soft and lonely-like, and of a sudden I knew I wasn't going back across that mountain, not that night, at least. With that haunt feeling upon me, the odds against me making it safe were about equal to the odds against that Lizzard-mule of mine being agreeable. Or an old maid showing good sense in the company of a sweet-talking man. Blast! The way I was feeling, the whole thing could get skimpier than tracking bees in a blizzard.

"Come on, hoss," I whispered, and even my whisper cracked, I was so nervous. "Let's g-get up into them trees and hole up till daylight."

Without a murmur those animals agreed, and quick as that we were skedaddling up that slope and into the black of the pines. I gave the swaybacked cayuse its head then, hoping it could see better than me, and we rode real quiet for the next five minutes.

Then Lizzard-mule got contrary and started pulling off to the right. I hauled on her lead rope to pull her back, she set her haunches, I yanked the rope hard, she opened her mouth to bray, I kicked her muzzle hard with my boot, she jumped away and pulled harder and set herself to bray again, and finally I gave in. She wanted so bad to go that way, fine! We'd all go.

And we did. For maybe thirty feet. The ground dropped away and sudden-like we were in a deep swale with trees rising black all around us and new grass growing belly-deep to the horses. And after we'd stopped and it got quiet, there was even the laughter of a small stream that I later discovered was a spring.

"Lizzard-mule," I said softly as I looked around, "I've been misjudging you right along, and here-and-now I apologize. This is about as fine a camping site as I ever saw. You've sure enough led us home for the night."

Moments later I had the saddle and the other gear stripped from my old horse, and it and the two mules were all staked out proper. I had hobbles on all of them, too, trail hobbles that I rigged on the spot. I may learn slow, but I do learn.

Dragging the saddle with me, I walked over to one side of the tiny swale, and there, where I somehow sensed it would be, was a pile of rocks set perfect for hiding a fire from anyone farther away than a few feet. Well, that set my spine to chilling again, for there was no way I could have known about those rocks, and I stood for a long time staring out into the darkness, wondering what it was I was feeling. My craw was so shrunk up it wouldn't chamber a piece of pea gravel, and I felt about as yellow as mustard without the bite.

Trouble was, all three of my critters were grazing real peaceful, and I knew that their senses of approaching trouble were to be trusted far more than my own. Despite I was feeling chousy as a screw-worm steer about whatever it was I felt was watching me, I knew I should trust my animals. So, setting my saddle down and dropping myself onto it, I did.

It was the fire, though, that finally tied it all together. Anyone who has ever been out alone in the far-up hills at night will say there isn't anything friendlier'n the bright flames of a fire. There they are, licking hungrily at anything a body can toss into them and lighting up a few feet of the world at the same time, making at least that little area of light civilized again, making it into a place where a man can relax and feel secure. A fire's a wondrous thing, I'll say that.

Anyway, I'd put together a tiny hatful of one there in those rocks, had water heating up, had checked the animals, and was out searching for a little more wood when I found what I now figure was my first clue. I reached for a wide piece of dead, white wood, picked it up, and realized I was holding the skull of an animal, a mule, I figured. I hauled it back to the fire, and sudden my skin started in to prickling again. For there, smack in the forehead of that poor critter, was a bullet hole that was at least fifty caliber wide.

Carefully I looked around again, staring out into the darkness. But my animals were still quiet, and suddenly I knew what it was. A haunt. Animals don't usually pay haunts much mind, but people-folks do, and I was one of that nervous species!

Searching carefully I moved out from the fire again, circling, for I had a feeling about what it was I was going to find. And sure enough, back in the trees I came on what had to be the remains of a tent and a bedroll. Second clue. I had been right. Someone else'd camped here, and the evidence was truly pointing toward the distinct possibility of foul play.

Way I figured it, someone had died there where I was camped, and I was feeling the haunt of it. Only a matter of time, I was certain, and I would come on the remains of that poor pilgrim himself, whoever he was.

Only that time I was wrong.

I searched high and low for the next couple of hours, found another shot-up mule skull, third clue, finally slept until daybreak, and commenced to searching again. Two more hours passed, and I was beginning to feel like if I didn't soon light a shuck out of there I'd be up to my hip pockets in Indians and no room to swim.

Disgusted and more than a little nervous, I sat down on an old log to try to reason things out one more time. I stared at the pack mules and my old horse, which was saddled and ready to go. I stared around the swale. I stared at the bullet-holed skulls. I stared at the remains of the tent and bedroll. No matter which way I twisted things, I couldn't puzzle it out.

Someone had died there sure, and I couldn't find him. Or them.

The skulls looked to be seven, eight years old. The fabric of the tent was rotted but still there, and that left me with a number of possibilities. Either the man had escaped and never returned for his gear, or he hadn't escaped. That also left a couple of alternatives. Either the killers had disposed of his body, or the wild animals had done so. Either way, robbery hadn't been the motive. Otherwise, why would the killers have left his gear and killed two good mules besides.

Indians, I wondered? Maybe, but—

Suddenly the mules lifted their heads and I came alert myownself, shifting on the log to see where it was they were looking. I leaned way out, and that old log, long rotted, of a sudden gave way beneath me. I yelped in surprise as I sank into the soft red pulp and then scrambled quick to get away from a whole army of big black carpenter ants that were swarming about. That was when I saw the small leather bag.

Clue four, and bingo!

For an instant I just stared. Then, real slow, I reached down and hefted it. Heavy. Gold, I wondered quickly? No I decided as I shook it slightly and heard no sound of clinking coins. Nor did it feel like coins. Turning the old pouch I saw the letters ER had been burned into the leather. ER. Initials, most likely. Other than that, there was nothing on the pouch that could tell me a thing.

Carefully I drew the top open and gazed inside. I was still staring, my breath stilled, when I heard a twig snap behind me. That was when I finally remembered that all three of my animals had been staring into the trees behind me.

"Maybeso white pup findum sacred money-rock."

Spinning with the sack still in my hand, I stared into the dark, cold eyes of my friend Zenos Hill.

"Zene," I whispered, "what are you—"

"What do, sacred money-rock?" Zene growled his question and stepped forward, and that was when I noticed the Winchester he held. Interestingly, it was pointed straight at me.

Looked like I'd been wrong about that Ute Indian, I thought. The Mormon white on the inside of him hadn't taken. It wasn't anywhere near so thick as I'd supposed.

"Speakum up, white pup!"

"I . . . uh . . . I don't know *what* I'm going to do with it, Zene. I only just now found it, and to tell you the truth, it was the last thing I was looking for."

"Umph."

"It was! Way I figure it, some poor soul was murdered right here in this very spot. I was looking for his remains when I sat down on the gold. See, I even gathered up the skulls of his mules and what little was left of his tent and bedroll. Don't you see?"

Zene didn't answer. He just stared at me out of those eyes that had suddenly gone so hard and flat and black.

"By the way," I asked, trying my best to get him to talking, "what'd you mean, sacred?"

"Carre shin-ob," he whispered. "Heap bad place! Money-rock from there sacred to Ute."

"No kidding? I never heard of it."

"Umph!"

Well, whether Zene believed me or not didn't change anything. I hadn't heard of it, or the name, at least. I had, however, heard about that gold. Or at least I thought I had. From time to time there were rumors in town of lost gold mines and rich strikes and fabulous

Spanish treasures here and there, and I suspicioned the gold I held in my hand was a bit of that.

My brother Ernest and I had talked time and again of finding some such lost mine, dreaming of easy wealth as most young fellers are likely to do. Lots of folks believe that the West is filled with buried treasure, and I like to think so myownself. In any country where there is danger, as from the Indians or from bandits, or where folks have to travel light and fast and might have a little trouble, they are apt to bury gold or whatever they value highly.

Sometimes they'll pick likely places to hide their goods, sometimes mighty unlikely ones, such as the Mormon Saints who dumped their fine china and other valuables down into their privys when they were being driven from Nauvoo. Now who on earth would ever look in such a place as that for treasure? Only polecats and maybe a few mobocrats, who were both of the same breed anyway, I reckon.

Anyway, sometimes the owners got killed, and sometimes they lost their nerve and never came back. Gold can look almighty nice, but a few hundred miles of sun-blistered desert or ragged-edged mountains full of angry Apaches or Utes can look mean enough to take the shine off almost any amount of gold. So there a treasure sits, waiting for the first feller with guts and smarts enough to go get it.

Ernest reckoned he was such a feller, and who was I to argue? He thought I was too, and I didn't argue with that either. Of course, Pa argued plenty, for he didn't like us wasting our time dreaming of lost gold and other such truck. Whenever he heard us, he'd shut our chatter down quick.

"Gold," he'd say, "is a hard-found thing, and even harder to keep. Lots of folks, good folks otherwise, will turn to murder for the sake of gold. Brother Brigham advised the Saints to be farmers and to leave gold and its troubles to the gentiles. Boys, should the unlikely need ever arise, my advice to you would be to do the same."

I thought on that now, thought of the heavy sack of gold bullion in my hand, saw the hard look in Zene's eyes and steady rifle he held watching me, and then and there I decided that Pa had been right.

"Sacred," I said quietly. "Well Zene, if that's the case, this stuff surely doesn't belong to me."

Carefully then I laid the pouch down on the rotted log. "Maybe you'd do me a favor, Zene, and see that it gets back to your people before someone else gets hurt."

Zene said nothing, so I turned my back to him and walked to my horse, my skin crawling the entire time. I mean, anyone who has walked thirty or forty feet with a hard-eyed Indian standing behind him pointing a rifle at his back will understand why I was jumpy as a bit-up bull in fly time.

Quickly I mounted, and though I didn't want to do it, I couldn't help myself—I was upset, and so I looked back. I had to take one more look at Zene, one more look to convince me that my old friend had turned against me.

It wasn't the gold I was upset about—it wasn't the gold at all. If it was sacred to the Utes, that was fine with me. I respected that. Some things were sacred to me, too, and I didn't like folks making a mockery of them. Besides, the gold *was* on their land, or at least I thought it was. So by right it should have been theirs.

No, it was Zene himself that upset me, turning redskin so sudden-like as he had. That's why I turned back, so's I could argue with him one more time.

Only, where Zene had been, nothing at all remained. Even the sack of gold with ER branded on it was gone. That mountain was silent and empty as the day after the good Lord had divided the light from the darkness.

Gathering up the lead ropes to the mules, I turned the old horse I rode, and all of us, horse and mules and myownself, departed from that swale posthaste.

"Lizzard-mule," I growled as we topped the rim and dropped down toward Currant Creek, "I take back my apologies! You are a stubborn and evil animal. You lead me into the valley of the shadow one more time, and the next thing you know'll be the *last* thing you'll know. That there's a promise!"

3

Strawberry Flats
Sheep Camp

It was early afternoon when I came down off the hills and started across the flat toward the sheep camp on the Strawberry. I'd been moving right along, both because I hated to leave Mr. Aagard's sheep alone and because I wanted to get shut of that reservation. The way Pa always said it suited me just fine. "The sooner the quicker," he'd yell when he wanted us to hurry, and, like I said, I couldn't agree with him more.

Of course, I knew the dogs could handle the sheep. But still, I'd been hired, I'd taken Old Man Aagard's money, and I was beholden to him for paying it. So, now that Zene was gone, I figured to pack camp and trail those woollies up into the Grandaddy area at the head of Rock Creek myownself.

Of a truth I was worried about Zene, but I was a whole lot more worried about his wife and kids. I'd have to tell them, of course, but blast! How would I do that? How could a kid like me tell a good woman that her husband had turned Indian on her? That was the bone I was worrying over as I topped that last little rise above the camp.

Drawing rein in a hurry, however, I just sat and stared. The camp was there, all right. But so was Zene's horse, grazing peacefully at the end of its picket rope. Zene was there too, sitting on his campstool and staring into the fire.

"No," I whispered as I stared, "this *can't* be! I ain't never rode so hard in my life, and that horse of his doesn't even look lathered!"

Nudging the horse forward, I rode down the slope and up to the fire, where I stopped again, staring down at the herder. Zene, however, didn't move, didn't even look up.

"How'd you get here so quick?" I finally asked.

"Rode," Zene answered, still not looking up.

"You got rid of that gold mighty fast," I declared. "You'd of had to, to beat me back."

"Umph."

"You weren't alone, were you." It was a statement. "Other Indians were there with you."

"Umph."

Well, I could see that Zene was back to his usual elocutionary ways, so with a frown I dismounted and set about taking down the tent and packing our gear. I'd finished, had the mules loaded, and was all set to mount up myownself, when Zene, who had not yet moved, finally spoke.

"Hy," he said quietly.

My back was to him, and at the sound of his voice I hunched like I'd taken a Ute bullet between the shoulder blades. He'd never called me Hy before, only kid and, lately, white pup.

"Yeah," I answered, doing my best to growl it.

"I'm afraid I owe you an apology."

Now I turned to look at the Ute herder. Suddenly he didn't sound like a reservation Indian anymore but was back to his old self. To say I was confused would have been putting it mildly.

"What for?"

Zene dropped his gaze and stirred at the fire with a stick. "You offended me yesterday, and you apologized."

"Yeah, I know. I meant it, too. The apology, I mean."

"I know that, and I appreciate it. Thing is, Hy, I also offended you, and I've been too stubborn to apologize."

"Zene, you don't need—"

"Hy, a boy has a right to be proud of his father, and yesterday I took that away from you. Your father is a fine man, and I truly admire him for living the Principle when it is so hard. I don't know if I'd be strong enough to be jailed for my beliefs or not. I hope I would, but I just don't know."

Zene poked at the fire again, and I stood there hipshot like my old horse. I felt like saying something, if only to ease off on Zene. To the best of my knowledge that was the longest speech he'd ever made, for he was of the firm opinion that if the ears were bent more often than the mouth was opened, the health of the scalp would be highly improved. But now he'd gone in real deep, and I didn't see how I could help.

Nor could I fault what he'd said. Sure us Soderbergs were having it a little rough, but despite the fact that we missed Pa and truly needed him, there wasn't one of us that wasn't busting our buttons with pride over Pa's strength and courage. No sir, Pa and Aunt Victoria and the baby were in jail because Pa and she held their beliefs and their family sacred, and Zenos Hill's ridicule or not, I was proud of Pa, proud of our family for sticking together, and I wouldn't abandon him or them nohow.

"Zene," I finally said, "your words were maybe harsh, but no more'n my own to you. Besides, such a little thing as what you said couldn't tear me away from Pa. He was disgusted with himself for being caught by those femininely attired marshalls, I was disgusted with him, and I reckon the whole family was disgusted. That doesn't change anything at all. We're still a family, and no matter what those marshals do, no matter even what Congress does, it won't change anything. Pa says our family is an eternal entity, and I believe it with all my heart.

"Besides," and now I grinned, "you were right about Pa and me being predictable. Ernest is telling both of us that, all the time."

Looking up, Zene smiled. "You'll do, Hy," he said quietly. "You'll do."

Slowly then he stood up and began fiddling with the double diamond I'd used to hitch the pack to Lizzard-mule. "It's hard, Hy, being an Indian and living in the middle of a lot of white folks. Mostly they treat me good, but now and then one of them makes certain I remember who I am, or was, or am supposed to be. I suppose you feel the same, being a cripple."

"Yeah, sometimes."

"I thought as much. I guess that's why I took to you. Thought you'd understand." He paused and looked over his shoulder. "Actually, I've never been an Indian, Hy. Not since I was about one year old. I was just born with their features, something I can't do much about. Like your leg, I reckon. I always thought that you accepted me as a man like yourself, nothing more, nothing less. That's why what you said hurt so much. I'd never expected it from you."

Well, I hung my head, and I don't recall ever feeling so low-down rotten.

"What's the bail against your father?"

"A thousand dollars."

"A *thousand?*"

"Yeah. Kinda high, ain't it."

"It is. But your father's a big man hereabouts. The marshals want him bad—figure to make an example of him."

We both looked at the trailing smoke from the fire. A thousand dollars was a vast amount of money, more than I could come up with in *five years* of camp tending, let alone one summer. Just thinking of it discouraged me. Pa's bail was steeper than a barn roof, and all the ideas I'd had of springing him from the calaboos when I found that gold came up gritty as dry-washed sand. Nothing smooth about any of them. Not with the gold gone back to the rightful owners. I—

"Hy, you should know I trailed you because I got worried about you. I didn't even mean to sneak up on you like I did. That just, well, it just happened is all. And I surely didn't intend to rob you of that gold. It wasn't mine, and I never thought it was."

"That's fine," I said, for truly I did not care that much about losing it. "At least it got back to the rightful owners."

Again Zene looked at me. "You really think I know those Lamanitish folks, don't you."

"Some," I admitted. "But so do Pa and my brother Jim. Zene, I ain't accusing you of being Indian or anything else. As far as I'm concerned, the only thing you are is one of my best friends. And as far as that gold goes, I'm with you. If it is sacred, then it ought to be treated as such. I'm just glad you were there to inform me."

Zene's eyes were glittering again, and I couldn't tell exactly what he was thinking. Fact is, I couldn't even tell if he was happy with what I'd said, or angry.

"Well," he finally growled, "you'd best be moving."

Now I raised my eyes and looked at Zene again, happen I hadn't noticed that with everything else he was also going blind. Either that or he was angry and setting in to have more words with me. Anybody, even a blind Mormon Indian, could see that I'd already struck and packed the tent and other gear, and he could also see that the only thing left to pack was his own campstool. My rough-gaited horse was even still saddled.

"Hand me the stool," I said, doing my best not to show my own sudden flash of anger. "Do that, and the onliest thing left to move will be you. This underprivileged camp tender will be long gone."

"Not with me you won't," Zene said quietly. "Here's where we go separate ways for a spell. While you're gone, I'd like you to pick up this list of supplies. And, happen you get to Fountain Green while you're away, stop in and say hello to my family."

"What? But—"

"Take this with you," he went on, reaching into his vest and grasping something. "I imagine the gold you found will cover your father's bail and then some."

Then Zene handed me the small leather pouch branded ER and filled brim-full of the purest gold bullion I'd ever seen. I stared, took the gold, and awkwardly made my thanks. Zene grunted stoically and packed his camp stool, and I was ready, as a matter of Strawberry Flats fact, to go and free my pa.

4

Provo—Territory of Utah

I followed the river past Bridal Veil Falls and down into Provo late the next day, and all the way into town I rode slow and stared. I'd been there before, but that still didn't change things. Provo was a *big* town, with nearly ten thousand folks living there, and I could hardly imagine a town as big as that.

The streets were wide and lined with trees. Homes were set well back, and all of them were fine homes, brick or adobe, and their trim-work was painted. There were also businesses everywhere, and to a feller like me who was used to the Co-op and maybe one or two other small stores and the blacksmith shop, it was a place to see.

Anyway, my first stop was the assay office, for I wanted to get that gold weighed and out of my hands. I mean, a feller never knew what sorts of antisocial criminals he might run into, and I wanted the gold safe.

The assay office wasn't much of an office, just a cluttered, dirty cubbyhole with a flyspecked window, a counter, and two tables. The man who ran it was small, hardly bigger'n a minute and a half. His name was Doolin. He had thin wispy hair and small beady eyes, and right off he made me nervous. Still, he took my gold quick enough.

He hefted it like he was weighing it, looked at the sack and then gave me a funny look, emptied the gold onto his scales, and worked himself around so his body was somewhat between me and what he was doing.

Now, I may be from a small town, and I may also be young, but right off I could see what this little feller was trying to do. The needle on the scales was in sight, my gold was even in sight, but the weight side was hidden behind him, and I knew immediately he was using his hand to make those weights go where he wanted them to go.

"Well, young feller," he whined all happy-like, "you've got yourself quite a fortune here. Comes to, let me see . . . yes, three hundred and two dollars and—"

"Mr. Doolin?"

"Yes?"

"Turn around, real slow, and while you're at it, take your left hand away from your scales."

Well, what followed was the biggest quiet since Giggles La Monte decided to show up for church on Easter Sunday. And seeing that Giggles hadn't heard a preacher, wore a hat, or been seen abroad in daylight for six years, that was some quiet.

"Say," he squeaked, and now his voice was truly high-pitched, "you haven't any right to come in here like this, giving me orders! I told you what the gold was worth, and I run a fair scales."

"Well," I replied, lifting my arm and hand, the one that had my old coat draped over it, and thrusting my hidden finger toward him, "maybe you do, and maybe you don't. Stand away from that scale and let's see that gold weighed square!"

"I won't do it!" he squeaked. "You have no right—"

"Mister, you got more guts than Custer's bugler blowing the second charge at the Little Big Horn. 'Course, you got about that many brains, too. This Navy Colt that you see in my hand says I got all the right in the world. Now *move!*"

That Doolin feller looked at my hidden finger, saw in his mind the pistol I hoped he'd see, and like some rare form of scrawny whiskered bird, he flittered right away from that scales.

The balance needle moved far over on the register, floated back and forth, and finally settled to a stop. "Read it," I ordered.

"S-sixty-four ou-ounces," he stuttered. "T-troy weight."

"Very good. And at twenty dollars an ounce, that comes to . . . let's see . . . yes, twelve hundred and eighty dollars. Pay me, please."

"No sir," he declared, growing suddenly defiant. "I won't."

Well, I was in a fix, and I knew it. I couldn't very well shoot the man, for my finger wasn't loaded. Nor did I know how much more of a bluff he'd go for. Still, it was all I had left, and so . . . "Mr. Doolin, lie down on the floor with your face away from me."

"Wh-what for?"

"I'm going to have to shoot you," I answered easily. "I don't mind that, but I do hate to see a man's face when he's dying. The eyes bulge out, the tongue rattles in the throat and turns the face a sickly blue, and all sorts of other ugly things happen. I just hate to watch that, so lie down with your face against that desk."

"Wait a minute! Wait a minute! I've thought it over, and maybe if we just came to a compromise—'"

"Mister, you got my gold. Just under five and a half pounds of it. Happen I don't have my money, *all of it,* within, say, sixty seconds according to that big old Regulator clock of yours, you'll be lying on that floor and feeling just as dead as that brave and foolish bugler of Custer's ever was. Pay up!"

I never did see a man who was so tight as that Doolin feller. He started to get my money and then happened to see the leather pouch, which I'd made the mistake of leaving in his possession. His eyes saucered up wide, and suddenly he stopped counting.

"Where'd you get the gold?" he demanded in a high squeaky voice.

"Found it," I answered.

"Them your initials?"

"Not hardly. Found the sack, too. Now let's have the cash and a receipt."

"No sir, young feller, I won't pay you. I've got to report this."

"Mister," I finally said, "I've plumb run out of patience. Lie down against that desk!"

"You'll never get away with this."

"Maybe, maybe not. But anything's better than coyoting around the rim of this thing with you all night long. Lie down!"

Doolin looked at me, and slowly he lay down. I stepped closer; his eyes were saucered up. I twisted his head so he was looking at the desk. I saw his body start to shake, and I was in a pickle for sure. My aimed finger was shaking worse than he was, and I knew this bluff was nearly up. For crying out loud, if only—

That was when I remembered one more of my birth defects, one that'd come along for the ride with my club foot. My tongue was extra nimble, and I'd learned as a tiny boy that I could make the strangest clicking sounds with it that a body ever heard, sounds that no one else I knew could make. I could do a single click, or a roll of them like a rattlesnake. I could click out tunes, and I had one sound that Pa said sounded just like the click of a pistol. I tried that then.

Click!

Doolin jerked, and suddenly I laughed out loud. "Mr. Doolin, I have a better idea. Shootin's too good for thieving assayers, but com-

ing down the trail today I ran onto a little critter that seems like
mighty appropriate company for a fellow like you. Lie still while I
put him on your back."

"No!" he screamed. *"No!* I—"

"I mean it!" I thundered. "Lie still!"

He did, and I reached onto his counter and took from it a short
length of half-inch rope, which I dropped onto his back, at the same
time making my rattlesnake roll of clicks.

"Wh-what's that?" he shrieked.

"Oh-oh," I whispered as I wriggled the rope. "Don't move, Mr.
Doolin. Was I you, I wouldn't even breathe. Rattlesnakes are mighty
touchy, and—"

"R-rattlesnake?"

"Yes, but—" Now I clicked again. "Don't move," I whispered
urgently as I twisted the rope. "The thing's coiling up, and is eye-
balling the back of your ear. Oh-oh, it's getting ready, and—" I
rattled again, and suddenly I could hear the small man sobbing.

"No . . . no . . . no . . ." he sobbed, "I can't stand snakes. I'll
pay, just as you asked, only get that—that snake—"

"Mr. Doolin," I answered, "I'll let you up just one more time.
Happen you don't pay immediately and give me my receipt to
boot, I will force-feed this rattlesnake to you head-first. Then you and
it will have a biting contest to see who can poison which the quickest.
Am I understood?"

"Y-yes sir," he whispered through his sobs.

"Fine. Now let me get hold of this snake . . ."

I lifted the rope slowly from Doolin's back, clicking my tongue a
couple of times while I did so, and then I stepped back. "All right,
you can get up, but remember, this Navy Colt is watching you carefully, and my rattlesnake is lonely for companionship. Get moving."

With terror in his eyes and sobs of fear still in his throat, Doolin
rolled over and stared up at me, and when I signaled with my hidden
finger, he scrambled to his feet like a fire had been built under him.
Instantly he started in to counting again, and it wasn't more than
thirty seconds before I had the full $1,280 in my hand.

I thanked him kindly, picked up my receipt, assured him that I'd
never recommend his business establishment to another soul, and
backed out of his office. Finally me and the old horse were on our
way. I had a bad feeling about that Doolin fellow, though. I couldn't
help it, I just did. He and I would meet again, I was sure, and when
we did, grief would come of it.

5

Territorial Prison— Provo

I put all but a little of my money into an account in the First National Bank, stuffed some more into a used moneybelt I purchased from the bank manager for two bits, and got a draft for a thousand dollars. Then that spavined horse and I made our way out Center Street to the jail where they were keeping Pa and Aunt Victoria and the baby.

The man in the office was big and some run to fat, but he looked competent. He had his boots up on the desk, and his main occupation seemed to be swatting flies. When I walked in, he didn't even look up.

"Umph," I said, imitating Zene.

"He'p you, sonny?"

Well, I hadn't been "sonny" to anybody for near two years, and that got my dander up. I don't know why I was so sensitive about my age, but I was, and it usually got me in trouble. "I reckon," I answered softly. "Fetch me your Boss. I don't do business with office boys."

The man got real quiet. Slowly his boots came down, and at last he swung around to look full at me, his eyes squinting. "Do I know you?"

"Not yet. Where's the Boss?"

"You're looking at him," he said, rising until he'd reached his full eighteen feet or so of height. I stared up at him, and, well, it wasn't too hard to tell that man could make mincemeat out of me eight days out of seven. Besides, if he was the Boss, he was the man I needed.

Yessir, I'd pushed hard enough for one day. Then and there, I smiled. "I should have known it," I said easily. "You do look like a man with authority. I'm right sorry."

"Umph," he grunted, and I thought how amazing it was that such a simple word could be so widely used by so many different people.

"I'd like to bail out my Pa."

"Your Pa a polyg," he asked, "or a horse-thief?"

"Those the only two kinds you keep in here?" I asked.

"Usually, though we got one murderer, one feller who's been selling the bed of Utah Lake for land development and doing a booming business, and Shin-bone Sally, who was picked up last night for soliciting inside territorial boundries, which puts her a minimum of two hundred miles off course, at least according to the laws of man. Which of the first two is your Pa?"

"There's some that claim both," I answered, grinning again.

That made the man smile too, and I discovered then that he was missing one of his two front teeth. I'd surely never forget him.

"What do *you* say?" he asked. "About your pa?"

"I don't say anything, but you boys have him locked up for unlawful cohabitation, and nothing else that I know of. I've got his bail."

"Cagey, ain't you." the man said, grinning wider. "Who's your pa?"

"Jons Soderberg."

"The bishop? Well I'll be. I mighta knowed it. You two talk alike. Bail, huh? I heard tell he was going broke."

"Not so's you'd notice. Who do I pay?"

"Cash money?"

"Same as. Bank draft."

"Lemme see it."

"You the man I pay?"

"I said I was the Boss, didn't I? I'm deputized and bonded both. Now let's see the color of your draft."

I handed the draft to him. He walked to the window and examined it carefully. "Where'd you get this?"

"First National Bank. It says right on it."

"Not the draft," he said, looking down from his lofty height and giving me the dark and evil eye. "The money for it."

"Found it."

"Smart, ain't you."

"I get by. I'm also passing honest, and that helps. When do I get my Pa?"

"Honest, huh. You know, young feller, I believe you are. There's too much brass in you to be otherwise and live very long. You sign this draft, I process it, and you pick your pa up in the morning."

"The morning! Why so long?"

"Rules. What you aiming to do about the woman and the kid?"

"Is there bail on them?" I asked.

"Nope. They're witnesses."

"Then for now I reckon they stay, though I surely hate to see that happen. This thousand-dollar draft is just for my pa."

Again the deputy looked at my draft. "You Hyrum Soderberg?"

"I am. Now give me a receipt for that draft, please, and I'll be back in the morning—eight o'clock on the nostrils."

"Eight-thirty."

"Fine. Let's have the receipt."

Well, that big, tall buzzard eyed me over, grinned again, pulled a tattered book of receipts from his beat-up desk, and wrote one out.

"This your name?" I asked when he tore it out and handed it to me. "Tinsdale?"

"Says so on my birth record," he answered.

"Fine, Mr. Tinsdale. I'll expect my pa to be a free man come eight-thirty tomorrow morning."

"Not free, young feller. Only loose. He's still got to stand trial. Otherwise you lose all this money." He grinned even more widely, showing that big gap in his teeth again, and so without another word I turned and walked out.

I took a room in a house on Academy Street, called that on account of it ran past what was shaping up to be the new home for Brigham Young Academy, which had been operating now for maybe fifteen years. With two meals, the room I took came to six bits, and I figured it was well spent. Then I went to the S. W. Sharp livery, stabled my horse, dickered over a couple of theirs, and finally gave ten dollars for a nag that looked even worse than the one I rode.

Come morning we'd have to make our way south to Fountain Green, and there were three ways to do it, if you counted walking. Pa hated walking very far, so I counted that out. That left horses or the train. If Zene was right, then Pa was predictable, and I reckoned he'd be so tired of being cooped up that eight out of eight chances he'd choose to ride a horse. That's why I bought that second animal.

For a time I walked around Provo, and truthfully I'd never seen so many busy people. The town was booming. There were land speculators in from the East, townfolks figured they had money to burn, and the *Enquirer,* Provo's newspaper, said it all with its head-lines of "Boom! Boom! Boom!"

They had new resorts out at the lake; rail cars were running out there every thirty minutes and jammed every run. There were housing tracts springing up everywhere, and I had no doubt that there were at least a dozen other fellows besides the man in jail who were also selling the bottom of the lake to gullible and unsuspecting buyers. Of course, they were throwing in for free the twelve feet or so of water above the land, so maybe it wasn't such a bad deal after all.

The Provo Woolen Mills on First North and Second West covered nearly the whole block, making it the biggest building I'd ever seen. Taylor Brothers Furniture was packed with cash-paying customers. There were both an east and a west Co-op that were both big businesses. And the Palace Saloon and other such establishments looked like they couldn't have handled another customer if they'd found one. Like I said, Provo was booming, and there weren't even any mines to help it along.

For a time I just looked around, but I had an idea, and though it made me feel mighty reluctant and uncomfortable, I finally made my way into the west Co-op building.

"May I help you?" a woman asked.

"Uh . . . I reckon," I answered, feeling conspicuous as a buffalo chip in a punch bowl.

"Well?"

"Well what?"

"How can I help you?"

"I . . . uh . . . well . . ."

"Let me guess. You want something for a girl."

Embarrassed, I dropped my eyes. "Yes ma'am, I do."

"You want jewelry maybe? Or a book?"

"No, that ain't exactly what I had in mind. I just . . ."

"I know!" she exclaimed. "You want something frilly-frally!"

Then I really turned red. I don't know if it was because I was thinking of buying Ida Mae someting as personal as frilly-frally clothing, or if it was because that woman-clerk had figured me out. But whichever, I was embarrasseder'n a fox caught feather-mouthed in a henhouse.

Well, that woman showed me things such as I'd never before seen nor even imagined, and it took me a good ten minutes to convince her I was after something a great deal less . . . well, frivolous. Finally, however, she went to a rack of dresses.

"How big is she?" she asked.

"About like you, only maybe quite a bit thinner," I answered honestly.

Right off I could tell I'd made a mistake. That woman went white as a January blizzard, her lips thinned down to nothing but red lines, and her eyes narrowed off until all I could see were black slits. "One moment, sir," she hissed, and her voice was so cold I could have sworn her jowls were dripping ice water.

"I mean . . . I . . . uh . . . ," I stammered as she glared frostily at me, "I mean, maybe a little taller. Not much, but a little."

Well, she looked at me as though I had no more social position than an onion, turned, and, with a glacier-like flourish, whipped out the prettiest blue taffeta dress I'd ever seen.

"This," she declared haughtily, "is far too expensive for such a *boy* as you. Still, I feel obligated to show even an uncouth person like yourself our *finer* products. Now if you'll step to the back with me—"

"I . . . I'll take that one," I blurted.

"This one? My dear boy, don't add further insult to my day! This is a fine dress, but *very* expensive. Now in the back—"

"Ma'am," I said, "I'll take that one. Wrap it, please."

Well, the woman looked at me and I pulled out a twenty-dollar gold piece and laid it on the counter. She stared at it and of an instant was all smiles once more.

"Yes sir!" she beamed. "Right away, sir!"

My next stop that evening was at a small bookstore just down the street from the Co-op. I walked in and nearly lost my breath, the sight was so grand. Along both walls were shelves, and those shelves were all lined with books, more books than I could hardly imagine. Like I've already explained, I had a hankering for learning, and I'd promised Pa and Ma that I'd do some reading while I was up with the herd. And though I'd already finished or nearly finished Farrar's *The Life of Christ*, Tacitus's *The Annals and the Histories*, most of the Book of Mormon for the third time, and was well into Blackstone's *Laws*, I intended to make my promise more than good. If I couldn't go to a proper school, that surely didn't mean that I had to go forth upon the face of the land in total ignorance.

Ambition was strong within me. I wanted to see, to become, but most of all, to know and to understand. Most of what scholars took for granted was new to me, and so I read at every opportunity, and herding sheep, at least, provided plenty of free time.

So I had read a little, and the wider my knowledge became, the more I realized my ignorance. It is only the ignorant, I decided, who can be positive of everything, only the ignorant who can become fanatics, for the more I learned, the more I became aware that there are shadings and differing points of view in all things.

Thank goodness, I remember deciding one night after reading the life of Simon Gerty, whom the Americans considered a renegade but whom the British almost deified, *thank goodness that God has the capabilities to judge that man, him and all others.* For myself, my goal was to avoid judgement unless it was thrust upon me, to accept the good in all men, and to learn good things from all who had good things to teach.

Therefore I sought knowledge from every conceivable source, for in knowledge lay not only power but freedom from fear. Pa had told me once that generally speaking, folks feared only what they did not understand. I believed him, and because I didn't want to live a life filled with fear, I tried always to seek knowledge, develop wisdom, and grow in understanding. One of the best ways to do that was by reading, and so I read.

For maybe an hour I browsed through that bookshop, and when I left I carried with me Plutarch's *The Lives of the Noble Grecians and Romans,* all three volumes of William Russell's *The History of Modern Europe,* a fine volume by John Gilmary Shea entitled *The Story of a Great Nation,* and a bound volume containing all the past year's issues of the *Juvenile Instructor* magazine, which was published by the Church.

Taking my books and Ida Mae's dress, I went up Academy Street to the new Academy building, where I stood for a time looking up at the huge spires that were even then under construction. The original Brigham Young Academy had burned down in '84, and the huge building I was looking at was scheduled for completion in another two, maybe three, years.

It was a beautiful edifice, stretching high into the air and covering what seemed like acres of ground. Looking at it sort of made me wonder what wondrous things I might learn in there that would go along with all that I was gleaning from my books.

At last, being truly tuckered out, I returned to the rooming house and turned in, climbing into the softest feather tick I'd ever felt. It surely beat all hollow the rocks and sticks of Strawberry Flat.

Then, just before I went to sleep, I thought of that beady-eyed lit-

tle man called Doolin who ran the assay office. He was trouble, and
I knew it. Thing was, I just didn't know how much. Had I known, I'd
not have slept at all. But I did, like a log, and at a quarter of nine the
next morning I watched as Pa was led out of the jail and into the office
where I waited.

He looked bewildered, but then I reckon I looked some misty-
eyed, so neither of us mentioned the other's discomfortable appearance.

"Howdy, Pa."

"Hyrum, what're you doing here? Is . . . is your Ma . . . everyone . . . all right?"

"Everyone's fine, Pa. Or at least so far as I know. I came to take
you home. Didn't the deputy tell you?"

"Tell me what? Hy, you know they aren't going to turn me loose.
Bail's too high. I could just as easy fly as raise a thousand dollars."

"I know, Pa. I took care of it for you." Then I turned to the big
gap-toothed deputy. "Could you give him his things, please? We've
got to get along."

"But Hy—"

"Not now, Pa. I'll tell you later. Mister?"

Well, the deputy grinned down at both Pa and myself, and slowly
he handed Pa his personals. Pa took them, looking like he was in a
trance.

"You . . . you mean I'm free?" Pa asked.

"Yes sir," Deputy Tinsdale declared. "Until your trial comes up,
you surely are."

"Then . . . then might I see my . . . I mean, might I see Victoria
Copley and her baby?"

Deputy Tinsdale grinned his Cheshire-cat grin. "Well, Soderberg, you almost had a witness against you. Almost. But now, so far
as I know, Miss Copley is a single lady, and I see no problem with
you visiting her for a few moments."

"Thank you," Pa said humbly. "Might my son here come with
me?"

"No, I think he'd best wait here," the deputy said.

"As you wish. Will you escort me?"

"Certainly. Young Soderberg, can you handle my fly-swatter for
a few minutes?"

I nodded and took up the swatter and the big Deputy Tinsdale
led my Pa off down another hall. As they went through a big door I

heard Pa telling the Deputy somewhat concerning my leg and the good things it had done for me. Well, I'm only human, and my head swelled a little. Had Ma been there, she would have taken me back down a notch or two. But truthfully, I don't think praise is always a bad thing. For instance, anytime that someone tells me I'm great, I'll bust a gasket proving he's right. That helps them and it helps me as well, for I become a better person. So, as you might have guessed, I do like praise.

A few minutes later Pa came back. He looked a little emotional, but I understood that, and so I paid it no mind. I handed the swatter back to Deputy Tinsdale, thanked him again for his help, and Pa and I walked out of that jail. For a moment Pa stood still and breathed deeply, and then I led him to the horse I'd bought for him the night before.

"This cayuse still alive?" Pa asked as he saw the animal. He sounded pretty disgusted, but I reckon he was still used to his eighteen-hundred-dollar plug, and so I didn't get my tail up.

"It ain't bad for ten dollars," I said easily. "Would you rather take the train?"

"Train?" he snorted. "When I can ride and breathe in all this fresh air? Not hardly."

"Fine. I figured as much. Now let's rattle our hocks on out of here."

Pa looked at me again, shook his head, and swung aboard. I did the same on my own pile of bones, and we were just starting to ride when a voice we both knew stopped us cold.

"Hold it, Soderberg, or I'll blast ya!"

Pa and I reined around, and there riding slowly toward us on his ugly piebald gelding, was Deputy Marshal Hebron Clawson, yellowed mustaches, filthy dirty clothing, huge bulging nose, and all.

"Soderberg," he growled when he had pulled to a stop facing us, "you're under arrest for breaking jail, not to mention numerous counts of unlawful cohabitation, etcetera."

"Hello, Deputy Clodson," Pa said quietly.

"That's Clawson."

"That's what I said, Plodson. Looks like you're missing your new duds."

"Duds?"

"You know. Skirts and petticoats and such other unmentionables as only women and people like you would wear."

Well, right off the marshal's face turned beet red, trying to match his nose, I guess, and I could see he was going to be about as sociable as an ulcerated back tooth.

"Marshal Clawson," I said, "I—"

"Soderberg," he growled, ignoring me, "get off'n that horse! *Now!*"

"Clawson," Pa replied easy-like and quiet. "I'll not do it. I've been bailed legally, and I'm going home."

"Bailed! Soderberg, you're so dad-blamed broke you couldn't raise a blister, let alone the thousand I demanded they set for your bail."

"So that high bail was *your* doing?"

"You're blamed right it was. You're sneakier'n a weasel after weiner pigs, and I ain't *about* to let you slip away from me again. That's why your bail's so high. Now dismount!"

Marshal Clawson glared at Pa, Pa glared back, neither said anything, and finally, when Pa wouldn't look away, Old Clawson dropped his eyes.

"I might've known," Pa said. "Come on, Hy, let's—"

The air was filled with the sudden click of a pistol hammer being pulled to cock. Pa and I both looked back, and Clawson's big .44 was aimed right at Pa.

"Down," the marshal ordered.

"Marshal," Pa repeated quietly, "I told you, the bail's been paid."

"And I told you there was no way you could raise that money."

"You're right. I didn't. It was raised by Hyrum here. Now if you'll excuse us . . ."

"In a pig's eye. Now git down!"

We got down, and Marshal Clawson bellered out to the deputy in the jail, asking would he please and pronto make an appearance outside.

"What do you want?" the gap-toothed man asked after he had ducked his way through the doorway and raised himself up again outside.

"This man says he's bailed."

"He is. Why you holding a gun on him?"

"Well, I . . . uh . . . . He paid a *thousand dollars?*"

"The boy did. Bank draft. Now Clawson, put that pistol away before I arrest *you* for throwing down on a peaceable citizen."

Well, Marshal Clawson looked about as cheerful as an old bull elk surrounded by sixteen wolves and a blizzard closing in. He growled and glared and did his best to look evil and instead looked only miserable. At last, however, he took that .44 off cock and put it back into his pocket. As for me, I was having whole new thoughts about the gap-toothed giant who had clipped Clawson's wings.

"Satisfied?" Pa asked.

"Where'd you get the thousand?"

"I told Mr. Tinsdale," I answered. "If he wants to tell you, I reckon that's his business."

"I don't," Tinsdale said quietly, winking at me. "Like I said, young feller, Marshal Dyer has resigned, so for the time being at least, *I'm* the Boss around here."

"Yes sir," I agreed, "you surely are. Adios, friend."

Pa nodded too, and then we remounted. "Have a nice day," Pa said politely to Marshal Clawson. That worthy scowled, and we spurred those two flea-bags eastward on Center Street. Within minutes we were raising a dust southeast around the lake toward Fountain Green and home.

It felt good, it did, riding once more with Pa, and even Marshal Clawson's parting yell that he would trace my money and get us both back in jail couldn't dampen our spirits.

I looked at Pa, and he was grinning, and for the first time in months I started feeling real good myownself. Pa had that effect on folks. He is the sort, Pa is, who makes a laugh out of being alive. Not a joke of it, mind you. Just a grin, a sly chuckle, or an outright belly-shaker that makes him, as well as the folks about him, feel good—especially when things are curdling to clabber in a hurry and it appears that there isn't anything funny to be found between Salt Lake and Manti. That's usually when Pa will open up with a shout or a shoulder clap or just a friendly bear hug to get things "elevated" as he calls it. Yessir, it was surely great being back with my Pa.

For some time he just rode and grinned, every now and then swinging his hat in the air and breathing deeply. Me, though, I was troubled, and Pa soon saw it.

"What's wrong, Hy?"

"Oh, nothing, I guess. It's just that I'm so upset at Marshal Clawson I can hardly think straight. I don't understand how you can be civil to him."

"He's only doing his job, Hy."

"Maybe, but if you ask me, he's doing it almighty poorly. Almost anybody I could think of would make a better marshal than Clawson."

"Well, you may or may not be right, but whether you are or not, I surely understand how you feel. However, there might be another side to it, and I'd like you to consider it."

"Pa, he's had you locked up, and—"

"I know, Son, I know. But think what it would be like without any law at all. Right now in Fountain Green, Hebron Clawson may be one of the most important men in our lives."

"Oh, come on! I—"

"I mean it, Hy. That man is all that stands between us and savagery. He's the thin line of protection, and when he mounts that piebald gelding and rides out, his life is always on the line.

"Now I know that this polygamy thing is hard on our family, and I'm certain it is just as hard on hundreds of other families who are living the Principle. But Hy, think what it would be like if we *weren't* living it. Would Hebron Clawson be our enemy then? Would he?"

Slowly I shook my head.

"Of course he wouldn't. Under those conditions, we'd be free to come and go, do business, buy goods, love our families, go sparking with a cute young gal, and we could do all of that because he is there. He is our first line of defense—in many respects, the only line."

"Defense against what?"

"Against savagery, Hy. The savage is never far from the surface in any of us, but because we know the law is here, we fight it down. I don't lose my temper and strike somebody at least partly because Hebron Clawson is there. The drifter with the chip on his shoulder avoids trouble, also because Marshal Clawson is there.

"The Athenian Thucydides, in his *History of the Peloponnesian War,* describes what happens when the savage within us is allowed to run free. He writes that men, because of greed and ambition, lust for power over others. That lust is carried out in continually greater excesses and atrocities, continuing until every vestige of normal civilization is done away with and all people are filled with the desire to take each other's lives."

"That sounds like the folks who were the last of the Jaredites and the Nephites."

"Exactly, son. People don't change. Once they allow Satan to rage within their hearts, freedom is destroyed and the evil of savagery and oppression reigns continually.

"With the exception of polygamy, we have freedom, you and I and your ma and the others, because Hebron Clawson and other law enforcement officers are out there with a badge. To tell you the truth, I think he is a fine man to be wearing it."

"Pa—"

"Hy, let me finish. I know Marshal Clawson has made mistakes, but who of us hasn't. Still, he's dedicated, he hangs on like a bull-terrier pup, and he won't buffalo for sour apples. His judgment's a little lacking sometimes, but so's mine, for that matter.

"Some people believe the law to be a restriction, Hy, and it is, but only against evil. Laws, if they are proper ones, are made to free people, not to bind them. As you know, improper laws cause pain, but never proper ones. They are only to tell us what we may or may not do without transgressing upon the equal liberty of any other man."

"It says that in Blackstone."

"I know, Hy. I read it years ago."

"You did?"

"Of course. Where do you suppose I got that idea? And I'll tell you something else. The longer I live, the more sense it makes. If this polygamy issue wasn't up and about, why, things would be just fine between Hebron and I. He's a good man, Hy. He's just on the other side of the fence when it comes to plural marriage, and he's bound by his oath of office to do his job, just as I'm bound by my oath to support and sustain my wives and my children."

"Who was that Athenian feller you mentioned a moment ago?"

"Thucydides."

"He's a man I've never read."

"You should, son. I have his book at home, and you're welcome to borrow it any time you like. Thucydides was a fine thinker as well as an able war correspondent, and a man can learn much from him."

For a time we rode again in silence, and I spent the time thinking about Pa and myself. Here I'd been bragging about wanting an education so I wouldn't be arrogant or bigoted or fanatical, and first thing I knew, in spite of all my reading, I was. Pa, though, who had gone through only the sixth grade, was intellectually and emotionally where I hoped one day to be, and again I was thankful that the good Lord had given me such a father.

We were clear down near Spanish Fork when Pa finally spoke again. "I don't want to ask, Hy, but I've got to. Where'd you get the money for my bail?"

I looked at Pa and could tell right off that he was serious about knowing. I'd thought all along of making up some whopper, just to spare his credulity, but now that it was on me, I couldn't do it. Soderbergs just didn't hold with lying, not in any from at all.

"From gold," I answered quietly.

"Gold?"

"Yessir. And I know you've told us never to go chasing gold, but I didn't. Chase it, I mean. Honest I didn't. I just sat down on that rotted log and there it was. I was surprised as—"

"Whoa, Hy. Now start at the beginning. Right now you're blubbering like a calf with the slobbers, and I can't make heads or tails of what you're saying."

Well, I grinned and took a deep breath, and for the next few miles I told Pa about my remarkable discovery. When I'd finished, Pa said nothing, and for another few miles we rode in silence once more. Finally, however, Pa spoke.

"First off, Son, you're a truth-teller. You always have been, so I believe you completely, and I have no doubt that Zene will verify your story. Still, I'm afraid you've got a serious problem."

"But why?"

"Greed, Hyrum. And possibly revenge. A few years ago a man disappeared up in those mountains, a man whose last name was Rhoades. The rumor had it that he had found a great deal of gold, much more than a fortune. Word'll somehow get out that you've found some of his gold, and you'll have more troubles than you ever dreamed possible."

I thought then of the beady-eyed Doolin at the assay office, and suddenly my skin started to crawl.

"What'll I do, Pa?"

"I don't know as there's anything you *can* do. But was I you, I'd get back to the herd, and quick."

"I'll go tomorrow. First thing."

"Maybe you ought to go today."

"Pa, I've got to see Ma and the little girls. I miss 'em awful. I also want to see Ida Mae. I bought her a pretty little frilly-frally, and besides, I miss her terrible."

Pa grinned. "I understand, Hy. Only, this time I think you—"

"Pa, I've just got to see her!"

Pa looked at me and shrugged. "Well," he said, "I taught you to skin your own cats. Reckon I ought to let you be about it."

He didn't say any more, and so we rode in silence.

"Pa," I suddenly asked, "what about Aunt Victoria and the baby?"

Pa looked off into the distance, and for a minute or so I thought he hadn't heard me. Finally, however, he answered. "How have the families been doing?"

"Uh . . . okay, I guess."

"Hy, I want the truth."

"We've managed, Pa, but I suppose it's been rough on Ma and Aunt Polly. We're all working, though, and—"

"Hy, I can't let that happen to my families. I need to be there to support them. If my case comes to trial, they'll convict me. I'll go to prison, and I won't be there where I'm needed."

I looked at Pa, wondering what he was getting at. I'd asked about Aunt Victoria, one of Pa's three wives, and—

"Do you see what I'm saying, Hy? I've got to jump bail, go into hiding, and run my homes from there."

"But Pa, that thousand dollars is a whole lot of money. You jump bail and you'll be throwing it all away."

"I know, Hy, and some day I'll pay it back to you. Right now, though, I can't risk a conviction and a three-year sentence. Besides, if I disappear, then the territory'll be forced to let Victoria and the baby go. After all, there won't be anybody for her to witness against."

That made sense, and though I was some bothered about losing that thousand dollars, I reckoned it would be worth it if Pa could go free. Besides, what was a thousand dollars? Riches is all. I'd been rich two or three days, but that wasn't enough to make it a habit. No sir, I still thought and felt and looked broke, so I might as well *be* broke to go along with it.

Again we rode in silence, with Pa now and then pointing out something that he wanted me to see and consider. When I was younger I loved that, but then I went through a spell where I hated it. I felt like every time Pa said something, what he was really saying was that I was dumb and didn't know enough not to eat rocks. Of course, that wasn't true, and now that I have a little more wisdom, I've come again to where I truly appreciate Pa. In spite of being human, he is a great man, and I can hardly get enough of listening to the things he has to tell me. In fact, I think that's what God meant when He said to honor our parents. Finally, by jings, I think I do.

Much later the two of us pulled rein on the hills above Salt Creek Canyon. The Sanpete Crawler was chugging up the grade below us, and I wondered if this was Amos Reed "Tucker Bill's" run. His eyes were going bad on him, and lately he'd only been working days.

We watched until all we could see was the black smoke belching up from beyond the hills, and then we hit the trail and went down into the canyon ourownselves.

Seeing the railroad tracks and the creek and that trail put me in mind of Pa's race, and I was thinking on that when Pa finally spoke.

"Makes a man think of the race," he said.

I nodded, pleased that our minds thought together like they did.

"Mungus is making a fine counselor in my bishopric," he said. "You and Ida Mae surely turned him around."

"With the help of your fists," I said.

"Usually," he responded, "I don't hold with fighting. Brother Brigham taught against it, and it generally doesn't accomplish anything. You remember that."

"I will, Pa. Still, Mungus would've never paid you no mind at all if he hadn't learned to respect your good right hook. Seems to me a knuckle sandwich would be a wonderful diet for old Marshal Clodson, too. Maybe *that's* what would teach him his judgment."

Pa looked at me serious-like, and suddenly we were both laughing. We laughed like that all the way to the top of the divide.

"How are you and Ida Mae getting along?" he suddenly asked.

"Last time I saw her, things were great."

"You like her a lot?"

"Yeah, I do. She's cute as a button, and she treats me right."

"How do you treat her?"

I looked at Pa. "Okay, I reckon. Probably even a lot better than that. To be truthful, I'm scared to death of her, and so I treat her pretty much like I would treat the king or queen of England. Is that good enough?"

Pa smiled. "I imagine it is. Just be certain that, for so long as you remain together, you treat her like a queen, and I guarantee she will always act like one for you."

For a few moments we rode silently. "Pa?" I finally asked.

"Yes?"

"Can I ask you a hard question?"

"Of course. I don't know if I can answer it, but I will try."

"How come the Lord doesn't let women hold the priesthood?"

Pa looked at me and saw immediately that I was serious and

wasn't interested in one of those dumb jokes about holding priesthood holders. "Why do you ask?"

"Well, lately I've been reading a book about Jesus, and it seems to me that of all the people who surrounded Jesus, the women were strongest and most steadfast. I know the apostles were great, but many of them wavered a little, at least right after Christ died. There is no evidence that the women ever did."

"What book are you reading?"

"Farrar's *Life of Christ*."

"That's a fine book. I'm glad you're reading it."

"Well, it is enlightening in lots of ways. Anyway, reading it got me to thinking a lot about Ida Mae and Ma and Aunt Polly and Aunt Victoria and my sisters, and I don't know that there are any finer people in all the world. I mean that, too. I'm not as good as them, not in hardly any way at all. So why did God single me out and give me His power, and leave them out in the cold? Why, for that matter, has He *always* done that with men and women?"

"Are you sure He did?"

"Well yeah! I mean, I know you say that Ma holds your authority hand-in-hand with you, and those are dandy words, but in lots of ways they don't cut ice, and you know it. You and I were ordained, Ma wasn't. You conduct all the affairs of the ward, Ma could never be a bishop, and on and on. That's what I mean. Why did God leave them out? Especially when womenfolks seem so much more righteous."

Pa rode quietly for a minute. Then he drew rein and I pulled up beside him. "I don't know that women are always more righteous than men," he said quietly. "But I *have* noticed that most women seem more inclined to want to be righteous. And you are right about the ladies in our family. In my personal opinion, they are much more deserving of God's authority than I am. That's why I think He gave it to them."

"What? But Pa, you know—"

"Hear me out, Son. God gave those sisters His authority just as He did us, but He gave us completely different assignments. Man's is limited and given only according to personal and immediate worthiness, and seems to be to conduct and preside and hopefully represent. Women's authority, on the other hand, is universal and is the power to conceive and nurture and give love to God's newly born children."

"Pa, every woman on earth can have babies."

"I know. And that seems to say something for their level of spirituality and worthiness in the premortal existence, doesn't it."

"I . . . I don't understand what you are saying."

"Hy, you already pointed out that you have noticed your mother's and Ida Mae's great personal worthiness. Isn't it possible that women, in the premortal existence, and I mean *all* of them, had developed to such a high degree spiritually that God gave them, in a blanket sort of way, the power and authority to bear His children into mortality?

"And if that is so, and it is my opinion that it is, then it seems to me there is *no way* that any woman should ever need to feel second rate to a righteous man, one who not only had to prove himself premortally but must do it again here in this life as well."

"And of course," I added, "if a man is *unrighteous,* then it would be impossible to feel second rate to him anyway."

"Absolutely. Now there is another problem that I should mention. We are beset by groups composed primarily of selfish people who claim that the bearing of children is demeaning and is an odious burden. These people would deny the God-given power to create life and are now even denying the sanctity of that life itself. Hyrum, these people are inspired by that same enemy of righteousness who once sought to overthrow God Himself. There are not many of these selfish people now, but I fear that they will multiply and grow more loud, and one day they will deceive even some of the elect of God. Make certain, my son, that you are not one of those who is so deceived."

"I'll be certain, Pa. Someday I really want to have a homeful of children."

"Good. Though they are a trial, children are also a great crowning blessing. Now, let me conclude this, and we'll be on our way. I believe, Hyrum, that *both* men and women have been blessed with great power and authority from God, gifts indicative of His love and trust. They are just here on different missions."

"I reckon what you are saying could be true," I said thoughtfully. "Still, those powers are surely not the same."

"Of course they aren't. But then, neither are men and women the same."

"Yeah, I remember when we talked about that last year."

"Good. Now remember, Hy, what I've told you isn't scriptural. As I've thought about it, however, it certainly seems to make a great deal of sense. What do you think?"

"Well, like you say, it seems reasonable, because I surely don't think God would favor me above a person like Ida Mae."

"No, He wouldn't, and that *is* scriptural. God is no respecter of persons. I believe that doctrine with all my heart and soul. I also believe the scripture that says that neither the man nor the woman can be without each other in the Lord. According to that statement, *no* gender is most important. It's comforting to me to know that, to understand that my God loves and honors and respects *all* His children."

We sat for a moment in silence while I thought about it all. Pa did have a way with words, and truthfully, though I wasn't certain I understood all he had said, I surely couldn't fault what he had.

The horses shifted restlessly in the afternoon heat, a long-eared jack-rabbit shied from a clump of brush a few feet away and bounded off to safety, and suddenly Pa spoke again.

"Hy," he said, pulling his horse around. "Suddenly I have a funny feeling. Seems to me it'd be a good idea if we split up and head into town from different directions."

"What's wrong, Pa? I bailed you out legal."

"I know. I suppose it's the gold that's worrying me. That and Hebron Clawson's threats. I've been nervous ever since he moved his wife to town and set up his base of operations there. Let's split up. You swing around and come into town by way of the depot, and I'll mosey around by Polly's Peak and come down that way."

"You going to Aunt Polly's?"

Pa nodded.

"I'll go home, then. Will I see you tomorrow, before I go back to the herd?"

"Unless things get hot I'll stop by your ma's. Hy, you be careful."

"I will, Pa. You do the same."

"Don't you doubt for a minute that I *will* be. Thoughts of those prison doors clanging shut would turn a ghost pale. Me, they plumb petrify. You can bet I'll be careful. And Hy, thanks for the bail. Words like this come hard to me, but . . . well, I love you, Son."

I blinked back my sudden tears. "I love you too," I said quietly. "And Pa, I'm proud of you. I truly am."

We separated, and had I known what was to befall, I'd have not been grinning so widely. Problem is a man can't read the future, so he marches into terrible trouble with a smile on his face and nary a care in his heart. And maybe that's the way things are meant to be. It's surely most often the case, I'll say that.

6

Ida Mae's Home—
Fountain Green

A few minutes later, as I approached the depot, I was startled to see Marshal Clawson's piebald gelding tied to the hitching post. At first I doubted it was his, for I knew he could not have ridden to Fountain Green faster than Pa and I had done. Then I remembered the train, and I knew how he had arrived so quickly.

Now I was glad Pa and I had made the decision to go by horse. No matter what Pa had said, riding on the same train as Marshal Clawson would have been somewhat less than wonderful, and that was a fact. Pa would've been skittish as the last flea on a drowning dog, and there was no telling how old Clawson would have reacted. Yes sir, I was glad we'd come the hard way.

Skirting the depot, I wondered whether I should go right home or go see Ida Mae. I debated with myself for maybe three seconds, and the decision made, I was instantly riding up the long lonely road to Sorenson's place outside of town.

I reckon Ida Mae saw me coming, for when I swung through the gate, she was on the porch, looking pretty as a field of new spring daisies. It's hard to explain what being around that girl did to me, but it was somewhat considerable. Just the sight of her got me all prickly under my skin, and she'd not even said yea or nay.

Her hair was down that day, something I'd not often seen before, and there was a lot of it, for a fact. It was all long and deep dark brown with red in it, and there were lots of curls cascading around her face and over her shoulders. They looked kind of like a fiery halo when the sun was behind her. Then she smiled at me and I forgot all about her hair.

Ida Mae had a smile that would've melted a revenue collector's heart. Her lips were bright red and full, her teeth gleamed white when she smiled and laughed, her nose was thin and turned up pert on the end, her cheekbones had somehow become a little more prominent in the past year, and all of that made her face seem more angular and lovely than ever.

And her eyes, oh my goodness if she didn't have the most wondrously mysterious eyes. They were a bright blue that somehow could turn to gray or green and could sometimes even be flecked with yellow. They were framed by the longest and the darkest lashes a body ever saw, and they danced, all the time they danced with their own sparkling light. When she looked at me, sometimes it gave me the fluttering fantods, for it felt like she was looking right through me. That was bad, but what was even worse was that when I got close to her that day, I saw a brightness, like a hot fire or something, that I'd never seen before. Spooky, that's what it was.

"Hyrum, what a surprise!"

I swung off the old horse, and Ida swept off the porch and without so much as a by-your-leave she was up to me and had both of my hands in hers before I could even be proper and remove my battered hat.

"H-howdy," I stammered, mesmerized by her incredible eyes.

"You look fit," she said, pulling back a little but not letting go her grip on my hands. "I don't reckon you came home sick or injured."

"You look mighty fit yourself," I said, grinning sheepishly. "Fitter even than I remembered."

Ida Mae suddenly blushed, and I was glad there weren't any mirrors hanging from her porch. Sudden I was sweating like a hog-butcher at frost time, and I know I was red from the crown of my hat clean to the soles of my boots. I couldn't believe I'd said what I had. I was glad I had, mind you, but still I could hardly believe I'd managed it.

"So what brings you back from the herd?" she asked, breathing deeply to cover her embarrassment.

"Business," I answered, not wanting to get too elaborate.

"Business? Hyrum . . ." and now there was so much honey in her voice I was afraid her tongue would stick to the roof of her mouth. Howsomever it didn't, and she kept on, ". . . that word has a *very* mature sound. Uh . . . what *sort* of business are you doing?"

Sweeter than ever. Oh my! How could a feller *ever* keep secrets from a woman like her? "Well . . . uh . . . I reckon I had to go into Provo and go Pa's bail."

"Bail?" Now her eyes opened wide, and looking down into them

I supposed I could see all the way to China, they seemed so deep. "Your father's out of jail?"

I nodded.

"How wonderful! My father will be so pleased. My, how he dislikes conducting all those meetings."

Well, I grinned and was stewing on what we could discuss next, this had all been so pleasant, when that Ida Mae girl rared back and hit me with her next question, the one I'd hoped she'd never ask.

"But Hyrum, his bail was a thousand dollars. Where on earth did you ever get that kind of money?"

Quickly I dropped my gaze and shuffled my boots in the dust, wondering how best I could answer her. Nearby a chicken clucked softly as she pecked in the dirt for her own sorts of treasure, and from out back came the noise of hogs worrying each other for the coolest spot of mud in the pen.

I heard all that, was aware of Ida Mae's hands holding my own, thought about how pleasant her touch felt, and suddenly I knew I couldn't tell her all of it. Like Pa had told me, gold came ready-packed with greed and grief and misery, and I didn't want to dump any of that on Ida Mae.

Still, I couldn't lie, and not be true to all my ma and pa had taught me. "I found a little money someone had stashed," I answered quietly, looking directly into her eyes.

"Stashed? But Hyrum, wouldn't that be theirs? Whoever hid it, I mean?"

"It would've, but this was stashed a long time ago, years and years, and that poor pilgrim won't never be back."

"Won't ever."

"That's what I said. By now he's long dead. That's why Zene and I decided the best thing to do with it was to go Pa's bail."

Suddenly I remembered what I had in my saddlebags, so reluctantly I let go of Ida Mae's hands and turned away. "That reminds me. There was a mite left over, so I picked you up a little something with it."

I handed Ida Mae the package. She took it, her eyes wide and serious, and slowly she opened it.

"Oh, Hyrum," she whispered as she lifted that frilly-frally dress up to her. "It's . . . it's . . . oh my, it's lovely!"

She held it like it was a dancing partner or something, spinning around with it again and again, and I stood there grinning like a jack-ass eating cactus. Suddenly, however, she stopped spinning and threw her arms around my neck, and once again I was the startled beneficiary of the munificent contraction of her oral orbicular muscles. Kissing, I was beginning to think, was such a wondrous occupation that a man ought to give careful consideration to entering into it on a full-time basis. Especially could he go into partnership with such a pair of lips as graced the beautiful face of Ida Mae Sorenson. Yes sir, I—

"Hyrum, did you know this is the first store-bought dress I ever had?"

I didn't, but I don't think she really wanted an answer. Leastwise she never waited around for one.

"This'll be *perfect* to wear to the dance tonight. Hyrum, you'll escort me to the dance, won't you?"

"I . . . uh . . . well, Pa suggested that I get back to—"

"Hyrum," and now her voice was sticky-sweet again, "you simply *must* take me to the dance! Why, I'll be wearing *your* dress."

She reached out then and put her hand on my arm, soft-like, and squeezed. I felt the gentle pressure from those slender fingers, and suddenly I knew they had closed on my arm and my will like a number 6 lynx trap.

I don't know, now that I think on it, why her words and her squeeze were so important. Nor do I understand why they affected me so. After all, the dress wasn't mine anymore at all, it was hers. And I *did* need to return to the herd. Still, Ida Mae made it seem like her wearing *my* dress to the dance, and me coming along with it, were about the most important things to happen to either of us since who flung the chunk.

"I'll go," I said, grinning widely again. "It'd give me great pleasure to accompany you. I'll pick you up at eight."

Ida Mae smiled sweetly and hugged that dress close to her in a way that made me think she was wishing it was me. I turned red again and hurriedly climbed back aboard Andrew Aagard's broken-down horse, and that was the way we parted.

All the way down the road I could hear her sweet voice singing "Darling Clementine," and all the way down that same road, I was grinning and feeling rosy as a chapped papoose. It was truly wondrous how good that little lady made me feel.

7

The Pavilion—
Fountain Green

The dance that night was held in the Pavilion, a big log building
that sat back a little way from what folks were calling State Street.
We in Fountain Green did about everything in the Pavilion except fix
supper and go to church, and I reckon they could've done those there
too, had they wanted. The floor was thick planks that had been hand
hewn; there were two possum-belly stoves, one on either side; there
was a stage at one end where traveling theatrical groups put on their
thespian performances and where the band sat when dances were in
progress; and there were two coatrooms near the front door, one for
men and one for women. The men's coatroom wasn't much shakes,
but I'd heard tell the women's room had setees and chairs and was a
wondrously comfortable place. 'Course I'd never been in it, as you
can understand, but that's what I'd heard.

I picked up Ida Mae in Pa's surrey, a fancy rig he'd bought when
we could afford such luxurious trappings. And it *was* luxurious, with
long fringes around the top and isinglass curtains and spokes painted
bright red and trimmed with black. It was up for sale, but so far Ma'd
found no buyers. That was why she let me take it.

I'd had a good visit with Ma and had told her all about the gold
and what I'd done with it. She was pleased for Pa, of course, but she
was worried plenty about me. She felt about gold like Pa, I reckon,
and she was certain there was trouble ahead for me. Between them
they had me some nervous, but when I saw Ida Mae in that frilly-
frally dress, all my worries vanished. She was truly a vision to be-
hold.

"Evening, ma'am," I said sheepishly.

"Good evening, Mr. Soderberg," she answered, and with a
flourish she twirled and handed me her cape. Her brother Curley was

watching all of this, and when I went to drape it over her shoulders, he rolled his eyes, grinned, snickered a little, and walked away.

Well, I got beet red, and it was a miracle I got the cape on her at all, I was so ventriculated. Finally, however, we were in the surrey and on our way to the dance.

"Do you like the dress, Hyrum?"

"Uh . . . yeah. I mean, that's why I picked it out. I always liked it."

"Silly. I mean, do you like it on me?"

Well I should smile I did. 'Course, I'd have liked burlap bags had Ida Mae been wearing them. In the past year she'd filled out in all the right places, and what she did for that dress was truly remarkable.

"Well?"

"I . . . I don't reckon I've ever seen a prettier gal," I responded finally. It sounded lame as a horse that'd thrown its left hind shoe, but by gum it was honest, and I reckon Ida Mae knew that.

"Hyrum," she said, taking hold of my arm and snuggling up close, "you do say the sweetest things."

"Yeah," I sighed, breathing deeply, "reckon I do."

And so, snuggled up next to *that* little slice of heaven, we arrived altogether too soon at the dance.

That dance was a lulu, too, as a matter of Fountain Green dust-stomping fact. The town band numbered four men and two women: two guitar pickers, two fiddle sawyers, one banjo-picking man that did licks like I'd never heard before, and one man who called and thumped the tambourine. We could hear the music from about a mile away, and by the time we got to the Pavilion, even our horse had found the rhythm.

Ida Mae hung her cape in the women's coatroom, we stepped out on that floor, and the way folks's heads turned to gape at Ida Mae, you'd have thought she was governor of the whole territory. Talk about belle of the ball! She was it that night, and for sure.

We managed to do-si-do our way through one Virginia reel and one square dance, and then by dingleberry if Pete Livingston didn't cut in. I didn't begrudge him none, though, for he'd only made it through one round of the next dance himself when *he* was cut by Miller Hansen, so called because there were so many Hansens in town and he was our miller.

From him Ida Mae whirled to old Hans Wegian, called that because he was a Norwegian. That brought up Hans Tinker, our local

repairman. He was followed by Andrew Aagard, my Boss, and then
by the banker, Harrison Short, who was always trying to get ahead of
Brother Aagard in the lofty world of high finance, something everybody but him knew was impossible. When that dance was over, Ida
Mae needed a rest.

Brother Short brought her to me, and she was flushed and laughing and basking in all the light of adoration. The way folks were
carrying on, it made me proud just being seen with her. I could tell
that I wasn't the only one who'd noticed her stunning good looks.

"Folks," the tambourine man called out after we'd all had a
couple of minutes breathing time, "the next dance is a special
number, named after the little lady in the blue taffeta dress. Pick your
partners, square them off, and let's begin the Ida Mae!"

Well, I stared at the caller, Ida Mae grabbed my hand, and the
next thing I knew, we were the head couple in the center square on
the floor.

"One, two, three, four," the man called out in cadence, thumping
his tambourine against his fist, and with the first screech of the fiddles
we were into it.

> *Gents form a circle, Indian-style,*
> *Ida in the middle and the gents go wild!*
> *Ida Mae, Ida Mae,*
> *We're in love with Ida Mae!*

Well, all around us folks were laughing and whooping, and even
sour old Dutch Hanner, so-called because she was from Holland, was
smiling and tapping her feet. I'll tell you, that was a round, and I was
skipping through it just like the rest of them.

> *Heading down to Shanty Creek,*
> *Hide your eyes and we won't peek,*
> *Do-si-do in the big barn dance,*
> *Ain't no gal that's got a chance.*
> *Drinking corn and salty dogs,*
> *Chasing through them soggy boggs,*
> *Fox in the henhouse I don't care,*
> *'Cause chasing Ida's free and fair.*

> *Fare-thee-well, Betty Lou,*
> *Fair-thee-well, I say—*
> *Ain't nobody chasing you,*

> *We're in love with Ida Mae.*
> *Ida Mae, Ida Mae,*
> *We're in love with Ida Mae.*

The caller stopped calling then, but the banjo and the guitar players started in on their licks, folks were really stomping, and the dust was rising so thick a body could hardly see across the floor. Nobody minded, though, and the dance just got hotter than ever.

> *She's gonna lead and we're gonna follow,*
> *Bay like a hound-dog through the hollow,*
> *Run, run, fast as you can,*
> *She can out-call a hog-eyed man.*
> *She can swim and she can climb,*
> *Ida's making double time—*

Again the music swelled, and even with my gimped-up leg I was fairly flying. Ida Mae's face was lit up like a Christmas tree, and I'd never seen anyone look so happy nor so beautiful as she did.

> *All the boys from miles around,*
> *Foller her from town to town,*
> *Round the tree and back again,*
> *She can't lose and we can't win.*
> *Do-si-do, Cotton-eyed Joe,*
> *Swing to the middle and I don't know,*
> *Foller that girl in a hollow log,*
> *Wind up kissing an old groundhog.*

> *Fare-thee-well, Jansey Ann,*
> *Fare-thee-well I say—*
> *We're going to catch her if we can,*
> *We're in love with Ida Mae.*
> *Ida Mae, Ida Mae,*
> *We're in love with Ida Mae.*

Just then, as I took Ida Mae and swung her around, I looked over to the door, and honestly, I about fell over. There, big as life, was my Pa and Ma. "By jumping jehosephat," I murmured happily, "he's with Ma, and he ain't even in disguise."

"What's that?" Ida Mae gasped happily.

"Nothing. Pa's here, is all."

"Oh good," she laughed, not really understanding, I'm sure,

about Pa's courage in showing up at a dance, and then we were off
again.

> *Swing her high and swing her low,*
> *Swing to the middle with a backhand roll,*
> *Swing her up and swing her down,*
> *Chasing Ida round the town*
>
> *Fare-thee-well, mother dear,*
> *Fare-thee-well I say—*
> *We'll get back some time next year,*
> *We'll be chasing Ida Mae.*
> *Ida Mae, Ida Mae—*
> *We're in love—with—Ida Mae.*

Well, the dance finally ended, with Ida Mae safely in my arms,
and as we both staggered toward the side, laughing and gasping for
breath and being back-thumped by about everyone there, I don't
think I'd ever been so happy. Despite that gimped-up old leg, I could
really dance. But even more important, I could dance with Ida Mae,
and that was what made it all so terrific.

"Oh Hyrum," Ida Mae gasped as we stood close together, "I had
no *idea* you were such a dancer. That was *wonderful!*"

I grinned sheepishly, the fiddle-players launched into a waltz,
and for the next three or four minutes Ida Mae and I drifted happily
around that old plank floor, close to each other as I'd care to get,
completely oblivious to the world around us and the cares it main-
tained. I was happier'n a centipede without bunions, and the way I
felt then, I didn't care if the night never ended.

When the music stopped, we drifted toward the door where I'd
seen Pa and Ma. Happen they'd taken in my fancy footwork, I was
figuring on doing a little boasting. Howsomever, when Ida Mae and I
got to the door, things serioused themselves down right quick, and I
didn't do any bragging at all. Fact is, I didn't say anything. I just
gripped Ida Mae's hand, she gripped mine, and we stared.

There were Pa and Ma, all right. But some ways behind them,
looking miserable as ever despite he had his lovely wife with him and
was dressed up in his Sunday best, was our own Deputy Marshal
Hebron Clawson, in the flesh.

8

The Pavilion—
Fountain Green—
Again

"H-hello," I said to the Marshal as I gripped Ida Mae's hand and did my best to stall the man until Pa might see him. Only Pa didn't look. I was shaking like an aspen leaf in a high wind, and I didn't know what else to say.

Marshal Clawson looked at me, scowled like he'd just bit into the greenest apple on the tree, grunted, and turned away.

Ida Mae looked up at me, and I shrugged desperately, for I was truly at a loss for words. I didn't expect her to help, but I was praying hard enough that I half hoped a legion of angels would come down and go to work on the marshal. They didn't, of course, but I was standing next to one that I'd not even thought of, and she took over for me.

"My, what a lovely dress," Ida Mae said sweetly to Marshal Clawson's wife, Amelia.

"Why, thank you, my dear," the woman responded, smiling. "Yours is beautiful too."

"Thank you. Hyrum gave it to me just today."

"How sweet. He has very good taste, in girls as well as in dresses."

Well, I colored up at that. I think Ida Mae did too, and so I made another stab at conversating with the marshal. "Nice dance, isn't it," I declared hopefully.

"Umph!"

"Good band, too."

"Umph!"

"Folks're really raising the dust."

"Umph! And *umph*!"

Well, I was getting disgusted with the man, but apparently I was no more disgusted with him than was his wife, Amelia. After the last "umph" she jabbed him with her elbow, and with a whisper that could be heard for a country mile, she called him to repentance.

"Don't be so rude, Hebron. Talk to the boy."

"But—but—"

"No *buts*! *Talk* to him!"

Hebron Clawson looked at her, looked back at me, and then with a sort of sickly grin finally spoke. "Pretty warm, isn't it?"

Well, I was about to make some inane remark of my own when Ida Mae suddenly answered him, and right away I could see the drift of her conversation. Not only that, but I hoisted my own sail and did my best to help it along, knowing that the more we talked the better Pa's chances were. Happen, that is, that he saw us, which so far he hadn't.

"What's pretty warm?" Ida Mae asked innocently.

"Why, the weather," the marshal responded, sounding surprised.

"What weather?" I asked, slipping quickly in.

"Why, this weather."

"Well, how's this different from any other weather?"

"Well, it's warmer."

"How do you know it is?"

Marshal Clawson looked at me with a strange look in his eyes, while his wife beamed happily as she watched the dancing from beside him.

"I—I suppose it is," he answered.

"Isn't the weather the same everywhere?"

"Why, no—no; it's warmer in some places and colder in others."

"What makes it warmer in some places than it's colder in others?"

"Well you little crippled pipsqueak! I ain't a'gonna—"

Marshal Clawson got another elbow in the solar plexus, and right away he was back in our conversation with all his heart and soul. "I reckon," he sputtered, "it's the sun—the effect of the sun's heat."

"Makes it colder in some places and warmer in others? Marshal, I never heard of such a thing."

"No, no, no. I didn't mean that! The sun makes it warmer."

"Then what makes it colder?"

"I—I believe it's the ice."

"What ice?"

"Why, the ice, the ice that—that was frozen by—by the frost!"

I could tell that the Marshal figured he had just won a major victory, and I probably should have let him claim it and just walked away. But I was enjoying myself so much, and I had just read a book about weather patterns besides, and so I was pretty anxious to show off. Then too, so far as I could tell, Pa *still* hadn't noticed us, nor had anyone else, and so I needed to give him more time.

"Have you ever seen ice that wasn't frozen?" I asked quietly.

"No—that is, I believe I haven't."

"Then what are you talking about?"

"I was just trying to talk about the weather. Amelia said—"

"And what do you know about it? What do you know about the weather?"

"Well, I been in it enough, so I ought to know something, you young whipp—"

"No sir, you don't, and that is a blue-tailed fact. Yet you come into this dance and begin to talk about the weather as though you owned it, and I find that you yourself don't know a solitary thing about the matter you yourself selected for a topic of conversation. Marshal Clawson, you don't know one thing about meteorological conditions, principles, or phenomena; you can't tell me why it is warm in August or cold in December; you don't know why icicles form faster in the sunlight than they do in the shade; you don't know why the earth grows colder as it comes nearer the sun; you can't tell why a man can be sun-struck in the shade; you can't tell me how a cyclone is formed nor how the trade-winds blow; you couldn't find the calm-center of a storm if your life depended upon it; you don't know what a sirocco is nor where the southwest monsoon blows; you don't know the average rainfall in the states or even in our territory for the past year; you don't know why the wind dries up the ground more quickly than a hot sun; you don't know why the dew falls at night and dries up during the day; you can't explain the formation of fog; you don't know one solitary thing about the weather, Marshal Clawson, and you are just like a thousand and one other people who always begin talking about the weather because they don't know anything else, when, by the Aurora Borealis, they know less about the weather than they do about anything else in all the world, sir!"

Well, the poor marshal was staring at me with his mouth hanging open, his wife was still smiling, though *mighty* stiffly, it looked like, and even Ida Mae had grown pretty quiet. Then with a loud and disgusted "*umph,*" the marshal turned away, and Ida Mae and I were alone once more.

"Where'd you learn all that?" she asked breathlessly.

"In a book. Would you look at my Pa. He *still* hasn't seen the danger, and—"

"Hyrum, how did you *remember* all that?"

"It's a trick Pa taught me. All it is is a matter of concentration. Focus on what you read, and once it is read, it will always be yours. I've been learning scriptures that way, too. Did you see ol' Clawson's face?"

"I'll say I did. He was humiliated."

"I know. Served him right, the sneaking coyote."

Now Ida Mae looked up at me, and her voice was quiet and earnest. "It may have, Hyrum, but I don't know. I hope you won't regret humiliating him like that."

"Why should I? He can't touch me. I'm no polygamist."

"You say you've been learning scriptures?"

"Yeah, and—"

"Hyrum, have you learned yet the scripture called the Golden Rule?"

Quickly I looked at the little gal who stood beside me, and suddenly I was feeling terribly guilty. I even— "Oh no!" I gasped. "Ida Mae, I think we've got trouble!"

Pa *still* hadn't seen the marshal, and was now right in front of him, laughing and visiting with Ma and a couple of other folks, while the marshal, right behind, was chewing on his dirty yellowed mustaches and just aching to reach out and clap some irons on Pa. He looked plumb miserable; his tight-fitting old suit didn't help him none, and his poor wife, standing next to him and reading his mind every bit as easily as I was, looked miserable too.

Then the band started up again, and Pa, with a laugh, took Ma's hand and together they headed for the center of the floor.

Well, I reckon Pa's flagrant violation of the Edmunds-Tucker Act had gotten to the marshal. Muttering, he gripped his fists together and started after my folks. Just then I caught old Hans Wegian's eye and he gave me a warning look, and I knew that once again it was up to me. Clawson had decided to arrest Pa, and somehow I had to stop him long enough so that Hans Wegian could warn Pa and get him out of there.

I nodded, took Ida Mae's unsuspecting arm, and dragged her into the path of the determined but misbeguided marshal.

"Marshal Clawson," I said bravely, doing my best to hide the quiver that was in my voice, "I apologize for not properly introducing you a few moments ago. May I present Miss Ida Mae Sorenson. She has requested from you, sir, the honor of the next dance."

Well, Marshal Clawson did a double-take and Ida Mae about clobbered me, but the whole entire plan, got together in considerably less than a minute, worked better than I'd ever dared to dream or hope.

Realizing what had happened, and seeing that he was fairly stuck with Ida Mae's truly ravishing beauty, Marshal Clawson decided to take advantage of the promising situation. Drawing himself up to his pompous best, sucking in his ample belly (which was evidence of his prosperity in the cohab hunting business), and smiling through his dirty old mustaches, the portly Marshal Clawson bent forward in a low and courtly bow of acceptance.

"Ma'am," he declared as he descended, "it would be my honor—"

And at the extreme depth of his bow, and in the middle of his little speech, we all heard something rip.

Instantly the marshal's mouth was closed and he was up again, his face even more red than usual. He backed up a step, then another, and while Ida Mae and I stood there staring, he called frantically to his wife.

"Amelia," he whispered loudly, "let's get out of here."

"What?" she answered indignantly. "Nonsense! We've only just arrived. I won't go to a dance and leave again without dancing."

"But—but—" he whispered frantically, "I tore my pants!"

"Nooooo. Let me see."

Mrs. Clawson stepped back and looked down, and the poor marshal almost swung down on her.

"Amelia, don't—"

"My goodness," the woman said, sounding surprised, "you certainly did. You should have listened to me about that suit. You've grown some in the last ten years."

"You're right," the marshal hastily agreed. "Now let's get out—"

"Don't worry, Hebron. I can fix it. I have a needle and thread, so come into the ladies' coatroom with me, and—"

"But Amelia—"

"Come on! Don't just stand there with your underwear airing out. Hurry!"

Well, Mrs. Clawson checked inside the ladies' coatroom, found it empty, and informed her husband of that fact. Then while Ida Mae

and I did our best to keep from bursting our gaskets, and while everyone else tried to keep from noticing, she dragged the reluctant deptuy
marshal through the door and out of sight.

Quickly Ida Mae and I stepped to the door, and without even
planning it, both of us pressed our ears to the wood.

"Hurry up, Hebron," Mrs. Clawson was saying, "take them off!"

"But Amelia—"

"Do it!"

Ida Mae grinned at me, and I grinned back, for through the closed
door we could hear the scuffling sounds as Marshal Clawson pulled
off his boots, dropped them to the floor, and finally dragged off his
britches.

"I'd never have guessed it," I whispered to Ida Mae, grinning,
"but that man's so henpecked he moults twice a year."

"Hyrum," Ida Mae responded with mock indignation. "that isn't
being henpecked. That's simply bowing to superior strength and wisdom."

"Yeah," I nodded, thinking again of what my Pa had told me up
on the divide. "I reckon most women *are* superior in one way or
another."

"*All* women," Ida Mae responded teasingly, and with a smile at
me she signaled that we should listen once more.

"For pete's sake," Marshal Clawson growled a few seconds later,
"hurry it up."

"I am hurrying," Mrs. Clawson answered. "I just need to thread
this needle . . . There! Now it won't take but a minute or two."

For a few seconds there was silence, and then the marshal spoke
again. "Amelia, hurry it up. What if someone comes in?"

"They won't," she replied quietly, and suddenly I had the most
wonderfully evil idea I'd ever had. I looked at Ida Mae—she knew
right off what I was thinking, and her eyes opened wide in protest. I
winked, and suddenly I knew she would go along with me.

"I don't want to hurt him none," I whispered quickly. "Let's just
scare twenty years off his growth."

"He *does* need to go on a diet," Ida Mae agreed, getting into the
fun of it.

We grinned at each other. I straightened up, lifted my voice to a
falsetto, and then I spoke."Well dearie," I squeaked loudly, "I'm for
a rest in the coatroom."

"Me too," Ida Mae sang out sweetly, making herself sound totally exhausted. "I'm so hot I'm about to *die!* Here, let me get the door for you, sweetie. That coatroom's just the place at a time like this."

We shuffled our feet a little, put our ears to the door again, and instantly we knew our dirty little ruse had worked.

"Amelia!" Marshal Clawson yelped desperately, "there's *women* coming!"

I grabbed the doorknob and gave it a little rattle, and Mrs. Clawson came to the immediate rescue of her terrified husband.

"Quick, Hebron," she ordered, "get into that closet!"

We heard her open the closet, shove the marshal inside, and slam the door closed behind him. I pushed the coatroom door open a tiny bit for further effect, Ida Mae and I started to congratulate ourselves for doing this one up proud, and suddenly things on the dance floor got real quiet.

Surprised, Ida Mae and I looked at each other. The band squeaked to a stop, for an instant the air was deathly still, and then from inside the coatroom we heard a furious pounding.

"*Amelia!*" the marshal's voice suddenly thundered, seeming to come from everywhere around us, "lemme in!"

"Hush, Hebron," his good wife called back.

"Open this door!" Clawson screamed, his voice pleading desperately.

"I can't Hebron. Those women are coming in."

"But Amelia," he wailed, "you gotta. This—this ain't no closet!"

"What? But Hebron—"

"Amelia, I'm in the *ballroom!* That—that *door* came into here!"

There was a roar then from the crowd, a mighty cheer, and Marshal Clawson suddenly pounded around the corner and thundered past us, all dressed up in his holey socks, red longjohns, and the upper half of his tight-fitting suit. The applause rose to just slightly short of deafening, and suddenly I was applauding too. Looked to me like Marshal Clawson wouldn't be pestering my pa any more, that night at least.

"Would you care for the next dance?" I asked Ida Mae politely.

"I'd be honored," she replied sweetly, and so together, with no more cares at all, the two of us waltzed back into our own little portion of heaven.

9

Hattie Soderberg's Home—Fountain Green

"Hyrum? Hyrum, wake up!"

Ma's voice sank into my tired brain, interrupting one of the finest and sweetest dreams I'd ever had. Ida Mae and I were down south of town, riding close up to each other in the surrey. I was home from my mission, and we were fixing on getting married . . .

"Hyrum!"

"Yeah, Ma, what is it?"

"Get dressed. Quick."

Well, the tone in her voice wasn't one I liked to hear, for she sounded afraid. Throwing back my covers I leaped up, pulled on my shirt and my pants, grabbed my shoes and socks, and headed for the ladder.

"What is it, Ma?" I asked as I climbed down from my loft with my back to her. "Is something wrong?"

"I'll say it's wrong," a man's voice answered.

Surprised, I spun my head and was startled to see Marshal Clawson standing there with his big old shotgun out and pointed at me. Even more surprising, and frightening as well, was who stood behind him. It was beady-eyed Mr. Doolin, the man from the assay office up to Provo, and he was jumping up and down like someone'd put a burr under his saddle.

"That's him," he shouted over and over. "Arrest him, Marshal. It's him. He held a gun on me, he tried to kill me with a rattlesnake, and he murdered for that gold. I know he did! Now I've earned that reward money you promised me. I have, I surely have!"

"Shut up," Clawson growled at Doolin out of the side of his mouth. "I know who the little crippled pipsqueak is, more's the pity.

"Off that ladder," he ordered then, holding his scattergun on me.

I stepped down slowly, and by then Ma was beside me, her face filled with grief. "Hy," she cried, "I told them it wasn't you! It couldn't be! You found that gold fair and square, and . . . and . . ."

"Back off, lady!" the marshal snarled. "That kid's caused me more grief and trouble than I can say. Besides aiding and abetting and the charges this man here has filed, I aim to prosecute him for defamation of character. He humiliated me in front of my wife, and I'm certain he had something to do with what happened in the . . . the . . . well, later on at the dance. No ma'am, I'm taking him in, and he's earned every bit of the misery he's gonna get."

Well, I thought about Ida Mae and that Golden Rule scripture, and right about then I started wishing with all my heart that I had been a little less smart and a little more wise. Usually, however, when we begin wishing for that, it's way too late. I know it surely was for me.

"But—but you can't just walk into a person's home and take him away," Mother sputtered incredulously.

"Shut up, lady. I'm the law, and I can do about what I want!"

"But—but—"

"It won't do any good, Ma," I answered quietly. "They'll believe what they want to believe. In spite of how Pa feels about him, Marshal Clawson doesn't like Pa, or me either, for that matter. I forced this Doolin fellow to be honest, and so he doesn't like me any more than Mr. Clawson does. Altogether, this must look like a good way to even up a few scores. That I really did find the gold doesn't even matter—"

"Find!" Doolin screamed. "Find, nothing! You killed for that gold, you smooth-talking young murderer! You killed Enock Rhoades, just like you tried to kill me, and then you stole it, just like you *did* steal from me!"

"Mister," I said, turning on him, "you say that once more in front of my ma, and scattergun or not, I'll clean your meat-house up thoroughly!"

Doolin backed up, whimpering, and then I turned to Hebron Clawson. "Marshal, I do have a receipt from him, if that—"

"I'll say he does, forced from me at gunpoint! Marshal, I demand that you arrest this young man right this instant!"

Well, Clawson looked at me. I shrugged and started to turn away in disgust, and suddenly the marshal moved. "Don't do nothing stupid, Soderberg," he growled. "This here double is bored full choke both tubes. She's loaded to the brim with number-one buck.

One false move and you'll look like somebody drove a snubbing post through your brisket, sideways. And frankly, I'd like that. Now where's your pa?"

"I don't know," I snarled angrily. "I haven't seen him since last night, just after you made your hurried departure from the dance."

Marshal Clawson growled hard and lifted his shotgun threateningly, and I thought he was going to brain me right there. Finally, however, with a supreme effort, he got himself under control. "No matter," he muttered. "We'll get him. Stolen bail money's no good. Now you're both in trouble. You were young when Rhoades was killed. How'd you do it?"

"Marshal Clawson, I don't know what you're talking about. I never knew that Rhoades feller, and—"

"Liar," Doolin screamed. "Marshal, he's lying. Look at the bag he had his gold in! You'll see. "

The bag! I'd not thought of that, but now . . . ER—Enock Rhoades. *That's* who that bag belonged to! I recalled the story now, or at least a little of it—Caleb Rhoades's brother disappearing when he was after secret gold. But that had been so long before, how could they suspect me? I couldn't have been more than eleven or twelve. Why hadn't they—

"Give me the bag, Soderberg!"

I looked at Clawson, then at my ma, and then over at the weasel-eyed Doolin. Then with a sigh I pulled that leather bag out of my pocket and handed it to the marshal.

"See," Doolin cried excitedly, "there it is, just like I said. See, there are those initials. ER."

"I see them," Marshal Clawson growled. "Now pipe down and lemme think. Soderberg, how old are you?"

"Seventeen, going on eighteen."

"That would have made you eleven going on twelve. Young, but you could have done it, especially with help. Ma'am," he said, looking at Ma, "where was your son the summer of '84?"

I looked at her, tried to warn her, but it did no good. Ma was a perfectly honest woman, and even if she *had* seen me she'd have said what she said. After all, it was the truth.

"Let's see," she answered thoughtfully, doing her best to remember what I was desperately hoping that she'd forget. "He . . . he was herding for Mr. Soderberg, up in the Uintah Mountains. That's right. I remember it clearly. That was his first summer as camp tender."

Clawson and Doolin looked at each other darkly, and then Clawson asked my mother one more question.

"Was he alone?"

"Alone? Of course not! He was herding with Dale Allred, God rest his soul."

"Is that man dead?"

"Yes, this past winter. We heard he died of consumption."

"Well," Marshal Clawson said as he prodded me with the shotgun, "that cinches it up tighter'n thirty-nine bugs in a bed. You and that other feller did the job, and as soon as he died, you made a beeline for the stash. Pretty cool, young feller, but it won't wash with me. You are herewith under arrest for the murder of Enock Rhoades, and for the alleged robbery of Mr. Doolin here. Now let's get down to the jail."

He pushed me ahead of him, and behind me I heard Ma cry out like she'd been hurt, which I guessed she had.

"Hy," she wailed, "say it isn't so. Say it, and I . . . I . . . ."

"Ma!" I yelled out, "You know me. I didn't do it! Help me, Ma. Get Pa. This ain't right—"

Clawson smashed me in the back with the muzzle of his shotgun, and I didn't say any more. I couldn't. But I'll tell you this: I made a vow then and there that I was going to get out of that jail, and when I did, sure as a belch after a big meal, I was going to clear myself, and then Doolin was going to pay dearly.

10

The Palace Saloon—
Provo, Utah Territory

Felix Ethelbert Friendlessman sat alone at a table near the back of the Palace Saloon, drinking slowly. He was frustrated, he was angry because he was frustrated, and his mood was growing darker by the moment. Somehow that old fool Caleb Rhoades had eluded him again, had vanished without a trace, and eight days of steady tracking and searching had not turned up so much as a new set of hoofprints. The old man had simply vanished.

Again.

Friendlessman stared at his drink and forced his mind to shut out the sounds of the tinny piano and a woman's shrill laughter. In age he was just past thirty, but he was so fiercely intent as to appear more than that. His dark eyes gleamed like live coals. Buried deeply in his head, they seemed to move constantly, making those who knew him think of the eyes of a stoat or ferret. He was full bearded, both hair and whiskers black as stove polish except where silver had touched his temples. His nose was thin and finely formed, his ears were small and lay tight against his head, his body was wire-tight and nervously strung, and his manners were impeccable.

A brilliant, erratic man, Friendlessman was handsome, witty, and elegant, an athlete and an intellect, fawned upon by those who knew little of his true nature. He had been called the Thomas Jefferson of his home county in Pennsylvania, and he was adored by women, yet he was a perjurer, a hypocrite and a manipulator.

When he had been younger he had gathered about him, as a means of furthering his own professed identity—for he was truly hungry to be recognized—what was considered by many to be the intellectual and artistic elite—actually a group of bored men and glib-tongued libertines who talked much of art, literature, and music but who were without any deep-seated convictions upon any subject aside from their own prejudices. Mainly concerned with their own posturing, they were creatures of fad and whim, seizing upon this writer or that painter and exalting him to the skies until he bored them, and then shifting to some other, with the same results. Occasionally the artists upon whom they lavished attention were of genuine ability, but more often they possessed some obscurity that gave the dilettantes an illusion of depth and quality. In most cases, what was fancied to be profound was simply bad writing, bad painting, or deliberately affected obscurity.

Yes, Felix Friendlessman was hungry. Not food-hungry; he cared little for that. Instead, his hunger was for wealth and power. In eastern Pennsylvania he had achieved moderate success in both farming and in intellectual circles. Still, he had felt restricted, not able to acquire the wealth or fame he sought. Others were always there before him, others who fought strongly to protect their own positions of strength. And no matter how he fought back, Felix Friendlessman always found himself left out of the biggest deals or the rarest circles of influence, just short in every race for positions of prestige and power.

Then had come the letter from Wyoming Territory, and his life had been forever changed. Friendlessman recalled the letter, written by the kid he had hired for a brief month in the cold spring of 1882. The kid, whose name was Harry Longabaugh, had moved on, to New York, then back to his home in Phoenixville, and finally west to the territories of Utah and Wyoming. In the letter he had told of his travels and of his new friend, a young man called Robert LeRoy Parker. That had meant nothing to Friendlessman, but according to Longabaugh, Parker had evidence that there existed a fabulously wealthy gold mine near the cities of Ashley and Price, in Utah Territory. Furthermore, if Friendlessman would come west, Longabaugh and Parker would point him in the direction of this mine. This was to be in payment for Friendlessman's kindness, given when Longabaugh had been down and out and only a penniless kid.

For a moment Friendlessman had held the letter and debated, but even in that brief hesitation, he had known that he was going west.

Gold! That was what he needed. Mountains of it. With wealth like that, none of the so-called elite would ever stand in his way again. And so, five years before, Felix Friendlessman had sold his property and had come west, seeking for himself the wealth of Caleb Rhoades's fabulous secret gold mines.

Leaning back, Friendlessman sipped his drink and recalled with bitterness the past five years. He had found Longabaugh, and from what he and Parker—who now called himself Butch Cassidy—had said, he had determined that the mines were supposedly on the south side of the Uintahs, both low down and high up. Yet nowhere in that area, Whiterocks, Ashley, Fort Duchesne, Price, or anywhere in between, could he find a single soul who could, or would, tell him more.

Discouraged, he had hunted down Parker again and had found him working at the FS Ranch, up in Wyoming. That had been in '85. Friendlessman had questioned him closely, and Parker had been very reluctant to give out any further information.

"Can't tell you no more," Parker had said.

"Why not?"

"That gold is sacred to the Utes."

"Sacred?"

"That's right. There's some old tale about Spaniards forcing the Indians to labor in the mines. There was a rebellion, the Spaniards were all killed, and now the mines and the gold are taboo."

"But you aren't an Indian."

"Nope," Parker had replied, "but I respect 'em."

"And you really are foolish enough to believe there is gold?"

Parker had looked hard at him, glanced around, and lowered his voice. "Listen carefully. I'll tell you this once, and if you ever say I said it, I'll flat-out deny it. One day I was heading up here to Brown's Hole, and I was crossing the mountains above Ashley to avoid meeting folks. It started to rain. I rode up a side canyon, dismounted, and crawled into some bushes. I'd been there maybe ten minutes when I became aware of an old tunnel behind me. I crawled in, lighted a match, and knew right off I'd stumbled onto something big. There were bones scattered around, human bones, and mounds and mounds of mined gold ore.

"I was just looking at it, holding a fist-sized piece of ore in my hand, when behind me I heard breathing. I turned, and in the light from my nearly dead match, I saw this big Ute. He wasn't armed, but still I didn't try nothing foolish.

"'Do not touch the gold,' he said in perfect English, 'for it is sacred. There is only one white man who can take it from here, and you are not he.' I believed him, set it back down, and asked him who the man was, and why. He told me, and told me too that I would be all right as long as I left their gold alone. I have done so, Mr. Friendlessman, and recommend that you do the same."

"But why?"

"The curse of God is on them that take that gold," Parker had answered solemnly. "I respect that curse."

Parker, or now Cassidy, had meant it, too. He'd apparently seen the gold since, and yet he had never touched a nugget. Still, in that same conversation he had hinted at a man called Rhoades, so as a last resort Friendlessman had gone to Price, bought some property, and concentrated on watching Caleb Rhoades. And that, finally, had given him his big break.

Vividly he recalled the dying Indian he had found on The Strip near Fort Duchesne when he had been trying to follow Rhoades out toward Whiterocks. He had almost passed the Indian by, for he felt no compassion for the man at all. Yet a sudden thought that this Indian might know something had prompted him to stop and to give aid. As things had turned out, it was one of the luckiest decisions of his life.

He had given the man a drink, and the Ute, with almost his last gesture, had ripped a small medicine pouch from his neck and handed it to the surprised Friendlessman.

"Sh . . . shin-ob," he had mumbled with his last dying breath. "Carre shin-ob . . ."

He had then died, Friendlessman had pocketed the pouch and had gone to notify the authorities concerning the dead Ute, and with one thing and another, it had been several days before he had gotten around to seeing what the Indian's medicine power had been.

The sight of the huge gold nugget had rendered him speechless, and it had also propelled him into what had become the one passion, the single true obsession, of his life. Longabaugh and Cassidy had been right! In spite of the fact that no one would talk of it at all, there was gold, a great deal of it, and nearby!

In the course of the next year, following one pitiful clue after another, Friendlessman had determined that Caleb Rhoades did indeed know where the gold was, but he was not talking. Still, Felix Friendlessman was certain that one day, in one way or another, he would find Rhoades's gold, and the wealth he craved, nay, *deserved*, would at last be his.

Thus were Friendlessman's thoughts as he sipped his drink and cursed the luck that seemed to constantly follow Caleb Rhoades.

Rhoades lived near Price, a town he'd helped to found, and for years it had been assumed that his frequent trips to the mountains were for hunting. But he always had money, a great deal of it, always gold, and his hunting trips always seemed to begin at night. Gradually Friendlessman convinced a few other men that Caleb Rhoades was not hunting but was going to secret gold mines, anciently discovered by the Spaniards, and gathering his wealth from them.

These men, who had come in with the railroad or to work in the coal mines, had been as anxious as Felix Friendlessman to find an easy way to wealth. Thus they had carefully laid their plans to follow Rhoades. They would wait near his small farm out on the Price River; he would set out and they would follow. And they had done this, time and time again. Yet each time he would disappear into the darkness and the mountain, and they would be left behind, both looking and feeling very foolish.

Lately the others had grown tired of the search, and that was fine. Felix Friendlessman had not. He would follow Rhoades alone until the gold was found, and then there would be no one he need share it with, no one but himself. He would not even share it with young Longabaugh, who had only recently taken upon himself the sobriquet "Sundance Kid," chosen because he had spent the past eighteen months in jail in Sundance, Wyoming. Why, even young Parker, or Cassidy, had turned to outlawry, and that very week the papers had reported that he had robbed the bank at Telluride of over ten thousand dollars. No, their pathways had diverged, his and Cassidy's and Longabaugh's, and Felix Friendlessman would never stoop to outlawry. There were easier, if no more legitimate, ways to wealth.

So he'd kept after Rhoades, actually set out alone to find his gold and take it from him, twice. But the first time he had become lost in a thick stand of willows, had left his horse for a moment to find the trail, and had come back to discover that his expensive pistol had been stolen from his saddlebags during his absence.

He had stared around, into the silence of the willows, and had shivered with wonder and even a little fear. Rhoades had been there all the time, playing cat and mouse with him! The old man was a wonder, he truly was!

Actually humbled and yet filled with bitterness, Friendlessman had been unable to do anything but mutter his thanks when, two weeks later, Caleb Rhoades had shown up on his doorstep with the missing pistol in his hand.

"Found this up a side canyon," the old man had said quietly, smiling as he spoke. "Knew it was yours, figured you must have lost it."

And now there was this last incident, the last straw, so to speak, the event that had brought him, finally, to Provo and to defeat.

He'd set out again, carefully, making certain that Rhoades did not know he was being followed. There was no moon, so he had followed closely, guided by the sounds of Caleb Rhoades's horses and mules' hooves striking stone on the hillsides and in the rocky creek-beds. When the clamor of the horses' hooves would stop, so would Friendlessman. When the sound would start again, so would he, carefully, quietly.

All night he had followed the tortuous path, knowing that at last he had managed to stick to the trail of the wily Rhoades. He'd known it would one day happen, and the sense of satisfaction he had felt was almost overwhelming.

At last the sky began to gray in the east, and Friendlessman drew rein in a clump of trees so that he could see without being seen. He could still hear the animals ahead of him, knew that he was close, and knew as well that he didn't want to get *too* close.

Rhoades and his animals were just beyond a small ridge that rose before him, and so patiently Felix Friendlessman waited, knowing that shortly they would come into sight, climbing the face of the next hill.

At last they did, and Friendlessman stared in wonder that turned to horror and anger and frustration and disgust. For there, making her way up the far slope, was not a horse and two mules as he had supposed, but instead an old Ute squaw, climbing slowly, banging two rocks together with her hands as she noisily moved forward.

For Felix Friendlessman, that had ended it. He could not bear to see Rhoades again, could not bear the humility he would feel when the old man would look at him and smile and nod in greeting.

No, it was time to go! Time to get on to San Francisco, where two of his former associates were doing so well. He'd thought of returning to Pennsylvania, but he could not, *would* not, go back, not until he could do so in the manner he felt he deserved.

Therefore—

"I'm telling you," a whiney voice declared, "he found the gold!"

At the word gold, Felix Friendlessman's head came up, and instantly he was listening. The man who was speaking was small, with wispy thin hair and bright beady eyes. He seemed to be drunk, yet he was still upright and was desperately trying to convince a man next to him of the truthfulness of his story.

"It was Rhoades's gold, all right," he went on, banging his fist weakly on the table. "The pouch had ER on it, for Enock Rhoades. I myself weighed it out at over twelve hundred dollars. It was pretty, mostly wire and five-niner pure."

"Ha!" the other man shouted. "Doolin, you do tell the tales."

"It's true. I swear!"

"Show it to me."

Doolin dropped his head. "I can't. The marshal took it for evidence. But that crippled kid done Rhoades in and probably knows right now where them mines—"

Friendlessman waited no longer. Quickly he stepped to the staggering Doolin, put his arm around him, and started him away.

"I'm sorry," he said politely to the man who had been arguing, "but he does carry on when he's in his cups. Why, I'll bet he's been muttering some foolishness about gold mines. It's a persistent nightmare of his."

The man stared drunkenly, finally nodded, and turned back to the bar, and Felix Friendlessman steered the little Doolin from the Palace Saloon and toward the hotel.

"Come, my inebriated friend," he muttered as he dragged him across the street. "You and I have a great deal to discuss, a great deal indeed."

11

July 1889

Ashley-Vernal—
Utah Territory

Leaning against an awning post in front of the general store, the outlaw Jack Moore watched as three men worked to change the sign on the bank across the street. The old sign, which read "Bank of Ashley," already lay in the dust. Now the men struggled to straighten the new one, which read "Bank of Vernal." Moore watched, but he cared little for which was used. His cares concerned only what was inside the bank, and he cared about that very much indeed.

Slowly he scratched the stubble on his jaw, glancing up at the cloudless sky as he did so. It was hot, probably the hottest day of the year so far. And it was only the first of July. Lowering his eyes, he pushed up his hat, wiped the sweat from his forehead, and looked again at the men who were trying to hang the sign. He wished they would hurry with their task and be gone. They were a complication he didn't care to deal with.

Down the street, the man known as Blue John, on account of his one blue eye, lounged in the shade of the hotel veranda. His feet were propped up on the railing, and he seemed to be asleep, but Moore knew that was not the case. Blue John was ready to move in on the bank and waited only for his signal.

Again Moore lifted his hat and wiped at his forehead, wondering for the thousandth time how much money the bank contained. He'd heard that the young fellow who was calling himself Butch Cassidy had taken over ten thousand from Telluride. That was a real haul. He doubted that there was even half that much across the street, but anything was better than the twenty cents he had in his pocket.

Pulling out the makings, Moore fashioned a cigarette, thinking as he did so how thankful he was that the man called Silvertip was not there. Silvertip, whose real name was a thing that was never mentioned, just didn't have what it took to be an outlaw. He was strong as a bull, but when it came to brains he was three bricks shy of a full load. The way Moore saw it, Silvertip's head was stuffed fifty-fifty with sawdust and cement. And given thirty days to do it, he still couldn't figure out how to pour creek water out of a wet boot. No, not even with the directions printed on the heel. And from what Moore had heard, Silvertip was the smart one in his family.

That combination of bedrock head, powerful body, and a strange inbred stubbornness made him about as safe to handle as a black Spanish bull. To get between him and wherever he might be going was deemed as sporty as standing barefoot in front of a trailherd stampede. Or lying naked across the tracks in front of the Sanpete Valley Crawler. Or crimping dynamite caps with your side teeth. Crossing Silvertip was as bound to lead to the rigors of mortis as shooting yourself through the roof of the mouth with an eight-gauge goose gun.

So now Jack Moore thought of Silvertip, smoked his cigarette, wiped at the sweat on his face, and felt only relief that the man had finally and of his own free choice gone his separate way.

Across the street, the three men were finally finished hanging the sign. One at a time they climbed down from the roof and entered the bank, probably to get paid. Moore thought of that, felt a momentary sense of loss that the three were getting some of the money he already considered as his own, and then forced the thought from his mind.

Be generous, he told himself. Let them have a little something. After all, it couldn't be very much, and he'd likely lose more than that on women and poker.

Glancing down the street, he saw that Blue John had lowered his boots from the railing. He still looked relaxed, but that was deceptive, and Moore knew it. Blue John was a grim man, lean and hard as jerked reservation beef, with hair and beard the color of snow melting in a chinook. He was never completely relaxed even when he looked to be—no man rode the owlhoot trail very long after he stopped expecting trouble, and Blue John had ridden that self-same trail for nigh onto eight years.

Moore shifted his gaze again and looked at his new horses. They were strong, had lots of bottom, and if held to their gait would run all day and then some. They were the most superiorly fine horses he'd ever managed to steal, almost as good as that blooded Belgian the Mormon bishop had managed to wrangle from him the year before.

Still, these broomtails were about as good, and with them he felt certain he and Blue John would shortly be safe and long gone from the newly named city of Vernal, bank money, stolen horses, and all.

His gaze shifted once more, attracted by movement in front of the bank. The three workers had stepped out onto the boardwalk, stuffing their money in their pockets as they moved. One of them said something funny, the others laughed, and Moore found himself itching to draw his pearl-handled revolver and relieve all of them of their new burden.

They stood for a minute in conversation; then they stepped off into the powdery dust of the street, mounted their dusty broncs, and were soon departing. Moore watched, saw them all out of sight, saw that save for an old woman and a few scratching chickens, the street appeared empty. Slowly he stretched and straightened from the awning post, flipping away his cigarette as he did so. From the corner of his eye he saw Blue John lift himself to his feet and light a cigarette of his own, and he knew the time was at hand.

Carefully he stepped down into the dust of the street, moving slowly so as not to attract attention. The sun struck him like a hot iron, and suddenly his mouth was cotton-dry. This was always the way it was, and in a strange way he liked it, the feeling of fear that turned to exhilaration when the job was done. Blue John had told him once that he never felt fear, and Silvertip, when he'd been asked about it once, looked blankly at Moore and asked what fear was.

"Silvertip," Moore then asked, "don't nothing ever faze you?"

"Why sure it does," Silvertip had replied, smiling openly. "Now don't press me, Boss, and I'll think of it directly."

Moore had given up. Silvertip, who would wrestle a boar grizzly barehanded just for fun, would go down grinning wherever he was when his bullet came along, and he probably wouldn't even be worried about it. Neither would Blue John, who by his own admission had the grit of a bear-dog and who would bet the devil that hell wasn't hot. No, the question wasn't them. The question, for a blue-tailed fact, was Jack Moore, him as the others called the Boss.

Moore was almost across the street and could hear Blue John angling in behind him when he first became aware of the clatter up the road. Turning, he stopped in amazement, staring at the spring wagon that was churning up the dust toward him.

"What the . . ." he heard Blue John muttering behind him, and then Jack Moore's own jaw fell wide open. Many things in this world were purely amazing, but nothing could beat the stupefying fact that, of all the days to show up, and of all the moments to appear in this one all-important day, good ol' Silvertip had chosen to appear just as he, Jackson T. Moore, and Blue John McGuire were about to pull off the biggest, most grand hold-up of their entire lives. Why, the chances of that happening, in Jack Moore's amazed and hastily considered estimate, were about two times double ought divided by zero.

"Boss," Silvertip shouted as he slowed the team to a stop in the middle of the road, "I got news! For you too, Blue John."

The two would-be bank robbers stared hard at the man they had thought was gone from their lives and wondered what worse could go wrong. Shortly they were to find out, for there was an altogether second rock in their road to robbing the Ashley-Vernal bank.

"Silvertip," Moore growled as he glared at the hulking man in the wagon, "if brains was leather, you couldn't saddle a bug!"

"Now Boss—"

"I mean it! I don't mind you being ignorant, but you sure don't have to work so hard making a perfect job out of it. You're so dog-gone dumb you couldn't teach a setting hen to cluck! Now what in thunder do you mean barreling up here and yelping our names so the whole blamed territory knows what handles we go by?"

Silvertip looked slowly from Moore to Blue John and then back again, and suddenly his face broke into a happy smile. "Say, you fellers were fixing on robbing that there bank, weren't you."

It was a statement, not a question, and it caught them flat. Moore and Blue John stared at each other. Moore felt the itch in his hand again, the itch to draw his revolver and blast away. Desperately he fought to control it, and slowly his fingers lost their curl and his hand fell away from the butt of his gun.

"Silvertip," he whispered hoarsely, "I asked you what is it you wanted. Happen it's nothing but a social chat, Blue John and I are some busy. Now let's *hear* it!"

Again Silvertip looked from one to the other, his smile still on his face. His answer, when it came, was as easy and uncovered as though he were admitting he had forgotten to close the backhouse door. Moore and Blue John looked at him three long drags, and Blue John, finally, flipped his foul-smelling cigarette away.

"You came all the way here to tell us *that?*"

"Sure did, Blue John. Been pumping this rig since before daylight. I got that wire from Mr. Friendlessman, down to Provo. He figures he's got the man who can take us to all that Injun gold."

Blue John looked at the dust that nearly covered his boots and shook his head disgustedly. Moore, just as purely amazed, hawked and spit to clear the gather from his throat.

"Silvertip," he finally growled, "do you have any idea how long Friendlessman's been looking for that gold? Or how many final sure-fire leads he's come up with in that time? Or how many horses and mules he's wore out tromping around in them mountains? Or how many Injuns he's had laughing at him all that time? Or how loud, for pete's sake, ol' Caleb Rhoades has been hee-hawing and hoorahing him these past five years?"

"Five," Silvertip answered.

"Five what?"

"Five years. You asked how long Friendlessman's been looking, and you just said the answer yourself. Must be so if you say it. You're always right. As for how many leads he's had, I don't reckon—"

"Silvertip!" Moore thundered, "get out of here before I . . . I . . ."

"But Boss, ain't you and Blue John coming with me? Friendlessman said this time it was a sure thing, and—"

"No I ain't coming! Blue John and I got work to do here! Now git, you chuckleheaded moron, before I—"

"But Boss . . ."

Moore, his face livid, turned his back on the still-protesting Silvertip and stormed into the bank, with Blue John directly on his heels. Instantly their pistols were out, and they were ready.

"All right," he shouted as Blue John closed the door and stood against it, "everybody get their hands up! This is a hold-up!"

There was no movement, and Jack Moore stared at the teller's cage and the office beyond, suddenly aware that there was no teller. Nor, for that matter, did there seem to be anybody else.

"Boss," Blue John asked quietly as he moved into the room, "where is everybody?"

"I don't know. I ain't seen anybody leave."

"Maybe they're at lunch."

Both Moore and Blue John spun about in surprise, their guns leveled at the innocent Silvertip, who had come in behind them.

"What're *you* doing here?"

"Golly, Boss. I just reckoned you might need some help."

"We don't, you dolt. Now—"

"Boss," Blue John's voice sounded urgent, "you hear that?"

"Hear what?"

"I don't know. Sounded like knocking, sort of."

Jack Moore looked around. "Since when do folks need to knock before they can go into a bank? Besides, see for yourself. There ain't nobody at the door at all."

Blue John shrugged, and then, while Moore and Silvertip watched, he stepped behind the teller's cage and peeked into the office.

"Boss," he whispered loudly, "there truly ain't nobody here."

Moore, deep in thought, suddenly brightened. "Boys," he said, grinning, "it's the perfect set-up. For a minute there I was confuseder than a blind dog in a butcher shop, but by jingo, I just found the bone. I got it all figured out."

"Tell us, Boss," Silvertip pleaded earnestly.

Moore gave Silvertip an evil look and then turned to Blue John. "The way I see it, these folks have been called out on some sort of emergency. So, let's us take advantage of the situation. There can't be no superiorly wondrous time to rob a bank than right this minute, when nobody's home to object. Blue John, you keep a watch on the door; Silvertip, you get the cash out of the teller's cage; and I'll strip the vault. Now go!"

With a happy smile, Silvertip stepped behind the cage and reached for the drawers, and Moore ran into the office, ready to open the vault.

"Boss," Silvertip suddenly called.

Moore, already examining the vault door, ignored the man's call.

"Boss, I got me a little problem."

"Little," Moore muttered as he looked at the door, "you don't know the half of it, you imbecile. You don't have the brains—"

"Boss, there ain't no money here!"

Jack Moore, just tugging at the edge of the vault door, which he had discovered was loose, stopped. So, too, did his breath. "What?" he whispered painfully.

Blue John answered him. "Blazes, Boss. Silvertip is right. These teller's drawers are empty!"

Urgently Jack Moore ran out of the office and, one at a time, yanked out all the drawers and tossed them onto the floor. "Cleaned out," he muttered. "Why in the . . ."

Hastily he moved back into the office while his two subordinates followed. "It can't be," he mumbled as he gripped the edge of the vault door again and started to swing it open. "They were workers, is all. They were hanging the sign . . ."

With the door open, Moore and the others stared incredulously into the vault. Then, almost mechanically, they moved inside. The vault contained nothing but bare shelves and trussed-up bodies, and carefully they untied the teller and bank president, both of whom lay bound and struggling on the floor.

"Oh, thank you," the president gasped as he rubbed his hands, "I thought nobody'd *ever* come. Those three cleaned us out! I've got to get a posse right away or they'll get off scott free."

Then, while Jackson T. Moore and Blue John McGuire and Silvertip stared in amazement, he ran out into the street, screaming for help at the top of his lungs.

The teller, still seated, sat and slowly rubbed circulation back into his wrists. "Boys," he said, "you've no idea how glad I was to see you come into that vault door."

"You . . . you mean those three pilgrims who hung your sign *robbed* you?"

"Sure as horsehair grows in winter they did. But we'll get 'em, don't you worry about that. Meanwhile, although the bank's closed, I'll do my best to help you with *your* business. What was it you wanted?"

Jack Moore stared at Blue John and then at Silvertip and finally looked back at the teller. I don't reckon you can help us anyway," he sighed. "We was just fixing to make a small withdrawal."

The teller laughed bitterly. "Well, you're right as rain about that," he declared. "We've already been withdrawn to about our limit. Sorry, boys, but thank you again for setting us free."

Dejectedly, Moore and the others stepped out into the street, where they stood watching the posse form down near the sheriff's office.

"Who'd have thought it?" Moore growled. "Them sign-hangers! Them dirty, no-account, thieving sign-hangers. I knowed we should've blasted them! I had me a feeling, but oh no, I've got to go be the nice guy. Talk about a Pecos swap if I ever seen one, hanging the sign and then robbing the bank. Ohhh, them dirty miserable low-down—"

"Golly, Boss," Silvertip said happily, "ain't it wonderful?"

"What, you numbskull?"

"Why, seeing that there posse taking off down there and knowing it ain't after us. Gives a man a right peaceful feeling. I'd most forgot what it was like. Why, now we can meet Mr. Friendlessman and go looking for all that gold. Come on, we can use the wagon."

Moore, finally driven beyond the tautly stretched limits of his frustration, was just getting ready to whip out his pistol and terminate Silvertip's benign stupidity when there was a clatter of hooves from behind him. Spinning, he was shocked to see a man ride his horse out from the narrow alley beyond the bank, the alley he had been certain that, only moments before, had been empty.

The man rode forward, drew rein, and sat looking down at the three outlaws.

"Well boys," he drawled quietly, "you was lucky, luckier'n you'll ever guess. Now was I you, I'd climb into that wagon and ride. I'd say the man with the silver hair has a truly fine idea."

Moore slowly turned so that he was facing the stranger, ready to draw. But there was something that stopped him, something—

Backing up a step, Moore eased his hand and looked the man over carefully, trying to discover why he sensed such great danger from one who appeared so singularly alone.

The stranger sat his horse like most men of the time, like a lean sack of loose oats. His long legs reached straight for the ground in the let-down stirrup leathers. Cradled under his offside was the ever-present Winchester. Slung across the cantle were his suggin and slicker, probably encompassing in their slender girth most all that the man held personal in the world.

Coming to his clothes, the pattern held. The trousers were faded blue, low-hipped, shotgun-barreled as to leg, and a man could bet his last twenty cents that their waistband was stamped "Levi Strauss." The full, choked tops of the Levis would be stuffed inside the pull leathers of sixteen-inch Texas boots, and if those boots failed to support cartwheel Mexican rowels, a man would lose the pockets that held his last twenty cents. His coat was black broadcloth, as was his vest. His shirt was white, or at least had been so at one time, and his bow-tie was black and neatly tied. The hat, too, was out of the clothier's bible, a genuine Six-X beaver Stetson, flat-crowned, four-inch-brimmed, and held on by a string under the chin.

As to his face, it was lean and leathery, surrounded by a long beard and even longer black hair that was stringy and streaked heavily with gray. He seemed a bit oldish, maybe, but it was impossible to tell exactly *how* oldish. Fact is, he might have been forty, and then again he might have been twice that. It was just impossible to tell.

He fitted, all right, and yet he didn't. There was something in his eyes, some glint or gleam—

"Who're you?" Moore demanded angrily.

"I'm your judge and jury," the man drawled, his voice more quiet than ever.

"Sure you are," Moore snapped. "And I'm Albert Sidney Johnston, back from the dead at Shiloh. Mister, you talk or I'll drill you."

"No talk needed," the man replied quietly. "And you won't be drilling anybody. Case has been tried and the verdict's in. You've done been found guilty."

"Guilty?" Moore cried, "guilty of what? We just went into the bank to do a little business and found it had been robbed. We was the ones set those fellers loose!"

"Mister," the man said, and Moore noted the hardness that had suddenly appeared around the edges of his voice, "I've been watching you eyeing that bank, so cut the act. You might be heros to these folks, but I know the kind of withdrawal you had in mind. Besides, when you put your foot out to steal them two horses yonder, you did not step into just *anybody's* cowchip. You lit hard with both brogans square in the middle of the grandaddy pasture flapjack of them all. Mister, them horses yonder are *mine!*"

"Wh-what horses?" Moore asked weakly.

Faintly the man smiled. "That's why you ain't pushing up daisies already. I hate to shoot genuine heroes. Nor do I take to wiping out folks who are smart enough to see the error of their evil ways. And mister, I reckoned right off that you was a mighty smart man, quick to repent and anxious to do so. Now the three of you climb aboard that rig and rattle your hocks on out of here. Happen you choose to do otherwise, why, come this time a minute from now, you'll be staring at the sky and seeing nothing but nothing."

"Now lookee here," Moore blustered, "you can't go around telling folks what to do! Blue John, get our horses, and—"

"*Whoa!*"

Moore stepped back, startled by the loud order and even more startled by the terribly sudden and horrifyingly unexplained appearance of the man's big Colt revolver.

"I reckon," the man went on, his voice once again quiet, "that I'll

have to read to you from the book. For the last time, them're *my*
horses. One of you touches either of them again, it'll be about as safe
as kicking a loaded polecat. Comes to them horses, I'm touchier'n a
teased snake. Them're my favorites. Now git into that wagon!"

"But—but our gear," Moore demanded, sensing defeat but still
fighting against it.

"Chalk it up to interest on the use of my horses," the man said.
"Just credit the account of a feller you might call Orrin Porter
Rockwell."

Jack Moore stared, and then felt his mouth go suddenly dry—
very, *very* dry. He heard Blue John suck in his breath and turn and
climb quickly into the wagon, and instantly he was scrambling
aboard himself. Defeat, after all, was nowhere near so hard to accept
as he had thought.

"I—I thought you was dead," he whispered as he settled onto the
seat.

"Not hardly," the stranger declared.

"But you are! Or I mean, he is . . . I mean . . . Listen, I got
friends who was at your funeral, and that was ten, eleven years ago!"

"Do tell," the man responded calmly. "Makes an interesting dilemma, don't it."

"What do you mean?"

"Just what I said, a dilemma. If you're right and I'm dead, you
got nothing to fear. On the other hand . . ."

"Mister, who *are* you?"

Slowly the stranger leaned over and spat. "I've said all I intend to
say. It's up to you to either call or throw in your hand."

"You're right," Moore growled, "and I ain't about to throw—"

"Moore," Blue John muttered, "it doesn't matter *who* he is. That
.44 is real enough, and it's already out and pointed your way."

"Maybe so, but if this gent ain't Port Rockwell—"

"Mister," the man said quietly, "it ain't in you, and you know it.
You'll never know who I am, and you'll likely die wondering."

"By thunder," Jackson T. Moore growled, "we'll see about that!
I'm gonna—"

"Mister Moore," the man interrupted flatly, "you're already
sucking on the front sight of this gun, and if you want the rest of it,
here goes. That sound you hear is a single–action Colt revolver being
cocked. The next sound that you *don't* hear will be your bodies flop-
ping out of that wagon and into the dust. You got that rig ready to
roll, amigo?"

It developed that Mr. Jackson T. Moore's mother had not wasted her cooking on any feeble-minded children. He had got the point of the hard-looking stranger's discourse, and instantly he had the reins and was nodding yes.

"Good. Now *git!*"

Silvertip looked from Moore to Blue John and back to Moore. Both men nodded quickly and vigorously, and so Silvertip, his face wearing a happy smile, climbed aboard, took the reins from the trembling Moore, and reached out and ticked the wheeler with the popper of the whip. He added a kind word for the off-wheeler, and the wagonload of outlaws turned and headed leisurely, in spite of Jack Moore and Blue John's urging instant greater speed, west from the empty Bank of Vernal and Taylor's General Merchandise, Vernal, Territory of Utah.

Happen they'd have thought about it right then, Moore and the others would have known they were going after Friendlessman's Indian gold. They didn't think about it, of course, for two of them could think of nothing but the empty bank and the dark-faced man who was behind them, he of the lightning draw who had claimed to be the notorious marshal Porter Rockwell. The third man, Silvertip, thought little about anything but taking care of his horses, and he certainly wasn't worried. He was merely happy, for he was once again with his friends.

Still, the three were definitely going gold hunting. For them, it was about the only option left.

12

Jailhouse—
Fountain Green

"Hyrum?"

Surprised at the sound of Ida Mae's voice, I started up from my bunk. The jail I was in was small, about ten by twelve feet. It was a single room with one heavy door and two small barred windows up near the ceiling. As near as I could tell it had been made of logs and then framed over with sawed lumber, and altogether it was a pretty dismal place. There was no office to it—the marshal's office was across the street, and once the door was shut, I was alone and more lonely than a man can imagine.

In the room was a bunk and a stool and a bucket, and scattered on the bunk were several issues of the *Deseret Weekly,* which I had been reading off and on ever since I had been locked up the day before. I'd also been reading the graffiti that had been scratched on the walls, and in some ways, that graffiti was a whole lot more educational than the *Deseret Weekly.*

I got two meals a day, which the marshal's wife, Amelia, brought to me, and other than that I got nothing and saw no one. Ma had been down and had talked to me twice, and my younger half-brother Ernest had come and talked to me for a few minutes the day before. But I couldn't see them even when we talked. The window was too high and I couldn't get to it.

"Ida Mae?" I asked, wanting to be sure it was her.

"Oh, Hyrum, are you all right?"

"Yeah, I'm fine."

"Is . . . is it bad in there?"

"Not too bad," I grinned. "I feel about as homeless as a lost poker chip and as lonely as a Wyoming winter sky, but other than that, I don't mind it."

"Oh, Hyrum, I can hardly stand the idea of you being in . . . in *jail!* You would never do *anything* so evil as what they're accusing you of, and I think that awful Marshal Clawson is a disgrace. Oh, how can you bear it in that tiny room?"

"Well," I answered, feeling mighty good that Ida Mae was so concerned about me, "it is somewhat confining. I reckon I can handle it, though."

"You are so brave, Hyrum. I'm . . . well, I'm very proud of you. I know what it means to you to be out and working, and now that you're cooped up in that little . . . little hen-house of a jail, well, now I see even more what kind of a person you are."

I shouldn't have to say that I was getting puffed up in my pride as a bloated heifer, but I was, and I couldn't help it. Now, we take care of heifers when they're bloated by sticking them, and I had no way of knowing that the Good Lord takes care of people the same way. In other words, I was getting ready to be stuck, and I didn't see it coming at all. No sir, in spite of my being in jail, I was still just a happy kid who was basking in the light of his girl's adoration and looking to maybe impress her a little bit more.

"It really isn't so bad, Ida Mae," I said modestly, "even though I do take kindly to open lands and sunshine and the far, lonely winds. I like to look far off. Then it seems like I'm free, even if I'm not."

"What do you mean?"

"Well, in a lot of ways I suppose I am more free than many others, but when you think about it, Ida Mae, are any of us who know something, who have an understanding of one thing or another, ever totally free again?"

"I don't think I understand what you're saying."

"Ida Mae, even when a man isn't bound by walls, he's still bound by knowledge and understanding. Those things tell a man that he is surrounded by duty; duty to the things he knows, duty to family and friends, duty to folks about him, duty to his church and country, duty to the law—such-like. If he ignores that duty, then there is no way that he can call himself a man."

Ida Mae was still, and I wondered for a moment or so if she had gone. "Hyrum," she suddenly said, "you really believe in this duty, don't you."

It wasn't so much a question as it was a confirmation of fact, and I squinted up at the window, wishing that I could see her and explain to her with my eyes as well as my words how I really felt.

"Yes I do. Without duty, Ida Mae, life doesn't make any kind of sense."

"I suppose. But you said law. Do you still feel duty to the law, even after you have been treated so shabbily by Marshal Clawson?"

"Of course. If folks are going to live together, they have to have rules and abide by them. The law is those rules. Now, there are always mavericks who can't or won't ride a straight trail, and so we as people need someone who can ride herd on them. I suppose that is who Marshal Clawson is.

"Under the right conditions, the law doesn't work against a man, it works for him. Without it, every house would need to be a fortress, and no man or woman would be safe. Like Pa says, almost everyone would revert to savagery, and we would all be either victimizers or victims. In fact, I'll bet that when Adam and Eve first got their eyes opened, they likely started making laws so they could live together.

"The law will work for me, too. When I go to court I'll get Zene Hill to testify for me, and this stupid charge won't hold water at all."

"Do you think folks will believe an Indian?"

Ida Mae's question surprised me, and I didn't know how to answer it. "I reckon," I finally said. "Why shouldn't they?"

"Oh, they *should,* but folks being what they are, I wonder if they will."

"Well, I don't wonder about it! Zene's a fine man, and probably a better Christian than 80 per cent of the people here. You'll see. When the conditions are right, the law will work for me and I'll be released pronto."

"And what if the conditions aren't right, like with polygamy?"

Well, Ida Mae had hit squarely the question that was ripping apart the Territory. Conditions were indeed bad, and evil, uninformed men had manipulated the law until we as a people were truly under siege. Pa had told me that hardly a day went by without one or more men, and sometimes even their wives, being sent to prison for adultery or fornication or unlawful cohabitation, whichever ridiculous, trumped-up charge the judges decided to press.

For instance, according to a torn-out news item on the wall of my jail, on Monday, last November 19, 1888, in the First District Court at Provo, Judge Judd had sentenced the following brethren: Hans Nielsen of Chester, Randolph H. Stewart of Moab, Jens Hansen of Gunnison, Eli A. Day of Fairview, John F. F. Doius of Ephraim, Oluf C. Larsen of Ephraim, Wm. Christiansen of Pleasant Grove,

John Spencer of Indianola, Samuel S. Cluff of Provo, Alfred Turner of Lehi, Richard Jenkins of Nephi, Oluf J. Anderson of Castle Dale, Albert Jones of Provo, Orlando F. Herron of Pleasant Grove, Soren C. Jensen of Mt. Pleasant, Lorin Harmer of Springville, and Wm. Gallup of Springville. All were convicted of unlawful cohabitation or adultery, fined up to three hundred dollars each, and sentenced to prison for terms ranging up to fourteen months. From what Pa had told me, that sort of thing goes on five days out of every week.

Then there is the issue of all the Church's property, which the government had seized and placed into receivership under the very greedy hands of now ex-Marshal Dyer. The government had done that because of claims that we are not, under the current laws of the land, a legal entity, which of course is nonsense and religious persecution in the land of the free besides.

Last November Dyer had received over $750,000 worth of Church property, including the temple in Salt Lake City and everything else he could lay hand to, and the crook was demanding a fee of $25,000 for handling it, to be paid, of course, by the Saints.

"I asked Pa about all this," I finally answered, "and he told me that our duty is to always follow the prophet, no matter what kinds of pressures Satan and his minions bring to bear. Pa says that Joseph Smith once prophesied that God would never let the prophet lead the Saints astray. Of course, you know that the prophet says to fight the plural marriage issue peacefully and to work through the courts to finally get the law changed."

What happens if the government won't change it?"

"Who knows? One way or another it will work out."

"But Hyrum, what if they keep throwing people in jail? Do the Saints just keep fighting them and suffering?"

"I don't know," I answered, leaning against the wall. "I've thought about it a lot, and I just can't imagine that the Lord will let that happen. Either the government will change the law or the Lord will open a way so that we can obey it without breaking God's law in the process.

"In Farrar's book about Jesus, he discusses the time when Jesus was forced, by Peter's innocent ignorance, into the position of paying a redemption and temple tax on his own temple and when he was already preparing to give his very life as the ultimate redemption. Farrar says 'He paid what he did not owe, to save us from that which we owed, but could never pay.'

"Jesus taught Peter that He, the Son of Man, should be exempt from the tax, but that if it was paid, it must be done freely and not compulsorily, as should be the case with the living of all religion. Then he told Peter that the tax would indeed be paid but not in the normal way. Peter was told to go and pull a fish out of the water, take a coin from its mouth, and pay the tax.

"Peter did so, Ida Mae, so that Jesus might obey the eternal laws of charity and self-surrender and yet still maintain his God-like majesty in the face of mortal law.

"Ida Mae, I truly believe that same type of thing will happen to us. The Lord loves the Saints for this great sacrifice they have been willing to make, and one of these days, in the very midst of our most difficult struggles, God will instruct President Woodruff to throw in his hook and pull out a fish. Some amazing new development will then occur, and we will once again be known as a law-abiding people, both of God's laws and of man's. Then I can truly speak to you of my duty to the law and mean it."

Ida Mae was quiet, and it was not difficult to hear the chuckling of the small creek that ran behind the jail. Oh, how I longed to be out there, either fishing or just sitting with my feet in the cold water, day-dreaming. I had spent many an hour in such pleasant circumstances, and—

"Hyrum?"

"Yeah?"

"I . . . I'm very proud of you. Yet I can't bear to see you remain in that jail. It isn't fair. I'm going to get you out. Somehow . . . yes, somehow, I will surely see that you are free!"

"Ida Mae, I—"

"I mean it! Sit tight, and I'll be back as quickly as I can find help."

Then she was gone, and I was left alone in the tiny jail, feeling proud as punch that Ida Mae Sorenson was my girl. Yet I was about to get stuck like a bloated heifer, and I had no idea of it at all. Nor was I ready. But then, who of us ever is?

13

Jailhouse—Fountain
Green—Again

"Hyrum, why . . . why did you do it?"

Surprised, I stared up at the window. "Do what, Ida Mae? Go to jail, you mean?"

"No, I mean . . . I mean, why did you *kill* that man?"

Well, I can hardly express my surprise and . . . and *hurt*. It hadn't been four hours since Ida Mae had been telling me how awful it was that I was cooped up and how proud of me she was for not fighting it. And now suddenly I was guilty until proven innocent, and my heart was running over with a bigger ache than I had ever before felt.

"Ida Mae!" I said, my voice filled with exasperation, "I told you what happened! I didn't kill nobody—"

"Anybody, Hyrum."

"Yeah, that's what I said. Nor did I help anyone to get killed. I found that gold just like I said, and—"

"Now I understand why you aren't really fighting it. You are guilty, you know it, and you know it would do no good to try and prove otherwise."

"Oh for pete's sake—"

"Hyrum, you can talk straight with me. I still care about you, very much. I won't get angry or anything, and I really think it would be good if you told the truth. That's the first step in repentance, recognition, I mean, and—"

"For crying out loud, Ida Mae, I *am* telling the truth. What makes you think otherwise?"

"Why, *everbody* says it had to be you, and—"

"*Everybody*? Who is everybody, other than old Clawson and that beady-eyed Doolin from up to Provo?"

"There are others, Hyrum, very influential people. But I don't want to talk about it if you're going to shout."

"I'm not shouting!" I yelled, hardly even able to control myself. "I just want to know who's the dirty underhanded sneak who thinks I'm a murderer."

"He isn't dirty *or* underhanded, and you are too shouting. In fact, he's the opposite. He is a perfect gentleman, something I haven't seen around here in some time. His grammar is absolutely wonderful, and his manners are . . . are . . . well, they're superb!"

Though I hated like blue blazes to admit it, Ida Mae had me there. I'd picked up a tolerable amount of poor grammatical and social habits during my brief mortal probation, and everything I was reading made me more aware of them. Time and again I'd determined to improve, but habits, once adopted, are hard to shed, and I'd found that to be especially true of my verbalogical difficulties. Given time, though, I'd do better. I'd made myself that vow, and knew I would. But convincing Ida Mae of it was something else altogether.

"What in tarnation are you talking about? Who is this . . . this . . ."

"I'm talking about help, Hyrum. Help! And you might be interested in knowing, *Mr.* Soderberg, that he has offered to help get you out of jail."

Well, that was all I needed, help from some feller who was going around telling folks . . . no, telling *Ida Mae*, that I was guilty. Happen he *did* use language that was so polished a feller could skate on it, I could care less. That was *my* girl he was tearing me down to, and I didn't like it one little bit!

"He? He? Who in thunder is he? What's this hombre's name?"

"Felix Ethelbert Friendlessman."

"*Felix Ethelbert Friendlessman*! Ida Mae, that ought to give you a clue right off that the man can't be trusted. I'd say you'd best watch out for him. There ain't a self-respecting man on earth who'd tell *anybody* he was called by a handle like that."

"Well, how rude! And he even wants to *help* you."

"I can tell," I snarled. "He's most surely helping me with you."

There was quiet for a moment, and when Ida Mae spoke again, her voice had a whole new tone to it.

"I declare. I do believe you are jealous."

Now that got to me quick. She was correct as a schoolmarm's manners, or maybe this Friendlessman feller's manners too, and though I hated to admit it, I hated even more for her to know it.

"Well," I growled, changing the subject as fast as I could, "I *would* appreciate all the help I can get, getting out of here. This jail's fast becoming pure misery."

"I'm sure it is," she answered, apparently as eager as I was to change the subject. "What on earth do you *do* in there?"

"Sometimes I sleep. Sometimes I think. And now and then I even think out loud. Most of the time, however, I read."

"Read? What on earth is there to read? Did the marshal give you your books?"

"No, but there's a whole pile of *Deseret Weekly*s, and those poor misbegotten pilgrims who have spent time here before me have scratched a good deal of literature of their own on these walls. Reading what they wrote has been an education all by itsownself."

"Hyrum," Ida Mae said, sounding shocked, "you aren't reading *that?*"

It wasn't difficult at all to catch the vivid edge of disgust that was lining her voice, and I caught it. Made me feel badly, too, it truly did.

"Of course I'm reading it," I replied, forcing a lightness into my voice that I did not feel. "A man needs to be educated, doesn't he?"

"You surely can't call all that . . . that *filth*, an education?"

"Filth? Now Ida Mae, that's being a bit harsh. I admit there's a touch of roughness here and there, but a feller's just got to skip over that. Pa says that's what a man has to do in life, too.

"Actually, I was thinking more on some of this other stuff. One feller must have had bad feet, for instance, for he wrote that the only difference between an oak tree and a tight shoe was that one held acorns and the other held corns that ached. Ida Mae, that there is truly an educational thought."

"I don't get it."

I grinned. "Yeah, it is some deep. Another feller must have been a poet, for there's a whole pile of these limericks. What do you think of this one?

> *There once was a man named Deeth,*
> *Who sat on his set of false teeth.*
> *Said he, with a start,*
> *'Oh, bless my heart!*
> *I've bitten myself underneath.'*

"Now Ida Mae, that's terrible fine literature, as you've surely got to admit."

"I'll admit no such thing!"

"Well, you should. It's better than a lot of stuff folks are passing off as literature these days. They write to make money or to aggrandize their own names before the world, and then they can't understand it when folks don't buy more than one or two of their books. The way Pa says it, if a man takes pen in hand to write something for other folks to read, he'd surely better have something significant to say. Otherwise he's not only wasting his time and money, but he's wasting the time and money of other folks as well. Besides that, he's fiddling with their minds, maybe even preventing them from learning something important that they might otherwise have learned, and that is a heavy responsibility indeed.

"Say, here's one written about us folks."

"Us folks?"

"Yeah, us Mormon folks. See if this doesn't make a little more sense.

> *There once was a young Mormon priest*
> *Who lived almost wholly on yeast.*
> *'For,' he said, 'it is plain,*
> *We shall all rise again,*
> *And I'd like to get started, at least!'*

"Hyrum, that's the dumbest thing I ever heard."

"Educational."

"It is not," Ida Mae declared disgustedly. "If you call that an education, then I'd recommend that a person ought not to have any education at all."

Well, I could tell that Ida Mae was getting riled again, but for some perverse reason I didn't much care. I mean, what did she *expect* me to do in that jail? Metamorphosize? Besides that, being in jail hadn't improved *my* temper too much either. I was there when I hadn't ought to have been, and there was some Felix feller outside who was impressing my girl all over the place, and because of that I was touchier'n a busted tooth and didn't care who knew it.

"I don't know, Ida Mae," I said, feeling evil but enjoying it. "Way I see it, education's like a mother's love or a married lady's morals. A feller don't dare question either one, especially in public. Now you just come out against education, and if folks had heard you, why you'd never get elected to nothing in this whole country. Not *ever*. Same with religion. You could likely stand in favor of them owlhoots who stole your pa's and my pa's horses, or maybe giving free liquor to the Indians, and be better off. Me, I'd rather run on a ticket of kicking stray dogs and pistol-whipping little old ladies than to utter a derogatory word against education or religion. Seems to me, Ida Mae, that you ought to be a little more open-minded."

"Well, I declare!" she stormed. Something banged against the side of the jail, like maybe her toe or something, and she cried out like she might have been in pain.

"Hyrum," she stormed, "I can't even *begin* to imagine what I ever saw in you! You are . . . you are absolutely *despicable!* It's a wonder I recognized the gentleman in Felix at all. I've surely never met one before. So good day, Hyrum Soderberg! And *good riddance!*"

And then she was gone and I was still grinning, only suddenly I was feeling miserable as a calf with the slobbers. Dropping back onto the bunk I sighed, picked up another *Deseret Weekly,* and read where maybe they had caught that feller in England they were calling Jack the Ripper. Then I laid down the paper, stared up at the ceiling, and sighed again.

Blast! What was wrong with me? That little gal was the best thing in my whole life, and here I'd driven her away. Driven her! Made a feller wonder if maybe someone hadn't jiggled the good Lord's arm when he poured in my brains. Blast again! Teasing her had been a sure-enough foolish thing to do. Now I truly *did* feel lonely, and there was no one to blame but myownself.

Yes sir, I surely did give me one miserable day. I'd been stuck but good for my puffed-upedness, and believe me, the gasses of my pride were dissipating fast. Somehow I had to get out of that jail, and I had to do it soon. Even if it was with the help of that Friendless fellow, or whatever his crazy name was. It was the only way I could see of finding out who *had* killed Enock Rhoades. Once I found that out, then maybe Ida Mae would believe me again.

14

Jailhouse—Fountain
Green—Still

"Hyrum?"

Quicker than a New York minute I was up on my bunk and as close to that window as I could get.

"Ida Mae? Hey, I'm sorry! I didn't mean—"

"Hy, you numbskull, this ain't Ida Mae. It's me. Ernest!"

"Oh," I growled sullenly. "Well, why didn't you tell me sooner, you little pipsqueak? You trying to make me look stupid or something?"

"Doesn't look to me like you need much help," Ernest replied. "Besides, I ain't little."

"Then you must have growed some since they locked me up. Yesterday you didn't come no more than hipbone high to a mired duck."

"Oh yeah? Well your head's so hollow you had to hold your hands over your ears to keep from going deaf from the noise of the one single lonely thought you had all last month."

I started to make another reply, even more nasty, but finally thought better of it and sank back onto the bunk. I could have said something, I surely could have, but Ma says us Soderbergs have been given quick tongues, and we have the responsibility of blessing folks with our words or of cursing ourselves by tearing those same folks down. I was tearing Ernest down and was so angry I didn't even know it. Thank goodness for an occasional cool breath of sanity and understanding.

"I'm sorry, Ern," I said. "I reckon this jail's just getting to me a little."

"I reckon," he replied, apparently also feeling bad about the tone of our conversation.

"Sure good of you to come see me."

"That's okay. It's better'n weeding Ma's garden."

I grinned at Ernest's honesty. He had to be one of the finest kids a body ever saw. And smart? Why, he was full of information as a mail-order catalogue. Like I might have said earlier, out in the hills he'd spook a normal person. He could count the sweat beads on a mule deer's lip at four hundred yards, and he could hear and just plain *feel* things like he was part varmint. Gave a body the fluttering fantods, just watching him moving through the brush.

I'd heard Pa telling Ma one day that I was some that way myownself, and I *do* feel things now and then that other folks seem to miss. But Ernest, well, I didn't hold even half a candle to that kid. He was something.

"Well, I still appreciate you coming."

"Hy, what do you do in there all day?"

Seemed like everybody had the same question. Might be a good idea if everyone in town got locked up a day or so, so's they'd know. Then I wouldn't have to spell it out so often.

"Read," I answered. "That and sleep."

"What do you read?"

"Papers and stuff that's on the walls."

"Walls?"

"Yeah. There's lots of poems and other literary explorations. Like this one:

> *Thursday's sure a long, long day,*
> *All filled with draggin minutes.*
> *I'd never thought so before being jailed,*
> *But there must be a* million *in it.*

"That feller knew what it was like. I hate it in here. I truly do."

"That's why I came to see you. Some fellers might be fixing to bust you out."

"What?"

"Deaf Man Hibbard told me to tell you."

"Deaf Man Hibbard? How would he know?"

Ernest giggled. "Hy, can you keep a secret?"

"I reckon."

"Swear it by every drop of blood in your body, Hy. You tell, and you have to cut off *every* finger, one at a time, and let your blood *all drip out!* Swear!"

Good grief. Where had he ever heard that gory stuff? Made a feller wonder what the world was coming to. "All right, I swear. Now what is this deep, dark secret?"

"Hy, Deaf Man Hibbard ain't deaf."

"What?"

"It's true. And I just today found out myownself. You know Ma's had me going over there for the past year to read to him, don't you?"

"I know. Pa says you was asked because you made your words good and he could make them out a little. Me, though, I always figured Old Man Hibbard was desperate for human companionship and finally settled on you, which was somewhat shy of the mark."

"Hy, you want this news or not? Happen you don't, I've got some *real* important things to do, like slop the hogs and take a nap."

"You've got a way, Ern, of getting straight to the point. I take it all back and humbly ask you to continue."

"Okay, I will. This morning I was over there to Deaf Man Hibbard's place, reading to him as usual. Old Lady Hibbard was fussing about like she always does, grumbling and growling and scurrying hither and yon with her broom and dustmop, fairly making that place sparkle.

"Sudden she stops in front of Deaf Man and motions that she wants him to go down to the Co-op to pick up some dry goods. Deaf Man, he just stares like he's trying hard to understand but somehow can't get the job done. Finally the old lady gets angry and gives up, motions that he's a useless so-and-so and that she'll go herself, wraps herself in her shawl, and out the door she goes.

"Well, Deaf Man he watches that screen door for maybe two or three minutes, and sudden he turns to me. 'Ernest,' he says, "I've got to let you in on a little secret. I'm not deaf. Fact is, I can hear as well as you."

"Hy, that stumped me. All my life that old man's been deaf, and here I thought all this time I was doing some great Christian act, reading to him like I did. 'But,' I says to him, 'you've been deaf ever since I knowed you. Did you have a miracle or a priesthood blessing or something?'

"'Nope,' he says. 'I never was deaf. Never would take a blessing for it, either. Ernest, about twelve years ago that woman I'm married to finally wore me out. She'd been fussing and yelling and nagging at me for near forty years, and I just couldn't take it any more. I considered the options—murder, suicide, divorce, leaving home, and so on—and every one left something or other to be desired. No matter what I did, I'd break one or another of the Lord's commandments and end up on the short end of the eternal stick.

"'Then one night I thought of going deaf, thought my way through it and couldn't see any major drawbacks, and decided that was the thing to do. When morning came, I was stone deaf.'

"'For real?' I ask him. 'Of course not,' he replies. 'But the same as, nevertheless. And Ernest, these past twelve years have been the happiest years of my life. It's wondrous how comfortable a man's home is when he can relax there.'

"'So why are you telling me?' I ask. 'Because,' says he, 'I heard some fellers talking. Folks do that around me. They figure I'm deaf, and that's about the same as not being there at all. So they just go ahead and talk. Sometimes its plumb embarrassing, but last night it was more informative.

"'You heard of this Friendlessman fellow?' 'No,' I says, 'I haven't.' 'Me neither,' he continues, 'not until last night. But I was up at the depot, and this Friendlessman was there, along with another man who seemed to be from up around Provo way. They were talking to George Loose-lip Lundstrum, and they were being mighty secretive. They stopped talking when they saw me sitting there, but Loose-lip said I was deaf. That satisfied them, and they continued.'"

"Ernest," I said, staring up at my window, *"I've* heard of Friendlessman. Ida Mae thinks he's mighty wonderful, but she might not, happen she knew he'd teamed up with Loose-lip. She doesn't like that man at all."

"Yeah, I recollect Loose-lip and her pa were closer'n two bobcats in a blanket, hunting lost gold all the time and chasing all over these hills on all sorts of fool's errands."

"That they did, and Loose-lip didn't like it at all when Pa and Mungus got to be friends. Mungus's wild days ended in a hurry. Anyway, what'd they have to say?"

"Hy, that's the strange part. All of 'em are convinced you know where that lost gold mine is, and they're going to bust you out of here and make you take 'em to it. Deaf Man Hibbard says they've wired some fellers out on The Strip. Hy, *do* you know? Where the gold is, I mean?"

"Of course I don't know. If I did, do you think I'd have quit gathering gold at just enough to go Pa's bail?"

"No," Ernest replied thoughtfully, "I don't reckon you would have. Hy, where's The Strip?"

"Out by the reservation. It's a strip of land that both Indians and whites claim, so it's a sort of no-man's land. Outlaws hang out there when they're not down to the Roost and out in The Hole. Figure the law won't touch 'em there."

"Outlaws! That's what Deaf Man Hibbard figured, all right. Anyway Hy, Friendlessman wired these fellers, and they should be here in the next few days."

So Ida Mae was right. That miserable Friendlessman *did* plan on breaking me out, only illegally, which she surely wouldn't believe. And here I sat, helpless as a frozen snake. Oh my, oh my, oh my. Life surely was getting complicated.

"Ern, I've got to get out of here, and quick. I don't have a clue to where that mine is, and if they get me and I can't lead 'em to it, then I'm a dead man for sure. Have you told Pa about this?"

"Can't. Pa's gone into hiding again. I told Aunt Hattie, though."

Well, that made me breathe a sigh of relief. At least Ma knew. And if anybody could get me out of that jail, it was Ma. She was little and dainty, but I'd seen great big men back down and crawl away when Ma got her dander up. There's just no stopping a good woman who knows she's in the right, and Ma usually was.

"What's she going to do?"

"I don't know, Hy. Last I saw her she was heading for the bank."

The bank? Now, that was a thought. Maybe Ma had some idea to borrow my bail. Trouble was, she'd be dealing with Banker Short, and everybody knew he was tighter'n a woodtick in a lobo wolf's tail. Money went into that bank, but so far as I'd heard, none had ever come out again. Just foreclosures and such as that. Still, there wasn't another place on earth where Ma could go. So all I could do was wait and pray and hope that Banker Short would come through.

15

Jailhouse—Fountain Green— and Still Again

"Hyrum?"

"Yeah," I said, scrambling up from my bunk. I'd just been reading in the *Deseret Weekly* about lost Spanish gold mines down in California and of how the padres were in the country long before the Americans, had located lots of rich veins of ore, and had enslaved the Indians to work the mines for them. Reading about it out in California made a feller wonder if maybe they were true, all those stories about gold up in the Uintahs.

"Hyrum, this is your mother."

"I know," I grinned. "How are you?"

"Worried, Son. Are you getting along all right?"

"Sure, Ma."

"What are you doing to occupy your time?"

Now I smiled again. I'd been right as rain. *Everybody* wanted to know about that. "Reading, mostly," I answered.

"Good things, I hope."

"Ma, would I read anything else? Marshal Clawson wouldn't get any of my books, but I've got piles of *Deseret Weekly*s in here, and there's poetry and lots of philosophy and such."

"Poetry?"

"You bet. There's even a poem in here called 'Ode from a Polygamist's Wife.' Want to hear it?"

Ma giggled just like a little girl. "Of course I want to hear it. Who's the author?"

"Some feller named I. M. Anonymous. Here it is:

> *I make a dress of cheesecloth,*
> *You buy a dress of silk.*
> *I wear mine most every day,*

> *Yours in the closet wilts.*
> *I patch mine when holes appear,*
> *I must ignore the silt—*
> *Everything should be thoroughly used,*
> *Or else I'm filled with guilt.*
> *And when the dress won't hide my bones,*
> *Is tattered as an ancient quilt,*
> *While your dress is scornfully thrown away,*
> *Mine's used to strain the milk.*

For a long moment there was silence, and at last Ma spoke. "My goodness, Hyrum. Maybe there *is* someone else in this world who understands. I've truly never felt so broke, nor have I felt so keenly the need to have money."

"Ma, we can get by."

"Hy, I went to see Brother Short about your bail. He turned me down flat, the pompous so-and-so."

"That's all right, Ma. They can't hold me here forever. I've been thinking that we could get Zene to come and testify for me. He saw me find the gold, and he knows how surprised I was by it. If he told that, then they'd *have* to let me go."

"Zene's a long way away, Hyrum."

"I know he is," I replied dejectedly. "He's also Indian, and I suppose there's a good chance folks wouldn't believe him anyway."

"I don't think Marshal Clawson would believe him," Ma said thoughtfully. "I think there's something more behind your arrest than the obvious. I'm worried, and I think we need to get you out of there as quickly as we can."

"Well, maybe that Friendlessman feller will get me out."

"Yes, and that's just what I'm afraid of. Hyrum, after listening to what Ernest told me, I'm afraid of that man. Somehow I feel that he is behind all this. He is evil, and I know it."

Well, I couldn't have agreed more, but I didn't say it. Probably would have looked like I was being jealous again. Which, as a matter of Fountain Green jailhouse fact, I was.

"So what are we going to do?"

"I don't know. I'll go see Brother Short again tomorrow. They've set your bail at two thousand dollars—"

"*Two thousand dollars!*" I shouted. "Ma, it ain't fair! I didn't kill that man. Everybody ought to know it, and now everybody's falling all over themselves calling me guilty. Mormons, non-Mormons,

everybody! Even Ida Mae told me I needed to fess up so I could begin
to repent. Criminentely, Ma, it's disgusting how pious folks suddenly are. Makes me feel like never setting foot in our ward meetinghouse again!"

Outside it was real quiet, and I could hear the cheeping of the
baby barn swallows that were in the nest high up on the back of the
jail. "Hy," a deep voice suddenly said, and instantly my heart was in
my throat.

"Pa, is . . . is that you?"

"It is."

"I didn't know you were there. I . . . I'm sorry. I—"

" I just got here. But Hyrum, you don't have to apologize for honest feelings."

"But Pa, you're the bishop, and I know what the Church means to
you. I wouldn't have said—"

"Hy," Pa interrupted, "listen to me. Of course you're right. I love
the Church, and I've covenanted to do all in my power to see that it
prospers. But Son, I am me, and you are you. That's obvious, but the
meaning of it is that because I have a testimony of the gospel it
doesn't necessarily follow that you also have one. Testimonies must
come individually. No one can take his from another person, no matter how much that person loves or is loved and respected. Do you understand?"

"Yeah, I guess. What I don't understand is how a person who has
covenanted through baptism to be Christ-like can do the things that
some of these folks are doing to me! How can a church with people
like that in it be true?"

Pa chuckled lightly. "Son, that's a powerful question, and better
men than you and I have struggled with it."

"You have?" I asked incredulously.

"Of course. How do you think I feel when a member of my ward,
whom I've just spent hours laboring with, either working in his fields
or providing financial assistance or counseling with his children, runs
straight to Marshal Clawson or one of the other deputies with the information that I'm spending a little much-needed time with one of
my three wives and *our* children? Don't you suppose I struggle with
that?"

"I don't know, Pa," I growled, "but I surely would! If I was you
I'd cut 'em off! Creeps like that don't deserve to be in the Lord's
church."

"And that, Hyrum, is the point."

The voice was now my mother's, and I looked up at the small window, waiting for her to continue. "Hyrum, your father and I have discussed this much, for, as you know, there is a great deal of persecution being waged against those of us who live the Principle, both from within the Church and without. We can deal with it, of course, but only because we have come to understand a principle that we now want you to understand."

"Hy," Pa continued, "we're going to make two statements that will sound like one, but are not. Listen carefully and we will explain. First: the gospel is true. Second: the Church is divine."

Well, mentally I scratched my head. They did sound the same, and I would—

"The gospel," Pa continued, "is the revealed word of God the Father and his Son, the Lord Jesus Christ. That word is eternal, and because it never changes except as God or his Son direct, it is total truth.

"The Church, on the other hand, is a divinely inspired organization made up of all sorts of men and women, not one of whom is perfect. It changes continuously, the people within it make all sorts of mistakes and do all sorts of foolish things, and it is anything but true. The organization is truly Christ's organization, but the Church itself is only a vehicle, with imperfect members. The Church is designed only to preach and promote and administer the eternal truths and ordinances of the gospel; it was never meant to *be* the gospel."

"Do you understand?" Ma questioned. "When you are confronted with the faults and evil deeds of Church members, then you must see that you are viewing the weaknesses of people, and not the gospel or the church of Jesus Christ. The Church is the vehicle through which mankind learns the truths of Christ's gospel and obtains authority to administer God's ordinances."

"Hyrum, does what we've said make sense?"

"Yeah, it does, though I reckon I'll have to think on it some."

"George Lundstrum is an example," Pa went on, "of what I am speaking of."

I thought of Loose-lip and grinned, for as bad as he was, somehow I could not bring myself to be afraid of him. He just didn't—

"As you know, Hy, George has been baptized and ordained to the priesthood. Now he has chosen to ignore it. In light of that, I would like you to consider this thought: Joseph Smith told us that no man, once he accepts the gospel of Christ, can ever return to neutral ground. From the moment of his acceptance, through all eternity, that man is either for Christ or else he is against him. No man can *ever* return to neutral ground. Now, where would you say that George is?"

"Pa, I don't want to judge—"

"Hy, the Lord said that we must not judge 'with unrighteous judgment.' That does not mean that we must not judge at all, for only by judging can we make decisions regarding our own lives. Now what about George, at least as of today?"

"Well," I said quietly, "the way it looks to me, he's against Christ."

"Yes, he is. Now of course he can change, and I for one hope that he does. I'm certain that the Lord still loves George and one of these days will see to it that the man is humbled sufficiently to make him at least consider such a change. But here is the great question: because George Lundstrum is a Church member and yet is choosing to ignore the gospel and to live wickedly, does it therefore follow that the gospel of Jesus Christ is false?"

"No, I don't reckon it does."

"You're right, Hy. Now suppose there were a *thousand* George Lundstrums, all laughing at the Saints and doing their best to make them appear foolish in their beliefs and in their faith. As far as the eternal gospel of Jesus Christ is concerned, what would that change?"

"Nothing, I reckon."

"Exactly, Hyrum. Nothing. Now remember this. When an elephant walks through town, all the dogs bark. But that neither changes the identity of the elephant nor of the dogs. There is a little noise and a little discomfort, but when it is all over, the elephant is still an elephant and the dogs are still no more than loudly yapping dogs. Do you get my point?"

"Yeah," I said, grinning. "I do."

"Good. Can you be an elephant?"

"You bet your sweet buttons," I declared firmly.

"Fine. Now remember that the way of elephants is to step carefully so that they do not injure the little dogs. Even when the dogs bite, elephants do not bite back. Such must always be the way of a disciple of Christ.

"And remember this as well. I am using dogs and elephants only as an analogy. I do not intend to call people who disagree with us, dogs. Actually, some of the finest men and women I have ever known choose to remain outside our church or choose to become inactive within it. Of course, I disagree with them and they with me, but they are still fine people and have the right to live as they choose. Someday God will see to it that active Mormons also have that right, and then we can live peacefully and happily as well.

"Now, I've got to leave, Son. Will you be all right in there?"

"Yes sir."

"I expected as much," Pa declared. "Hyrum, both your mother and I are proud of the way you're standing up to this. No matter what happens, you have a family that believes in you. When worst comes to worst, as it very well might, we will be there pitching in beside you, and you can count on that!"

"Thanks, Pa," I whispered, suddenly so choked up I could hardly talk. "And thanks for coming. I know it was a risk—"

"Oh, pshaw," Pa growled, and I could tell that he was grinning and doing his own best to cover up a few tears. It's funny how us men-folks try to hide our emotions, but we do, and I don't reckon it's going to stop, not at least in this generation.

"Meanwhile," Ma said, "your father needs to be going."

"Bye, Pa," I muttered.

"Bye, Son. I love you and pray that God will bless you."

"Yeah, I pray so myownself. Take care, Pa."

In the stillness I heard him move quietly away toward the willows that lined the creek, and when he was gone, Ma spoke again, "He's a good man, Hyrum. I am a lucky woman to be his wife, and you are a lucky boy to be his son. It seems that, in spite of our trials, we are very lucky people.

"Now, what are you and I going to do to solve that ridiculous bail? Banker Short is the only man in town who has access to that much money, and I don't know how to shake him loose."

"No he ain't, Ma."

"Isn't, Hyrum. Will you please learn to speak properly?"

"I'll try. Anyway, Ma, Old Man Aagard probably has lots more than two thousand."

"Why, you're right, he does. Many times that. If there was one man in town who could afford it, that one man would be Andrew Aagard. But you know how he feels about lending money. He just won't do it. Even your pa tried to borrow from him, figuring it was a fair return on the money he'd once lent Brother Aagard. Brother

Aagard didn't see it that way, however. Jons got lots of advice but no money."

"Yeah, Old Man Aagard's so tight he wouldn't pay a nickel to see a hundred-dollar earthquake. You should see the horse he's been having me use. Doggone thing's gaited like a hybrid buffalo. That's probably why he's trying so hard to get Jim to marry his daughter Ellen. Maybe he figures it will be cheaper to have her gone."

"Hyrum!"

"Well, maybe she eats a lot."

"She could eat all day and not eat as much as you do. Now stop carrying on so shamefully about Brother Aagard."

"Yeah, I reckon I ought to hold my tongue about him. He *did* hire me, and besides, maybe he will also be family one of these days, happen Jim gets his way."

"Ellen is a lovely girl. I hope it works out."

"So do I, Ma. It'd be nice to have money in the family for a change."

"Hyrum!"

I grinned. "Ma, you know I'm joshing. I wouldn't want another man's money. It'd sure be nice, though, if we could get a little of it for long enough to get me out of here."

"It would, but we can't—not from him *or* Brother Short."

"I'll say amen to that! Banker Short is worse than Old Man Aagard ever thought of being. He wouldn't loan a feller a nickel unless that same feller got all the angels in heaven to go on his note."

Ma giggled again. "Hyrum, you're just awful."

"I reckon," I said, feeling pleased to have been so judged. "It's too bad, Ma, that we just couldn't make a bet with those two and then see that they lost. Brother Short is a betting fool, and Old Man Aagard likes a little game of chance now and then himself. You recollect they were the first ones to line up after Pa announced he wanted to race his horse Ingersol."

"That's right, Hy," Ma replied, sounding like her thoughts were a thousand miles away. "That's right. Of course, the Lord doesn't hold with gambling, and you know how much trouble your pa got into with *his* bet."

"Yeah, but Pa still did it."

"Yes, he did. Much to his own sorrow. No, I don't believe gambling is the way. There must be something else . . .

"But don't you worry. I'll have you out of there before

Friendlessman can break you out, and that's a promise. Just relax, and maybe you can write a poem or two of your own on that wall while you're waiting."

I grinned again, Ma left, and I sat down with a pencil, ready to begin my career in creating fine literature.

> *The polygamist's wife was a honey,*
> *Though she hardly had any money.*
> *But she glowed like the sun,*
> *Getting by on just none,*
> *And the results were really quite funny.*

Not bad literature, and prophetic too, though at the time I didn't know that at all.

16

Hattie Soderberg's Home— Fountain Green

Hattie Soderberg stood in the middle of her small log home, gazing about. What did she have that could possibly be worth two thousand dollars? Why, even the house was worth less than five hundred—at least Jons had paid much less than that for it just a couple of years before.

Two thousand dollars! Why had Marshal Clawson ever put that much bail on Hyrum? Meanness? No, that wouldn't be likely. Probably he thought Hyrum really did know where the gold was, and wanted to stop anyone from getting his bail. But that wouldn't stop her, Hattie knew. One way or another, she was going to raise that money—

"Ma?"

Startled, Hattie looked down at LaRue, who at seven was her youngest child.

"Ma, will Hyrum have to live in jail for the whole rest of his life?"

"No, silly," Lucille answered quickly, while Hattie's thoughts drifted back to her son. Lucille was ten and considered herself very mature. "He'll only have to stay until his trial. If he's found not guilty, they'll have to turn him loose. If they decide he's guilty, they'll shoot him."

"Will not," LaRue fumed.

"Will so! Won't they, Ma?"

Shocked, Hattie realized what the girls were arguing about, and instantly she lashed out at them. "Hush, you two! I won't hear such talk as that! Lucille, how can you bear to say such things?"

"Well, it's so, Ma. Pa said that's what happens to people who murder."

"Hyrum didn't murder!"

"I didn't say he did. I only said that's what would happen if they decided he was guilty."

"Well he *isn't!* I'll get him out on bail, and then he can go find out who killed that poor man. Maybe then the marshal will believe him."

"But Ma," Lucille questioned, "where are you going to get all that money?"

"I . . . I don't exactly know. Hyrum said something to me today, and I might have the beginnings of an idea. I'm going to go see Brother Short again in the morning, and—"

"Banker Short? " LaRue exclaimed. "But Ma, he's closer with a dollar than the satin on a can-can dancer's seat!"

"LaRue! Where do you hear such terrible things?"

"Hyrum taught me," LaRue answered proudly as she looked up and smiled. "He's my favoritest brother."

"He's your only brother," Lucille declared scornfully."

"He is not! There's Ernest and Johnny and Jim and Lyman and—"

"I meant *whole* brother, dummie. Half brothers don't count."

"They do too!"

"Betcha they don't."

"Betcha they do, don't they, Ma?"

"Of course they do," Hattie slowly answered.

Bets. The girls were fighting each other with bets. It *was* a powerful way to fight. That's what Hyrum had said. Bet and bet. And even though the Lord frowned on gambling, maybe . . . "Now, you two stop arguing and get on those dishes," Hattie ordered. "If I'm not back when you finish, then peel some potatoes for dinner. Please."

"Oh golly, Ma. Do we have to?"

Hattie Soderberg gave Lucille a withering gaze, and instantly the girl dropped her eyes. "Okay, okay. We'll do it. Will Pa be here?"

"No, he's gone into hiding again."

"Is he out in the desert?"

"No, I don't think so. He went to Sa— Listen, it doesn't matter where he is. Just remember him in your prayers."

"We will. Where are you going?"

"To see Brother Short," Hattie replied as she tied on her bonnet. "I may have one other stop as well. Now be good, and I'll see you in a little while."

And with that, Hattie Soderberg gathered up her skirts and her courage and determinedly set out for the bank.

17

The Bank—
Fountain Green

"Hattie . . . uh, Sister Soderberg, I think we've been through all this. Naturally I'm pleased to have our bank considered by the bishop's wife, but frankly, two thousand dollars is far more than we are prepared to go."

Hattie Soderberg gazed levelly into Harrison Short's eyes and didn't say anything.

"I . . . uh . . . I realize you want to get young Hyrum out of jail, and I believe I understand why. After all, I *am* a father, and . . . and . . . But my dear sister, where there's smoke there's fire, I always say, and well, perhaps he ought to stay right where he is until a judge hears all the facts—"

"Are you judging my son guilty, Brother Short?"

Suddenly the man coughed. "Of course not. I . . . uh . . . well, to be perfectly frank . . ."

"I wish you would be, sir."

"Uh . . . yes, of course. To be completely candid about it, you are too great a risk for us to make such a loan."

"You don't believe I would pay you back?"

"Well, actually I didn't say that. I have no doubt that you would. Or would intend to, at least. No. It's just that . . . that . . . well, you're in no position to do so. Your husband is in hiding, it's no secret that his affairs are in a shambles, and now that Hyrum is in jail you have no income at all. You have no collateral that is worth anything near two thousand dollars, and frankly, unless Hyrum does know where that gold is, I'm certain we would never see our money again. No, Sister Soderberg, the bank simply cannot extend itself in such an irresponsible manner."

"Very well." Hattie paused and gazed directly and openly into

Banker Short's eyes. "Then, Brother Short, I would like to propose a *different* sort of business arrangement."

Harrison Short, unused to women taking such a forward and direct approach, was suddenly cautious. It had been his experience, infrequent as it had been, that such women usually had something on their minds that would not be good for him. Furthermore, in spite of his caution, such women usually prevailed. Nevertheless, he *was* curious.

"Uh . . . what exactly did you have in mind?"

"A bet, Brother Short, I would like to make a small bet with you."

Harrison Short smiled. "Surely, Sister Soderberg, you cannot be serious. I'm a banker, not a gambler."

"Even on a sure thing?"

"Have you forgotten so quickly how near to disaster your husband came just a year ago?"

"No. Neither have I forgotten that you were first in line to place your bet against him."

Harrison Short started to turn red. "Well . . . uh . . . well, that bet did seem like a sure thing. However, it wasn't, and truthfully, madam, I have learned my lesson."

"I'm speaking of a *very* sure thing, Brother Short."

For a full sixty seconds Harrison Short, his gaze level and his expression blanker than that of a hard-boiled egg, stared at Hattie Soderberg, trying to make her drop her gaze and her confoundedly tempting conversation. But she wouldn't, and so at last he capitulated.

"What, exactly, is this 'sure thing'?"

"Brother Short, I would like to bet you that tomorrow morning, when you come to work, you will be wearing polka-dotted underwear."

"What?"

"Would you like me to repeat myself?"

"No," Harrison Short declared, settling back in his chair with a slight smile on his face. "You mean here, at the bank?"

"I do. Tomorrow."

"Uh . . . Sister Soderberg, I don't wear polka-dotted underwear. Ever!"

"You will tomorrow."

Harrison Short drummed his fingers together as he gazed past

Hattie Soderberg and out of the window. The day was nearly over, and he had to get down to the field to irrigate one of his farms, a farm upon which a payment was nearly due. There were also those headgates he had to buy and that new buggy his wife was pestering him about, the one that was going to cost even more money than had Andrew Aagard's . . .

"How much is the bet for?" he finally asked.

"Two thousand dollars."

"Two thousand dollars! But . . . but you have no collateral. How can you cover such a bet?"

"I'd say that was my problem, wouldn't you?"

"Not altogether. If I bet, and win, how can I expect to be paid? And when?"

"Tomorrow, when the bet is concluded. But Brother Short, you won't win."

"You seem very confident, Hattie. Is there some trick to this little wager? Some play on words or something?"

"None." Hattie smiled brightly. "I'm simply willing to wager two thousand dollars that tomorrow morning you will wear brightly colored polka-dotted underwear when you come to work."

Harrison Short now smiled himself. "Sister Soderberg, I hate to do this, but you have made the wager, and I think you must be taught the lesson. I will take your bet. Be prepared to pay."

Hattie Soderberg smiled sweetly as she rose to her feet. "I'll be prepared, Brother Short. But you'll be the one who pays. Good day."

"Good day, Sister Soderberg."

18

The Bank—Fountain
Green—Again

Harrison Short couldn't concentrate on a thing. Work was piled a foot deep on his desk, and all he could do was look from the clock on the wall to the door and back again to the clock. His secretary kept looking back at him, expecting him to get at the dozens of tasks she had laid out for him to do. And he'd tried, he really had. But all he could do was pick at them, first one thing and then another, not really accomplishing anything toward the completion of any of them. All he could think of was his wager with Hattie Soderberg.

Nor had he slept much during the night. For hours he had gone over that bet in his mind, and nowhere could he find a flaw, a weakness, a way that Hattie could trick him. He couldn't imagine that it was an honest bet, for it was was too sure, too simple. Yet that was all he could discern about it. The whole thing *was* sure, and very, *very* simple.

Again he looked at the clock. Nearly ten-thirty. Of course, she hadn't set a time, but he did wish she'd hurry. Not that he really wanted to win, though indeed he did. But even more than that he was curious; he wanted to know how she would come up with that much money. Especially when she needed that exact sum so badly to get her son Hyrum out of jail.

And that brought up another thing. Was it possible, he wondered for maybe the thousandth time, that the boy *did* know the location of that lost mine? Under given conditions, he knew that all things were possible, even that. Could *that* be where Hattie planned on getting her money? After all, he'd checked on her the day before, and she *had* visited the jail. Maybe Hyrum had told her—

"Good morning, Harrison."

Startled, Harrison Short quickly lifted his eyes. "Hattie, I didn't see you come in."

"Yes." She smiled. "I noticed that you seemed rather distracted. And I understand perfectly. It *is* difficult to lose such a large sum of money. You *are* prepared to pay, I assume."

"Uh . . . Sister Soderberg," Harrison Short replied, making his voice as gentle as possible, "it's you who must be prepared to pay."

Hattie Soderberg laughed. "I fear you are mistaken, sir. You see, I wagered that you would wear colored polka-dotted underwear to the bank today; you did, and now you must pay."

Harrison Short was surprised but admitted to himself that he truly admired the woman's gall. "No, Sister Soderberg," he declared, "I did *not* wear polka-dotted underwear, and it is you who must pay."

"Sir," Hattie Soderberg asked, her face suddenly more serious, "are you certain?"

"Of course I'm certain! I'm wearing those . . . uh, my underwear, aren't I? My underwear is white!"

"Brother Short, I don't believe you."

"What? But . . . but . . . this is ridiculous! I say my underwear is all white, with no colorful polka-dots, and so it is. Now be a man and . . . I mean . . . uh, well, just pay the money!"

"I'm sorry, but with such a large sum at stake, I simply cannot accept your word. I'll have to ask for proof before I even consider concession."

"Proof? Woman, my word is as good as—"

"Proof, Brother Short. Proof, or immediate payment in full!"

"But . . . but . . . how . . ."

"Show me."

Harrison Short stared at the woman who stood calmly before him.

"Sh-show you?"

"That's right. I'm not asking you to remove your trousers entirely. Simply lower them for a few seconds. That will give me ample time to discern the truth."

"Well, I never! Sister Soderberg, such a request is . . . is downright *immoral!* I will do no such thing!"

"Then, sir, I must ask you to pay me immediately, for it is obvious that you *did* wear polka-dotted underwear, and that you fear—"

"I did not, I tell you! But neither will I—"

"Brother Short, folks do their banking here because, first, it is the only bank in town, and second, because for the most part, they trust and respect you. Now by nature I am a quiet woman, but if I get riled

up, I will start screaming like a she-bear in a dog-fight. On the other
hand, if you show me your underwear and it is white, I will pay you
and be gone before you can brush off your shirt. What do you say,
Brother Short? And remember, men come quickly when a lady starts
screaming, and I have a voice you will think came out of a split can-
non muzzle. I'll count to three; take your time.

"One."

Desperately Harrison Short looked about, but there was no help
in sight, no help at all. Nor, thankfully, were there many people in
the bank. The teller was busy with a man at the window, there were
a couple of folks by the door, and his secretary, thank goodness, had
her back to him. Oh, if only—

"Two."

A quick look into Hattie Soderberg's cold, level eyes told Harrison Short that he was only seconds away from terrible embarrassment and even possible social destruction. Nor would it matter that
he was in the right. Folks would claim that he had taken advantage of
a woman, that he had known all along of her plight, that she had been
duped because of her desperation—

"Three."

With a grimace of pain, Harrison Short closed his eyes tightly,
rose to his feet, and pulled his suspenders over his shoulders; then he
unbuttoned his trousers, jerked them down to his knees, and just as
quickly yanked them back up, trying his best as he did so to shut from
his mind the sound of some commotion over by the door and the sight
of Hattie Soderberg, smilingly watching his humiliation.

"There," he growled as he worked feverishly to redo his buttons,
"are you satisfied?"

"I certainly am," Hattie Soderberg replied brightly. "And Brother
Short, I apologize for doubting your word. You are truly an honest
man. Here is your money."

Hattie Soderberg reached into her purse, pulled out a thick wad of
bills, and placed them carefully on Harrison Short's desk. "If you
would like I will count it out for you. However, I can assure you that
the two thousand is all there."

Harrison Short slowly sank to his chair behind the massive desk,
too stunned to speak. "N-n-no, that . . . uh . . . that won't be . . .
be necessary. I . . . uh . . . I will take your word."

"Good. Thank you, Brother Short," Hattie Soderberg declared,
and quickly she turned and started toward the door.

"Hattie . . . uh . . . Sister Soderberg?"

She paused and turned. "Yes?"

"I . . . well, I don't understand."

"What do you mean?"

"I mean you lost. But doggone it, how could you afford to do it? I don't understand."

"It's simple, Brother Short, I didn't lose."

Harrison Short slowly picked up the bills. "Sister Soderberg, this two thousand dollars says you did. Yesterday you came in here broke and desperately needing this exact amount of money. Today you happily give it away on a very foolish bet. That, sister, is called losing. It's also called insanity. To me, the entire episode is very confusing. Would you please be so kind as to explain it?"

Hattie Soderberg stepped back to the desk. "Well," she replied in a confidential tone, "since you asked so nicely, I will. And Harrison, I promise I will also keep it quiet. I can't guarantee the silence of the others, but you have my word concerning myself."

"O-others?"

"Well, other, I mean. You see, I bet you two thousand dollars that you would wear brightly colored polka-dotted underwear this morning; you showed me your white drawers, and I won."

"Lost."

"Won. Did you happen to notice Brother Andrew Aagard?"

"Well, yes I did see him. But—"

"Did you see him fall to the floor in a faint?"

"Faint? No, by thunder, I—"

"Brother Short, last evening I bet Andrew Aagard *four* thousand dollars that you would pull down your trousers in front of me, right here in the bank, sometime before noon. He laughed, told me you were too pompous ever to do it, and made the bet. Yet you did, he fainted—with laughter, I think—and I won."

And with that, Hattie Soderberg smiled sweetly, gathered her skirts up, turned, and left the bank, its dazed owner, and the still gasping but slowly reviving Andrew Aagard altogether behind. She was on her way to the marshal's office, and that poor soul was about to be as shocked as the rest of them. And that little detail didn't bother Hattie Soderberg one tiny bit.

19

The Lane—
Fountain Green

"It's a lovely evening."

"Yes it is, my dear. And it is doubly so because you are here to share it with me."

Ida Mae smiled into the gathering darkness and shivered a little with the excitement she was feeling. Felix Friendlessman stood beside her, very near, and she had never felt quite so conscious of a man's presence.

"Thank you," she replied, almost whispering. "You do say the sweetest things."

"My dear," the man stated firmly, "I would never say them if they were not altogether true." Then, without warning, he placed his arm around Ida Mae's waist and drew her close.

Ida Mae gasped a little with surprise, and suddenly she was aware of the desire she felt to have this man hold her even more tightly and say more of those sweet things to her. She had never had such an experience, not even with Hyrum, and now this man—who was much older and much more polished and refined than Hyrum—was giving her the attention she had always craved. It was exciting, it made her feel like a woman, and with a start she decided that all those things equaled love. She was falling in love with this tall, dark-haired man from back east.

"There," he suddenly whispered, pointing with his free hand, "there was a meteorite, a shooting star. Did you see it?"

Ida Mae gazed up into the dark, star-filled sky. "I didn't. I'm sorry, I was—"

"No, don't apologize. Just watch for another. It is said that if one makes a wish during the fraction of a moment when such phenomena are visible, then that wish will surely come to pass."

"But how can a person wish so fast?"

"Simple, my dear. Have the wish in mind, think of it constantly, and wait for another meteorite to show. Shall we do it?"

"Oh, yes. And I have just the wish in mind."

"Tell me."

"Oh, no," Ida Mae declared. "That would be bad luck. Even *I* know that."

"Well, do as you please. But since I don't believe in such things as good and bad luck, I'll tell you *my* wish."

"Would you? Really?"

"Of course. My wish is that you and I might go on, like this, forever."

"Oh, Felix . . ."

"Don't say anything, Ida Mae. Just think about what I've said, and let us both hope for another shooting star."

Eagerly Ida Mae stared up into the darkness, her mind floating gleefully and her whole being almost dizzy with excitement. In the grass around them a thousand crickets sang their own love songs, while above them a bat flitted by, dancing in a manner that was suddenly terribly beautiful. Somewhere in the darkness a screen door slammed, there was a distant murmuring of laughter, and Ida Mae would have sworn she had never been so happy.

Almost reflexively she snuggled a little closer, and suddenly she was in the man's arms and their lips were together and she had never before experienced *anything* so wonderful, so breathtaking!

"Felix," she whispered when at last they separated, "I . . . I can hardly speak. What you have said is . . . is . . . well, I don't have the words . . ."

"Then hush," the man declared quietly. "Don't speak. Just think of my everlasting love and know that my coming absence will give me greater pain than I can endure."

"Absence?"

"Why yes, didn't I tell you? Very early in the morning I must leave on business, and I will be gone for several weeks. There is a chance that I will be gone even longer."

"Oh Felix . . ."

"I understand, my dear. I feel the same, and my poor heart is nearly broken with grief. I would almost rather die than be separated from your sweet presence. It is just that this trip has been arranged for so long, and it is so vitally important to *our* future . . ."

Ida Mae's mind whirled. Why, this was like a dream, but it was happening so fast, so very fast. Still, what harm could there be in that? He was such a good and sweet man, and he made her feel so, well, so *special*. Yes, she *did* love him, and would gladly wait for him always.

"There is also the matter of my dear grandmother," Friendlessman continued. "She is gravely ill, and there is no one left but myself. I must see to her."

"Oh dear, I do hope that it isn't serious!"

"Well, I'm afraid that it is. Very serious, in fact. Nevertheless, I have considered staying because of you—"

"No, you must go to the dear old soul!"

"But Ida Mae—"

"Yes, Felix," Ida Mae declared firmly, "you must! I would expect nothing less of such a dear man. And don't worry about me. I am well able to care for myself, and I will wait eagerly, no matter how long you are gone from me."

Felix Friendlessman held her tightly once more. "My dear, sweet Ida Mae, how like an angel you are!"

They kissed again, and then Felix Friendlessman drew away. "My dear," he said sadly, "I really must be going, but know this: I will return."

"I . . . I will be waiting." Ida Mae whispered.

Friendlessman took two steps away and then suddenly turned, almost as though he had forgotten and suddenly remembered something. "Ida Mae, there is one other thing. I have almost concluded the arrangements for securing the release of young Soderberg."

Ida Mae started, thinking suddenly of Hyrum. It was strange that she had hardly thought of him since she had been with Felix. Yet now that she did, there was such a feeling of guilt—

"There has been a great deal of expense for me in doing this, my dear, for I have hired several men to break him out during the darkness tonight. Yet still—"

"Break him out? But . . . but I thought he would be going to court."

"Ida Mae, if he goes to court, he will spend the rest of his life in prison, for he is guilty as sin. Therefore, I have encouraged him to flee."

"To flee? But—"

"My dear, I have done this because of his obvious guilt. Still, he was only eleven when he made this terrible mistake, and I do not think he should be forced to pay for it all the rest of his life. Therefore, I have convinced him to leave immediately upon his release, with the hope that the marshals will let the matter drop. I hope," Friendlessman continued gently, "that it will not be important to you that you don't see him. Possibly for quite some time?"

"N-no," Ida Mae stammered, "no, of course it won't."

"Good. I have told Hyrum to return to his sheep camp in . . . in . . . oh my goodness, I seem to have forgotten . . ."

"The Uintahs," Ida Mae declared helpfully.

"Yes, yes, I knew that, but I have forgotten exactly where . . ."

"Last time Hyrum and I talked," Ida Mae volunteered, "the camp was on the Strawberry Flats."

"That's right. That is near where he allegedly found the gold, isn't it? Oh, if only he had enough decency to admit his guilt. It would make things so much more easy. For him, I mean."

"Yes, I feel the same, poor boy. I can't imagine why I ever thought that he and I . . ."

"Now Ida Mae, don't say those things. You were innocent. How could you know what he was really like? Besides, I am certain that there are many qualities about him that are good and decent, qualities that a pure young lady such as yourself might find irresistible."

"Oh Felix, you are so sweet to defend him as you do."

"Well," Friendlessman smiled, "my motives are not entirely selfless. Quite honestly, I am thinking primarily of you, for I know how close the two of you have been. Ida Mae, that is why I wish to be of help."

"Thank you, my dear."

"You are most welcome."

"Will . . . will you get in trouble for breaking him out of jail?" Ida Mae asked fearfully.

"Possibly, but I hope that no one will find out I have been involved. I have considered meeting with the marshal and the justice of the peace, but frankly, I do not think they would understand. Anyway, before morning . . . Well, needless to say, plans have been made."

"But you do not mind taking this . . . this risk?"

"Ida Mae, how could I mind? Such a risk is as nothing so long as it makes you happy and so long as ultimate justice is served."

Friendlessman smiled sincerely, and Ida Mae beamed with pride that she should be privileged to know and to be loved by such a fine man.

"Uh . . . do you suppose Hyrum might move his sheep camp in the near future?" Friendlessman suddenly asked.

"Why yes. In fact, I am certain that it has already been moved. Hyrum told me that Zene would be—"

"Zene?"

"Yes. Zene Hill, the herder. Hyrum is only the camp tender. Anyway, Zene was heading the herd up toward Wolf Creek Pass, and, according to Hyrum, they will summer in the Grandaddy Basin."

"That's right," Friendlessman said thoughtfully, forgetting for the moment that Ida Mae was even there. "That's what he told Doolin, as well. But there is no doubt that the gold would be lower down, near where he was camped. That's where we must concentrate our efforts—"

"Gold? Efforts? But Felix, I don't understand. Your grandmother . . . she is . . ."

Quickly and sincerely Felix Friendlessman laughed. "My dear, you are delightful! How quick your humor is. I see now that I must look forward to a lifetime of teasing. But, more importantly, you will never know how it thrills me to see that you are so interested in my aged grandmother. Thank you, my darling!

"Now truly I must be off. But first, I would give you this small trinket as a memento of my love."

Ida Mae stared as Felix Ethelbert Friendlessman took her hand, held it out, and slipped a small ring onto her finger. "There," he said. "Do you like it?"

"Oh, yes . . . yes!"

"Good. May you think of me each time you see it on your finger. Now *au revoir,* my sweet, until we are together in each other's arms again."

Ecstatic and filled with sweet dreams concerning the nebulous future, Ida Mae kissed Felix to seal the promise of the ring and then stood dreamily as he vanished into the darkness.

"Oh my dearest," she murmured softly, "I love you so, and I promise that I will wait until—"

"Ida! Ida Mae! You'll never believe what happened this afternoon!"

Spinning around, Ida Mae was startled to see her brother Curly come bounding across the fence toward her. "My goodness, Curly, you startled me."

"You think I startled you, wait until you hear about Hyrum and his Ma and Brother Short. That'd startle anybody!"

"Hyrum? Brother Short the banker?"

"Yeah. I can't wait to tell Pa, this is so good. Hyrum's Ma bet Brother Short that he would take down his britches or something, and Brother Aagard was there, and I don't know how it all worked out, but anyway ol' Short done it and she got tons of money from Old Man Aagard and she bailed Hyrum out of jail and he's gone and—"

"Hyrum's gone?" Ida Mae asked quickly, her breath catching.

"I'll say. Gone as the wild geese in winter. Would I like to have been there in that bank."

But Ida Mae was no longer listening. She was hurrying down the lane, searching vainly for Felix Friendlessman, hoping to prevent the true love of her life from wasting his time, his efforts, and his money to secure the release of an evil and unrepentant boy who was no longer even around.

20

Granary and Jailhouse— Fountain Green

"Silvertip, you idiot, stop whistling!"

The outlaw Silvertip looked up from where he was working on the rigging of the harnesses. "Ah, Boss," he moaned, "my ma always told me to whistle while I worked. She was real smart, and—"

"Well don't do it now, you imbecile. Why do you think we're doing this in the dark? We're trying to keep people from knowing about us. Do you suppose your whistling helps?"

Silvertip sat in the moonlight, surrounded by harnesses and the running gear of a wagon, and shrugged. "Beats me," he replied honestly. "But say, Boss, if I can't whistle, what *can* I do?"

Jack Moore looked up at the star-filled sky as if praying for divine relief. Then, without waiting for such aid to manifest itself, he growled, "I don't know, but I'm fairly sure you'll think of something." Then he spun about and stalked toward the granary where the others were planning.

"Did you get him to shut up?" he was asked as he stepped through the door.

Moore looked at the questioner, the man named Felix Friendlessman. "You can't hear him whistling, can you?"

All listened, and suddenly Blue John threw his hat onto the floor. "You're right. He ain't whistling. Now he's out there singing 'Streets of Laredo.' I'm telling you, Boss, that man ain't altogether here, if you know what I mean."

"I do," Moore answered. "Trouble is, I just couldn't help myself from bringing him along."

"But Moore," Loose-lip Lundstrum added, "we've got troubles enough without a man like that to ruin it for us."

"Don't I know it," Moore replied sourly. "If you'll recollect, this wasn't exactly my deal. Nor did I ask Silvertip to come into it. That there was Friendlessman's doing."

"Yes, it was," Friendlessman stated quietly. "He was the only way I had of getting to you and Blue John."

"I understand that," Moore agreed. "I also understand how terrible hard it is to get shut of somebody like Silvertip. Yes sir, especially when that somebody looks at you with eyes that would make a kicked hound feel happy and asks only to warm his hands in the flickering warmth of your companionship. Yes sir, Mr. Friendlessman, I understand fully why Silvertip is here. I just don't like it.

"Nor do I like taking on Bishop Jons Soderberg again. I've had enough dealings with that man and his kith and kin to last me a lifetime. That feller's got him a purely direct connection to the powers of heaven, I swear it, and a man can't fight that for sour apples. When I heard we was after ol' Soderberg's son, I voted to drop the whole idea and go to barbering out in California or to butchering up in Oregon or Canada."

"But Moore," little Doolin whined, "think of all that *gold!*"

"I have thought of it, a whole lot, and the odds in favor of us seeing one ounce of it are poor as a desert grasshopper."

"You think that," Doolin argued, "because you didn't see any of the gold. I *did!* That kid had it, and he knows where the lost mine is located."

"Maybe, maybe not. But you fellers are getting set to spring that jail and unleash a storm that'll make a Wyoming Blue Norther look like a Saturday afternoon picnic. You'll have the law after you; you'll have the Mormons after you; the good Lord will probably join in with a few of His angels, happen He still favors the bishop as much as He did a year ago; you'll be hip-pocket high in angry Indians; and ol' Caleb Rhoades will probably figure in there as well.

"What I'm saying, boys, is that come this time tomorrow, all them forces will be snapping at your tails like a trapped weasel. No sir, gold or not, Mr. Doolin, I'm not altogether sure this gambit is worth the risk."

"Are you through, Jack?"

All eyes in the room turned toward the still form of Felix Friendlessman.

"Yeah, I reckon, other than to say that I got a bad feeling about things. This is going to end in a whole lot of pain and trouble, and you all will remember that I said so. That's all."

"Good. You might be interested in knowing that I heard about your encounter with the man in Vernal who claimed to be Porter Rockwell. I also know about last year's posse and the promise they made you out at the Roost. Something about sending you dancing up the golden stairs on the end of a rope, as I recall. Seems to me, Jack, that your choices are most severely limited. Need I go on?"

Slowly Moore shook his head.

"Good. Then I recommend we get on with our plans. As soon as Silvertip has the harnesses rigged to the running gear and the team harnessed, then we go. Blue John, you work the horses. You're the best man with teams I ever saw. The rest of you, pay attention. The old jail was dragged to that spot by the creek. It's made out of logs, and the folks who dragged it left their iron hoops buried in the wood. We will use those hoops the same as they did, for our ropes and chains. With all of us as well as the team pulling suddenly and together, the jail should come apart quite easily.

"Moore, when it does, you get inside and throw down on young Soderberg. Pop him on the head if you must, but no matter what else, he cannot be allowed to escape or to shout for help, nor do I want him hurt badly. If we can get away with no more noise than the breaking down of the jail, then the lead we build will be significant and should be sufficient.

"Now, are there any questions?"

"Yeah," Blue John said quietly, "I've got one or two. The Boss mentioned the law and the Mormons, and I'm altogether as worried as he is. Clawson's not too hot, but I truly fear that bishop. He ain't all human."

Friendlessman smiled coldly. "So the Great Blue John is afraid."

At those words Blue John stiffened, his fingers curled above the butt of his pistol, and there was a sudden stillness in the room as all eyes went to him and his gun. "Friendlessman," he whispered, "I don't take that from *any* man, let alone a city-slicker dude!"

There was instant silence. Blue John was ready to draw, and he would have, too, except that when Friendlessman's left elbow jerked and he started, he suddenly found himself staring into the yawning mouth of a left-handed .44 that had come from nowhere into Friendlessman's hand. His own pistol, meanwhile, was still only half-way out of its holster, and so Blue John let it slide slowly back down.

"Nor should you," Friendlessman replied, still smiling icily as though nothing had happened. "My point, Blue John, is that you of all people should have no need to fear."

"What . . . what's that supposed to mean?"

"Just this. Hebron Clawson is inept, and from him we have little to fear. Besides, Loose-lip here will stay behind and plant plenty of seeds of cautious wisdom in the marshal's ear. That should take care of him. Nor, for several reasons, do we need to fear the Mormons."

"Why not?"

"First, the bishop is in hiding. He's out of it. Second, I have made great strides in developing a, shall we say, romantic association with young Soderberg's girl. Ida Mae is naive and innocent, very lovely, and firmly convinced that I am breaking the young man out in order to save him from certain conviction. I am more than confident that, come morning, she will explain all that to the proper church authorities as well as to Soderberg's family. They will merely sit by, then, and wait for all this to blow over and for young Soderberg to return.

"Any more questions?"

"I have one," Doolin whined. "How are we going to split the gold?"

Friendlessman gazed levelly at Doolin. "Why," he replied softly, "I'd say that would depend on who does what during the recovery of it and who is left among us after it is recovered. Wouldn't you agree, Mr. Doolin?"

Hastily Doolin nodded, and shortly thereafter the small group was moving through the darkness toward the rear of the tiny jail. Quietly they moved through the creek and up to the building, and there Blue John turned his team, stretched out the harnesses, and silently went to work.

The tugs from the horse collars and hames were connected to the singletrees, which, of course, were attached to the doubletree, and that was firmly in place atop the tongue of the running gears. These, consisting of the front wheels and axle stolen from a heavy wagon that had been found nearby, were used to secure the chains.

Quickly Blue John looped the chains over the axle and back to the iron hoops imbedded in the rear wall of the jail. Silvertip, Friendlessman, Loose-lip, and Doolin worked rapidly to secure their ropes, which were then checked for tightness. Moore pulled his pistol and made ready, and suddenly Silvertip broke the silence.

"Boss," he said innocently.

"Quiet," Jack Moore whispered angrily.

"I'm sorry," the big man whispered back. "But Boss, I don't like this at all. That boy in there's a good boy, and besides, his pa's the bishop in these parts. You know it don't do no good to go against the likes of them, what with all that happened last year, and—"

"Will you shut up!" Friendlessman hissed. "Boys, get ready!"

They all did, including the reluctant Silvertip, and then the signal was given.

As one the team snapped the harnesses tight and the men on their mounts raked them with spurs, sending the animals lunging ahead. The old jail skidded slightly, creaked, and groaned, and with a loud tearing sound the rear wall burst out and disintegrated. The horses plunged forward, carried along by their own momentum, and Jack Moore, ignoring his struggling partners, stepped through the dust and into the sagging remnants of the jail.

"All right, Soderberg," he growled, "Get outa that sack, and . . ."

And for the second time in not too many more days than that, Jackson T. Moore found himself holding a loaded gun on an empty room. Hyrum V. Soderberg was long and permanently gone.

21

The Sorenson Home— Fountain Green

"Ida Mae!" I whispered loudly.

Hearing no answer, I stood silently outside Ida Mae's window, wondering what in Job's turkey I was doing there. I'd set out for the herd after saying good-bye to Ma and the girls, thinking to get back on my job with Zene and work from there on who killed Enock Rhoades. But I'd felt so bad about my rudeness to Ida Mae that I had doubled back so I could see her and apologize and maybe warn her concerning just what kind of a miserable rascal that Friendlessman feller was. But now it was the middle of the night, and I had already tossed two pebbles against her window besides calling her name, and nothing had happened. And with my luck, nothing would. Not unless I woke her pa or maybe her brother Curly and got shot for my efforts. I'll tell a man, I was feeling lower'n a snake's jaw in a wagon track.

"Ida Mae," I whispered once more, just for luck. Still nothing happened, and I was just turning away when I saw the curtain move at her window. Then the sash lifted, and Ida Mae pushed her head out from between the curtains.

"Who is it?" she whispered, straining to see down into the darkness.

"It's me," I said, stepping out from the haw-bushes where I'd been hiding. "Hy."

"Oh."

Well, there wasn't much excitement in her voice, but I'm the eternal optimist. Pa always told me to look on the bright side of things, and I did then. She might not have been very enthused to see me, but at least she hadn't called me names or pulled her head back in or yelled for her pa.

I was just gathering my thoughts to apologize when she suddenly disappeared from the window. Not knowing what she was up to, my mind instantly began telling my heart what a fool I'd been, and I was having a fairly major battle with myself about whether or not to flee from the premises when I heard the front door creak open.

After what seemed an eternity but which was probably not more than five or ten seconds, I saw Ida Mae's form beside the lilac bush near her door. With one hand she motioned for me to be quiet and with the other she signaled for me to follow, and like a lonely little lost puppy, I hastened to obey.

"Ida Mae," I stammered when we had reached the corner of the tack shed, "I . . . uh . . . I came to say I was sorry."

"I heard you were out of jail."

"Yeah, Ma got me out."

"I heard about that, too. The whole town's laughing about what your Mother did to Brother Short, but I think it was just awful! What a horrible way to get money! I don't understand how a woman could *do* such a thing."

"Now hold on, Ida Mae. You're talking about my ma now, and I won't stand for it!"

"Well, I'm sorry it is your mother, but I *still* don't understand how she could do that. Besides being lewd, it was an immoral way to get money—"

"Listen," I interrupted, feeling all sorts of emotions that I was not liking at all. "That was a deal where nobody got hurt. Brother Short is two thousand dollars richer for dropping his trousers and is altogether more popular than he's been in years. And Brother Aagard was at our home all evening, laughing his head off. He told Ma that he'd gladly give another four thousand to see two or three others in this community with *their* pompous purity let down.

"Finally, Ma has already told Brother Aagard that she will give at least the two thousand back the minute I appear in court for my trial. Brother Short has finally decided to become friends with Brother Aagard and will likely give him back his money as well. So you see, everything *is* working out for the good.

"Besides," I continued, searching frantically for some way to get at least equal footing in our conversation, "happen it was up to you to get me out, how would *you* have raised the money?"

"Truthfully," Ida Mae replied scornfully, "*I'd* have let you stay. From what Felix has told me about poor Enock Rhoades and his murder, you deserve everything you're getting."

Well, by this time I was more frustrated than a starving sparrow watching an empty wormhole. As Ida Mae gathered her shawl even more closely about her shoulders, I desperately tried again.

"Dad-gum it, Ida Mae, I told you I was *innocent*. I never even knew a murder had been committed until this week!"

"Yes." Ida Mae responded, looking off down the lawn as though I was not even there, "Felix was right, as usual. He told me that a sure sign of guilt was when a person kept bringing up his own innocence. Hyrum, you surely do keep digging yourself into a deeper hole."

"Ida Mae, you're daft. *You* brought it up, not me. And besides, that Friendlessman feller ain't altogether clean hisownself."

"Hyrum, don't you talk against that man!"

"Somebody's got to. I'm telling you, Ida Mae, there's something about Friendlessman that smells fishier than Friday in St. Patrick's parish."

"That shows all you know! Why, he told me that he's been working for days on how to get you out of jail—he was planning on doing it tonight, a little later on. I've tried to find him and tell him ever since I heard you were out, but I couldn't. He's off somewhere putting himself at great personal risk and wasting his money to secure your release. And a thankless task *that* will be, the poor soul."

Well, I was getting plumb sick to my stomach, and I was starting to feel mean again. I knew why Friendlessman wanted me out of jail, but how on earth was I ever going to convince Ida Mae of what I knew? I mean, it's bad enough when a feller's girl tells him that his mother is lewd, but then to have her fall head over heels for a purely dispicable excuse for a man, well, that's *really* tough.

"Ida Mae, I have a thing or two to say that you need to hear, and I don't want you to take it wrong. I ain't saying it because I'm jealous, though I'll own up square to the fact that I am. But mostly I'm telling you this because I like you. A lot."

"It hadn't better be about Felix."

"Well, as a matter of fact, it is. Ida Mae—"

"Hyrum, I won't listen to this!"

"Ida Mae, have I ever lied to you? Have I? You know doggone well I ain't never told you nothing false before. Not ever!"

"Oh, but you have terrible grammar!"

"Maybe. But my heart's clean and innocent, which is more than I can say for Friendlessman, no matter how fine he can speak."

"Hyrum, I'm warning you!"

"Hear me out, will you? Please?"

"Well . . ."

"Please? Just for a minute?"

"Oh all right, but hurry!"

"Thank you. Ida Mae, I have proof, confidential but reliable, that Friendlessman is pure crooked. For honesty he's ganter than a bottleflied colt, and he's tied in with some thoroughly mean hombres, including a Mr. Doolin, who happens to be the man who tried to steal my gold and who got me arrested."

"Which you thoroughly deserved," Ida Mae declared. "You'd best put up that proof you mentioned."

"Well, uh, I can't," I mumbled, mentally cursing Ernest's dumb oath. "I made a blood vow never to tell how I came about that knowledge, and—"

"And you expect me to believe *that?*"

"I'm hoping you will. Ida Mae, there's more sand in one of Ma's biscuits than there is in Friendlessman's craw. I'm telling you, he is purely a cowardly crook, as is Doolin and who knows how many others. Why, they've even got old Loose-lip Lundstrum tied in with them."

"Hyrum, I won't listen to another word of this. I've never heard such a rambling pack of lies. Felix warned me the other day that you'd try to do this, and now I can see how truly wise he is. And mentioning Loose-lip isn't going to make me believe you either. You *know* I don't care for that man, so naturally you'd throw his name in for effect."

"Ida Mae," I pleaded, "it's all true! They figured on busting me out of jail so they could drag me into the mountains and have me show 'em where Enock Rhoades's gold is hidden. Happen I couldn't take 'em to it, which I can't, they'd likely kill me."

"Oh, Hyrum, stop being so . . . so melodramatic! Murder you? What a lot of nonsense."

Well, I could see that I wasn't making much headway, and even worse, I could see that Ida Mae had been stricken harder than I'd thought. I don't know what Friendlessman had, besides that he could color up the facts redder'n a Navajo blanket, but it surely did seem to be what it took. I'd never seen anyone so confounded moonstruck in my life as Ida Mae Sorenson. Maybe it was time I tried coming into this from another angle.

"Ida Mae, I . . . uh . . . I thought, well, I had it in mind that you was my girl."

"Whatever gave you *that* idea?"

Brother, talk about a cold, cold voice. Ten minutes with her and a feller'd end up with frostbite or his death of pneumonia. Still, I'd gone too far to back off now. Frostbite or not, for her sake I had to go through with it.

"Well, we've had a lot of talks about it, and a couple of times we've even kissed."

"That, Mr. Soderberg, was long before I knew what you were really like."

"Ida Mae," I growled, "I told you before, and I'm telling you for the last time, *I'm innocent!* How in blue blazes could I have—"

"Don't you swear in front of me!"

"Oh, for crying out loud, that ain't swearing!"

"Isn't!"

"Yeah, *isn't!*"

"And stop shouting!"

"Well you . . ." I stormed, finally and most completely losing my temper, "I ain't *shouting!* But I am most assuredly ready to start! You . . . you're ornerier'n a rat-tailed horse in fly-time. I sincerely wanted to warn you, I truly did. I know what Friendlessman is like while you don't, and let me tell you, he's so crooked you could twist him into the ground like a corkscrew. But no, you won't listen! Instead, you fight me, and all I get is . . . *this!* As far as I'm concerned, you deserve that miserable misbegotten whelp of a hydrophoby skunk. More and more it's beginning to look like you and he are two of a kind! Good night!"

Well, Ida Mae gave me a look that was as cold as the stare of a gila monster, gathered up her gown or whatever it was she was wearing, and headed back to the house. Me, I strode back myownself, grabbed the ground-hitched reins of Old Man Aagard's sway-backed cayuse, scrambled into the saddle, and spurred the horse hard down the dark road.

Blast! Why on earth had I *ever* thought that little gal liked me? Sometimes it seemed like I didn't have the brains the good Lord gave a stinkbug. Trouble was, I truly did love Ida Mae. She was a fine girl, and I loved her in spite of everything she'd said and done. I'll say this, it surely was discouraging.

22

Hyrum's Bedroom
Loft—Fountain Green

That ribbon of road stretched off into the warm June moonlight, and I followed it blindly, not even thinking about which way I was going. I was churned up inside worse than a fresh batch of Ma's butter, and that was some churned up. Fact is, I felt awful. It truly looked like everything was over between Ida Mae and me.

Like I've said before, that little lady meant a great deal to me, falling only behind my family in that regard. Nor do I think that's much different from folks everywhere.

Pa says that when kids start to become adults, they fall in and out of love pretty regular. It's painful, but Pa says it's necessary, for that is how a person discovers what trusting means and who truly and completely loves whom.

Once that discovery is made, trust is established, two folks pair off and get married, and the family as the point of reference—something that I think I mentioned earlier—is established once again. Then those two who are now joined together can sort of let their hair down in front of each other. They each see the other's true person, and they love and trust in spite of all the superficial daily annoyances.

Then when babies come along, they too feel the trust, and as they grow they always know there is a least *one* place where they can find security and support.

As far as Ida Mae and I were concerned, I suppose I was still learning who really loved me and who I could trust. But now I was in misery, for all along I'd had such good feelings about her. I'd been certain as death and tithing that I loved her, and here I'd learned that I couldn't trust her at all! She'd turned against me like I was kith and kin of Governor Lilburn W. Boggs (the good Christian gentleman who had issued his extermination order against all Mormons in Mis-

souri, back in 1838), and that was about the same as saying I was
linked up personal with the devil. It made a feller want to lie down
and lick his wounds, it pained that bad.

"Well, ol' hoss," I growled, "I reckon you and I ain't needed too
badly here in Fountain Green. Not after tonight. Suppose we take
these supplies Zene asked for and get on up to the herd—"

And that was when I realized I had accidentally ridden home. I
hadn't meant to. I'd meant to leave town and strike out for Zene
Hill's sheep camp up in the Uintahs. But now that I was home, the
thought of my feather tick was too much, and I couldn't turn away
from it.

Of course, the house was dark, for it was near two in the morning. I put my old horse in the corral, took off his saddle, and rubbed
him down, and then I headed for a few hours of real comfortable
sleep.

Once on the porch I carefully removed my boots and then quiet-
like I opened the door and stepped into the inky blackness of the
kitchen. Quietly I closed the door and latched it, and carefully I
threaded my way past the table and chairs and over to my ladder.
With my boots under my arm I went up and into my loft, careful to
make no sound that would disturb Ma or the girls, who would be
sleeping below.

For a moment I thought of lighting a candle or lantern, decided
there wasn't any point in it, stripped off my duds, and hit my knees
for a quick good-night to the Lord.

I reckon it could be said that I was a praying man, for Ma and Pa
have taught me well, and off and on through my young life I've had
to lean pretty heavily on the powers of the Almighty. I believe in
prayer, I've had many prayers answered, and yet lately I'd noticed
that my prayers were getting scarcer'n ducks in a desert, and they
were mighty thin on content when I did say them. Seemed like I was
just too all-fired discouraged and there were too many things going
on against me for me to take the time to pray.

I did pray at night, I mean usually, but every time I did, it made
me think of something Pa had once told me. "Prayers," he'd said,
"are like telegrams. Most folks send 'em at night so's they can get the
low rate. The Good Lord probably answers them the same."

Gave a body something to think about, it did, especially happen
he was interested in a real powerful answer. But that night I wasn't,
though I surely should have been. I was just miserable and tired and

feeling worse than a poorly sheared sheep about my fight with Ida Mae. So I whipped through my prayer, pulled back the covers on that big wide feather tick, crawled in on the side where I always slept, twisted my pillow until it was comfortable, snuggled down under Ma's soft sheets with my back to most of the bed, closed my eyes, and—

Suddenly a soft arm came out of nowhere and snaked itself around my shoulders, and instantly an altogether too feminine body snuggled up against my backside!

Well, for an eternity or so I froze up solid as Nephi Robertson's stock pond in January. Then a soft and sleepy voice that I'd never heard before started whispering into my ear, and I realized that I was in real trouble.

"Hi, sweetheart," this altogether feminine voice purred, and I could feel an awful lot of warm breath in my ear and on the back of my neck. "I thought you weren't coming over."

Well, I was speechless as an Egyptian mummy. It was obvious as little red apples on a big green tree that I wasn't alone in my bed, and I should have been, I truly should have been!

"I'm glad you came," she went on. "This loft is so awful—tight and cramped and untidy. It just *isn't* what I'd expected. I'm so glad you're here to make it comfortable."

Well, saying such things about my room was plain rude, and that made me mad! That there was a fine loft, with the best fixings Ma and Pa could provide. Besides that, it was *mine,* and I wasn't about to let no female hussy go running it down.

I was just ready to tell her, too, but then she kissed me on my neck, and of a sudden rooms and rudeness were altogether forgotten. I was out of that feather bed faster'n chain lightning with a link snapped.

"Wh-wh-who are you?" I whispered haltingly.

"Why dear, I'm your new wife."

I caught my breath. "L-lady, I ain't got no wife, new or otherwise!"

There was a instant of total silence, and then that loft of mine was pierced with the doggonedest scream a body ever heard. It was so loud it would've driven a whole pack of wild wolves straight to suicide. The way she was carrying on, I even gave suicide some thought myownself.

Instead, however, I controlled my shaking fingers, struck a

match, and tried to light my lantern, and all the while that lady was screaming like a scrub calf caught in a briar patch.

I finally got the lantern lit and dropped the chimney down, and my chin near broke a hole in the floor, it hit it so hard.

There was this woman, a total stranger, kneeling in the middle of *my* bed, with *my* covers wrapped up around her, screaming that *I'd* attacked her.

Well, I saw and heard that, saw that her eyes had saucered up big as barn owls, saw the cavernous pit where her mouth had probably once resided, saw that she was still yelping like a run-over sheepdog, and suddenly I realized that I was standing there all exposed in my red long-johns, the ones that had one of the rear drop-seat buttons missing. Worse, I was gracing the vision of some strange and likely evil woman whose morals weren't no straighter'n a willow in a high wind.

Quick as I could, I grabbed up my covers and threw them around my unclothed form. Then I realized that the screaming had grown abruptly worse.

I looked, and discovered to my horror that the quilt I had whipped around me was the self-same quilt that had originally been covering the frantically screaming woman. Now, of course, she was screaming more but was covered with a great deal less, and that was a purely naked fact.

For an instant I considered sharing my quilt, for from the sudden way she had huddled down she did appear to be mighty cold. However, right off I knew that would never work, not her and me together under the same quilt again. No sir, Ma hadn't raised no foolish children that lived in *my* loft. Happen I tried that, I reckoned there'd be a lot worse than screaming going on. Why, I'd be about as welcome under that quilt as a polecat at a Sunday school picnic.

So, being the wise and true gentleman that I am, I settled on the next-best course of action. I picked up my trousers and started climbing into them. That done, I figured on giving my quilt back to the screaming stranger, and then we'd both be happy.

I'd have done it, too, but just as I was fixing to do so, I saw Ma come churning up the ladder with her broom in her hand. The sight so unnerved me that I dropped the quilt, and quicker'n scat that woman was off the bed and onto the floor, with them covers up and around her once more.

By cracky, I thought, that woman could certainly galvinate.

She'd got under that quilt faster'n a lizard off a hot rock. I'd not seen anything move so swift and shameless since Euphemistic Lynn Barnes had gone to treat his saddle gall in the dark and got the undiluted sheep dip out of the medicine chest instead of the soothing, comforting bear grease.

Then that woman, now that she was once more covered, commenced to screaming again, and I decided that her resemblance to Euphemistic was even greater than I'd first supposed. My recollection was that he'd hollered some too.

"What is it?" Ma gasped as she tried to adjust her eyes to the light from my lantern. "Who is it, Cordelia?"

Then she glimpsed me, her eyes hardened, and instantly I knew I was buzzard bait. Without hesitation Ma was onto me, whacking me with that broom, joining her screaming with that of the woman Cordelia, and instantly my room was noisier'n an empty wagon running fast on a hard-froze road.

"Ma!" I screamed myownself, and about then Lucille and LaRue were up that ladder and they were screaming too, and both of them little female wildcats who had always and heretofore been my sweet little sisters had also lit into me and were biting and tearing me further asunder with every passing mouthful.

"Ma!" I yelped again. "Its me. Hyrum! Ma, its your *son!*"

At that Ma slowed down enough to look, saw that I was telling the truth, and gasped, and then her lips thinned down with anger and she started swinging that frightful broom again.

"Hyrum, you . . . you . . ." she sputtered angrily. "Why, this is *awful!* What on earth are you doing in bed with Cordelia?"

Well, I thought of several answers, but I didn't give them because I was too busy ducking that swinging broom and pulling my legs out from between fiercely chomping teeth. Why, the whole up-scuddle made a feller wonder about what I'd said earlier concerning families and love and trust and about kinfolk coming to the rescue whenever there was trouble. If this was what it was like to be rescued, then I never wanted to be involved in such a horriferous extricative event again.

"Ma," I yelled, "it's *my* bed and *my* room. I don't even know this woman! And I *surely* didn't mean to go climbing into bed with her! It was *dark!* Now doggone it, *leave me alone!*"

That must have done it, for Ma suddenly stopped and stepped back and looked at me. Then, as I winced from the loss of a major

portion of my left thigh to LaRue's dripping jowls, Ma reached out
and pulled both LaRue and Lucille away.

"For heaven's sake, Hyrum, I . . . "

It was impossible for either of us to converse, however, for Cordelia whatever-her-name-was was still carrying on noiser'n a strong
wind blowing over an empty barrel bung.

"Cordelia!" Ma finally shouted, "Will you please be *still!*"

That did it, too, and for the first time in what seemed like a
hundred years, my room got quiet.

"Well?" Ma asked, stern as I'd ever seen her.

"Well what?" I countered.

"Well, what are you doing here?"

"It *is* my room."

"Maybe so, but you are supposed to be on your way to the herd."

"I decided not to go tonight. Besides, who is this woman, and
how'd she come to be in my bed?"

Ma looked strangely at me, looked down at Cordelia and then
back at me again, and it seemed, thank goodness, like maybe her
eyes had finally been opened to the light of truth and understanding.
"Well for heaven's sake," she declared. "You *wouldn't* know, would
you."

"No ma'am," I agreed quickly, "I surely wouldn't. Now *what*
wouldn't I know?"

"Hyrum, your Pa has taken himself another wife. Please meet
your new Aunt Cordelia. Cordelia, meet my son Hyrum."

Well, I was shocked, to say the least. You'd think Pa had him
enough troubles with three wives and every marshal in the territory
after him for having them. Of course, with Pa a body could never tell.
He seemed to like trouble, maybe even to thrive on it. Like I've said
before, my Pa has maybe three interests in this world: the Church,
money, and lovely women. And no doubt about it, this new wife was
lovely. I guess he figured four wives would be altogether better, for
escaping from the law, than three.

"When was this decided on?" I asked.

"While you were in jail. Both Jons and I forgot to tell you. Polly,
Victoria, and I got telegrams from Jons while he was hiding in Salt
Lake City, giving us the details and asking our approval. We talked it
over and decided in favor of it. Cordelia came into town late today on
the train.

"I told her that since you were away, she was welcome to stay here in your room until Jons could find her a better place. She seemed quite happy to accept, and she dearly loves your room."

Well, I looked down at Pa's crouching new wife, Cordelia, and recollected what she'd said about my room whilst she was snuggled up against my back. She knew right off what I was remembering, and sudden she was redder'n a fiery sunset after a dust storm. That did my heart good, seeing her embarrassed. Sort of put us on equal footing, if you know what I mean.

"Aunt Cordelia," I declared magnanimously, "I'm pleased to make your acquaintance. You are most welcome to my cramped and untidy room. Whilst I spend the night outdoors where the air is not so stuffy, I would be honored to have you stay here."

Aunt Cordelia got redder, but then politely and very subdued, she replied, "Hyrum, I . . . I'm sorry about . . . about . . . Well, I accept your hospitality with pleasure. And now, well, I can tell that your room is much more spacious than I had at first supposed. Thank you."

Ma gazed from Cordelia to me and back again, somewhat confused I imagine. The little girls sat down on the bed and started to giggle at Cordelia huddled on the floor in Ma's quilt, and we were all finally starting to smile when of a sudden there was a terrible pounding on the door.

"Open up in there! Hurry it up! Open up or we'll break down the door."

"Who is it?" Ma called.

"Never you mind, lady. Just open up and let us in!"

"Ma," I whispered, "I gotta get out of here."

"Hyrum, what have you done?"

"Ma, I ain't done nothing but find a little gold. I think it's Friendlessman and those outlaws, and they're after me!"

Ma gasped. "Oh my word!" Then suddenly she was angry again. "Well, I won't have it! I simply won't stand for this! Hyrum, I'll get the door and will do my best to keep them busy. Cordelia, take Hyrum's shotgun there—you do know how to use it, don't you?"

"I do," Cordelia declared, rising to her feet with the quilt still firmly in place.

"Good. Let's hope you won't have to. Hyrum, load it for her. You little girls get into your beds downstairs. Quickly.

"Now Hyrum, as soon as the gun's loaded, you get out that window. I've seen you do it for Ida Mae, so I don't imagine you'll have too much trouble now."

Well, I grinned. Its purely amazing how much a mother's apt to know about her children. And mine was a wonder, I'll tell you that. "Okay, I'll go. And Ma, thanks for trusting me."

Ma looked up at me, reached up and softly touched my face, and then she hugged me. "I love you, Hyrum," she whispered, and then she was on the ladder and going down.

Quick as I could I grabbed a handful of shells, loaded two into the scattergun, handed both gun and extra shells to Cordelia, saw that Ma was downstairs watching me, saw too that she was holding Pa's pistol out in front of her, and saw finally that her hands were very steady. Feeling proud as punch of that little lady who was my ma, I grabbed my boots and shirt, waved and smiled at Ma and at Pa's new wife, blew out the lantern, and was out that window and gone.

I heard the door open around front, I heard Ma's cold voice order those men to stand tight, I heard Cordelia's firm voice echoing Ma's, and I knew Pa had got him another good woman. I was glad there were still some around. Gave a feller like me a little hope, happen things continued to stay sour between Ida Mae and me.

Instantly those men were quieter'n a used-up feather duster, and I waited to hear no more.

Thanking the Good Lord that I had a family I could trust and depend upon happen there was trouble, I was off and away across our night-dark pasture, my bare feet making no sound at all as I ran.

23

Brush Canyon—
Sanpitch Mountain,
Sanpete County

There was a new moon above me, and the small amount of light suited me fine. I knew where I was going, but those hombres back at the house didn't and so the darker it was, the better.

In my bare feet I ran to the back fence of the pasture, and there I stopped long enough to pull on my boots. That done, I was through the barbed wire and climbing the gentle, sage-covered slope to the west of town, going just opposite to the way I hoped they'd expect me to go.

For maybe thirty minutes I ran and walked, and that old crippled clubfoot of mine hardly slowed me at all. In fact, I suppose it helped, for all my life it had forced me to develop muscles on my muscles just so I could drag it along.

It's passing strange how things like clubfeet and other problems usually also turn into blessings. It sort of verifies the Lord's promise in the book of Ether, where He says that He gives men weaknesses so that they will be humble, and then if men *will* be humble, He will make their weaknesses become strong unto them. Now I'm not saying I am humble, but I am saying that my gimped-up leg hasn't lost much because of atrophied muscles. No sir, it carries me right along.

Finally I came to a small hill at the mouth of Pole Canyon, one that seemed to stand sentinel over all that passed below. I didn't climb it but angled up the slope toward the north, worked my way through some fairly thick scrub oak, and so crossed the ridge and dropped down into Spring Canyon. There I stopped for a drink at what folks called the Big Springs, those that had given Fountain Green its name.

There were a whole passel of stories about those springs, which came gushing out of the side of the mountain like a big green fountain, and I'd heard them since I was knee-high to a short stump. First, the springs seemed to bear no relation to the snow-pack on the San-pitch Mountains, which lifted above them. Folks had speculated for years as to their origin, and no one seemed able to decide where the water truly came from. Some fellers had even poured dye into the waters up above, and none ever came out in the springs.

That led to the other story, which was probably my favorite. According to that account, when President Brigham Young, whom folks usually just called Brother Brigham, first called settlers to the northern end of Sanpete Valley, it had been drier'n the dust in a mummy's pocket, and the settlers had been pretty nearly droughted out. In fact, only two or three families had managed to stay.

When Brigham Young heard about it, it was told that he came south from Salt Lake City, stopped his buckboard down below the Big Springs, stood up, and, looking up at the mountain, declared that so long as the settlers in our town lived their religion, the springs would always be of sufficient size to supply the needs of the community.

We must have been doing all right living our religion, too. The town had grown from a couple of families to sixty or seventy, and each year the springs had grown larger. Truthfully, we always seemed to have plenty of water, and in our country that was saying something. Made a body feel good just thinking about that. Maybe there was a little hope for us recalcitrant sinners after all.

There were a lot of stories around concerning Brother Brigham and his prophecies, and who was to say which of the stories, if any, were correct? He'd been dead since 1877, and to the best of my knowledge he'd made no public appearances since then, either to confirm or deny what folks were saying he'd once said.

Lots of the stories of his prophecies concerned gold and gold mines, and I've always found it interesting that for a man who tried so hard to keep the Saints away from gold prospecting and busy on their farms, so many prophecies abounded about the nearby locations of the fabulous wealth he was always telling the Saints to ignore.

For instance, the story is told that in Salt Creek Canyon, which is just north of Fountain Green, Brother Brigham pulled his team to a halt one day so that his animals might drink. They were then at the confluence of Salt Creek and Hop Creek, and as his horses guzzled the water, the Prophet is supposed to have stood up in the wagon, looked around, and pointed north up the canyon. "Brethren," it is claimed that he said, "someday the Saints will find gold up there, more gold than is found in any other mine in the territory. The location of that deposit is within one mile of where I now stand."

Well, there was always a little placer gold turning up in Salt Creek, and Loose-lip Lundstrum and a few others had churned up the mountains for miles around in their search for the mother lode, but to the best of my knowledge no one had ever found Brigham Young's deposit. Of course, Loose-lip and those others weren't exactly what might be called Saints, and the active Mormons were too busy making a living to go burrowing around in the hills after improbable wealth, so maybe that was the problem. After all, Brother Brigham *had* said Saints.

From Spring Canyon I kept moving north, climbing partway up a steep ridge and then moving across the brush-choked sidehill until I finally came to the edge of the small defile that most folks called Brush Canyon. By then I'd been pretty torn by all the scrub oak, and my clothes were ragged as one of LaRue's dolls. I was also tired as blue blazes, for I'd come near five miles over mighty rough foothill country. I'd done it in the dark of night, and such a climb would wear a body down even if he didn't have a clubfoot. So just where the ridge dropped off, I squatted down into a soft, inviting sagebrush, and there I took my first real breather.

Behind me, up on the slopes of Sanpitch Mountain, a coyote took his last couple of yips at the sinking moon. Then it was silent and I sat still; my own breathing was the only sound on the quiet hillside.

For sometime I closed my eyes and rested, thinking of that woman Cordelia who was Pa's new wife. That had been something, her thinking I was Pa and snuggling up against me like she'd done. It had truly startled me, but now that I thought on it, I grinned. No sir, it hadn't felt altogether bad. In fact, it made a feller understand a little why folks seemed to look forward to marriage like they did. In a way I even looked forward to it a little myownself, happen I could get through my mission and find a gal who would love me as much as Cordelia seemed to love my Pa.

And that got me to thinking of Ida Mae. Though I'd had no right, I'd thought all along that when my mission was over, why, she and I would happily enter into the state of wedded bliss together. I'd even seen a wedding dress in that Co-op in Provo, and I'll tell a man, it was a thing of surpassing beauteous wonder: veil, trail, and the whole regale. I could even imagine Ida Mae in it, providing of course that she'd be willing to wear it with me beside her. Which event now didn't look too likely, I had to admit.

Way over east the sky had taken on a rosy cast behind the East Mountains, or the Wasatch Plateau, which was what the mountains on the east side of Sanpete Valley were properly called. I watched as the mountains grew into focus, knowing that I had to cross over into them, and knowing too that the odds against my succeeding were only just barely short of stupendous. Especially would it be difficult with Friendlessman and his boys on my trail like they were.

Down in Fountain Green a rooster crowed, a dog barked, and somebody's door slammed, and in the intense stillness of the morning I heard the screech of a pump as someone drew water for their breakfast.

Here and there a light showed, for the town was still in darkness, and suddenly I got a real lump in my throat. That little town wasn't much on size. In fact, it was downright small. I'd even heard folks joke about that, one saying that when his pa had died, the town had had to hold an election for mayor, sheriff, justice of the peace, and town drunk, all at once. Another had said that when Fountain Green was surveyed, the man hadn't even bothered to use a scope. Pa always said that in Fountain Green a man could have his face shaved and his shoes shined at the same time, and the barber shop was across the street from the shoe shop. I didn't know about that, but I did have it on good authority that when our town's first and only sightseer stopped by last summer and asked for a local map, they gave him one and furnished a magnifying glass to go with it.

So, like I said, as far as towns went, Fountain Green was small. Still, it was home, and that means something to a man. It was where the folks that I loved lived, and it was where I felt at home and secure.

Down below me the smoke lifted from Cornelius Collard's blacksmith and wheelwright shop, and I thought of the last time he'd fixed Ma's wagon and wouldn't accept any pay. Down the street was John Green's brickyard, where he had molded, fired, and then donated all the brick in the ward tithing office. Then around the corner was Rees Lewellyn's home, which also served as our post office. Brother Lewellyn was a fine man and a real leader, and folks were already talking of running him for the Territorial Legislature. Besides that, he was Pa's friend, and he did all he could to keep Pa informed about the activities of the marshals. Then right below me was Pa's mill, which he called the Phoenix Mills and which was just beginning to come to life. Ole Sorensen ran the mill, and he did a good job of it, too. The winter before, he had gone out of his way to teach me all about milling, and I thought the world of him for that. A boy can always tell which adult folks like him; the ones I've mentioned liked me, and I can't even say how such an understanding helped me on the way to growing up.

So looking down on that little village made me think of a whole lot more than a few small cabins and adobe homes, several barns and corrals, and a couple of withering businesses. That's why I had that lump in my throat.

It was coming on real daylight by then, and I decided it was time to get down into the old tunnel in Brush Canyon where I planned to hide out for the day. I stood to go and started to turn, and just then a sudden movement above and behind me caught my eye. I looked, and there, not more than three hundred yards off, a man sat on his horse staring at me.

Suddenly he lifted his rifle, but I was already in the air and diving down the hill when the *whap* of the passing bullet assailed my ears.

How had they found me? How on earth had they tracked me in the dark and going opposite to where they should have expected me to be going? I didn't know, but that bullet had been evidence enough to convince even an eternal optimist like myself that they had. I hadn't fooled them one little bit.

Down the slope I hurriedly scattered leaves, hoping to confuse them a little and maybe gain some time. I rolled a big rock off toward the bottom, and then, careful to keep my feet on rocks and dead wood, I quickly descended in another direction. I went fast, but I was careful as conditions permitted, and I did all the things Pa and Zene had shown me in the way of hiding a trail.

At last I came to the mouth of the old tunnel I sought, and there for a moment I paused. The tunnel had been dug years before by a fellow who had come into town, learned that we all got our water from the same spring, and decided to tap into it, divert it, and sell it to us out of *his* canyon.

The story went that he'd dug, the bishop had warned him, he'd kept on digging, and then even Brother Brigham had warned him. Still the poor fool had kept on digging. By then he had quite a hole into the side of Brush Canyon, and folks said they could hear the water through the rock, he was that close.

Finally he'd been warned one last time, some said by Brigham Young again, and he had laughed and declared that it was his canyon and he could dig as he chose. Just days later there was an accident, either at a saw mill up Ephraim Canyon or in the tunnel, depending upon who was telling the story, and when things had settled, the poor misbegotten soul was minus one arm.

Well, it's pretty tough swinging a single jack with one hand, so that was the end of that fellow's attempted piracy of the Big Springs. The way it looked to me, it didn't seem to be a very wise proposition, going against Brother Brigham Young. Nor any of the rest of the brethren either, for that matter.

Samuel Brannan, who I read recently had died a pauper down in Sonora, Mexico, last year, had tried that and had also lost. When Brother Brigham settled the Saints in the valley, Sam Brannan had come along and declared that the place to go was California. Brigham Young had said no, Samuel had argued yes, the Saints had stayed, and off Samuel Brannan had gone to prove the Prophet wrong. Well, he did have lots of experiences that the world would probably call successful, but none seemed to last, and worst of all, he never seemed able to throw a rope around being happy. Finally, as I said, he died alone and a pauper down in Sonora, a witness to the fact that it doesn't pay to fight against the prophets of God.

Carefully I worked my way down the side of the gaping mouth of the tunnel, moving through the thick brush, doing my best to break no tree limbs and skin no bark. They had a tracker with them that must have come from the high, deep woods, and it was going to be difficult enough to shake him if I was perfect. Mistakes would kill me sure.

At last, near the floor of the tunnel, I found good footing. I leaped out and came down on a large rock just behind the thick stand of oak that hid the tunnel from view. So far, so good. Happen they didn't know of the tunnel, I just might get away with hiding there. Happen they did know of it, well . . .

Stepping backward, I pulled a few oak limbs down to better cover the small opening I had jumped through, and then I stooped and shuffled maybe a dozen feet back into the tunnel and sat down to wait it out. I could have gone deeper, but there had been a cave-in, and I didn't want to chance another one. Besides, the deeper I crawled the more I knew the hole would feel like a trap, and I didn't like that feeling at all.

I dozed for a time, and it was maybe two hours later when I heard the first of the men. Right off I knew I had been correct about that tracker. My attempts at hiding the trail had been futile at best.

"Boss," a voice called from somewhere above me, "I think he came this way. There's a scratch on this rock that looks fresh, and I reckon it's him."

"Good work, Blue John," another voice called from farther off. "Silvertip, get Friendlessman and Doolin. He's gone this way."

There was silence then for maybe thirty minutes, and I was surely starting to sweat. A fly buzzed in the tunnel, around and around and around, and watching it, I felt more trapped than ever. They'd find me sure, and there was nothing I could do about it. I debated making another break for it, gave that up as suicide, thought of giving myself up, decided that was suicide as well—just the delayed kind—and so I simply sat, hoping for a miracle and knowing there wasn't going to be one.

"Boss," the voice suddenly called again, this time from on past the tunnel mouth, "this kid's a slick one. I've lost him again."

"Stick to it," the Boss's voice called out, sounding so near to me that I actually jumped. "He can't vanish into thin air."

"Boss, you know that and I know it. I just wish the kid who's vanished knew it. I tell you, cripple or no, this Soderberg kid's some spooky. I'd have sworn that Friendlessman nailed him first off this morning, but there ain't been no sign of blood, not anywhere. Then there was that false trail he made with the rock, made like a wounded man might make, and at the bottom it wasn't no trail at all. I tell you, he's slick. Now he's come to here, and whoosh, he's just lifted up and gone."

"It can't happen!"

"Maybe it can, happen a feller believes in haunts."

The one called the Boss laughed, and it was not a pleasant laugh to hear. "You can't be serious," he said scornfully.

"I'm getting serious."

"So am I," the Boss snarled. "And I'll haunt you, happen you don't raise that kid's trail mighty quick."

There was another brief period of silence. I sweated some more and thought on what those two had said to each other, and then from across the canyon on the north slope, another voice called, a high, thin, reedy voice that I'd never forget as long as I lived.

"Say, Moore," the man whined, "there are tracks over here, and they look to be fresh. I'll bet the kid came this way."

Doolin! Why that miserable little skunk! More and more I was growing to dislike that man.

"Blue John," the Boss shouted from nearby, "get over there and follow that trail."

"Oh, for . . . " Blue John's voice called out from so close to the tunnel mouth that I was surprised I couldn't see him. "That ain't his trail, Boss. It can't be! I've followed it to here, and I'll lay odds the kid's within fifty feet of me right now!"

Fifteen feet would be more correct, I thought as I wiped my forehead, hunkered down, and looked around for some rock to duck behind. Fifteen, or maybe even ten. That Blue John fellow was *close*.

"You go on over there, Blue John," another voice suddenly declared, a deep booming voice that sounded kind and friendly and not at all like an outlaw. "See what Doolin has found. Moore and I will stay here and keep looking."

"Yeah," Blue John growled, addressing himself but doing it loudly enough so that I could easily hear. "And a fat lot of good that will do, you knucklehead. Silvertip, you wouldn't know dung from wild honey happen you stood neck deep in it.

"No, boys," he called out, "I'm staying—"

"Blue John," a new voice suddenly ordered, the same ice-cold voice I'd heard order Ma to open her door, "you go join Doolin! Now! Moore, you go with him. Silvertip and I will stay right here and watch the slope. That way we'll have everything covered so tight that even a rabbit couldn't move without being seen. One way or the other, we'll get the boy this time."

There was a scurrying in the brush as the man descended past the tunnel, and instantly I breathed easier. That Blue John fellow had about located me, but now with a little luck, maybe—

"Friendlessman," the deep booming voice of the man known as Silvertip suddenly called, "you reckon he's holed up right around here somewhere? You reckon maybe he can even hear us?"

"Of course I don't," that snow-chilled voice stated flatly. "Why would he have stopped here, when he might just as easily have kept on to his destination?"

"Uh . . I don't know. I just thought maybe . . . well, maybe he's got him a hole or a cave or something."

"In this canyon? You ninny, of course he's in a cave, or more properly, a tunnel. We all know that, and we know as well that it is in Gammett Canyon, not here. Why, in this gully we could *see* a cave, providing there was one. Which there isn't. This ravine isn't large enough to conceal a rabbit burrow, let alone a tunnel."

Now how had they known about my tunnel in Gammett Canyon? I'd not said a word to anyone, and even Ma and my new Aunt Cordelia hadn't known where I was going. It made no kind of sense, but it did give me a great deal of concern.

"But Mr. Friendlessman," the outlaw Silvertip argued, "there's patches of thick brush that could hide anything. Like maybe that there patch of oak right below you."

Well, my heart nearly stopped, I was that scared. I knew what was below that Felix Friendlessman, and it was no more and no less than me, hidden up in that old and concealed tunnel. If anyone got any closer than Blue John had done, they'd literally fall into my hiding place. Trouble was, there was nothing I could do about that, nothing at all.

I stared at the entrance where the morning sun filtered down through the oak leaves, and I wondered how far I could get if I made a break for it. Not far, I feared. There were rifles behind me and rifles across the canyon, and I was fairly boxed.

No, the only thing to do, if they even gave me the chance to do it, would be to surrender peacefully and then to wait for another time. There were a lot of miles to cover before the Uintahs, and maybe—

"Well," the cold voice of Friendlessman asked, "are you going to check out that brush or aren't you?"

"Mr. Friendlessman, I was only suggesting—"

"Silvertip, look into that brush!"

"Yes sir," Silvertip replied immediately, and I heard clearly the scuffle as he rose and started down the slope toward my thicket.

It's purely amazing how sound carries in a mountain canyon. I could even hear the man's breathing as he approached. I could hear the tune he was suddenly humming, and for the second time I thought of this particular enemy as a man, a person who might, at another time and in another place, be my friend.

In the gloom of the tunnel I looked again for a better place to hide, considered crawling back into the debris from the cave-in, and gave it up. That way I would be trapped for sure, and happen the roof gave way again, I'd also be dead. No, at least with the outlaws I'd have a chance.

Outside, the man was within just a few feet of the tunnel mouth, and I knew the game was up. He was still humming "Sweet Betsy from Pike," he was already at the edge of the brush, and he had just parted the first of the limbs when from the earth beneath him, almost under my own nose as well, broke forth the most awful yipping and wailing a body ever heard.

It was a she-coyote yelp of anger and pain and fierce determination to protect her young, and it burst so near to Silvertip, as a matter of Brush-Canyon Sanpitch-Mountain fact, that the outlaw believed he had stepped on the very coyote that was giving the wild-crying alarm.

With a shout of surprise and fright he lunged backward; the trees closed up again, there was a flying up of earth toward his retreating form, and suddenly a small body hurtled into the tunnel and crouched down, staring outward.

There was more yipping and snarling; Silvertip kept moving away, and suddenly he laughed and spoke.

"Mr. Friendlessman," he called, "I reckon I was right. There *is* a hole down there, a coyote hole. Mrs. Coyote's to home, too, with a whole passel of pups. Reckon that means the kid's gone. No wild animal will stay holed up and quiet like that if it's close to a human."

"I suppose you're right," Friendlessman agreed, and abruptly he issued new orders. "Let's cross over. I'm certain that the kid has moved into Gammett Canyon, and that's where we'd better go as well."

I listened as they left, but I didn't move my eyes from that still-crouching form, I didn't move them at all. Nor did the small body move until the two men had crossed the bottom of the canyon and were thrashing their way up the north slope. Then it slowly turned toward me . . . and grinned.

"Howdy, Hy," was all it—he—said.

24

Fountain Green Vicinity—
Sanpete County

"Criminentely, Ern, how'd you get here?"

My younger brother kept grinning, but at last he spoke. "I declare, Hy. You're predictable as rain water running downhill. I knew right where you'd be, and it looks like Ida Mae did too."

"Ida Mae?"

"Yeah. I reckon it was her told Friendlessman and the others that you'd likely hide out over here. Nobody else knew, and them boys came a-fanning it right on your trail. *Somebody* surely told them. Hardly gave me time to lead them astray."

Well, I studied on what Ernest had said, and bad as it made me feel, it did seem right. I'd thought they had a good tracker, and they did. But even good trackers have a hard time of it at night, and like Ernest had said, those boys had come a-fogging. Besides that, it surely answered my question about how Friendlessman had known I would be hiding in a tunnel. Yes sir, I'd been pointed out, and it had to have been by Ida Mae.

She and I had talked of this tunnel often enough, for it was where Pa hid out if things got real bad between him and the marshals. It wouldn't be any trick at all for her to put two and two together. Of course, she'd never been to the tunnel, and so far as I knew she didn't even know it was in Brush Canyon; I'd only told her that it was north of the Big Springs. That's why those hombres had been looking in Gammett Canyon. Somehow they'd assumed a tunnel would be in a larger canyon, and that assumption had saved my bacon.

That, and Ernest.

"Little brother," I said, "I surely do admire the way you coyote around these hills." I shuffled forward to shake his hand, and as we gripped, the breeze brought a whiff of something that smelled powerful awful.

"Ern," I gasped, "You're whiffy as the national skunk convention. Where in tarnation you been?"

"In a coyote hole. Where'd you think I yapped from out there? Horseback or something?"

"I . . . I don't know."

"That hole was the only place left between them outlaws and the tunnel, and given about three seconds to make a decision, I took it. Gave me the idea of yapping, too."

"Well, Ern, you did it up good. You the one who laid that trail out across the canyon?"

"You bet." Ernest was proud, and I didn't blame him. For a runt-sized kid, he'd done more than fine.

"Now those boys won't be in Gammett long, Hy. I had to dead-end the trail and get back here in a hurry. Seems to me we'd best depart."

"Shanks-mare, Ern? You know I don't have much foot speed, and this gimped-up leg is about as wore out as the path to the privvy in chokecherry time. I just don't—"

"Just to the bottom, Hy. No farther. I got ol' Ingersol tethered there, and he'll carry us both."

"Ingersol! Ernest, what'll Pa do when he hears—"

"I told Ma to ease it to him gentle, happen she sees him again before we get back. Besides, when Aunt Hattie came and woke us up and told us about you and them fellers who were after you, I knew there wasn't an awful lot of time to spare on getting approval. And Pa always says that it's easier to repent than it is to get permission. I was just sort of applying his teachings. Now I reckon we'd best be on our way."

I reckoned the same, and shortly two young Soderbergs were hoofing it down the gully to where Ernest had hidden Ingersol, Pa's Belgian stallion that had run over a hundred miles on that one day the year before.

"How'd you ever catch this plug?" I asked after we were mounted and moving easy-like down the deep gully toward town. "He's kid-shy as any horse I ever saw."

"Luck," Ernest replied. "I've been around horses all my life, and what you say, big brother, is the gospel truth. Horses altogether are peculiar, and this one in particular, well . . . it's come to me that no matter how spavined or broken down horses might look, no matter how gentle is the look in their eyes, all horses are a little *loco en la cabeza*. Ever since I was throwed by that fool mare belonging to Deaf Man Hibbard, which is the slowest looking nag I ever saw, I've watched horses careful as rattlers in a sack. They'll go out from under you or come down on top of you or just plain up and run off from you for no good reason at all. And that's if it is your own personal horse, one you happen to know like a brother. Coming to a monster like ol' Ingersol here, which I've never rode nor even throwed a blanket on, well, it's Katie bar the door, for sure."

"So how'd you catch him?" I asked, grinning.

"It was tough," Ernest grumbled. "I walked up, took his reins in my hand, climbed up on the fence, and swung aboard."

"He was saddled?"

"And rearing to go. I reckon Pa had him ready for a quick get-away happen ol' Clawson or some other marshal showed up while he was asleep."

"I hope they don't," I breathed.

"Yeah, me too. If they do and if Pa can't find his getaway horse, and if he ever gets out of jail after they throw him in again, I reckon we'll both be dead men."

"You're a comfort, little brother, you surely are."

Ernest was silent, so I kicked Ingersol into a run, and moments later we were down on the lane running from the Big Springs down into Fountain Green. I was some worried about Friendlessman and the others seeing us, but as we rounded the first turn in the road we came onto old Deaf Man Hibbard driving his wagon full of water barrels back home from the springs.

Quickly I pulled Ingersol to a walk beside his wagon, and for the next few minutes we had perfect cover. To anyone up on the mountain, it would look exactly like we had all been after water. Or at least that's how I hoped it would look.

"Hello, Brother Hibbard," I called.

"Eh?" he grunted, cupping his hand to his ear and staring at me.

"I said hello," I shouted, and suddenly I remembered that the old man was no more deaf than I was. Why was he—

"Speak up, sonny, I can't hear a word the way this rig is rattling about."

"Brother Hibbard, Ernest said quietly, "I told Hyrum about you."

Deaf Man Hibbard looked hard at Ernest, my younger brother squirmed behind me, and at last the old man grinned. "Well, a man never knows," he laughed. "Besides, I'm so used to being deaf that sometimes I forget I ain't. Whew! Which one of you fellers is polluting the morning breeze?"

"It's me, I reckon," Ernest answered. "I got a little scented up back there on the hill."

"Well, get that horse to the lee-side of this wagon. Deaf or not, I never claimed to have lost my sense of smell."

I smiled, reined Ingersol around, and soon we were riding smoothly again.

"Ern," Deaf Man Hibbard then asked, "did you tell Hyrum about Loose-lip and those others?"

"Yes sir, I did."

"Is that you they've been chasing around up there this morning?"

"Yes sir, I reckon so."

"Looks like you two was a match for 'em."

"Anybody'd be a match if they had Ern with 'em," I said. "Out in those hills he disappears quicker'n a full-blooded Indian."

"So I can tell by the odor," Deaf Man Hibbard declared. "Coyote holes, skunk holes, nothing's too good for young Ernest, I take it." Then, "What you aiming to do now?"

"I've got to get back to the herd," I answered honestly. "Maybe from there I can figure out who killed that Enock Rhoades feller."

"Well, good luck, young man. And look sharp. You're about as wanted by now as your pa is, and that's some wanted."

I grinned and pulled rein, Deaf Man Hibbard clucked his horses down the road, and Ernest and I sat and watched him go. "Now what?" Ernest asked.

"Now," I answered, unbuckling my money belt as I spoke, "I've got one quick stop. Then I'll be on my way."

"One stop?" Ernest asked as I counted out a double handful of silver dollars from my belt and stuffed them into my pocket. "Hy, I hope it ain't to see that no good Ida Mae Sorenson. That girl's useless as—"

"Ern, don't you say no more. Happen anybody runs Ida Mae into the ground, it'll be me. Besides, her home's close, just through the field. It'll only take but a minute, and then I can pick up Old Man Aagard's horse and be gone."

Ernest didn't say anything to that, so I kneed Ingersol around and a couple of minutes later we were coming to a stop in Ida Mae's yard. I dismounted, and when Ida Mae came to the door I was standing in almost the exact same spot as I'd occupied just a few hours before.

"Good merciful heavens," she snapped, "haven't you given yourself up yet?"

"Not hardly. Can I talk to you back by the tack shed?"

"What about?"

"I'll tell you there. Come on."

I started walking, and reluctantly Ida Mae followed. I rounded the corner so that Ernest and whoever else might be watching from the house couldn't see, and then I leaned against the wall of the shed and looked at her.

"Well?" she snapped again as she stopped in front of me, and I could see that she was surely put out. I reckon she'd hoped I would hasten up to ol' Friendlessman and plead to be captured. Now that I hadn't, and now that he hadn't come up with me anyway, Ida Mae was probably figuring out some other way to get me into Friendlessman's graspy little paws.

"Well what?"

"Well, what do you want?"

"I just wanted to take a good look at you," I answered honestly. "You are awful pretty when you get riled."

Ida Mae colored up quickly, and to cover it she stamped her foot and glowered at me. "Hyrum Soderberg, that isn't funny!"

"Wasn't meant to be. Neither was what I said last night, both about liking you and about my innocence. So far I ain't . . . haven't done anything wrong. No killing, no robbing, no nothing. Not even anything exciting. I was just kind of hoping that you'd changed your mind and had decided to believe me."

"I haven't, and I'd suggest that you place yourself into the hands of Felix or his men right away. Believe me, Hyrum, they have your best interests at heart, and it will be for your own good."

"And if I don't, then you'll do your level best to point out to them where I might be hiding, just as you did last night."

Well, she colored up again, spun angrily away, and started walking back toward the house, and I knew Ernest had been right.

"Hold up a minute," I said quietly. "I'm not quite finished."

"Well, hurry it up," she declared frostily as she stopped. "As far as I'm concerned, we have nothing left to discuss."

Quietly I took out the silver dollars that I had removed from my money belt, and slowly I counted out thirty of the big coins. These I stacked carefully on the windowsill of the tack shed. Though she still had her back to me, the sound of the coins proved too much for Ida

Mae's curiosity to withstand, and she half turned so that she could see what I was doing.

"Pick 'em up," I said when I had finished. "They're for you."

"For me?" Ida Mae frowned as she turned the rest of the way back and started toward my three stacks of coins. "What for?"

"Remember Judas in the Bible?" I asked her. "The same wages for the same work."

I watched her face go pale, and then I nodded, touched the brim of my old hat in farewell, and hobbled past her and around the corner of the tack shed. I did not look back, nor did I think I needed to. She had surely got the message.

25

The Divide and the Wasatch Plateau—Sanpete County

"Hyrum," Ernest shouted as I appeared in sight, "hurry it up! There's riders coming from town, and that piebald gelding out in front looks awful familiar."

I looked, and sure enough, there was Marshal Clawson's horse and the good marshal himself leading a group of about five other horses and riders, and they were all pounding the dust toward Ida Mae's place.

"Look out," I yelped as I swung up onto Ingersol, "we've got to skedaddle, and quick!"

Ingersol took the bit, and instantly we were out of there and headed toward the Divide. I didn't stop to realize that I had nothing to fear, and I think most other folks would have made the same mistake. When a feller gets used to running, then he always will, even when there's no need to do so. I'd been bailed out legal, my trial wasn't for another two weeks, and there was nothing on earth that Marshal Clawson could have wanted me for. Yet still I was running.

"Hy," Ernest asked after we'd gone maybe two miles, "I was just wondering, why do you suppose ol' Clawson is after you?"

"Beats me," I replied. "I reckon it's because his heart's just naturally colder than an Eskimo woman's feet."

"Has he got anything on you?"

"Not that I know of."

"I wonder if—"

Ernest was interrupted by the distant shouts of Hebron Clawson, and when we finally understood them, we grinned and slowed ol' Ingersol's pace a mite.

"Soderberg," he was screaming, "you lousy dirty polygamist, hold up there, so help me, or . . . or . . ."

"Ern," I said, grinning, "Clawson thinks he's chasing Pa."

"But that ain't so, Hy."

"I know, but this is Pa's horse, and from the back . . . Say, I'll bet one of the marshal's spies—some active member of Pa's ward, no doubt—saw Ingersol at Ida Mae's, knew that Mungus was Pa's counselor, put two and two together, and came up with about nine."

"I'll bet so too," Ernest called into the rushing wind. "Now what?"

"Well, let's let him run until his horse is good and winded and then let him catch us."

"Hy, you're gritty as eggs rolled in sand. What'll you do if he's after you too?"

"Take that chance, I reckon. If he isn't, we've helped Pa out a little. If he is, I'll rely on you to help me out. You've done good so far, and I'll bet you've got another rescue or two tucked away, happen I need them."

Ernest grinned, and so for another mile we stayed just out of rifle range of Clawson and his deputies.

"Soderberg," the marshal finally screamed at the top of his lungs, "you'd best stop, and I mean pronto."

I reckoned it was time myownself, so I pulled back on the reins, dragged the just-warming Ingersol to a stop, and pulled him around to face the lathered mounts of Marshal Clawson and his deputies.

"Soderberg," he panted, straining to see through the cloud of dust his sliding horses had created, "I arrest you for unlawful cohabita—"

"Howdy, Marshal," I said easily, doing my best to force the quiver of fear from my voice. "I appreciate your yelling. Otherwise I'd not have known you were trying ride with us. Is there something I can help you with?"

Clawson's face was a study, and I'd have laughed if I hadn't been so afraid that he'd haul me back to town and lock me up where Friendlessman and his cronies could try again to get their greedy little hands on me. He looked from me to Ernest, then at Ingersol, who was hardly breathing heavy, and then back at me and Ernest again.

"I . . . uh . . . I . . . Well dad-gum it," he sputtered, "where's your pa?"

"I don't know," I answered truthfully. "I ain't seen him in some time. Ern and I were just giving his horse a little workout, and I happened to hear you yelling."

"And your pa wasn't never with you?"

"No sir. He doesn't even know we're working his horse. I'll swear to that, and so will Ern here. Ain't that so, Ern."

"Right as rain," Ernest declared. "Pa, he's probably long gone, over to Emery County or down to Robber's Roost. Ma says that's where he likes to hide because no marshals dare go down there."

Clawson's face turned beet red, and with his big nose and his straggly yellow hair and mustache, he suddenly reminded me of one of them circus clowns. I grinned a little, and Clawson suddenly turned on me.

"You figuring on leaving town?"

"No sir, I'm not."

"You look like you are to me, and that there is against the conditions of your parole. Maybe we'd best ride back together, all of us. Let's go!"

Well, I was surrounded, and I couldn't see any way out of it. Clawson and his deputies were sober as the ladies at a Thursday night testimonial, and I reckoned they meant business. Fortunately they had all put their weapons away when they had discovered we were not who they had expected, but they were all around us, and—

"Say!" shouted one of the posse, "who turned loose the skunk?"

"I don't know," another complained, "but things sure are foul!"

"I don't smell nothing," a man next to Clawson declared.

"Well, come over here, and—"

"Boys," I said, "it's my brother Ernest that's odoriforizing the air. He got in a tangle with a whole passel of polecats this morning, and we were hoping the fast ride would sort of air him out."

The men stared, and then as one they pulled their mounts around until they were all near the marshal. "Clawson," one of the men stated, "that kid's considerable whiffy on the lee side. If we ride back with him, I aim to lead out with him following far behind."

"I'm with you," another declared. "I wouldn't—"

"Hy," Ernest suddenly hissed while the men were complaining, "look down the valley!"

I did, and my insides suddenly went cold with fear. About two miles back—maybe a little less—and coming fast was a boiling cloud of dust. It was still too distant for Clawson and his men to have seen, but my little brother could count the flies on a window-sitting pie-crust at two miles, and I didn't doubt his ability now. With dreadful certainty I knew that Friendlessman and his men were churning up that dust cloud, and with just as dreadful certainty I knew that unless we got out of there, and pronto, I'd be magpie fodder for sure.

"Hang on," I whispered back to my younger brother. "We're about to depart."

"Now?" Ernest whispered questioningly. "But Hy—"

"Have to!" I whispered acidly. "Seems to me there ain't no superiorly good time that a cripple and his runt-sized brother could pick to bid adios to the marshals and the outlaws of Sanpete Valley. Not unless you'd prefer to see me pushing up daisies and alfalfa and maybe join me there yourownself."

"I wouldn't," Ernest answered quickly, and I could tell he was grinning again. "Let'er rip, big brother! I'm hanging tight."

"Here, you two!" Clawson growled. "What are you whispering about?"

"Not much," I answered brazenly. "We were just deciding it would be a wise thing to accompany you back to town, happen there might be Indians or other malcontents about."

"Malcontents? What's that mean?"

"Bad men, marshal. Like maybe those fellers yonder who are fogging it toward us."

Clawson and all his men turned their heads to look, and instantly I sank my heels into Ingersol's sides as far as they would go. With a wild snort he crouched down, and then like a shot we were gone— through the huge gap that Ernest's scent had opened up for us, up a small rise, and down the other side and away.

"Hey!" we heard the marshal or someone else yell, and by then it was too late. Ingersol was running flat out, and like Pa had told the members of our ward the year before, that big old plug could *move!* Clawson and his men plunged after us, but by the time they reached the top of that small rise and started firing, we were nearly out of range. A few shots whapped by, but they weren't as close as they sounded, or at least that's what I told Ernest, and by then we were out of range and hauling out.

I never did see a horse that could run like that Belgian plug. His big old feet pounding against the earth sounded like thunder, the dust he churned up was something awful, and his legs were so long that from a little way off it didn't look like he was running fast at all. But he was, he truly was, and the wind in our faces that was taking Ernest's scent away told us so immediately.

Across the Divide we raced, and by the time we entered the mouth of Water Hollow, we had outdistanced the marshal and his deputies by nearly a mile. Friendlessman's men were hardly even in sight. Ernest was shouting and whooping it along, and I was enjoying it a little myownself. However, I had me a worry, and I didn't know what to do about it.

For a time I kept Ingersol running full out, but then as the bottom of the hollow grew steeper I slowed him down and sort of gave him his head. The animal still ran, but now he picked his own way, and I didn't have to concentrate so much.

"Ern," I said then, "we've got us a problem."

"Lots of them, looks to me like."

"I mean an immediate one. I'm heading for the Uintahs, and I don't know what to do about you and Pa's horse. I mean, I need Ingersol desperate bad, and I don't feel good about setting you afoot clear up here in Water Hollow. Neither do I want to take you with me. Things could get bad, and—"

"Things are already bad, big brother. Besides, I ain't going home, not without Pa's nag."

"Why not?"

"He'll murder me is why. Against outlaws and Indians and marshals I've got me a fighting chance. Against Pa I ain't got none at all. Him I don't dare fight back."

"He'd get over it," I declared without conviction.

"Not so's you'd notice he wouldn't. Hy, let me go with you. Pleeease?"

"Ern, what'll Aunt Polly say?"

"You're right, by jings! That's another reason I can't go back. Ma'll kill me too. I didn't get down to the tithing office today to kill all them turkeys Terry Johnson donated, and she said just last night that I'd better or face the consequences. Hy, you wouldn't want me to die twice, would you?"

Well, Ernest sounded so funny with his whine and his serious pleading that wasn't serious at all that I couldn't put him afoot. I knew if I did the marshals would probably find him and drag him back on the end of a rope so he wouldn't offend their olfactory senses, and that might even slow them down a mite. But doggone it, I was lonely, and Ernest was better at weaseling through the brush than most anyone I ever knew. Time might come when I needed his help and for sure. Like that very morning, when I'd never have gotten out of the old tunnel if it hadn't been for Ernest and his quick thinking.

"All right," I growled, "I'll take you along. But remember, it was your idea, and one of these days you'll have to face both Pa and Aunt Polly. Coming with me is only delaying the inevitable."

"I know, I know. Maybe if I'm up there all summer, things'll blow over."

"All summer! Good grief, Ern, you can't do that! I'm thinking a few days, no more, and even that's pushing things. Agreed?"

"Hy—"

"I mean it, Ern. Agreed?"

Ernest spit off into the brush, and I knew he was disgusted. "I reckon," he finally grumbled.

"Good. Now we still need to figure some way to get word to Pa and your ma that you're with me."

"What for? They'll figure it out, and you know it. The way Ida Mae's been so full of verbal lather lately, she'll bust a gut getting it spread around town that she saw us escaping together. Sooner or later that'll get back to 'em."

"Ern, I warned you—"

"Doggone it, Hy, I got to call it like it is! You know I'm right."

I did, and that bothered me. Ida Mae would likely do exactly as Ernest said, and somehow I couldn't get upset at her for it. In spite of everything, my thirty silver cartwheels included, I still loved that lady and truly hoped that some day soon she'd come to her senses and be my girl again.

All morning we pushed ahead, up Water Hollow and over the top into Big Hollow, which we followed down and through The Gap toward the tiny community of Milburn. After skirting town we headed up Dry Creek to the top of the East Mountains, which as I said were really called the Wasatch Plateau, and then we turned north along the rolling top and rode through the heavy stands of pine and quakies.

The air was sharp and clean. Now and then a mule deer bounded off and down into some secluded draw. Twice we passed summering herds of sheep, camp-robber jays followed us off and on, several times we passed trees that had been scratched and marked by territory-establishing bears, and altogether it was a beautiful ride.

There is no more beautiful country in all the world than the top of that plateau, and if I were to die today, I'd go to my reward convinced that I'd already seen God's greatest kingdom at its finest. I mean, a man can stand on the rim of one of the canyons that drops steeply away from the top, with thick stands of pine marching down all around him, and the blue of shadow is so thick in the bottom that he can't even see where the timber ends.

And quiet? It's like the day after the earth was created. Even breathing sounds loud and out of place, and many's the time I've found myself holding my breath without even realizing it, just listening to the beauty and feeling the power of the silence.

Every little way we'd come to a giant snowbank melting in the warm summer sun. Those banks are forty to fifty feet high, with tiny rivulets dancing away from the bottom on all sides. Downhill those little freshets join up, and by the time they've dropped a few hundred yards they've become some of the prettiest little streams a man will ever see. The water is crystal clear and sparkling in the sunlight, and it's cold enough to cause headaches happen a feller drinks too much too fast.

There're fish up there as well, fine native trout that flash from rock to rock when a shadow of danger appears. They fight like crazy when hooked, and spread out and fried up right those fish make some of the best eating this side of anywhere.

And beaver? Goodness but they build up that mountain with beauty. Some folks claim beaver are nuisances because they chew down a few trees, but let me say this: Those quakies grow faster than any beaver can ever chew them down, the trees'd die anyway after a few seasons of growth, and the dams the beaver make with the trees, well, those dams stop flooding, provide catch basins for the topsoil that the streams would otherwise carry away, provide habitat for fish and other water critters, and finally turn deep eroding canyons into grass-filled meadows that feed herds of wildlife and are places of surpassing beauty besides. No sir, God didn't make any mistakes when he created mountains like that Wasatch Plateau.

Of course I may be a mite prejudiced, but happen someone ever sees those mountains, he'll know what I'm talking about, and he'll know my prejudice is well placed.

At the first beaver dam we came to, I reined Ingersol over, rode him into about two feet of water so he could take a drink, and then I spoke.

"Ern, ain't this a pretty place?"

"Yeah, I reckon," he answered, sounding uninterested.

"Doesn't it make you think of clean things?" I asked.

"Clean things?" he responded, sounding puzzled. "I don't know that it does, Hy. Like what, maybe?"

"Like you, maybe," I answered, and with no further ado I pushed my younger brother off Ingersol's back and into the water of the pond.

He went quickly under and came up even faster, sputtering and fussing and wiping water from his face, madder than a rained-on rooster.

"Doggone it!" he snarled. "What'd you have to go and do that for? I oughta—"

"Because you smelled so bad, Ern. I had to do it, don't you see? Ingersol and I couldn't take no more. Now and then this horse likes to go slow, but with you up here it just wasn't possible. Every time he'd slow down, your pleasant scent would catch up, and the horse and I would both get dizzy. Still, I'm mighty sorry I had to do it."

"Well, you should be. You might at least have warned me so I could be holding my breath. I like to have drowned."

"Oh, I wasn't sorry for you, Ern. I didn't mean that at all. I was just feeling sorry for the fish and the beaver in this pond. With all that awful scent in the water, them poor critters'll probably be laid up for a week."

"Why, you dirty no good, low down . . ." Ernest growled, and then he started in to really throwing the water. I couldn't let that go on, so I ground-hitched, or I mean water-hitched, Ingersol, and then I was in the water fighting back, and when we climbed dripping and laughing onto Pa's horse a few minutes later, we were both tolerably cleaner.

We slept under the stars that night, huddled together under Ingersol's saddle blanket. We'd even had a couple of fish for supper; so as far as roughing it went, we weren't too bad off. Still, I knew that with Ernest along I needed more supplies. I just hoped we could get to Soldier's Fort and the general store before the next night.

All the next day Ernest and I rode north along the top of the mountain, drinking in the beauty and thinking hardly at all of the men who must surely be following. We didn't do anything special to hide our trail; we just counted on Ingersol to keep us out in front. And that he did.

Late that afternoon we descended the slope of Spanish Fork Canyon and rode into Galula, a railroad town that wasn't more than a few shacks and a saloon. Turning east we pushed on up the canyon, and it was coming onto sundown when we came over the top and rode into the town of Soldier's Fort.

As towns went it wasn't much, but it was a whole lot more than Galula had been. There were several shacks scattered back on the hills, and there was a railroad station and building, several saloons that lined the main drag, and one general store.

Soldier's Fort, which was called that because soldiers from Johnston's Army had established a post there years before, was in reality a railroad town, or at least that was the case when we were there. Whatever, it surely wasn't the typical Mormon frontier settlement, which had straight, wide streets; clean, well-built homes set back uniformly from the ditches; very few saloons; and an atmosphere that was so quiet a person could usually hear daylight coming.

Soldier's Fort, on the other hand, was what some folks called a Gentile town, and in most ways it was just the opposite of the Mormon communities. Men had been killed there, or at least that's what folks said. And though times were changing and violence was no longer so easily tolerated, it was still pretty firmly entrenched.

For death to occur was natural, and in a violent land a violent death was more to be expected than otherwise. Such was even the case in Mormon communities. Of course, what I'm saying does not necessarily mean that men would die by the gun or the arrow, for there were multitudes of other ways to die, each just as violent.

To fall ahead of stampeding cattle, to be gored by an angry steer or cow (which had happened to my Grandmother Caroline one morning when she went out to milk), to be thrown and trampled by a wild horse, to be frozen to death or to die of thirst, to fall off a steep mountain trail in the iciness of winter—these were the order of the day. And there were dozens of other ways that I haven't even mentioned, all just as deadly and each just as easily accepted.

Outside of Mormondom it was customary to settle disputes between men with weapons, and it had been so for hundreds of years. In my time the pistol was the most accepted weapon, and so it was the one most often used. There were even cases where disputes were settled in such a manner among Church members, but fortunately such instances were rare and were quickly dealt with.

Murder was quite another thing from two men holding a powder-burning contest between each other, and that was one of the reasons why folks were so het up about what I had been charged with. Murder was more than a crime against an individual; it was also a crime against society, against its accepted customs, its way of thinking. To permit a murderer to go unpunished would be to tear a hole in the fabric of the society we were trying to build, and so it was vital that murderers be caught and disposed of according to law.

"Ern," I suddenly said, "we've got to get you a few things. Let's stop at the general store."

"You got any money?"

"A little."

"I'll tell you, Hy, it's mighty handy having a brother that's rich."

"I'll bet," I grinned, and with that I pulled rein in front of the store, a ramshackle building of weathered wood that had never yet seen a coat of paint. I stiffly dismounted, stretched, and moved out of Ernest's way so he could jump down, and then the two of us went inside.

There's nothing on earth like an old general store, and these days they're disappearing so fast that folks a few years from now will hardly know what they were. The smell hits a feller first, that and the darkness. It is the smell of food and leather and salt and dry goods and who knows what all, but it is one of the finest smells I've ever encountered. The darkness isn't so fine, for it is caused by too few windows, and those few are likely coated black with fly specks. In those days the land was alive with flies, and there wasn't much a body could do about them except ignore them as best he could and try not to eat or breathe more than a dozen or so a day. Like I said, in those days, flies were *bad*.

After our eyes had grown accustomed to the dark, Ernest and I stepped forward to the counter, which ran all the way around the narrow inside of the store.

"Help you?"

A smallish, friendly looking man rose up from behind the counter.

"You bet," I replied quickly. "I need a couple of blankets for my new hand here, who is otherwise known as my younger brother. He could do with a new shirt and a pair of those made-for-boots Levi Strauss trousers. Can you fix him up?"

The clerk looked Ernest up and down, grimaced, and then winked. "I reckon so. He's a mite small, but so are some of them Chinamen we get up here working on the railroad. If nothing else, I've got a fine Chinese cone hat he'll surely enjoy."

Ernest made a face. The man grinned, and then, while he scuttled toward the back to put our order together, Ernest and I looked around. On the counter were baskets of eggs—three dozen for a quarter. There was a big jar of butter, quite soft from the heat, that sold for twelve and a half cents a pound. There was cheese both from nearby and from New York and a bucket of hulled corn hominy with mosquito netting over it to protect it from the hordes of flies.

On the floor were barrels of flour of two grades, white and with shorts, and meal, very coarse—the kind that made a man sometimes want to scratch his back. There was a barrel of withered apples, sacks of soft potatoes, turnips, cabbage, and one withered pumpkin. And back of those were barrels of molasses and vinegar and a barrel of salt pork with a big stone on top to keep the pork under the brine.

There were also kits of mackerel of two grades—big and fat, and otherwise. Additionally there were dried codfish hanging by the tail, hams, shoulders and slabs of breakfast bacon, strings of red peppers, and, finally, fresh meats, mostly venison, which were also protected from the flies with more netting.

Back of the counter on the shelf were large boxes of big square soda crackers, crocks of honey, coffee—green Rio and Mocha (folks had to parch it and grind it themselves), tea, starch in bulk, bottles of catsup, cayenne pepper, and soda and cream of tartar instead of baking powder. There were also spices, rice, and two big jars of striped candy.

Further back were things for women, like bolts of cloth, white dishes, steel knives and forks and pewter spoons, jars, milk crocks, pans, wooden tubs, pails, brooms, and those conspicuous pots that always end up under beds. There were also things for the men, such as Levi trousers and shirts, boots, hoes, rakes, spades, ropes, kegs of nails, a whole shelf of tobacco, and one entire wall of leather goods and saddle tack. All in all, a man could find about anything he might ever need in one of those old general stores.

"There you go, young feller," the clerk finally said as he rolled the clothes and two cans of peaches up inside the blankets. "That'll be three dollars and eleven cents."

I gulped at the high prices, paid him, and grinned as he handed Ernest a stick of candy. Ernest almost didn't take it, because he didn't want to play the role of a kid. But it was peppermint, his favorite kind, so sheepishly he reached out his hand and snagged onto it.

Moments later Ernest and I were back on Ingersol and headed out of town and on up the mountain, eating out of the same can of peaches and happy as two kids who didn't know any better had a right to be.

It was nearly dark by then, but we pushed Ingersol on anyway, turning north and following the White River into the mountains beyond.

I wanted desperately to reach Strawberry Flats, but it was long after midnight when we came at last to a small seep where I had camped once before, and I knew we could go no farther. Ernest was asleep against my back, I could hardly hold my eyes open, and ol' Ingersol was about done in. I drew rein and helped Ernest down. Then I took the saddle from Ingersol and let him roll, and then while he drank and cropped at the thick grass, I rubbed him down. That finished, I spread out the blankets, Ernest and I curled up together between them, and the last thing I heard was a coyote somewhere out in the darkness who was complaining of insomnia. Poor critter, I thought as I yawned widely, it's pretty tough being tired . . . And then I was gone, and the silence of the night was the only sound left.

26

Strawberry Flats— Utah Territory

"Hy, wake up!"

Somewhere far off I heard Ernest's urgent whisper, and groggily I opened my eyes. The sun was an hour high, and that told me right off how tired I'd been.

"Hy, we've got trouble."

I rolled over, looked at my brother, and saw his eyes staring straight ahead. I followed his glance, and abruptly I sat up. Around us on all sides, seated on their horses but still and silent as a treeful of owls at noontime, were nine Ute braves. They were watching us as intently as we were watching them, and the only difference between them and us that I could see was that they had weapons of one sort or another, all leveled in our general direction, and we were unarmed.

Instantly my mouth was cotton dry, and as I climbed slowly to my feet I noticed that my palms were wet with sweat. Ernest was already standing, and before I could do anything about it he stepped forward and solemnly raised his hand in the universal sign of peace.

"How!" he declared.

There was continued silence, and all nine men sat without expression. "How!" Ernest tried again, louder, and this time also there were no visible results.

Well, I should maybe have mentioned previous to this that none of us Soderbergs were known for our patience and long-suffering. And to be perfectly honest, Ernest was the worst of the lot. Of course *I* could see that in a situation like this prudence was the better part of valor. I mean, I was old enough to understand that they had us so far outnumbered there wasn't even a chance of a Mexican standoff, a fair and even draw. Even before anything started, I could see that we had gone down to a burning defeat.

Ernest, though, was too young to understand that, and I reckon the fact that the Indians had ignored him was just too much for him to bear. Before I realized what he was about, he reached down, grabbed a fist-sized rock, and let fly at the Indian who sat on his horse directly in front of us, an old man with almost snow-white hair.

"Ern!" I cried in alarm, but I was too late, way too late. The rock was already on its way. Ernest's aim was a little low, however, for the stone struck the pony on the withers and bounced up, smashing into the jaw of the ancient brave.

There was a terrible squeal from the horse, who was already into the air and sunfishing around, and that and the blow from the rock became the perfect combination to unhorse that elderly Indian.

I saw him fall, heard his grunt, and saw the dust puff up from where he had hit; I saw that he didn't move, and I knew that my younger brother and I were dead men. Rifles were suddenly lifted and brought to bear on us, bows were bent with arrows at the ready, and I was already saying my prayers and seeking forgiveness for all I had done that might have been wrong, when that Indian who was on the ground rolled over and sat up.

He shook his head to clear it, felt his jaw—and his posterior, which is what he had used as his point of contact when he had so rudely greeted the earth, and then he rose slowly and somewhat staggeringly to his feet. Without looking to the right or the left he fixed Ernest with his dark and fierce scowl, drew his huge knife from its scabbard, and started forward.

"Run, Ern," I whispered urgently.

"I'll be darned if I will," he snarled. "I ain't scared of no Indian!"

"Do it! I'll do my best to fight them, hold them up. Get on Ingersol and they'll never catch you."

"I ain't running from no old Indian!" Ern declared. "Especially one so rude as that one is." Then, defiantly, he reached down, snagged another rock, cocked his arm, and let fly.

The Indian ducked and came on. Ernest grabbed a third rock and stood ready, his face filled with defiance and anger and absolutely no fear, and suddenly the ancient brave stopped, lowered his knife, and started to laugh.

I was shocked, Ernest was just as surprised, and before we could do anything other than just stare, the group of braves were laughing and pointing at the tottering Ute who had been knocked from his horse. And, strangely, he seemed to be laughing the loudest, enjoying the joke on himself, whatever it had been, most of all.

Suddenly, as if someone had given a signal, though I certainly saw none, all of them stopped laughing and were still. Then the old man who had been thrown from his horse smacked himself on the chest.

"Me Tabby," he declared proudly. "Me the sun!"

Well, Ernest probably didn't know enough to be impressed, but I did, and my mouth probably fell open, I was so surprised. Of all the people my little brother could have picked to knock from his horse, he'd had to go and pick one of the greatest chiefs of the entire Ute nation, an old man who was the long-dead Chief Wakera's brother. Oh, no! How come we had to go and have all the blessings . . .

Suddenly Chief Tabby stepped forward and grabbed Ernest's arm, twisting it a little. Ernest flinched but then held his ground and stared up at the wide-faced Ute. "You brave warrior," the man declared. "You be my son!"

"I will not!" Ernest retorted, pulling his arm away. "I already got a pa!"

"Him?" Tabby asked, motioning toward me.

"No sir, that's Hyrum. He's my brother."

"Brother. Ungh. He no brother. He coward. He no fight."

"He would've," Ernest declared, "happen you'd tried to hurt me. Why, Hy's worse than a den of riled rattlers and harder to stop than a wounded grizzly! He's a warrior for sure."

The old man looked doubtful, so Ernest motioned for me to step forward. I did, and after about the second step I heard gasps from the Indians around me, and I saw Chief Tabby's eyes go big in his weathered face. Then quickly he took a step back, then another. I stopped, and there was a rapid exchange between the Utes. I took another step forward and extended my hand so the chief and I could shake, and again Tabby recoiled in fear.

Ernest was as surprised as I was, but he was more blunt. "What's the matter?" he asked. "I told you, he's my brother. He won't hurt you none."

Tabby still stared, but at last he stuck his shaking finger out and pointed at my crippled foot. He chattered again so that neither Ernest nor I could understand him, and then finally he reverted to his limited English. "Him great medicine," he declared. "Him favored by great Spirit Mormonee call God with foot that is not like foot of other mans. Him filled with power!" And again he backed away.

"Hy," Ernest whispered, "you reckon they're scared of you?"

"Seems like it," I whispered back. "Ern, I'm getting awful jumpy."

"You're a poor liar," Ernest answered without looking over at me. "You could sleep in a sack of snakes without twitching. What do you reckon's going on?"

"I don't know. Just tell this ancient chief we ain't meaning to look his Ute gift horse in the mouth, and that you're right thankful that he wishes to be your pa. And tell him that we're glad to leave him our undershirts and our blankets and our single can of peaches with no hard feelings. I don't know about you, little brother, but I feel sort of surplus to this entire hastily called meeting. It ain't uplifting to anything but my hair. Now be nice to him, but hurry up, and let us be long gone!"

"Well then," Ernest answered, "I'll second that. Motion's now been moved and carried, and we're off."

We both took a step backward, the Utes stopped talking and stared at us, we took another step toward our horse, and old Tabby raised his knife again.

"You go," I said low-voiced. "Just jump on Ingersol and take off. I'll keep 'em busy for awhile."

"You make leaving you sound slick as a Kansas City snake-oil salesman," Ernest replied. "Hy, I can't do it. We had 'em there for a minute. Don't you think we can bluff 'em along again?"

"I don't know, Ern. Indians are notional, but I'd say you might be right. A bluff seems to be our onliest chance. Happen it works, we may live. Happen it doesn't . . ."

"So how'll we do it?"

"Just like what you was doing before. I reckon we'd ought to play my bad foot and my strength for all they're worth. Tell the old Chief I won't hurt him if the others will put down their weapons."

Ernest grinned, and suddenly he stepped forward. "O Tabby," he said dramatically, "you are right. Hyrum is filled with great power. Just yesterday we came to a great cliff that we could not get down. Hyrum saw this, and so he took me in one arm and our horse in the other, and he carried us both to the bottom."

There was a great intake of breath, and I was shocked that these powerful men could believe such a pack of lies. I was also embarrassed that my own little brother could come out with them so easily.

"I will show you," he went on. "He wishes for two braves to come and stand on either side of him."

There was a gasp. Tabby looked around; then he signaled, and two warriors reluctantly slid from their mounts and moved carefully toward me. Well, I grinned, for this was an old game of Pa's, and because I'd had a weakness in my legs, I'd practiced it some myownself. I'd been blessed by the law of compensation, for while my legs were born weak, they were weak no longer, and I truly did have some real power in my arms and shoulders.

Stooping down, I wrapped my arms about those two stout Utes, felt them shaking with fear, and then I rose up with the two of them leaning rigidly against my shoulders and actually making little whimpers of fear.

"You see, chief?" Ernest declared. "He has great power. Now he has them, and if you'd like, he will throw them so high that they'll smash into Tabby, which you call the sun. Of course, they'll die, but that's up to you. What do you say?"

"Ern!" I hissed, "that's the dumbest thing I ever . . ."

"My brother says he would rather not kill these men," Ernest declared quickly. "He says that good warriors should live."

"He is wise," Tabby declared softly. "Wise and good. It is enough."

Relieved, I lowered the men to the ground, and they madly scrambled back up on their horses. There was another long silence, and I could see that if I didn't do something quick, we'd likely be there staring at each other all day long. Stooping, I gathered our two new blankets and the remaining can of peaches, and stepping forward, I placed them upon the ground.

"Gifts," I declared, "for the great Chief Tabby."

I stepped back, Tabby stared, and then slowly he stepped forward and took up the gifts. "Me thankum great warrior Hy-mum," he said awkwardly. "Me thankum Little Warrior too. How you called, Little Warrior?"

"Ernest."

"Enn-nest. Good. Good Indian name, Enn-nest. Come. We go."

He turned, and one of the braves leaped down and helped him aboard his pony. Ernest and I looked at each other and shrugged. Quickly I bridled and saddled Ingersol, and moments later we were on our way, surrounded by Chief Tabby and his eight Ute warriors.

For hours we rode, across Strawberry Flats, over the low hills to the east, and down the Strawberry River, almost the same way I had gone when I'd chased down Old Man Aagard's mules and found the gold. Thinking of that, I was amazed that only a little over a week had passed. So much had happened that it seemed like months, and it was hard to wrap my mind around the fact that circumstances in my life had changed so quickly.

Before I'd stumbled onto that gold I'd been a pretty normal young man, head over heels in love with a gal who loved me and doing my best to earn a little extra cash so our family wouldn't be in such dire straits. Now I was still the same age, but most of the marshals in the southern half of the territory knew of me and were after me, a gang of outlaws had sworn in their wrath to take me and force me to lead them to some gold I didn't know anything about, and the girl I still loved had turned against me and would no longer even talk to me.

Talk about change! Pa had always said that gold was a hard-found thing, was even harder to hold, and always came hand in glove with trouble. Now, for a fact, I could say "Hallelujah, amen" and mean it wholeheartedly.

We turned south along what I think was Willow Creek, followed it up for some time, and then rounded a bend and came face to face with the camp those Ute braves were calling home. There were a few tipis and a couple of brush wickiups, some dogs and dirty little kids that had to announce our arrival all at once, and a couple of old men and several squaws who just stared at us.

We dismounted, and Tabby in great solemnity took us to his tipi and bade us welcome. There were two women there, I think both of whom were his wives, and with short instructions he sent them scurrying. He hauled out his pipe then, and though I am thoroughly against the use of tobacco, I did puff on that foul-tasting weed and send smoke off into the four directions so that he would know that my heart was good toward him.

Ernest did the same, but I noticed the smell of the knickinick in the pipe pretty much turned him green. And if it hadn't, the meal the women served up a little later surely did.

Now I need to say that as a whole the Utes seem to be a sincere and wonderful people. Still, they surely don't live life as we do. Nor do they seem to want to, and as far as I'm concerned, that's fine. Folks should have the right to live according to their traditions. But that doesn't change the fact that it's hard for a couple of fellers like Ernest and myself to sit down and be perfectly comfortable with them.

As far as my own tastes went, their filth was awful. Chief

Tabby's oldest squaw passed the antelope hair around in the lid of an old chamber pot that looked like it had been used all day for its natural purposes, and it was all Ernest and I could do just to take it in hand and pass it by. Later we had some stew that we ate with our fingers, and I knew full well we were eating one of the little dogs I'd seen running around earlier. And of course they expected us to stay the night, sleeping on those vermin-infested robes.

Both of us were reluctant but couldn't see any way out, so after dark we retired. In the lodge where we tossed and turned and tried to sleep were also six or eight more dogs, but before morning a couple of litters of pups had come into the world on our beds and had increased the number so materially that Chief Tabby, the aging proprietor of the wickiup, thought it necessary to have his wives remove the mess while he knelt and lead out in offering morning prayer.

"See," he said as he thumped himself on the chest, "Tabby prayum good. Brigham say prayum, Tabby prayum. Tabby good Mormonee."

I was impressed with Tabby's innocent faith, and to this day I believe him to be a good and kind man who was probably closer to the Spirit than I am. I thought then of Brother Brigham's prophecy that the Lamanites would one day be redeemed and become a delightsome people. Frankly, I believe that to be true, and I think that, in their own way, they already are. I just hope that white folks, even good-intentioned ones, don't ruin them first.

Still, as far as the saying goes that cleanliness is next to godliness, it looks to me like the Lord is going to have to accept those folks on their own terms and not His. Happen, that is, that His terms are somewhat akin to my own. And that there opens up a whole new can of worms, which can I'm not climbing into at all.

"Hy," Ern said quietly after more stew had been served up to us for breakfast, "we've got to get out of here before I starve to death."

"But they've given us plenty of food," I protested.

"Yeah, and all these dogs are getting fat from mine. How can you stand to eat that stuff?"

"Easy," I lied. "Dog meat's good for the system."

"Dog meat? Oh *no*, I th-thought that was v-venison. That's the only part I've been eating."

Ernest started gagging, and I decided my brother was right. I'd enjoyed about all of Tabby's hospitality I could stand. Rising to my feet, I smiled at the toothless old woman who seemed to be the boss wife. She smiled back and cackled something that must have been meant to amuse me, and I snorted in response, smiled and nodded at the still-breakfasting Tabby, stooped, and went out through the door-flap and into the clear air of the morning.

Ernest quickly followed. Together we walked to where Ingersol was tethered, and I began saddling him up. I had only just started, however, when a rider came churning up the creek, threw himself from his heavily lathered pony, and rushed into Tabby's wickiup.

Ernest and I looked at each other, shrugged, finished saddling and bridling Pa's horse, and suddenly Tabby appeared, striding toward us.

"Ho, Mormonee brothers," he called in his old man's cracking voice. "Bad thing happen. Heap bad thing. No good for Indian. No good for brothers. Enn-nest come, Hy-mum come, showum maybe so quick."

"What is it?" Ernest asked quickly. "What's wrong?"

"Goum with braves," Tabby said. "They showum!" And with that he turned and pointed off toward the mountains to the north. We mounted, the messenger and three other braves joined us (the messenger on a fresh horse), and soon the whole bunch of us were headed back down the creek.

"What you reckon it is?" Ernest asked as we rode forward.

"Beats the dickens out of me. That brave looked worried, though, and for that matter, so did the chief."

"Yeah, he looked anxious as a young buck lifting his first scalp. What do you reckon it has to do with us?"

I didn't particularly like Ernest's choice of metaphors, for scalping was not an altogether dead art, no pun intended. He had hit the spike square on the head, however, and I couldn't help him.

"I don't know, Ern, I surely don't. Howsomever, I do have me a bad feeling, and the last time I felt this way, I found my poke of gold. I truly don't need any more trouble like that."

"Me neither. I'm getting fidgetier'n a chicken drinking out of a rusted pie tin with a herd of hungry coyotes waiting in line behind, and I ain't exactly anxious to know why."

"Yeah. Happen I know Indians, little brother, this is going to lead to where she squeezes down like a tight-choked side-by-each."

"Like a what?"

"A double-barreled scatter-gun bored full-and-full."

"Ah."

"Yes sir, Ern. I'm feeling miserable as a steer in a herd of heat-struck heifers. A man can't sleep a full night in a Ute wickiup full of vermin, smoke himself over a green-pine fire, and feed himself on half-cooked dog to boot without building up for himself some trace of what every *real* Indian is born natural with—a sixth-sense nose, touchy as a blistered heel, for impending disaster. I hate to say it, but I do believe we're heading for trouble."

Ernest didn't answer, so we rode in silence for a time and lived with our unhappy thoughts. We went down Willow Creek, crossed the Strawberry, and rode on into the wild and tumbled country that formed the western end of Currant Creek Mountain. We were climbing then, through cedar and sage, up into thick hillsides of pinion and oak, and finally into the quakies and pines and firs of the high-up country along the flat top of the mountain.

Skirting a mess of huge boulders that had gathered from who-knew-where, our guide turned abruptly and started down the sharp edge of a dry wash that dropped steeply away to the north. We followed, and Ingersol took that hairline trail like he'd been born to it. We came to the bottom, rode out, and crossed what had to be either Wildcat or Deep Creek, and right off we were climbing again.

"I'm beginning to see why that messenger's hoss was so lathered up," I finally said. "We've come a far piece."

"Amen," Ernest replied. "You don't suppose there's any way we can rig two saddles onto Ingersol, do you?"

"What's the matter? You getting sore?"

"Hy, I got saddle sores on my saddle sores. Besides that, I'm like to split right in half, Pa's hoss is so wide."

"Well, don't fret. We're likely nearly there, wherever *there* is. Then, once we get back to Zene and the herd, some of that sheep dip we'll have to use to kill Tabby's dogs' lice will do wonders where you're galled."

"Yeah, and kill me, to boot. You ever been really galled?"

"Once."

"What was it like?"

"Ern, being galled's a mighty personal thing, and a feller doesn't discuss it. I will say this, though. Bear grease is the thing. Don't never let my ma talk you into putting some of that white Dr. Shields Cure-All Wonder Powder on it."

"Why not? Does it hurt?"

"No, not so's you'd notice, but it sure spreads the word that you've been galled. Everywhere you walk you leave little white clouds, and Ern, that there is a purely embarrassing experience."

Ernest giggled, and suddenly, from up on the mountain, we heard a distant gunshot.

"Oh-oh," I breathed. "I've got that bad feeling again."

The Utes had heard it too, and all of them pulled rein and bunched up together, talking to the messenger. Finally after what seemed like hours of discussion, all grew silent, and the messenger, a tall man with a scar on his face, turned to us.

"Bad," he grunted, "heap bad, Utes good Indians. All-the-same Mormonees. No fightum Mericats. Very bad."

"Mister," I said soberly, "I am confuseder'n a blind bear in a bramble patch. What exactly is the trouble?"

The tall Ute looked at me, then up the mountain, and then back behind him and down the slope. "Me good Indian," he declared with finality. "Utes good Indians. We goum back. No fight. You go, heap strong, you fight."

"Fight? But what—"

"Heap Chief Hy-mum, little warrior Enn-nest, fight bad Mericats. No should be here. We driveum out, more bad Mericats come. You driveum out, bad Mericats no getum angry with Indians. You strong. You Ute's friends. Saveum Cale, all-the-same helpum Utes. There."

He pointed up the mountain, and I had a sinking feeling like I'd never had before. He was sending Ernest and me up there alone, into what I had no idea. "Now see here," I protested, "I don't think—"

"We go," the scar-faced man declared, and before Ernest and I even had a good idea that they were leaving, the warriors had gone. We were alone on the mountain with not an idea in the world as to why we were there or what we were expected to do.

Mericats was the Ute word for Americans, as opposed to *Mormonees,* which is what Tabby and all the rest of them called Mormons. I'd heard Pa talk of that and of the Ute way of speaking, which he had picked up somewhat during what folks called the Blackhawk War, back in the early '70s. Even with the crazy lingo, however, there was no mistaking that tall Ute's orders. There was someone up there needed fighting, and if the Utes did it, they'd be in real trouble from Washington. Happen we did it, however, we'd likely be in trouble only with the law. And since that was already the case . . .

"Ern," I said softly, "Pa used to allow that if you wanted to collect stuffing for a featherbed, you'd put two young cock birds in the same pen of pullets and stand back with your cotton sack spread wide. He guaranteed you a toteful of ticking fodder inside five minutes flat."

Ernest nodded his head. "Yeah, I recollect. He also says that it takes only two growls and a back-leg scratch to turn a nice sociable sniffing into a first-class dogfight."

"You're right, Ern. He does say that. Now I reckon we've had our two growls and are only waiting for the leg-scrape."

"Yes," agreed Ernest as he suddenly strained his eyes up the slope, "and big brother, yonder she comes."

27

Windy Ridge—
Utah Territory

"Ern," I whispered, "who is that feller?"

"Don't you know?"

"Would I be asking if I did?"

"Reckon not. That's Friendlessman, him that's been sparking Ida Mae."

"Friendlessman," I breathed as I stared up the slope. "So that's Felix Ethelbert Friendlessman. Don't look like much from here, does he."

"Nope, not much. Is that his name for true?"

"It is," I grinned.

"Man's folks ought to have been whipped," Ernest declared soberly.

"Don't see why," I argued. "The Felix and the Ethelbert parts are okay, but the Friendlessman fits him like a glove. Altogether, I'd say they go together mighty well. I'd also say that the name's about right for a fellow like him."

"Maybe you are right," Ernest replied slowly. "In fact, I do believe you are."

We were down on our bellies on the slope, looking upward through a patch of sparse brush. Ernest had kept watch while I had sneaked Ingersol back into some oak and tied him, and now we lay together, watching.

"What's he doing?"

"Watching, like us."

"Yeah," I responded, "but who? He ain't seen us, has he?"

"Naw, he ain't even looked down toward us. He's watching something on the other side of that ridge."

"What, you reckon?"

"I don't know, Hy. Can't see through hills yet."

I grinned, Ernest smiled back, and suddenly I was glad he was there with me. He was young and he was small, but come to what we seemed to be doing, there was nobody, only Pa and maybe Zene Hill excepted, that I'd rather be with.

Time and again I'd been hunting with Ernest when he'd spot game and instantly get a strange look in his eye. Johnny, one of our other brothers, always said that Ernest was daft and stranger'n a lost wolf whelp. He claimed Aunt Polly doted on Ern, claimed in fact that she *had* to because he was teched.

Me, I didn't believe that. Not after I saw Ern track down a deer Pa had shot, *after dark!* He said he smelled it out, and I for one believed him. Like I said before, that kid was part varmint, and he could spook a man sure.

"What you reckon we ought to do?"

"Well," I answered, "since you can't see what's over that ridge, and since neither can I, it seems fitting that we Indian on over there and see what Scarface sent us up here for. With Friendlessman involved, we know it's going to be bad, and that's certain as mud clings to Sunday shoes."

"You want me to go alone?"

"No thank you, little brother."

"Afraid for me?"

"Nope. For them fellers up there. I saw what you did to them poor pilgrims the other morning, Ern, and being naturally soft-hearted, I don't want to see them come to any more grief than they already have. No, you mosey along, and I'll do my best to follow."

Ernest grinned, and seconds later I was being hard-pressed to keep up with him as he wormed his way silently up the slope. Thirty yards along he paused and waited for me to catch up. I did and then rested until my breath was nearly back to normal.

"You part Ute?" I gasped.

"'Course not, but here and there I learned me a thing or three."

"You learned 'em good," I declared. "You don't make no more noise than a winnow of wind in fresh wolf fur."

Ernest looked back at me, and his face was serious. "Don't mean to," he said quietly. "Let's go."

We did, and shortly we were on the ridge, about fifty yards below where Friendlessman was crouched gazing down into the ravine below. There was another shot, from somewhere below us and off to our left, and then someone shrieked with joy.

"I think I got him!"

Well, it was no trouble at all for me to recognize that whine, and suddenly I was storming mad. That there was that miserable little Doolin again.

"Hey Doolin, tell you what. You walk down there and make sure!"

That was the one called Blue John. He was also below us, off to the right a little, and I figured he was holed up behind a twisted pinion I could see down the slope.

"Now see here," Doolin whimpered, and then Friendlessman spoke.

"Be still, you two. We're in no hurry; we've got plenty of water and he doesn't, so let's let the sun do our work for us. Meanwhile, shoot only to wound, not to kill. Remember, we need him."

"I'll say," someone growled from right above us on the slope. "Especially since we lost that crippled Soderberg kid!"

Well, Ernest and I hunched down like we'd been shot at. Neither of us had seen Loose-lip Lundstrum up there, and the closeness of his voice gave us a shock.

"You see him?" I whispered almost silently.

"No, but I think I can see that feller down in the bottom, the one these owlhoots are shooting at."

"Where?"

"Down there between those rocks, the pink and yellow ones. A moment ago the shadow got darker for a second, and I'm sure it was the feller they're hunting, shifting position."

"I've got Loose-lip spotted," I whispered. "He's in that manzanita right up there. I saw his head move."

"Yeah, I did too. Wish we had Pa's rifle."

"I wish we had any kind of gun," I hissed. "I wouldn't kill no one with it, just maim a little. I feel mighty naked up here unarmed."

"I've felt that way my whole entire life, Hy. I wish Pa'd give me a gun. I can use one sure."

"Yeah, and maybe too fast, Ern. You know the Lord don't hold with shooting folks up."

"I know, I know. But there're times . . . "

For an hour or more we lay without moving on that bare-boned ridge, and it was hot enough to raise a blister on a rawhide bootsole. Things in general were touchier'n a teased snake, but somehow Ernest and I had to keep our thinking straight and hang onto the only cards we held. We simply couldn't afford to make any wrong moves.

We had three of those outlaws within fifty feet of us in three different directions, and maybe more than that who hadn't spoke up yet. In short, we were surrounded and had crawled ourselves right into the middle of it.

Still, faint heart never filled an inside straight, as Pa sometimes said, and I'd be doggoned if I was going to stampede as though I had bought a ticket to Hades and was running to catch the first train out of the depot. No sir. Somehow we were going to find us a way to get to that feller down in the bottom and get him out of there. Trouble was, I just didn't know how.

"Hy, you hear that?"

"Hear what?" I asked, straining my ears against the silence of the late afternoon.

"Horses. I reckon I know where these outlaw fellers hid their horses."

"So?"

"So the way I see it, we need horses. You have Ingersol, but I need a horse, and happen we get that feller out down there, he'll need a horse hisownself. Besides all that, those outlaw fellers don't need no horses at all. Fact is, we'd all be considerably better off if every last one of them was set afoot."

"I see what you mean. Think you can get to their horses?"

"Can birds fly? Or snakes crawl? Or you forever and always beat me at checkers? I hope to shout I can. Can you?"

"Maybe, but I doubt it."

"You want to try?" Ernest asked sincerely. "You're older, and you're maybe the best sneak in the family."

"Except for you," I declared. "Next to you, owl feathers and milkweed fuzz ain't in it. You could outstalk a housecat wearing goosedown shoes. No, you go, and you'd best do it fast. Night's fixing to come on, and I've got me a feeling these fellers are starting to get anxious."

There was a sudden shot from down below, the first that had been fired in over an hour. A white puff danced away from the rock down in the bottom of the draw, and I knew I had been right. Those fellers *were* getting anxious.

"I'm gone," Ernest whispered. "I'll get Ingersol too. When these fellers take off, happen things work out and they do take off, you be ready to shag hide down into that bottom."

"Aye, aye," I grinned, "and 'Yes sir' to boot."

Ernest smiled wide and twisted around, and seconds later he was slithering back down the way we had come. He was loud about it as a buzzard's shadow scraping mesa rock, and I surely did feel proud as I watched him go. Why, in a spot where a noise as loud as a cricket's cough could cost a man his life, that little brother of mine fairly sailed along.

I turned back to look, and suddenly I saw a figure rise on the hillside directly below me. The man stood crouched over, and then, carefully, he eased down the slope, screened by a wide old juniper.

Right off I could see that he was trouble to the feller who was hiding down below, but it took me a minute to figure what I could do about it. Then I noticed a small boulder a little above me on the slope, and I knew.

Worming my way up to it, I hunkered low against the hill and took a small stick; then I carefully eased the stick down and commenced to push the boulder. At first nothing happened, but then the rock gave a little, teetered, and finally fell loose and began to roll. Instantly I rolled too, under a small bush, and there I waited.

For a second or two the rock clattered; then it bounced into the air, made no sound, and crashed down, and suddenly that feller below me started shouting.

"Hey!" he whined, and right off I was grinning. *"Hey!* What you trying to do up there? Kill me?"

"Oh shut up, Doolin," Loose-lip snarled. "It wasn't nobody at all. The rock just came loose is all."

"Yeah? Well, it nearly got me, and now the old man knows right where I am!"

"Maybe he wouldn't if you didn't make so blasted much noise," the man called Blue John declared quietly from down below. "I declare, you're worse than Silvertip. Now be still and wait for Friendlessman to give the orders. Then we'll all move in together."

There was more grumbling from below, and I only felt bad because my rock had missed. Now I know I'd promised Pa that I'd be an elephant during my stroll through life, and I know too that elephants aren't supposed to step on the dogs; meaning, I suppose, that we true Christians are to be properly considerate of those who are trying their best to do us in. Still, I felt mighty badly about rolling that rock down at Doolin. At least I felt badly about having missed with it and not putting the poor misbegotten soul out of his misery.

So, next time, I vowed. Next time—

Suddenly there was a deep booming shout from off below, the sharp crack-cracking of a pistol, the thunder of hooves, and then that same deep bass voice cried out loud enough that all the mountain could hear.

"Blue John, Boss, *help!* Some two-bit kid got our horses!"

Instantly Doolin and Blue John and Loose-lip and even Friendlessman, high on the hill above me, were on their feet and running. Friendlessman even passed so close that I could have reached up and caught him. I didn't, and right away I was glad, for on Friendlessman's heels came another man who was probably the one they called the Boss. Anyway, they were all hotfooting it down the back of the ridge, and so without further ado I was on my way myownself, sliding down the face of the ridge toward the nest of boulders where the unknown man had spent the day hiding.

28

Windy Ridge—
Utah Territory—Again

"Mister," I called quietly as I neared the bottom of the steep slope, "don't shoot. I'm friendly."

There was no response, so I moved forward through the shadows and cautiously approached the tumbled boulders where Ernest said he had seen movement.

"Mister, you in there?"

The only answer was the cry of a crow from somewhere far off, and I grinned, knowing that was Ernest's way of telling me that things had worked out. Slowly I moved up to the boulders, crouched down, and squinted into the darkness.

"Mister," I said low-voiced, "I'm friendly, so if you're there, sing out. Happen you want to leave, we're going to need to do it in a hurry."

"I'm here, son," a quiet voice answered from way up under the rocks. "Who're you? And what became of those bushwhackers?"

"Name's Hy Soderberg," I answered. "And my brother Ernest lured them off. Now let's be gone, for I've a bad feeling that they'll be back."

"Oh, they'll be back, all right. Felix Friendlessman's like a bulldog when it comes to hanging on to a bad deal."

"You know him?"

"'Course I know him, worse the luck. Son, we got us a problem, a real bad one. My horse fell on me and then spooked, and so far I can't walk on my leg at all. Can't tell if it's broken, but it might as well be. You got a horse?"

"Yeah, but not here. Happen we make it, Ernest and the horses will be waiting up at the top of this draw. Can you get to me?"

"I can, but what good will that do?"

"If you can get out of there, I'll try and carry you to the top."

"Noooo," he said slowly, his voice filled with disbelief. "Son, it can't be done! I'm a big man, near one sixty. You'll never make it."

"Maybe not, but I'm open for suggestions. You got a better one?"

The old man chuckled. "You got a way of aiming direct, haven't you. Well, let's get at 'er and see what you can do."

There was a quick shuffle, and soon the man was there beside me, struggling to his feet. He was big, all right, not as big as Pa, but big. He was hard, too, and a body could tell he'd spent the last fifty years or so doing plenty of hard work. He had a long beard and lots of hair, and it was mostly gray with just a little black left in it. I reckon that's why Friendlessman and the others had called him old, for his eyes, his face, his hands, none of that looked old at all.

"How you aiming to do this?"

"You'll have to sit on my shoulders," I answered as I moved around in front of him. "Then—"

"Hold on there! You . . . you're a cripple!"

"Yes sir," I answered, looking right at him. "Have been since birth. Now shall we get on with it?"

Well, his face reflected his doubt, but, like I'd pointed out previously, neither of us had too many options—happen, that is, that we both wanted out of that draw together. "Here," I said, squatting down. "Get on my shoulders."

That old man pulled himself up to his feet, took hold of my shoulders, squeezed like he was testing to see whether I was prime or not, and then he hiked himself aboard. "All right, son," he breathed, and I could hear the pain in his voice. "I'm there. Now let's see if you're up to your brag."

I grinned and rose to my feet. "No brag," I said. "Just facts. Ern told Chief Tabby—"

"You saw Tabby?"

"Yeah, him and maybe eight other braves. That ain't counting all the folks at the village where we slept."

"You *slept* with the Utes?"

"We did, with old Tabby himself, and I ain't ever going to brag about that, either. It was awful."

"Was one of the Utes tall, with a long scar down the side of his face?"

"He came in today. In fact, he's the one that led us here."

"Ungh," the man grunted, exactly like the Utes had done. I listened for him to say more, but when he didn't, I went on with my little tale.

"Anyway, Ern told Tabby that I could throw two of his men clean to the sun. That was stretching it a bit, but ol' Tabby took it in, and I reckon I did too. You hang on for yourself now, leaving my hands free, and I'll do my darndest to get us out of here."

I started out, climbing slowly but easily, doing all I could to keep from getting winded. The way was rough, but that was almost in my favor. I had plenty of good footholds, and where the slope was steep and loose, the bottom of the draw was firm and staggered like a set of stairs. Except that the steps weren't even—it was almost like climbing into the tower of our meetinghouse.

"I'll be dad-gummed," the old man breathed after we'd climbed maybe thirty yards. "Young feller, I do think you might do it. Where'd you learn this stunt?"

"My pa. He'll carry two men and a cedar post on a dead run and still beat most of the kids in our ward. I used to look at him and figure there wasn't a stronger man in the world. Then one day I decided I wanted to be strong too, and so lately I've been working on it. Pa's given me some pointers about balance and lifting, and that's helped a good deal. Still, he beats me all hollow with what he can carry."

"Who's your pa?"

"Jons Soderberg. *Bishop* Jons Soderberg."

"The polyg from over in Sanpete?"

"One and the same."

"Well, don't that beat all. The *Tribune* says they arrested one of Soderberg's sons for the murder of Enock Rhoades. Your brother?"

"Nope. Me."

"You? But I thought they had you in jail."

"Th-they did. Ma got me out . . . on bail. Mister, normally I like ch-chewing the cud like most fellers, but not now. I just got to quit talking. This hill's . . . getting steeper'n the price of imported ginseng at the Co-op, and I just gotta . . . save my breath."

What I'd said was true, too. I was panting like Lyman's dog after it had been chasing rabbits, and for the first time I was beginning to have my doubts. That hill loomed above me maybe fifty more miles, and I truly didn't know if I was going to make it.

"You're right, young feller. I'm sorry for making all this chin music. Just one more question and then I'll be through. Did you kill that young Rhoades feller?"

I snorted and almost threw the old man down. "'C-course not," I grunted. "Would I have . . . admitted to being who I was if I'd been guilty?"

"Then how's come you got arrested? The *Tribune,* which I don't hold much truck with anyway, never did say."

"I th-thought you only had . . . one more question."

"I did! But dad-gum it, this here's important."

"So's getting out of here," I panted. "I . . . I'll tell you all about it . . . when we do."

"All right, all right," the old man muttered. "Reckon I can wait."

He did, and in an agony such as I had never before felt, I pushed myself and that old man up the slope. I could see the top by then, and that gave me a little hope. I could also see blood when I spit, and that scared me. My chest had never hurt so bad, and my legs were like sticks of wood that felt like they were going to break into pieces with every step I took.

I staggered, almost fell, stumbled forward, staggered again, and was thoroughly ready to admit defeat and lie down and die when the rock to the side of my head suddenly exploded. I jerked back, heard the powerful boom of the rifle explosion, and saw more rock chips go flying from the impact of another slug. Right off I was no longer quite so tired.

For the rest of the way up that draw I fairly ran, and that's something for a crippled kid who's packing a big old man on his shoulders. The man I carried was whooping and hollering like he was astride a racehorse, and I'd have joined in and whooped some myownself if I'd only had the wind.

Finally, maybe thirty feet above me, I glimpsed the frightened face of my little brother peering over the edge. "Ern," I gasped, and then something smashed into my leg and I was down and the old man was gone from my shoulders and I was rolling. I slammed into a rock, shook my head to clear it, and lunged to my feet, but instantly my leg buckled and I was down again.

"Hy, what's wrong?"

"I don't know, Ern. I must've wore my leg plumb out. It don't hurt, but I can't use it for sour apples."

"If it don't hurt yet," the old man called out from where I'd dropped him, "it will. You've been shot, young feller."

"Shot? But . . ." I looked down then, saw blood all over the rocks, and realized that the old man was right, and then I found out even more how right he had been. Instantly the pain set in, and it wasn't too long before I was wishing harder than ever that I'd never seen that blasted gold. Trouble, trouble, nothing but trouble. And I hadn't even stolen it.

"Hy, can you crawl?"

"Yeah," I gasped, "I can crawl. Trouble is, I can't crawl and carry the old man too. Ern, we're in a real fix, and—"

Another bullet smacked into the rocks beside me and whined away, and involuntarily I cringed.

"Son," the old man called, "don't you worry none about me. Get yourself on out of here!"

"But—"

"I mean it. You done all you could, and I'm beholden. Now scat!"

"Hy," Ernest called, "do as he says. Rattle your hocks on up here as best you're able. I'll take care of the old man."

Well, the old man snorted in disbelief, but he didn't know Ernest like I did, and so he was entitled. Before we were through, though, my brother and I were going to make that old buzzard a believer in Soderbergs, and that was for sure.

I inched my way up the bottom of the gully, which fortunately was dark with shadow, and I shook every time a rifle exploded and a bullet whined away from somewhere nearby. I came abreast of the old man, did my best to smile at him, crawled on, and suddenly I heard a whirr in the air behind me. I turned in time to see the old man open his mouth in surprise as the rope Ernest had tossed settled squarely around him.

"What the—" he called out.

"Sorry, mister," Ernest answered, "but it's the only way. Make sure it's under your arms and get ready. I'm going to pull you up."

Grumbling, the old man worked the loop down under his arms and pulled it tight. "Where'd a kid learn to throw a rope like that?" he asked of no one in particular. "First toss and downhill to boot, and it was right on the money. Maybe he ain't a kid. Maybe he's one of them midget fellers that does trick roping in the sideshows.

"Say, young feller, is that brother of yours a midget?"

Well, I was hurting something awful, and I was so weak that my head was swimming. Still I had to grin, the old man was that serious. "He is s-some shy of full-growed size," I answered honestly but weakly.

"Then how's he going to haul me out of here?"

"Mister, don't let Ern's size . . . fool you none. That kid's got more gall than a grizzly bear's bladder. He . . . he'll get the job done, providing it's do-able at all."

I started crawling again and heard a grunt behind me, and next thing I knew, that old man was past me and skidding up that hill slicker'n a Bible-thumpin' preacher with the devil on his tail. I followed fast as I was able and ignored as best I could the two or three rifle shots that whined by; moments later I was lying on the far side of that ridge holding my leg and doing my best not to bawl with the terrible pain of it.

"Ern," I moaned, "I . . . I got to bandage this."

"Can't do it, Hy. Not now. Them outlaw fellers will be coming, and we've got to make tracks. Plug it up with something and let me help you up onto Ingersol."

I scowled, but Ernest paid me no mind. He just took my arms, staggered, and then lifted me and started pushing me upward. Next thing I knew, I was astride Pa's big horse. Ernest did the same thing for the old man, and while that was going on I tore a strip from my shirt and stuffed it down into my pants and over that ugly-looking bullet hole. It wasn't much of a patch, I reflected, but for then it would have to do.

Ernest had chosen two fine mounts, and once he had the old man into the saddle of one of them, he scrambled aboard the other. "Come on," he urged, "let's get—"

"Hold up there," the old man ordered. "Where you figure on going from here?"

"Who cares, as long as it's away?"

"I do. It just so happens I know these mountains better'n I know the back of my own hand. We go thataway." And with his finger he pointed upward.

"But . . . but that's up into the high country," Ernest protested.

"That it is. We climb and Friendlessman will have to climb too. That's hard work when a man's afoot, and hopefully he'll get tired and give it up. Besides that, I've got somewhat of a hole up there a piece, and I aim to crawl into it and pull the edges in after me. Are you boys ready?"

We looked at each other, Ernest allowed as we were, and scant seconds later we were fogging it out of that country like three turpentined cats. Or dipped sheep, maybe. Or Euphemistic Lynn Barnes, now that I thought of it, who had run full-bore for an hour after he'd lathered up his saddle gall with undiluted sheep dip. Whichever, those horses were moving flat out, and soon, despite the fact that two of us were crippled, we were long gone from the unhealthy vicinity of Windy Ridge, Territory of Utah.

We rode until after dark and were high up and still climbing. I was pretty tuckered out by then, and it was all I could do to keep my thoughts in one place, let alone stay in the saddle. I'd long since stopped feeling all the pain, but I was weak from the loss of blood and knew that I couldn't go very much further.

What really worried me, though, was that I knew the old man was even worse than I was. To this day I don't know how he stayed in the saddle, but he never complained, never murmured. He just kept on riding, reeling and swaying and somehow every time pulling himself back aboard. Every so often he would give Ernest directions; most of the time, however, his teeth were clenched tight, and I did my best to ride that way myownself.

Finally, just after we had topped out on some ridge that was covered with boulders and a thick stand of timber, I saw the old man sway and sag down, and suddenly he was gone from the saddle. His horse shied and danced away, and I knew we'd come to the end of our trail.

"Ern? H-hold up. The old man's . . . down."

Ernest heard me and turned back, and together we rode to where the old feller lay sprawled in the dirt and rocks of the ridge. Ernest jumped down, and I started to do the same. The next thing I knew I was on the ground myownself, and Ernest was holding my head and patting my face.

"Wh-what happened?"

"Hy, Hy," he said softly, and in the dim light I could see the tears that were streaking his face, "I . . . I thought you'd bought it sure."

"Naw," I whispered, "there's l-lots of fight in me yet. H-how's the old man?"

"Still out. Hy, what we gonna do?"

"I don't know, Ern. Reckon we got no choice but to keep on going. Those outlaw fellers will be coming sure, and Marshal Clawson won't be far behind them."

"We can't do it, Hy. Not like this. You're in no shape to travel, and it's for sure this old feller beside you ain't. No sir, we've got to stay here."

"Here? But Ern, this ain't no p-place to camp. Besides, we've got to get on to . . . to . . . Oh doggone it, little brother, I don't know what to do."

There was a moment's stillness, and finally Ernest spoke. "I've been thinking, Hy. I hate to admit it, but we've got to have help. You and I might could have done it, but not now, not with you all shot to doll rags. Not especially with that old man in such a bad way."

"You're right, Ern. There's also another little rock in the road that I ain't mentioned, and I reckon I ought to. We're onto the reservation for real now, and the Utes won't like that. Zene Hill told me how riled up they were this summer, and I don't imagine anything's changed. I don't reckon we'll be lucky enough to run into a tribe of good Indians twice running, no matter *how* fine our luck's been so far."

Ernest sat still and let the silence mushroom. "Criminently!" he finally said. "I never even thought of that."

"I have, and I'm scared."

"Hy," Ernest suddenly declared, "I'm going for help!"

"What?"

"I mean it. It's our onliest chance."

"But how'll you do it? It's dark, and neither of us has a ghost of an idea where we are. No, I think we'd best—"

"Hy, I'm going. I'll take Ingersol and give him his head, and I know he'll take me home."

"But that's more than a hundred miles! It's got to be!"

"Better'n two, ain't it?" Ernest asked, and I could tell he was grinning. "Hy, I'll get you and the old man set up in a camp, stake out your horses, wrap your wounds as best I can, and then I'll be gone. Come on. Let's get over into those rocks."

Well, we did. Ernest got a small fire going, and by its light he washed and wrapped my wound and splinted the old man's leg. Then he went through the saddlebags of the two horses he had borrowed from the outlaws. Besides the bedrolls and two canteens, he found more than a pound of jerked meat, three cans of peaches, and a pistol and one round of ammunition. It wasn't a great haul, but it beat finding nothing all hollow, and I was thankful.

"You set, Hy?"

"I reckon. You sure about this?"

"I'm sure," Ernest answered, sounding confident as a skunk going for a stroll in the moonlight.

"All right. You be careful, little brother."

"I will. I'll even tie myself into the saddle, happen I get tired. I ain't stopping, Hy, until I fetch help. That's a promise!"

"It's appreciated," I whispered, suddenly choked up with emotion. "Ern, uh . . . t-take care."

"I . . . I will," he sniffed.

"Ern, I . . . well, I sure do love you."

"Yeah," he responded brokenly, "I love you too."

There was quiet then, brittle as glass. A log popped on the fire, and the old man stirred and groaned and was still again. "So long!" Ernest whispered. Then he scrambled onto Ingersol and lifted his hand in farewell, and with that he and that big old horse were gone into the darkness with all the noise of a couple of cutthroat trout sliding out of a sundapple and into deep water. Yes sir, that little brother of mine was something, he truly was.

29

Hilda's Basin Creek—
Utah Territory

Ernest rode Ingersol like he had never ridden another horse in his life, and for the first time in that same life he was beginning to feel like maybe horses, or at least this one particular horse, was something other than an enemy.

"Hey ol' boy," he called softly into the darkness, "you and me, we're gonna do it, ain't we. Yes sir, I can tell that you feel it too. We got to do it. Happen we don't, Hy and that old man will be dead as a couple of cans of corned beef."

Ingersol seemed to respond, and Ernest grinned. In the black of the night he was certain he saw the big horse's ears flap back, and he took that as a sure and certain sign of brotherhood.

There was also the route the big Belgian was taking. Right away Ernest had given the horse its head, and right away he could tell that the horse was weaving down the mountain and heading in the general opposite direction from what the old man had led them earlier.

"Good for you." Ernest whispered as he patted the Belgian's thick neck. "You and me, we're two of a kind. No matter what, we'll make it."

Ernest rode then in silence, steadily and with his eyes wide open and alert, and deep within him he felt better and better right along. He could do it! Yes sir, he and Pa's horse were a team, and provided the two of them could last, in one way or another, help was assured for his older brother.

"Ingersol," he grinned a little later, "for a time there, I figured we had about as much a chance as a one-legged man in a kicking contest. Now, though, I reckon we can do it. Yes sir, we surely can. This'll take a while, all right, but on the other hand, it'll be a piece of cake. Let's get on after it!"

All night Ernest rode down the mountain. He crossed Shale and Iron Mine Creeks, thundered across the meadows at the top of Wolf Creek Pass, splashed through Wolf Creek itself, and then turned and made his way down Trail Creek. Ingersol then turned, climbed Vat Creek Ridge, and continued south along the ridge that separated Bill's and Jimmie's Basins. Finally he dropped off again and followed Hilda's Basin Creek, and by then day was coming on and Ernest was finding it hard-pressed to stay even halfway alert.

If he had been, what happened next would never have occurred, for Sanpete County farm boys are smarter than ordinary run-of-the-mill outlaws, especially run-of-the-mill outlaws like Loose-lip Lundstrum, who was not a good outlaw and was a terrible Mormon besides.

But Ernest was swaying with fatigue in the saddle, the willows right there were tolerably thick, and for the life of him he didn't see George Loose-lip Lundstrum stooping down on the bank of Hilda's Basin Creek and scooping himself up an early-morning face-wash and drink.

Loose-lip saw Ernest, however, or rather he heard him coming. Hastily he mounted one of the two horses the outlaws had managed to recapture, and which it was currently his turn to ride, and from that vantage point he discovered the identities of the approaching rider and gigantic horse.

He thought of signaling his compadres in crime, who at that moment were slightly behind him, and suddenly he thought better of it. Nosiree Bob! That kid and his family had caused him grief enough for two men, and here was his chance to get even, but good.

Kneeing his horse closer to where Ernest would pass, Loose-lip loosed the piggin strings on the saddle and took up the rope that was tied there. Quickly and expertly he shook out a loop and held it ready, and then he waited, holding his mount quiet with tightened knees.

The big stallion and its small burden came on, Ernest too tired to see and the wind wrong for the stallion to catch the scent of the waiting enemy.

Loose-lip grinned his wolf-like grin and thought of what Friendlessman and the boys were going to say when he showed them his catch. They wanted the boy, that was certain. But there were two or three of them who would be more than excited to see that horse. Loose-lip remembered vividly the race of the year before, and he knew more than anyone else in Fountain Green the full story of that horse. Now, he thought quickly, he could get that nag back for the boys who had originally stolen him, and things would be truly fine.

Finally Ernest and the stallion trotted past, and expertly Loose-lip flipped an overhand loop, cinching the dozing youth low over his arms. Instantly Loose-lip threw two hard dallies around his saddle horn, sat his horse back on its hocks, and waited.

Ernest cried out, flew high into the air, and came down on the flat of his back, breath-bursting hard.

Suddenly Loose-lip paled. The boy wasn't moving, and he knew full-well that Friendlessman didn't want any of the Soderbergs, or that old man either, killed. Not yet, at least. They still had things to tell, and it was almighty hard to tell them when a feller was dead.

"Hey," he accused the flattened youngster, "you ain't kilt!" The declaration was rewarded by a stirring from Ernest, together with a little creative language that would have surprised his mother and maybe brought a tight smile from his Mormon bishop father, happen either one would have been there to hear it.

The affront relieved Loose-lip's fear of having killed the boy, and so with an oath of his own that was truly profane, he spun his horse about and dragged the boy, still on the flat of his back, across the sandbar and through the willows to where Felix Friendlessman and the others were squatted down over a small fire, planning.

Loose-lip had fully expected the big stallion to follow, for he knew that horses liked company and they also liked to remain close to their riders, especially far away from their home corrals. But Ingersol wasn't any run-of-the-mill horse, not by a long shot. For an instant only the animal hesitated after Ernest had been unhorsed, and then with a buck and a snort it was off and gone into the willows downstream.

Loose-lip finally realized that the horse was gone, and so he cursed again, but still he wasn't really worried. The animal wouldn't go far, and he and the others could rope it down any time they chose. Of course Loose-lip Lundstrum didn't know Ingersol very well. He only knew *about* him, and that was nowhere near enough.

Meanwhile Ernest was spitting sand and rock and other bits of mountain debris, and slowly he came wobbling to his feet. Loose-lip, greeting his fellows with his hoarse laugh and his brag of roping "the smallest and meanest of all the Soderbergs," made the reflex cowboy motion of slacking his loop. He had brought the kid back to the others and had busted him good doing it. By all rights the little brat had

ought to stand still and shake where he was. But, as has been mentioned, Ernest Soderberg wasn't any run-of-the-mill kid. He was
Soderberg through-and-through, Sanpete Mormon breeding,
courageous missionary stock, full of faith as a Book of Mormon
prophet, and slick in his think-box as a greased snake. He came up
shaking, all right, but not from being busted and dragged. Ernest
Soderberg came up mad clear through!

"Who's that?" Jack Moore asked of the glaring boy.

"The youngest Soderberg brat. Found him sneaking past and
thought maybe you fellers would like to ask him a few questions.
When you're done, I got you another little surprise."

"Where's your brother?" Friendlessman growled, looking up
from the sketch he had drawn in the dirt.

"Up there," Ernest answered, nodding his head in the direction of
the mountain.

"Dead?"

"Not so's you'd notice."

"You'll take us to him."

"Ha!"

"You will." Friendlessman turned away and began scratching
again at his plan, totally ignoring the roped and beaten kid. But that
was fine, and Ernest was glad. Why, the man was puffed up as a frog
in a cream can. More and more this was beginning to look like fun.

Ernest had felt the slack that Loose-lip had unwittingly given
him, and with his coyote's instincts for the sliding maneuver, and silent as a sleeping baby, the boy slipped the noose and stepped from
it. He was free then, but the thought of fleeing had not even occurred
to him. Ernest Soderberg had other solutions in mind.

Leaving the empty loop behind, he glided down the length of the
lariat as it lay on the ground trailing behind Loose-lip's horse. Picking up the rope no more than ten feet from the owner's saddle, the
boy swiftly coiled its length until he had the loop up to his hand
again. Beyond Loose-lip, the others were commencing to crowd in
on Friendlessman, who was showing them where he was certain that
Hyrum and the old man were holed up.

Ernest heard two or three things said about his brother that
brought the furies to his blood, and that was enough and more. Yes
sir, he was fairly itching to get on with what he was about to do.
Nothing would distract him now, for the weapon of deliverance was
at hand.

Directly at his feet was a large and meandering clump of mountain prickly pear, thorny cactus of the sort that had given more than one man a lot of grief. It was an old patch, but many of the leaves were big and thick, and Ernest was glad for that.

Stretching his foot, he managed to break loose a big, thorny, pear-shaped leaf. It wobbled, appeared about to fall the wrong way, then wobbled back and fell right at Ernest's feet. Reaching down, he grabbed it and juggled it until he had it by the broken joint. Hefting it, he eyed the target. Distance seemed about right. And trajectory. Time to be moving, for sure.

Quickly he shook out a smallish loop of the rope, whirled it once, and threw it to fly over the head and settle mid-body of Loose-lip Lundstrum. In the identical moment and with all the accuracy his amazingly natural abilities gave him, Ernest shoved the thorny pear of the prickly cactus up under the tail of Loose-lip's unsuspecting and quietly standing horse.

The poor animal squealed as if shot, and then it jumped like it was dying from the same nonexistent bullet. And for that matter, it probably felt like it was.

The horse went up not only straight into the air but horizontally sideways and out from under its dirty rider as well. When the poor creature lit once more upon the earth, it did so in full gallop and still squealing. And as Loose-lip had not bothered to unwrap the dallies from about his saddle horn, he was nearly cut in two when his horse reached the full length of lariat going away from him.

The wrench jerked the man out of midair with a hair-raising scream that was cut off somewhere just shy of dead center, and then it slammed him down onto the hardpan of the stream bank with fearsome force. All that saved his miserable life was the application of the ancient law of irresistible momentum against movable body, and move he did. Loose-lip followed his runaway horse at the far and worst end of his own dallied rope, bouncing and slamming about like a barrel rolling loose downhill.

He struck dirt, rock, sand, gravel, more cactus, adobe mud, natural gas, and everything but oil, and he surely would have been worn down to a human nubbin had not the horse turned in its own fright and run back toward the startled group of outlaws.

Doolin and Friendlessman dived frantically for cover, but the Boss, Blue John, and Silvertip, well versed in the fine art of subduing panicked horseflesh, ran out to wedge Loose-lip's horse between their own bodies. In that manner they slowed the animal and finally brought it to a stop only scant seconds before the hapless outlaw would have been ground completely lifeless.

Even so, all hades was immediately owing.

When the rock chips and streambed detritus had ceased flying and the gritty dust had settled again to earth, it was not alone the worn-raw parts of George Loose-lip Lundstrum's hide that were missing.

Not only the big Belgian stallion Ingersol but now even little Ernest Soderberg who had ridden him were both gone entire from the bank of Hilda's Basin Creek, Territory of Utah.

"Now that," Silvertip reflected softly as he stared about at the empty wall of willows, "is *my* kind of kid."

"Bah!" Blue John growled disgustedly, and together he and Silvertip and Jackson T. Moore began administering some much-needed aid to the hapless George Loose-lip Lundstrum.

30

Various Locations—
Utah Territory

The friendly proprietor of the general store at Soldier's Fort was not at the moment feeling very friendly. Others in his narrow store obviously were, though.

"Say Frenchy," one of the dozen men called as he waved a bottle drunkenly in the air, "grubstake me to another bottle of that there snake-oil whisky you got out in the back! It's like to do me in."

"That there Turley's prime gin," another man howled, a big man with a thick, black beard and a shirt that hadn't seen a location other than the wearer's back inside the last six months. "The demons get you, there's still a smile or two left in the bottle."

"Yes," the proprietor muttered, altogether afraid of the big man and his crowd of companions, "and it's a foolish rat that goes back to the same poison. No sir, boys, I grubstaked Tranch here and a couple of the rest of you enough and more, and all I ever seen from it was more empty promises. You want more of my goods, let's see *l'argent,* the cash money."

"Aw, Frenchy," the man with the bottle whined, "trust us. You know that gold's up there. That Lundstrum feller swore it when he came through! Why, they've got that kid and the old man trapped—"

"Trapped?" Frenchy Dupont declared with scorn in his voice. "Did you see how Lundstrum looked when he staggered in here? I'd of swore he'd trapped a she-grizzly in the back of a cave where she had two cubs to protect. And he was whining like a puppy full-up with porky-hog quills the entire time he was here. Boys, I'd as soon be caught in a room with no doors and no windows and eighty-three angry catamounts as to be up there with Friendlessman and them others."

There was a snort from the big man in the filthy shirt, he who was called Tranch. "Yeah, and that's why you're clerking in this hole of a store instead of out there where the *real* money is. Now Frenchy, I've run plumb out of patience—"

The door suddenly screeched open and a man entered, a big, clean-looking man who had a black beard streaked with gray. He wore a black broadcloth suit, the kind a minister might wear; he had a white shirt and bowtie, and his hat was low-crowned and flat-brimmed, the kind worn by most preachers. He was rangy, sort of, and somewhat gaunt. As mentioned, he stood fairly tall above his bunions and had wrists like the knucklebones on a four-year-old steer and hands the size of stove lids. He was gangly, maybe, and lanky, but both Frenchy Dupont and even dirty-shirt Tranch got the distinct suspicion that the Good Lord had not cut the gawky figure standing before them precisely to fit the cloth of the ministry.

The man nodded pleasantly at the others and then turned his back and began examining the leather goods that were hanging on the wall.

"Hey, preacher," Tranch sneered, "you're lost. The church is down the road."

"Yeah," the man with the empty bottle agreed sarcastically. "About forty miles."

"Better get to it," a third man giggled. "You're liable to miss your meeting with all the other sisters."

There was crude general laughter, and several of the men clapped each other on the back.

"Hey, boys, maybe this feller's a Mormon preacher."

"No, an upstanding preacher-man like this?"

"Well," Tranch declared, "if he is, then for sure we've found ourselves a female pansy."

"Boys," Frenchy Dupont whispered, "don't start any trouble."

"Frenchy," Tranch laughed, "you worry too much. That pansy ain't gonna cause no trouble for us. Why, he's on his way to church. Ain't that so, preacher?"

The black-suited man in the beard slowly turned and gazed at the crowd of men. "In a manner of speaking," he replied gently.

"Ha!" Tranch declared, turning from the man and forgetting that he was even there. "What'd I say? Man's a coward, pure and simple. Now Frenchy, about them supplies."

"Tranch," the store-keeper replied, "I told you already. I've grubstaked you for the last time. Besides, you fellers don't have a ghost of a chance of finding that gold. I told you what Lundstrum looked like, and it was considerable worse than I said. Additionally, that kid stopped down the street two . . . no, *three* days ago. He was riding that big Belgian stallion he and that other kid had ridden out on, and he stopped at the telegraph office."

"So what?"

"So this: I don't know where he sent his telegram, or to whom, but I'd take odds he was calling for help."

Tranch laughed derisively.

"You wouldn't laugh," Frenchy declared, "happen you'd seen that Lundstrum feller. He wouldn't say much about what happened, but it looked like he'd been throwed so high that St. Peter had whittled his initials in his boot-soles. I'm telling you straight, he was so beat up he had to lean against the counter just to spit."

"Anybody can get lucky, and those two kids did. They won't hurt us. Why, once we get that gold, we'll just plant 'em shallow without a reading. Won't nobody be the wiser."

"Maybe. But the one got lucky with Lundstrum was the little kid on the stallion, all by himself. And he was little, too. No more'n knee-high to a long stirrup. Think what those growed-up fellers who are trapped up there could have done had they tangled with him. Boys, you'd best watch your P's and Q's."

"Bah!" Tranch sneered, suddenly pulling a pistol. "Frenchy, I'm tired of asking and I'm tired of waiting. Fill up a burlap bag with bacon and canned goods and other supplies, and don't forget a couple of bottles of that Turley—"

"Is there a problem here?" the tall man in the black suit asked, stepping forward. He had a mule-skinner's whip in his hand, one he had been examining, and none of the others had noticed that he had been listening to the conversation.

"N-no, sir," Frenchy Dupont stuttered, as afraid for the tenderfoot as he was for himself. "I don't need no help at all, especially from you. Me and these boys were just working out—"

"See here, preacher," Tranch growled, thrusting himself forward and thumping the black-suited man on the chest, knocking him back a step, "keep your long skinny nose out of things that ain't none of your affair."

"But I thought—"

"You ain't paid to think, pansy. All you Mormons and preachers is alike. All gurgle and no guts. Now shove off!"

"Did I hear you say," the man turned to Frenchy, suddenly ignoring the glowering Tranch, "that the boy who stopped at the telegraph office rode a big Belgian stallion?"

"You did."

"Did he or the young feller who was with him earlier happen to mention a name? Like Soderberg, for instance?"

"They didn't, but they did say they was brothers. They looked kin, too, and they—"

"Say," Tranch shouted, "what is this? I told you to beat it, preacher, and when Tranch says beat it, he means—"

He never got the rest of the order out, for one of those stove-lid fists smashed full bore into his own sensitive proboscis. It showered bright red blood, but that was only the beginning. Tranch had only just noticed the new coloring of his shirt when the other stove-lid tunneled into his midsection, which was softened and bulging from years of holding quart upon poison quart of snake-oil Turley and other nefarious brands of booze.

Tranch doubled over; on his way down he met a long, wide-boned kneecap coming up, and the next thing dirty-shirted Tranch knew, he was flat out on the floor, covered with blood, and with not a desire in all the world to get back up.

"Well," the preacher said almost apologetically as he leaned over him and tossed away his pistol, "you *did* say to beat it. Frankly, I couldn't think of a better thing to beat.

"Now," he declared sternly, rising to his feet and looking at the other men, who were suddenly very sober, "I did tell you I was going to do a little preaching. Happen the bunch of you and your misfortunate partner aren't out of here in sixty seconds, the sermon will proceed. I will commence reading all of you from the Book."

The men looked at the tall gangly man in the black suit, and they were puzzled indeed. With one look the man was milk-toast as they come. With the other he looked gritty as fish eggs rolled in sand. If they cocked their heads one way, the feller appeared so helpless he couldn't drive nails into a snowbank. Cocked the other, he appeared like he might haul hell flat out of its shuck. All of them decided instantly that in a tight election, they wouldn't bet on him either way.

One thing was certain, however, and Tranch's cronies decided they would take bets on it all summer. That black-and-gray bearded man hadn't been raised in the territory. No sir. He wouldn't know a whiffle-tree from a wagon-tongue or a whey-belly bull from a spring-

bred heifer. He was as out of place there as a cow on a front porch.
As far as the decking of Tranch was concerned, the preacher had
been lucky indeed.

"Let's take him!" one of the men shouted, and they started toward
him. Suddenly the door screeched open again and another man entered, a small man in range clothes who had the swarthy skin of an Indian.

"Excuse me," he said softly as he removed his hat, "but this looks
like a lopsided dance. Would you mind if I bought a ticket and joined
in?"

The tall, dark-suited man grinned. "The more the merrier," he
declared, and then he turned again to face the men.

"What is this?" one shouted. "A preacher and an educated Indian? Come on, boys, let's learn 'em a thing or two!"

And so they tried. They surely did. He of the bottle broke it off at
the neck and took one swing with the jagged edge; the next thing he
knew, he was lying in a whole lot more broken glass on the
boardwalk out front, all of it fly-specked windowglass, and that general store was getting more light than it had seen in years. He started
to get up and then saw the man of the stove-lid fists gazing levelly at
him, so he quietly laid himself back down in the glass. It was, he suddenly decided, an altogether more comfortable bed than he could find
inside.

From that moment the battle truly raged. Fists splattered into
noses, ears, and bellies; blood flew, and so did bodies; and of a truth
the black-suited man and the Indian were having a mighty fine time
of it. The Indian was not large, but he was faster almost than sight,
and he jumped those men one after another like a roadrunner jumps
a rattler, pummeling them into the floor. He whom they called the
preacher, meanwhile, was smiling with pleasure as he picked a man
up and easily threw him into a knot of the others, sending them rolling like ninepins. Then, before any of the men were even certain
what had happened, stove-lid fists were tapping them on their jaws or
behind their ears, and one after another they rolled over and lay still.

Then it was quiet in the store, and the one they had called the
preacher straightened and started to turn to see how the Indian had
gotten along.

"Jons," the Indian hissed. "Behind you! A gun!"

The black-suited man quickly reached out to the counter and then
turned, ready. Tranch, staggering to his feet, was drawing his spare

pistol from his rear pocket, and in his eyes was the desire to kill. Suddenly something ice-like and painful curled around his wrist, and he screamed. His hand flew upward; the pistol discharged and blew a hole in the ceiling, and then it went clattering from his deadened grip.

With terror-filled eyes he watched as the tall black-suited man wielded the mule whip like he'd been trained to it all his life. First an open gash appeared on one of Tranch's cheeks, and then, more quickly than he could imagine, his other cheek was laid open. He raised his hands to protect himself, then watched in horror as the trigger finger on his shooting hand vanished with a sharp snap of the whip, and then he screamed again.

Long and loud his cry wailed, continuing until a sharp slap brought him momentarily to his senses.

"D-don't hit me with that again," Tranch wailed in fear as he gripped his bleeding hand.

The man did not answer. Instead he laid down the whip, took out his white handkerchief, and began to bind the man's mutilated appendage.

"Wh-who *are* you fellers?" Tranch then whispered, his face pale with shock. "Who'n—"

"That's Zenos Hill," the man in black answered quietly as he finished with the hand. "My name is Soderberg, Jons Soderberg, from Fountain Green. Those two young fellers you plan on killing, the ones up on the mountain? They happen to be my sons and Zene's friends. Just thought you'd like to know. When you kill 'em, you'll be coming over me and Zene to do it."

Carefully then he stepped back, picked up the whip, and placed it upon the counter. "I'll pay for the damage," he said to the stunned storekeeper.

"The dickens you will," Frenchy Dupont chortled. "No matter what this costs, it won't be near what I'd of paid for a ticket to see the fight I just saw! That Tranch is a mean man, and he's had that coming for a long time."

"Well," Zenos Hill declared, "he surely won't be shooting anyone for a spell."

"If we can't pay for the damages," Jons Soderberg said, "then I'd surely like to buy a horse. That, a saddle and blanket, a bridle, and a good rifle with plenty of ammunition. And yes, I'll take the whip here, too. Happen we get visitors up there on the mountain, I do want to receive them properly."

The men on the floor stared, and then hastily they scrambled to their feet and, with Tranch leading out, departed.

Moments later Jons Soderberg and Zene Hill stood in the street, waiting for a horse to be delivered.

"I'm glad you happened in," Jons Soderberg said quietly. "They had me a little outnumbered."

"I doubt it," Zene Hill replied.

"You here for the same reason as I am?"

"I reckon. A feller stopped by the herd this morning on his way up to, as he said, 'gather in the gold.' I brought him back in somewhat less than glowing health and thought I would send a telegram and let you know of the situation while I was here. I was some surprised to see you."

"Ernest sent me a telegram already," Jons Soderberg replied, "and I came a-running. I have two fine boys on that mountain, and until this is over, I aim to stand beside them."

"You want help?"

Jons looked at the smaller man. "The older boys are scattered all over the country, Zene, or they'd be here as well. I reckon you know that. If you can spare the time, and if Andrew's herd can get by for a day or so without you, why, I can't think of anybody's help I'd rather have. I know that Hyrum would feel the same."

The two men looked at each other and grasped hands, and then together they turned and strode up the rutted street of Soldier's Fort.

The saloonkeeper in Nephi laughed outright, and so did the five men who stood at the bar. "You fellers want to know what?" he asked, waving a glass in the direction of the two young men who had just walked in through the doorway.

"Do they still have that Soderberg kid pinned down up in the Uintahs?" the tall one asked quietly once again.

"Either pinned down or dead, and I hope he ain't dead. Maybe he deserves it, but if he's dead, it'll be mighty tough getting him to lead us to the gold."

"Us?"

"Yeah. Me and the boys here are figuring on joining that little war. The odds are good—just a kid and an old man. They're both hurt, and the stakes are high enough to make it interesting."

"Who's the old man?" the other of the two near the door asked quietly.

"Beats us. Likely some stray the crippled kid snagged onto for help. What's all this to you young fellers?"

"Well," the tall one answered as he lifted his hat and scratched his scalp, "we figured on going on up there and maybe getting involved just a mite ourownselves."

There was a chorus of laughter from the five who were standing at the bar. "Young fellers," one of the men scoffed, "you're a mite too late. What that boy's bought hisself on that mountain is one life less than a Mexican standoff—maybe two, happen the old man gets in the way. No sir, there's maybe half a hundred fellers up there right now. We figure to be on our way as soon as the train comes through, and the train's sold out. There just ain't no room for two more."

The two young men looked at each other, and then carefully they stepped apart. "You fellers notice the cracks in the ceiling?" the taller of the two suddenly asked.

The men, as one, looked up, saw no cracks, dropped their eyes, and found themselves staring down the yawning muzzles of two Colt .44s.

"Grab yourselves some of those cracks you don't see," the shorter of the two said quietly. "Good. Now with your right hands, reach down, each of you, and unbuckle your gunbelts. Careful now . . . gently, gently . . . that's the way. Now drop them to the floor.

"Bartender," he continued, "take your shotgun in your left hand and bring it around front of the bar, real easy like."

The two young men watched as the orders were flawlessly carried out. "You brethren are doing right fine," the short one continued. "Lyman, gather up their weapons."

"Now see here—"

"Mister, we do see. We see five growed-up men ready to head out into the hills to kill some poor innocent crippled kid and a beat-up old man. Well, we ought to let you at 'em just so they could learn you a *real* lesson. But time's short, so we'll have to do it ourownselves. Take off your boots and your britches, all five of you."

"Our boots and britches! Now, that's right unneighborly, boys."

"Yep, it is. But so is killing folks. Now get on with it!"

"Jim," the taller of the two young men questioned, turning to the other, "what for you want their boots and trousers?"

"You ever heard of tenderfeet, Lyman? Naked tenderfeet? If these fellers ain't the bashfullest tenderfeet yet, they will be by the time they get home, crossing all them rocky roads barefoot and in their long johns. They'll also have missed the train. Gather up their boots and britches, Lyman, and we'll give'em to John Ord. If these fellers want 'em back badly enough, they can fish them out of John's watering trough, up east of town."

Lyman grinned and began gathering up boots and britches. Jim, meanwhile, held his .44 steady, and the men did not move.

"You fellers won't get away with this," one of the men fumed.

"Oh, I think we will." Jim smiled laconically. "We ain't stealing, we're just evening up the odds."

"The odds? What're you talking about?"

"That boy on the mountain, mister. His name, in case you don't know, is Hyrum Vincent Soderberg. Just happens that last name's ours too. We're a couple of his brothers."

There was a deathly quiet in that high-ceilinged saloon, and the muzzles of the two .44s looked wider and darker than ever.

"Now," the tallest of the two brothers said quietly, "if you'd like to serve papers on us, we'll be right up on that mountain, just a-waiting to open an extra session of court. If you're feeling lucky, why, look us up and do it."

Johnny Soderberg cussed as thirty-eight head of horses skirted the brush-built neck of his makeshift corral and thundered away.

"Blast," he said as he smashed his hat against his dusty Levi Strauss britches. "Second time this week! If I don't get them horses rounded up, Brother Cook's going to fire me."

Hopefully the young man rode to the corral and looked inside. Seven. For two days he had chased that herd, and all he'd managed to catch was seven head.

The sun along the Green River was hot, and Johnny reached up and wiped his forehead. Off in the cottonwoods a chorus of cicadas split the morning air with their shrill buzzing, and a wandering breeze bent the grass on the bar of the river before him. But Johnny didn't notice that—he didn't see the beauty of the place at all. He'd failed to round up thirty-eight of Brother Cook's horses, and if he didn't have them by the end of the week, he'd not get paid. That meant that with his mother in prison the little ones would go hungry, and Johnny just couldn't stand—

"Johnny!"

Quickly he spun around and stared at the bluff above the river.

"Johnny, come quick! I got news!"

"Mattie Butts," he muttered in surprise. "What are you doing way out here?

"Just a minute," he called, turning his horse and spurring it into action. "I'm coming!"

Moments later, Johnny reined his mount in on the top of the bluff overlooking the muddy Green River. Swinging to the ground, he lifted the young lady down and took her into his arms.

"Mmmm . . ." she mumbled, trying to work her way free.

"That's what I say, sugar. I been seeing your pretty-eyed face in my dreams for nigh onto a month now. Our wedding is still an eternal sixty-nine days and three hours and twenty-six minutes off, and I'm powerful glad you came to see me! Let's have another kiss—"

"Johnny, for heaven's sake, this is important!"

"I'll say it is! Now let's—"

"Johnny, listen to me! Hyrum's in trouble, and everybody thinks Ernest is up there with him."

Johnny Soderberg was suddenly all business. "Up where?" he asked as he released the girl and stepped back.

"The Uintahs."

"Well, he's supposed to be working there."

"Johnny, he's been in prison for murder since you left, which was a trumped-up charge if ever I saw one, and there're folks after him trying to kill him. Ernest sent a telegram for help, and I thought . . . well, I hoped you'd want to know."

"You came all this way alone?"

"It was the only way to reach you, Johnny, and I knew it was what anyone else in your family would do. I took the train to Thompson, and then I borrowed a horse and rode south . . ."

Quickly Mattie explained, and within five minutes Johnny was on his way to the railroad, escorting beside him the courageous girl. When a Soderberg needed help, a lonely and frightening ride for a young woman who was marrying into the family was expected, for frontier women were anxious to stand beside their men and never cower behind them. Johnny knew that, and for the first time he also knew that Mattie Butts was a woman he could be truly proud of.

Additionally, in Johnny's mind, thirty-eight uncaptured horses belonging to Scott Cook suddenly seemed awfully unimportant. Those animals had gotten along fine for nearly a year, and another couple of days wouldn't make any difference at all.

U.S. Deputy Marshal Tinsdale sat in the coolness of his office at the Provo Jail, swatting flies. Outside, the sun beat down mercilessly, and he was glad that the walls of the jail were thick. Even so, the heat was bad, and he was forever—

The sudden beating of hooves against the hardened street caught his attention, and he was already watching as the door to the jailhouse swung inward and Marshal Hebron Clawson stormed into the room.

"Mr. Tinsdale," he said. Sweat dripped from the ends of his dirty yellow mustache and stained his already filthy shirt. "I just got word, and I got to get me a posse right away."

"Whoa," Tinsdale urged as he swung at another fly. "Come at this from the beginning, Clawson. You got word about what, and you need you a posse for who?"

"Mr. Tinsdale, I ain't got time for this! I got to catch that train!"

"The only thing you'll be catching is my boot in the seat of your pants," Tinsdale said easily. "Now let's hear it all, from the beginning."

Marshal Clawson ground his yellowed teeth in frustration. "Oh for—" he growled, but when he looked at Deputy Tinsdale he did not continue with his complaint. "Yes sir," he said quickly. "The whole story. I just heard down at the saloon that some fellers have that murdering Soderberg kid pinned down up above Wolf Creek Pass. He's wounded bad, I hear, and I figure if I can get me a posse and get up there pronto, then maybe I can get him before—"

Suddenly he stopped and stared upward at the giant who had risen before him. "B-be . . ." he stammered, "b-before . . ."

"Is that the boy who came in here and freed his pa?" Tinsdale asked sternly.

"Y-yes sir, it is one and the same. He killed that poor Enock Rhoades—"

"Has that been proven?"

"Well no, but—"

"Clawson, that kid wasn't more than ten or eleven when Rhoades disappeared!"

"I know, Mr. Tinsdale, but he had his gold, besides which—"

Deputy Tinsdale slammed his huge hand down on the desk. "Besides which, that Soderberg kid ain't no killer! I talked to him here, twice, and he don't have the eye for it! I know! Now who has him pinned down?"

"M-Mister Doolin," Marshal Clawson stuttered. "H-him and a fellow name of Friendlessman."

"Doolin? Friendlessman? I can't be hearing this! Clawson, you are dumber than I thought, and that is some dumb. Doolin, as you ought to have heard, is a known crook. Friendlessman, on the other hand, has remained on the right side of the law, but only just barely. Only a month ago Caleb Rhoades reported that Friendlessman was hounding him worse than ever, breaking into his barn and trespassing upon his property. On this very desk I have a warrant against him.

"Clawson, I order you onto that mountain to arrest those two men and any others who may be with them."

"Mr. Tinsdale, I won't do it!"

"You won't?"

"No, by thunder, I won't. That Soderberg kid and his pa and the rest of that miserable family have given me more unrighteous grief over the past three years than any man had ought to take in a whole entire lifetime. Whatever that kid's getting up there, he purely deserves! I just won't go!"

"Very well," Deputy Tinsdale responded mildly, "I suppose you are right."

Marshal Clawson looked up at the huge man, his face a study in surprise. "You . . . you mean I can gather my posse and—"

"I didn't say that," Deputy Tinsdale said as he held the flyswatter out to the filthily clothed marshal. "I merely said that you were right. You won't be going onto that mountain. You'll stay here, swatting flies, while *I* go."

"But . . . but . . . ."

"No buts, Marshal, but a word of warning, nevertheless. Jons Soderberg was arrested for unlawful cohabitation and for nothing else. In my own opinion that does not make him a criminal. Now there are folks who say the Edmunds-Tucker Law is constitutional and a fine law, but there are others, just as smart, who say the law itself is illegal and shameful. Happen that second bunch is right, and I personally am amongst them, why then you and me and every other polyg hunter in the territory could be imprisoned for harassment of innocent, law-abiding citizens. My advice, marshal, is to go easy on that good bishop. And marshal, he *is* a good bishop.

"As far as Soderberg's son Hyrum goes, both you and I know that murder charge was trumped up. Caleb Rhoades himself told me he knew the identity of the Indian that had killed his brother. Did you catch that, marshal? Indian. Spelled I-N-D-I-A-N. Not S-O-D-E-R-B-E-R-G.

"Now, take this flyswatter, hold it in your hand like this, and use it liberally. Flies you may chase down freely, but not Soderbergs. Happen there is any trouble at all while I am away, you will be back there swatting flies *behind* bars instead of up here where I am sure you would prefer to be. Do I make myself clear?"

Apparently he had, for as the gap-toothed Deputy Tinsdale was making long-legged strides toward the railroad station on the south end of town, with his hastily albeit carefully selected posse following, he could hear behind him the very rapid slapping of the fly-swatter against the walls and desk of the Provo jail.

Marshal Clawson was certainly a good hand against those flies, Deputy Tinsdale thought, grinning. Of course, with those filthy clothes he could probably be arrested for entrapment, but still . . .

Hattie Soderberg was busy straining the milk she had just taken from Hepzibah, the family cow. "LaRue," she said sternly, "hold that cheesecloth tight, for heaven's sake."

"I am, Ma, I am!"

"Well, it isn't tight enough. I'm in a hurry, and—"

"Sister Soderberg, excuse me."

The timid voice behind her surprised Hattie, and she almost dropped the container of milk she was holding.

"Oh!" she said, spinning around. "You startled me, Ida Mae."

"I . . . I didn't mean to. I just . . . well, I need to talk to you for a minute—alone, if I could."

"Very well, dear." Hattie turned to hide her smile, and with a wave of her hand she gave quick instructions to her daughter. "LaRue, hand Ida Mae the strainer, and you run along.

"Now, hold it tightly, Ida Mae. That cloth has a way of pulling free every chance it gets, and you know what the milk is like then."

"Uh, Sister Soderberg, I—"

"You may call me Hattie, my dear. All of the girls in the ward do."

"Thank you, ma'am. I . . . don't really know where to begin, but I've said some pretty cruel things, and I must apologize."

"Cruel things? I'm afraid you'll need to clear those up with Hyrum."

"No, I don't mean . . . I mean . . . well, I said some terrible things about you as well."

Now Hattie Soderberg slowly stood upright and gazed into the eyes of the young girl. "About me? Whatever for, my dear?"

"It was when you raised the money to pay Hyrum's bail. At the time, I thought it was a horrid thing to do to Brother Short, and I said as much to Hyrum. I said things to a few others, as well."

"Words on the wind, I take it?"

"Yes'm. I feel just awful and want to apologize. I hope I haven't done you damage."

"Of course you haven't. I did what I did with my eyes wide open, and I knew there would be criticism. That there has been so little has surprised me. Still, I do feel badly about what I had to do."

"You do?"

"Of course. What good Latter-day Saint woman would feel good about gambling or about deceitfully using two fine men? Thank goodness Harrison Short and Andrew Aagard are understanding people. Both of them know it was the only means I had of raising that money, and neither of them has been anything but kind and sweet.

"You see, my dear, when a mother is put in a position of protecting her child against overwhelming condemnation, especially when she knows of his innocence, she will go to nearly any lengths to save that child. Even now I would do it all again if it meant I could free my Hyrum from the clutches of those evil people."

Ida Mae stared at the container of milk. "Are . . . are you sure he's innocent, ma'am?"

"Ida Mae, I have known that boy for quite a while now, and he surely isn't perfect. Still, to my knowledge he has never lied to me. As far as I know, Hyrum Soderberg doesn't have an evil or dishonest bone in his body."

"But Felix said—"

"Ida Mae, I'm going to tell you something that you must swear never to reveal. Do you so swear?"

"Why . . . uh . . . yes, I guess I do."

"Very well then. I would like to tell you about Polly's son Ernest and Deaf Man Hibbard."

For the next fifteen minutes, a very sober Ida Mae Sorenson listened intently as Hattie Soderberg taught the young lady about her son and about a man who was supposedly deaf but who had overheard one Felix Ethelbert Friendlessman and one Loose-lip Lundstrum and one Mister Doolin of Provo plotting to kidnap and possibly kill her son.

Ida Mae gasped when the other had finished. "Are you certain?" she asked.

"As Hyrum would say, I'm as certain as flies head for new butter. If you'd like, ask Deaf Man Hibbard yourself. But make sure he's alone or you'll never get a word from him."

"No," Ida Mae breathed. "I . . . I don't think I need to do that. Deep down I've known it all along. It's just that . . . well, Felix is so convincing, so refined . . . "

"Ida Mae, Hyrum could be just as refined if he didn't have to support our family. Did you know his goal is to read at least six books this summer? He reads books that I can't even pronounce the titles to, let alone the authors. He has a fine mind, Ida Mae, and given the right friends and the right chances, one day the world will hear of him.

"Now, however, he may never get the chance to learn all the things that seem to set his mind afire. I have heard that he is seriously wounded, and Friendlessman and the others—"

"Wounded?" Ida Mae gasped. "Hyrum is *wounded?*"

"Yes, so I have heard."

"But they wouldn't—"

"Ida Mae, did you think they would chase him down for fun? Did you think that this was some sort of children's game? Those men are selfish—evil. They are murderers, and they will stop at nothing to destroy my son. In fact, he has been in a battle for his very life since the moment he rode into Provo to bail his father out of prison. He is alone in that battle, and I'm certain he feels that loneliness even more strongly since you have abandoned and condemned him.

"I am on my way now to catch the train to Spanish Fork and Soldier's Fort. If I can get no closer, at least he will know that I stood by him as well as I was able."

"Oh, Sister Soderberg," Ida Mae sobbed as she threw her arms about the older woman, "I'm so sorry. I never should have . . ."

For a moment the two women held each other tightly; then Ida Mae pulled away, wiped her eyes on her apron, turned, and ran to the gate. "I'm going to him," she declared as she climbed onto her father's white mare. "Hyrum needs me now more than ever before, and I'm going to find him."

"But Ida Mae . . ."

Without waiting to reply, the determined young lady spurred her mare and was gone.

31

Hades Pass, Uintah Mountains— Utah Territory

"Do you think they're still coming?"

"It's hard to tell."

Exasperated, I looked at the old man. "I know it's hard to tell," I growled. "I was just wondering what you *think*."

"At a time like this, it doesn't much matter what I think or even *if* I think. Like I told you, a fellow can't never tell."

"Criminently," I grumbled as I poked the fire, "you wouldn't admit water was wet."

"Not if I was drowning," the old man answered grimly.

I stared at the old man and realized that he wanted to say no more, so I threw another branch onto the fire.

Four days had passed since Ernest had gone, four days in which the old man and I had seen no one. Both of us had started to regain our strength, though things were mighty slow going. I was still hobbling and reeling around like a pup trying to find a spot to lie down on, and the old man moved like he was drunk as a fiddler's clerk. Still, as far as being our old selves was concerned, both of us were coming close.

"Do you think he made it?" I asked as I flipped over the mess of fish we were roasting for supper.

"Your brother?"

"Uh-huh."

The old man looked at me, then reached out and poked a small stick of his own into the fire. "Might've," he replied quietly. "I know one who didn't, but yours might've."

"One who didn't?" I asked.

The old man ignored my question, so I asked it again. "What'd you mean, one who didn't?"

"Brothers," the old man answered obliquely. "Yours was small, but he was knowing as a bunkhouse rat. Maybe he did."

"Ern's slick, all right. 'Course, so's that Friendlessman feller."

"That he is," the old man mumbled. "Besides that, he's shuffled himself in with a powerfully stacked deck. I'll tell you this, young feller: you *do* pick the enemies."

"I didn't pick 'em. They came after me—them and who knows how many others. It all started the minute I found that blasted gold."

"Gold can do strange things to a man, all right. It can destroy friendships, tear apart families and loved ones—all sorts of things."

"Yeah," I agreed. "I truly understand what you're saying. You know, that poke of gold cost me my girl, and it nearly cost me my friendship with Zene Hill."

"Zene Hill's your friend, huh? I know him. Indian, ain't he?"

"He surely is. He's also white and delightsome as any man I ever met. The Indian side of him, though, that's what shows up first. Why, he don't leave enough tracks to trip up an ant. I've learned things from Zene that ain't written down anywhere in a book, like how to float pack horses across a swollen stream and how to track game and how to doctor a mule or horse what's been snakebit and a lot of other things.

"Another thing I learned is that there isn't anybody who wants to hear about the hard times you've had, so if anything goes wrong, just keep it to yourself."

"Good advice. Speaking of Indians, did you know they're out there now?"

"I didn't know, but I reckoned they might be, since this is their land. Are they friendly?"

"Who can tell? They're notional folk, sometimes willing to give you their very lives, other times just as willing to laugh and take yours. These ain't friendly, but we've done nothing suspicious, so they ain't killing mad yet either."

"Why're they out there?"

"Watching us. They don't know about us, but they do know that most of them other fellers are after gold. That gold's sacred to them. Right now, they're waiting for us to make a move, but once the waiting ends, it's Katie bar the door.

"In my time, young feller, I've had my share of doings with Comanches, Kiowas, Arapahos, Cheyennes, Utes, and almost every kind of Indian there is. With most I got along fine; but when he's fighting, no Indian needs take a back seat to any man. I've heard that a European general called the Indians the finest light cavalry under the sun, and I believe him.

"When a man travels in Indian country, he'd better just sort of sift through gentle-like and take up no more room than need be. When you're on their land, as we are now, it's best to keep out of sight and sleep without a fire, unless it can be well hidden. On top of that, a man had better do a little praying, happen he's a praying man. And the deeper a man gets into Indian country, the more of a praying man he becomes. Young feller, where Lamanites are concerned, you just can't afford to miss any bets."

I sat silently, thinking of all he had said. Tabby had befriended Ernest and me, but why? And what of Zene Hill? How did he fit in with all this? As if reading my mind, the old man suddenly spoke again.

"What'd Zene Hill tell you about that gold you found?"

"Well, first he took it from me—said it was sacred to the Indians. Then when he found out what I was going to do with it, he gave it back, the whole poke."

"Gave it back, did he? What *were* you going to do with it?"

"Get Pa out of jail, and if there was any extra, give it to Ma to help her out. I done 'er too, except for a bit I gave to Ida Mae Sorenson."

"Seems like a good use. Young feller, tell me straight—did you kill for that gold, or have anything to do with the killing?"

Reaching down, I turned the fish over on the rock we were using for a frying pan. "Mister," I answered, looking him squarely in the eye, "I was eleven years old when that happened, so what would you think? No, I didn't kill, and I didn't even know there'd been a killing until just before I found that gold."

"Then how'd you find it?"

"It was crazy," I answered, frowning, "the worst streak of luck I ever had. And the gold didn't change my luck, either. It was almost three weeks back when I was hunting Andrew Aagard's mules. It came on dark, I needed a place to camp, and those mules took me to a swale down near where Currant Creek flows into Red. It was a dark night, but there was something besides dark in that swale. I could feel it. Ma says both Ern and I have the gift—I think she means for feeling things beyond the veil. I don't know if we do or not, but right away I knew *something* had happened in that place. I started looking around, and before long I found the remains of a tent and a bedroll, two mule skulls with bullet holes in them, part of a pack frame, and, the next morning, inside a rotten log on which I'd sat to rest, I found that poke of gold."

"What'd it look like?"

"The gold or the pouch?"

"Both."

"The gold looked mostly pure. It was in long, thin strands, almost like string. There were some other shapes too, like chunks, and a little rock was caked on them, but not much."

"So he did get there," the man murmured. "That does say something. What about the pouch?"

"It was long and narrow, made of leather that had mostly gone black and hard, and it had ER tooled into it. That's what Doolin from down to Provo got so het up about."

"I know Doolin. He's a bad one. He's also a coward, but that just makes him more dangerous. You do pick 'em, young feller."

"Him and Friendlessman and how many others? Old man, looks to me like the two of us are up to our navels in crooks who want that gold." I paused and looked the old man square in the eye. "And I *still* don't know who you are. You got a name?"

"I do, but it's not very important. Old Man's good enough, I reckon."

"Maybe, maybe not. I have a feeling about you too."

"A feeling?"

"Uh-huh. Kind of tight, here in my stomach. Makes me wonder *who* I can count on."

"Well, son," the old man said, leaning back, "Brother Brigham told my pa never to count on nobody but the Lord and his own good sense. Seems like sound advice."

I stared even harder at the old man. Was he trying to tell me something? Was he trying to set me up? Who was he, really, and why had Friendlessman been shooting at him? They were all good questions, but I had no answers, and that worried me a great deal.

"Well," I said as I forked over a fish to the old man, "I don't know if you're after that gold or not, and to be honest, I don't care very much. Personally, I don't want any more of that gold at all. Every bit of this trouble started down in that swale on Currant Creek when I found the first poke."

"You don't want the gold?" he questioned, eyeing me closely.

"No sir, I don't."

"You just don't know, young man. Either that or you are a liar. *Everybody* wants free gold."

"There isn't any such thing," I said quietly. "Everything has a price, *everything!* And the price of that gold is just too high."

The old man squirmed around and adjusted his hurt leg. "Hyrum, you seem to be uncommon smart, so let me warn you. Stick to what you've just said. Don't go chasing after the gold up here. It's cursed, and it only brings misery to the folks who aren't supposed to have it. I know. I've seen it happen time and again . . ."

The man stared off into the darkness of the trees, and for a minute I thought I saw tears in his eyes. But the smoke from the fire was blowing his way, and I decided that that was what had caused his waterworks.

"I felt it too," he said quietly as he finally peeled some baked fish from its bones and began to eat, "and now I know where, and why."

"What did you say?"

"Nothing, young feller. I was just thinking out loud. Somehow that sacred gold causes trouble for folks, and there isn't *anybody* who escapes it."

The quiet wrapped itself up and around us. I studied on what the old man had said, and finally I spoke. "Well, this has been a wondrous review, up to a point, but it seems to me we have skirted clear around the real issue."

"Real issue?" asked the old man.

"Yeah, you know, the answer; the Rosetta stone of the whole thing."

"The what?"

"Rosetta stone, old man: a piece of black basalt found in 1799 near the Rosetta mouth of the Nile, bearing a trilingual inscription in hieroglyphics, demotic characters, and Greek, famous for having given the Frenchman Jean-Francois Champollion the first clue toward deciphering Egyptian. It was a truly important piece of rock."

"Kid," the old man growled, "I went to the fourth grade. Not through it, just to it. We didn't get to that rock. We didn't even get to the Nile. All I remember about Egypt is a picture of Cleopatra advertising cigars. Now, if you'd care to come again with your complaint that my poor memory missed the real issue, I'll give it a whirl on that basis."

Well, I grinned, for occasionally I did get a mite carried away with the things I had read. Still, it was fun, and fun just might be the only thing I got out of that wonderful education I was giving myself.

"Okay," I responded, "think of it this way. Since neither of us has a Urim and Thummim to provide a pure translation of what I have just expostulated upon, here she goes in more simple terms. The moving finger writes, and having writ, moves on. I see its surreptitious cipher engraven on the rock of time. I see the basaltic key appear and unlock the secret meanings of the message. Its words stand forth in letters of fire and brimstone. They are simple words, simple even to folks such as you and me. They say, 'Having each of us got the other to this point, and beaten off the savage foe, what then proposes the unknown man with the game leg?'"

"How's that?" demanded the old man, his eyes wary and yet curious.

"I said," I replied quietly, "that I still don't know who you are or why you are here, and you've never yet suggested what you think we should do happen those fellers come at us again."

The old man bit down on my question hard. He chewed doggedly but it would not chew. Finally he spit it out dejectedly.

"Those are good questions," he admitted.

"And the answers?"

"I ain't told you who I am because—"

Whap!

Both the old man and I rolled into the darkness as the rifle slug tore our fire apart. "What in the . . . " I muttered.

"Hyrum?"

"Yeah, I'm over here."

"Work your way down to our horses. I'll try and meet you there."

I grunted to acknowledge the old man's whisper, and immediately I set off into the darkness. My eyes were blind from staring into the flames, and I cussed myself for breaking such an important rule. Twice I slammed into boulders and once into a fallen log, and then gradually my eyes adjusted to the dark and I was able to make better time.

Our horses were down off the hill in a small stand of pine, sheltered and with good grass, and from a few yards away that clump of pine didn't look thick enough to hide a jackrabbit. I hoped it had been good enough to hide our horses.

In the darkness I worked my way down the slope, slipped through the notch in the boulders that had become my own trail, entered the trees, and found nothing there. The horses and saddles were gone!

"Ssst," I whispered, staring about me. "Old man? Where in blue blazes are you?"

I listened, and nowhere could I hear a response. For a moment I felt fear, and then, suddenly, I got mad. The old man had played me for a fool, and now I could see it clear as day. He'd crippled himself up and let me do for him, and gradually, without ever telling me who he was or what he was about, he'd wormed out of me the location of where I'd found that gold.

Yes sir, that made me mad as a razorback hog stropping himself on a fencepost. Hone me down enough, by gumbo, and I would fix it so that old man would hear from me again!

Uphill, he'd said. That was the way to flee. All right, I'd go uphill. Happen I ran into the rest of the outlaws, well, that was just more the pity for them. I couldn't look out for *everybody* on this mountain!

Back I went up the slope, struggling, quiet as I could with my gimped-up foot and bullet-holed leg, and I was almost back to the fire when I heard voices. I hunkered down, inched forward, and found three men seated at our fire and eating *my* fish.

I was hungry, and seeing those fellers eating set my stomach to growling. Then wasn't the time to do anything about it, however, so I tightened my belt, opened my ears, and backed off, waiting. I didn't know any of those men, with the notable exception of one Mr. Doolin, whom I had previously become acquainted with. It was him that was eating the biggest fish of all.

"I wish Friendlessman would get here," he whined as he chomped on my dinner.

"I guarantee you he will," a man said quietly.

"I'll second that," a deep-voiced giant of a man declared. "If Felix Friendlessman wasn't hotter to get to that young gal down in Fountain Green than a hungry dog to grab a knucklebone, then my name ain't Alpha."

"Alpha, you say?" asked Doolin as he worked on his fish. "I thought your name was Silvertip."

"Nope. That there's just a handle, because of my hair. She's *Alpha*—the first letter in the Greek alphabet. My mother was an educated woman."

"Too bad she didn't pass it along," the quiet-voiced man said.

Silvertip smiled at him and said nothing.

"What's the rest of it?" Doolin asked idly.

"You knuckleheaded pea-brain," the quiet voiced man declared. "Don't you know that out here in the west a man's name is his own personal business?"

"Blue John," the big man said easily, "it's all right. I don't mind. If this feller Doolin's on the wrong side of the law, and if I'm on the wrong side of the law, then why shouldn't he know?"

Blue John rolled his eyes and said nothing, so Silvertip went on. "My name's Garrett, Mr. Doolin. Alpha R. Garrett."

"I don't suppose I should ask what the *R* stands for?"

"I sure wish you wouldn't. It's embarrassinger'n *Alpha*."

"Don't see how it could be," Doolin wheezed. "Tell me, please?"

"Silvertip," the quiet-voiced Blue John warned, "I wouldn't do it."

"Ah, Blue John, he asked nice."

"Maybe. But you tell him, it'll be the same as telling every runny-mouthed granny in the Territory."

"Gee whiz, Blue John—"

"Oh, go ahead, you numbskull. You ain't got the sense to spit downwind. I don't know what else I should expect. Just remember I told you what would happen if you revealed such a shameful thing as that to this flannel-mouthed weasel."

Silvertip grinned. "I'll remember, Blue John, I surely will." Then he turned to Doolin. "He don't mean nothing bad. It's just his nature to be suspicious and cantankerous. It's Rachel."

"What is? What's Rachel got to do with anything?"

"That's what the *R* is for. My full name's Alpha Rachel Garrett."

Doolin, his mouth full of fish, stared. "Why, that there's sinful," he finally muttered.

"Not according to my mother."

The men sat quietly, thinking over what Silvertip had told them. So was I, but I wasn't about to make any comments, not from where I was hiding.

"Do you mean to sit there and say," one of the men suddenly spoke up, "that your actual true name is Rachel Garrett?"

"Alpha Rachel Garrett. My mother wanted it all there. It's wrote square in the Bible and all. You see, Pap, he wanted a gal, and so did Mother. 'Course, I didn't come out with the right plumbing, but they decided they'd do their best with what they had. They covered me up with a double set of wet-pants and let my hair grow, and it was years before folks figured it out, myself included."

"Your folks wasn't educated," Blue John declared. "They was crazy!" Then he stood up and looked around. "Doggone it," he growled, "I wish Friendlessman would get here! I thought he was just stringing that Sorenson girl along."

"He was," Silvertip answered, "except I think the string's got mighty thick. From all I've heard, that there is a fine girl."

"Not too bright, though," Blue John responded. "She couldn't be, letting herself be hoodwinked by a man like Friendlessman. Blast! Where is that man? Now that we got the Boss down there with their horses, those two pilgrims are fairly well grounded."

Well, that gave me a start! That old man hadn't taken our horses after all. Which meant the horses were still around, and probably the old man too. That brought the score back to zero-zero, and we were in a whole new game that seemed an awful lot like the last one. The way it looked, if I was finally going to get me and maybe even that old man to safety, I was going to have to resteal those already-stolen horses.

Easing back into the dark, I stood up and listened. Nothing. Not a sound that might tell me where horses would be hidden. Oh, if only Ernest was here, I thought. He could hear bees snoring at five miles, and horses breathing at ten.

All right, he wasn't, so I had to think. Pa had always told us to reason things out. Most folks don't take time to do that, and they usually end up on the short end of the stick, acting on their emotions. I could have done that very thing when I heard what those outlaws said about Ida Mae, for it made me angry enough. But I could also have been dead. This way I wasn't, and there was still a small chance, hidden down . . .

The cove!

If I were going to keep several horses for a few days, I'd put them into the small cove I'd found down near the lake below us. There was plenty of good grass there, and no end of water, and whoever watched them had weeks' worth of deadfalls for firewood. Yes sir, that would be the place. It was also close to where the old man and I had hidden our own mounts, so they wouldn't even have needed to saddle them up to move them. That was why they'd done it all so quiet. I'd wondered about that, and now I knew, or at least I thought I did.

Hastily I started down the steep hill, going as quietly as possible. Then I thought, what the heck? If I was sneaking they'd likely hear me anyway. It'd only been dumb luck that the three at the fire hadn't heard me. On the other hand, if I just walked up like I wasn't hiding anything at all, then I could likely get close enough to cause some real headaches for the one called the Boss who had been left as guard.

That's exactly what I did, too. I wasn't armed, but I wasn't unarmed either. As the fire came in sight, I reached down and picked up a solid-feeling pine limb with a round knot on one end, and that was what I carried into the camp.

"Blue John," Jackson T. Moore said as he lifted his cup of coffee and turned to face me, "I was just thinking that maybe one of those two fellers might sneak up here and—say, you ain't Blue Jo—"

He didn't finish his sentence, at least not right then. The heavy knot on the end of my limb caught him square on the chin as I swung it upward. He did too, swing upward I mean, coffee, gurgled mouthful of sentence, everything, and the last I saw of him he was diving for pearls or other such treasure in some two or three inches of Heart Lake shallows.

"You're right," I said quietly. "I ain't."

Smiling grimly, I rolled the man onto his back so he wouldn't drown. Then I took his pistol and threw it out into the lake, instantly feeling bad that I'd done that because I was still unarmed. Then I turned and moved through the lush meadow grass to where the horses were tethered. I had no trouble at all picking out the mount I had been riding, for with the blaze on its face and its two white stockings, it did show up.

I saddled the horse, swung aboard, and started looking around for the old man's. That way I could lead it to him and help him mount, and we could be off again. I circled that meadow twice before I finally admitted what I hadn't wanted to admit all along.

I'd been right all along, and that dirty old man was just that— a dirty, sneaking old man. While I'd been eavesdropping up above and taking out the hombre who was at present totally committed to shallow-water swimming lessons, that old man had snuck down, stolen his own blasted horse, and taken off. He'd not thought of me, he'd not tried to help me, he'd not even told me he intended to leave me behind.

Suddenly I was mad enough to chomp a chunk out of an ax! That old man had done it to me, and I wouldn't stand for it. No sir, I'd trail him if it took until I was eighty and he was in Hades, and not the pass I was dropping off of either. I deserved an explanation, and he, by gumbo, deserved to give me one.

With that decision made, I turned the other two horses loose, whapped them with my hat to set them running, and found where the grass had been crushed in a pretty straight line. Then downhill into the darkness I followed.

32

Grandaddy Basin,
Uintah Mountains—
Utah Territory

With the first gray light of dawn, I squatted beside my small fire and thought. A fish roasted in the coals, and I was grateful for it, though with four more I'd have been four times as grateful. Above me rose a steep slope, and I adjusted the yarrow dressing on my throbbing leg and pondered the slope thoroughly.

There was no trail up it at all. Here and there were rocky outcroppings and there were clumps of brush, a maze of fallen logs, slides of broken rock, and scattered aspen. It all ended at a wall of rock thirty feet high or more, an old fault line that extended along the face of the mountain for over half a mile. And what buffaloed me most of all was that the old man's tracks led exactly to where I was camped. Then they started up the slope, and—nothing.

He'd had to climb it, though, for there was no other way he could have gone that made any sense. Trouble was, climbing it didn't make any sense either.

I planned my route carefully, for I was going to climb that hill myownself, aiming for what seemed to be a fracture in the face of the rock, a shadow only, a possible way to the top without going around to the far end. If that old man could get up through those rocks, then so would I.

In the saddle I started out, holding the reins up tight and weaving a precarious way up through the obstacles on the mountainside. Twice I paused to give the horse a breather, and both times I tumbled rocks down behind me, hoping to slow down those outlaw fellers who would be following.

Finally I rode near the high rimrock, and there my heart sank. The shadow had been just that, a shadow. There was no crack that I could see, and no way up but around.

Weary and discouraged, I turned the horse, felt it resisting, fought the reins even harder, and suddenly had a thought. That horse was likely mountain-bred, and if it had it a notion, why, who was I to argue? It kept pulling toward the cliff, and that was also where I wanted to go.

So—

The shadow was still a shadow, but directly behind it, invisible from more than a few feet away, was a steep fissure up through the cliff. Looking up at it I had my doubts, but dismounting I examined the ground and found the hoof prints from the old man's horse, and so on foot I started to climb.

I had a rough go of it, too, but no more so than my horse. I kept hold of the reins, and that mountain horse I'd borrowed lunged up right behind me, going where I'd never have guessed a horse could go. But it did, and shortly we topped out on one of the flattest and prettiest tabletop mountains I'd ever seen.

A trail led off through the trees, so I followed, not right on it but a few feet off to the side. Zene had told me once that Indians and other antisocial sorts baited those trails, and one was safe only if he wasn't on it.

Suddenly I noticed a small stump showing the marks of an ax. Carefully I walked the horse over and stepped down. The stump was about four inches in diameter and had been cut off about a foot above the ground. Nor was the wood of the cut white any longer, but gray. It was not new then, at least not this season.

Either that was cut for firewood, I thought, or it had been cut for a pole. My guess was firewood, for even the chips had been picked up.

I walked my horse in a widening circle, and it took only a few minutes to find a small lean-to and the remains of a fire. The bits of charcoal lying around had been worn smooth by wind and rain, and so I knew that the fire was old.

He's been here, I thought. *That old man has been here, and this was his fire.* Again I rode in widening circles, but now I found no tracks. I studied the distant ridge where the sun shone bright upon the sullen and silent rocks; then, filled with an idea, I started toward it. On the plateau there was no sound except the footfalls of my horse— that and the sound of the wandering wind, a wind uncertain of itself, prowling among the trees as if looking for something lost.

Again and again I drew up to look about, to listen, and to watch the trail behind. For all its beauty, there was an eerie something about this plateau that made me wary—something I had not felt on the Wasatch Plateau. I had the feeling that eyes were watching me, eyes that might be looking along a rifle barrel.

I changed course several times, veering suddenly to put a rock, a tree, or a bush behind me. I was trying to offer no target for a marksman, and my sudden changes would be useful, I knew, in making my trail difficult to follow. Instinctively, I chose the way that would leave the fewest marks behind, for I felt that even if I was not followed now, I soon would be.

Here and there I passed pits in the earth, diggings made by the old man or someone else in an endless search for wealth. Some of the holes were small and shallow, others much larger, and many had the appearance of great antiquity. I thought again of the Spanish padres who had come into this land so long ago, the black-robes who had enslaved the Indians and bled the land of both gold and life. Perhaps it was their ghosts I felt, theirs or the trusting Indians who had been slain by them.

Quite suddenly I dropped over a small ledge, and in front of me lay a tiny lake, its blue waters ruffled by the wind. I skirted the shore and, seeing that the water was shallow, rode in and walked the horse close to the shore for several hundred feet. I left the lake by a small stream that came down the ridge toward which I had been traveling, and I followed it upward.

In the woods along the course of the stream and in the clump of pine I was in there was no sign of man, but on the flanks of the ridge beyond the creek I noticed a hatch of sage sparrows hopping and flitting over something on the ground. Riding swiftly upward to the place, I found horse droppings that were still soft and, when broken open, faintly warm in the center. The old man had been there, then, and not an awful long time before.

Until dark I searched for further sign but found none at all. That old man could hide a trail, and more and more I was admiring his skill. That didn't mean I liked him any better, but I did appreciate his way in the woods.

In the gathering dusk I made camp in the corner of the ridge, picking up dry wood from old deadfalls that would make an almost smokeless fire. It was a good camp, too. The cove was higher than the land in front of it, offering a good view for perhaps a quarter of a mile. The camp itself lay in a slight hollow under fir trees that would help to spread any smoke the fire might make. Nearby, a stream tumbled toward another lake, and by feeling carefully under the rocks of the stream, I managed to catch a half-dozen small trout. After I had roasted them in the coals and eaten them, I felt considerably better about everything—everything that is, except the old man, the festering bullet hole in my leg, and, way back in my mind, Ida Mae Sorenson.

Four miles away, another fire burned fitfully behind some rocks on an open hillside. A slip of a girl sat huddled over it, doing her best to keep warm. Nearby, her father's white mare chewed contentedly on the thick grass, and for the first time in her life, Ida Mae Sorenson found herself envying a horse.

"Peppy," she whispered to the animal, "You'll never know how lucky you are. I'm so cold and hungry I feel like I'm going to die."

Out on the mountain a coyote began serenading the moon. The stanza was picked up by another of the small carnivores, and soon an entire chorus was yelping a cappella. Ida Mae shivered from more than the cold, put two great chunks of wood onto the fire, and stared fearfully around her.

"Peppy," she whispered, "how can you be so contented? I've never seen anything so dark as this mountain. I'm scared to death! How can Hyrum stand to be up here all the time? I . . . I've never thought about . . . what it would be like to work with the sheep. Oh dear, I—"

Suddenly from nearby came a shrill scream of death as a small animal became the evening meal of a larger predator. Ida Mae was instantly upon her feet with a limb in her hand, her breath stilled, staring outward. The silence was intense, and suddenly she could hear the clear and unmistakable sound of bones being crushed by powerful jaws. She shivered again, and, her eyes wide with fear, she ran to the mare and clung to its neck.

"Oh, Peppy," she breathed haltingly, "what am I doing here? How did I ever think—"

Suddenly she thought again of Hyrum, and in her mind she saw his quick and ready smile, his shuffling walk that he tried so hard to hide, the pain in his face as she told him of Felix, and the deep courage of total despair in his eyes as he told her to pick up the thirty silver dollars, hoping in that way, because there was no other way left, to finally get her attention. Never before had she felt as she did at that moment, nor did she ever wish to feel that way again! She would do *anything* to make things up to Hyrum. Even if he never spoke to her again, she would spend her life trying to be a better person because of him. She owed him that; perhaps she owed him even more. Hadn't he been the one who had brought her father back into her life?

"Peppy, I'm more scared than I've ever been, but I'm staying! I mean it! If I can help Hyrum in any way at all . . . besides that, my heart's about to break with sorrow and loneliness for that young man. Oh, Peppy, how could I have been so blind? I just . . ."

And once again she trembled in fear as the chorus of coyotes began their shrill yipping at the thin new moon.

Not quite three miles away, and at the base of the steep hill Hyrum had climbed earlier, yet a third fire burned. Felix Friendlessman squatted there, staring up into the darkness. "You idiots," he snarled, "how could you let them do it again?

"Let them," Blue John repeated quietly. "Friendlessman, take a look at Jack Moore there, and tell me once more that we let them."

Felix Friendlessman sensed the pulsing of danger within Blue John's voice, saw his fingers curled over the butt of his pistol, and intentionally he cooled the atmosphere. "Oh, I know you did what you could. It's just hard to believe that a crippled boy with a bullet hole in his leg and a crippled old man could manage to steal and stampede your horses. Twice!"

"Well, like I said before, that Soderberg kid's a slick one—always has been. He and the little one that almost killed Lundstrum are two of a kind, and a rare kind at that."

"I like 'em," Silvertip suddenly declared. "Like I've always said, I like kids like that."

"Shut up," Blue John ordered. "Look at the Boss lying there, and then say you like 'em."

Silvertip looked to where Jack Moore lay on a pallet of blankets, moaning softly. His face was swollen and black and blue, and he looked the picture of perfect misery. "Ah, the kid only broke the Boss's jaw," the big man responded easily.

"Yes, and like to drown him, to boot."

"No he didn't. I could see where Soderberg turned him over so he wouldn't drown."

"Well, maybe so," Blue John admitted. "Still, poor Jack Moore won't never eat a regular meal again. I'd like to know what that crippled Soderberg kid clubbed him with."

"I don't know," Silvertip admitted, "but still, I like him for it.

The kid's brave, and he won't quit nohow. I truly do like him, and, like I've been saying since we tried to bust him out of jail, I hope he wins out."

"Blast it, you . . ." Blue John swore. "I never did see a man so doggone dumb and loyal in my entire life!"

The big outlaw looked at his partner and slowly shook his head. "I never could see what was so dumb about being loyal," he frowned. "But then if a man isn't bright he wouldn't see it, would he?"

Blue John stared up at Silvertip and turned as Jack Moore groaned pitifully; then he shook his head disgustedly and was silent.

"Well," Silvertip declared brightly, "I don't reckon the Boss ought to complain none, even if his jawbone *is* broken. He'd have done the same thing to the Soderberg kid as was done to him, and he probably wouldn't have kept him from drowning, either. The way I see it, when we signed on to become outlaws, we knew it was liable to get a mite dangerous. Now it has."

"You meaning to suggest," Blue John questioned, his heavy voice scraping like a burro with a bad cold, "that we're all doing this by choice?"

"Yep," Silvertip replied smugly. "We was all maybe forced into it in the beginning, or maybe we fell into being owlhoots all accidental, but none of us was ever forced to *stay* in it."

"Why, you're balmier'n you look, man. It's no wonder you was named Alpha Rachel. You think we need you to tell us about outlawing?"

"I reckon *you* do, at least."

"Why, you're nervier'n a busted tooth," Blue John snarled, and his fingers curled toward his gun. Suddenly a loud metallic click sounded in his ears, and his hand froze in mid-air, suspended, waiting.

Felix Friendlessman got slowly to his feet, and his .44 Colt revolver was out and not moving. "That's enough," he said quietly.

"No it ain't. I'm going to put this moron out of our misery."

"Not now you aren't. Look around you, Blue John. We've already lost two good men, and that leaves just the four of us. Believe me, we'll need every man before this is over."

"We won't need this—"

"Blue John, already the vultures are gathering to the scent of the carcass. Lundstrum talked continuously about us and the kid and the mine, and when I was down in Provo today, men were gathering to the railroad from far and near."

"So what? I don't—"

"Ida Mae Sorenson's gone too. No one knows where, but she's gone. There's also talk that the Soderbergs are gathering and heading here."

"Not the bishop?" Silvertip interrupted. "Why, that feller's thorny as cactus! I hope we don't have to tangle with him again. Once in this life's more than enough for any man!"

"For once," Blue John growled, "I agree with this idiot. If that bishop is on his way here, then I'm on my way to Canada."

"Nobody is going anywhere," Friendlessman said quietly. "He may be coming, and he may not be coming. If he is, we'll just have to take care of him."

"Judging by his two young sons," Doolin stated, "that bishop will be dangerous. We'll have to kill him too."

"Lots of luck," Silvertip drawled easily. "It can't be done. Me, I'm with Blue John. Let's either leave altogether or else leave the Soderbergs alone and go look for that gold ourselves."

"You are not the first who has had that foolish idea," Friendlessman stated, "nor would you be the first to fail. No, to find that gold we must first find the kid. Now, if you are thinking of flight, listen to this. I also heard talk about the law today. Maybe they are coming as well, and they are looking for five men who have pinned that kid down.

"You see, Blue John, our only chance is to remain together, for only then will we be strong. Additionally, we've got to work fast, very fast, and it will take every one of us to do it. Now leave that pistol in its holster and let's do some planning."

Blue John glared at Friendlessman, Friendlessman looked calmly back, and slowly the thin outlaw relaxed. "All right," he said quietly, "what do we do?"

"We follow them."

"Up that? No way, not in the dark, at least."

"Are you certain their tracks go up?" Friendlessman asked.

"Not theirs," Blue John replied. "His. The kid's tracks go up that hill, and the tracks of that old man start up, then vanish."

"Can't we follow them?"

"I told you, not in the dark."

Friendlessman walked to the base of the hill. For a long moment he stared upward; then he took a step to the side, then another, and suddenly he spun about, his face filled with excitement. "How much light do you need before we can start up that hill after them?"

Blue John gave the man a sharp look. "Why are you so anxious?" he questioned.

"I've been here before," Friendlessman replied, "right *here*. I just didn't realize it until I saw that cliff above me. Boys, right now we are within five miles of the richest deposit of gold ore in the world."

"How do you figure that?" Doolin questioned. "You ever seen the mine?"

"No, not exactly. But I saw Caleb Rhoades vanish one afternoon from right here, and less than four hours later he appeared again with two mules loaded with gold."

"Well, I'll be forever . . ." Doolin breathed excitedly, poking his stick into the fire and jumping to his feet. "Let's get up there after them."

"Don't be stupid," Friendlessman growled. "We could all be killed. There are old mines and glory holes all over this country, some that don't even have bottoms to them. Besides, there are that old man and the Soderberg kid, both of whom are likely expecting us. No, boys, we stay here until first daylight. Now, let's get some sleep."

Doolin watched as the men gradually crawled into their bedrolls and fell asleep. *Stupid,* he thought. *It isn't me that's stupid, it's them. I saw the gold, and that Soderberg kid had seen it too, and I ain't waiting around another night when I can get at it now. Besides, why should I share it with them, anyway? What have they ever done for me?*

Carefully Doolin eased himself from the log upon which he sat. No one moved, and so without a sound, he slipped into the trees and away. He thought of taking Friendlessman's horse but decided against it because of the noise. If the gold was really within five miles, he'd walk to where it was and use the kid's and the old man's horses to pack it out. Yes sir, he was finally on his way to becoming a mighty wealthy man.

33

Grandaddy Basin, Uintah Mountains—
Utah Territory—Again

At first I thought it was the wind. Somewhere out in the forest was a distant wailing, a sound unlike anything I had ever heard. It woke me from my sleep. I listened and almost pushed it out of my mind. Then it came more loudly, and suddenly I knew the cry was human, the cry of a man in trouble.

Carefully I arose and made my way up the hill behind my camp, coming finally to the level plateau I had crossed the day before. The trees around me were thick, rocks were plentiful, and deadfalls made progress increasingly difficult. Besides all that, the moon had set, and under the trees it was darker'n Lucifer's disposition. Yet I was making progress, for the man's screams and cries for help were getting louder, though he himself sounded weaker all the time.

I hurried, wondering what might have befallen the poor soul. The voice sounded familiar, and suddenly I thought of the old man. Was it he who screamed? Might he be in mortal danger?

Plunging ahead I stumbled over a deadfall, rolled down a small incline, lunged to my feet, and pushed on, my heart filled with fear for the old man. Suddenly a group of boulders loomed ahead; I skirted them, and on the other side I found the man.

"H-help!" he whined over and over as I cautiously approached.

I paused, staring into the intense darkness, unable to see a thing. "Where are you?" I called.

"Oh, thank the Lord," the man gasped. "I'm here, in this hole. Get me out!"

Well, right away I started grinning, for now there was no disguising the thin, reedy voice of beady-eyed Mr. Doolin, my erstwhile enemy. Nor was there any disguising the genuine fear he felt.

"Aren't you Mr. Doolin?" I asked.

"Yes, *yes!* Get me out of here, quickly! I can't hang on much longer, and—"

"It's awful dark," I said, "I can't see you. Tell me where you are and what happened."

"Oh for . . . There's no time, man! I'm falling! Help me, please help me!"

"What happened, Mr. Doolin? How did you get into that hole?"

"I . . . I fell in! I heard something—someone *laughing.* It . . . it frightened me. I ran . . . I . . . I fell in. Oh, *help me!* I think this is one of those bottomless pits, and I can't hold on . . ."

"Hold on? Mr. Doolin, I don't understand. What are you holding on to? If that is a bottomless pit, why aren't you still on your way down?"

"There's a tree lying across the hole, and I'm hanging on to it. Now give me a hand, man, or I'll fall. My hands are slipping, and you've got to hurry. Please . . ."

"So that's a real bottomless pit, is it? I've heard of them, heard they're all over the mountain up here. Some are old mines, but the others, the blackest ones with the cold air up near the tops of them, are old volcanic tubes that drop all the way down to the fires of hell. I once heard of a man who fell into one of them. He screamed all the way down, and folks say that two weeks later the echoes of his screams were still coming up. Mr. Doolin, is there cold air in that hole?"

Doolin gurgled and sputtered, and I crawled a little closer to the hole, picking up a couple of pebbles as I did so.

"H-help! I . . . I can't hold . . ."

While Doolin was crying and pleading, I tossed the two pebbles past him into the blackness of the pit. Satisfied, I grinned and sat back. "Is the air cool, Mr. Doolin?"

"Yes. *Yes!* Now help me, for—"

"Oh dear, I was afraid of that. There's no doubt that you're hanging above one of the bottomless holes this mountain is famous for."

"Are . . . are you sure?"

"Sure as can be."

"Well then, help me! Give me a hand so I can get *out!*"

"I can't get to you, Mr. Doolin. I just tried, and the side started to crumble. So far as I can tell, there's no other way for me to reach you. And we surely don't want *both* of us incinerating in the fires of hell, do we?"

Doolin groaned. "Do we?" I repeated quietly.

"Oh please! Help me—"

"Do we?"

"N-no," he answered weakly.

"Good. I hoped that you'd understand."

"But . . . but . . . oh, please help me!"

"I can't do it. Too dangerous. Why don't you just swing your legs up and around that old log and then hoist yourself up and crawl out on top of it?"

Doolin gnashed his teeth like a man who could stand a thing no longer, and I was reminded of how the scriptures say that in the last days there would be weeping and wailing and gnashing of teeth among the wicked. More and more I was seeing evidence of the scriptures being fulfilled.

"I tried!" Doolin wailed. "For heaven's sake, man, don't you think I tried. The log rolls every time I do that, and . . . Man, help me. My hands are slipping again."

"Mr. Doolin, I'd like to, I truly would. Trouble is, I'd be afraid of another bullet in my leg if I got you out."

There was instant stillness, and then, after maybe ten seconds, Doolin spoke again. "W-who is this? Who are you?"

"It's only me, Mr. Doolin. Hyrum Soderberg. You know, the evil, vicious killer you tried to cheat and whom lately you've been trying to eliminate."

There was a long gasp and then a choking sob from the weasel-like man in the hole. "H-Hyrum . . . Mr. Soderberg, I . . . I'm sorry, I truly am. Get . . . get me out of here, and I'll swear you are innocent before every court in the land. I will, I mean it! I'll even leave the mountain. Immediately! You can have all the gold. I don't want any at all. I just . . . Oh, my fingers are going! Help me! *Help me!*"

"It's an interesting thing to think about, isn't it, Mr. Doolin?" I asked casually as I leaned back and prepared to philosophize. "The endless fall, the volcanic fires? And think too of the reward you'll be facing for all the dishonest deeds you're so famous for at that assay shop. Ah, Mr. Doolin, you've been calling upon the Lord pretty regular the last little while, and that's good. You'll likely meet Him soon, and I think it is a fine idea to let Him know that you are on your way.

"How do you think He'll respond when He hears how you've

hounded a poor crippled kid like myself, one with a pure heart who's never on purpose done any real harm in his whole life? I'll bet He'll—"

"He'll judge you for murder too," the little man whined. "You let me die and it'll be murder, and you know it! Now help me, please . . ."

"How can I murder you, Mr. Doolin? I've never touched you, and I can't even see you!"

"Yes, but you'll let me fall—"

"Straight to the devil, I expect."

Doolin cried again, sobbed some more.

"You are a thief, Mr. Doolin. Is that not so?"

"No! I never—"

"Mr. Doolin, the truth! Remember the hole gaping open below you, and let me hear the truth."

The man groaned again. "Yes," he whispered, "yes, yes!"

"And you tried to steal the largest portion of my gold from me?"

"Y-yes . . ."

"And I am but the lastest in a long line of victims?"

"W-why are you doing this?"

"Satisfaction, Mr. Doolin. Am I not right?"

"Yes, yes, *yes!* Now *help* me! I can't—"

"Mr. Doolin, I am sorry to hear that," I said, interrupting his plea, "but you see, I knew it was true. Thieves are always known. To a man with little money and no honor, the obvious way to riches seems to be theft. Thievery, however, is a crime only for the very ignorant and in which only the most stupid ever indulge. There is a crass vulgarity in theft, Mr. Doolin, a definite indication that a man lacks intelligence and wit. Without even considering the moral implications, Mr. Doolin, the penalties of theft far outweigh any possible gain."

Doolin was silent, and so for a moment or two I let him stew. "Did you mean what you promised?" I finally asked.

"Oh yes, yes!"

"And if I let you live, you'll leave this mountain immediately, close up your shop in Provo, and go somewhere back east or out to California with all the other crooks?"

"Close . . . close my shop?"

"Of course. That must be part of the deal."

"All right, all right! I'll do anything you say."

"Swear it!"

"I . . . I swear!"

"And Mr. Doolin, there's something else. Us Soderbergs are naturally contrary, and it just isn't in us to lie down and roll over. Real honestly, we don't care whether school keeps or not. One of us gets mishandled, the rest of us will still keep a-coming. Now you do as I've said and leave, everything will be fine as oriental silk. Happen you decide otherwise, you'd better start going to Sunday School and acting like it. Otherwise, the law will be around, and so will *we*. You hear?"

"I . . . I hear."

"Very well," I said then, rising to my feet. "I now decree that you will not die tonight. See you around, Mr. Doolin."

There was a strangled cry. "You . . . you can't—"

"No, Mr. Doolin, you're wrong. I can. Adios."

Again he screamed. There was a slight scuffling sound on the log, and Doolin's scream was cut short in a desperate gasp. I heard his fingers slip further, and suddenly with a soul-piercing screech, Mr. Doolin, hopefully lately of Provo, was gone.

34

Between Lodgepole Lake and
Fern Lake—Grandaddy Basin

The thud came about when I'd expected it to come, not more than two seconds after Doolin's hands had lost their grip on the log. I heard him hit, heard his scream cut short in surprise, and then I heard him moan and fall to the earth in what sounded like a swoon. I looked at the hole and grinned wickedly, for the tossed pebbles had told me the hole was not more than seven or eight feet deep, and *all* holes have cold air in them, for cold air always settles.

Doolin had expected to drop a long way, and I'd done my best to help that expectation along. I reckon when he'd fallen only a foot or two and hadn't been hurt at all, the shock was just too much for his weasely system to endure.

"Like I said," I murmured into the darkness, "see you around, Mr. Doolin. And next time, you'd better think twice before you take on a Soderberg."

Slowly I made my way back to my camp, careful to avoid the same problem encountered by Mr. Doolin. In spite of my brave words, I'd been shot full of luck as far as Doolin was concerned, and I knew it. I hadn't dug that hole, and I certainly hadn't led him into it. And there *were* some deep holes around, very deep ones. If he'd fallen into one of them, I don't really know what I'd have done. Probably helped him, I reckon. I couldn't have lived with myself and done otherwise. Of course, maybe I couldn't have lived with myself then, either. He was surely a miserable little man.

When I was nearly to my camp, however, I got my own set of fears and chills and fluttering fantods, and for a minute or two I felt sorry for Mr. Doolin. Off in the woods, sounding high up but somehow real close, I heard laughter, or what sounded like it. I stopped, waited, heard only the wind, decided I must be imagining things, started on, and then heard it again.

Haunts, I thought, the same haunts that had driven my friend Doolin into his "bottomless" pit. Why was it that everywhere I went I ran into haunts? I stared about me; the wind whistled through the pines; down at camp my horse snorted and stomped its hoof; and I knew it would do no good to go seeking the haunt out. Haunts can't be sought but have to come out on their own. If this one wanted me to, I'd see it soon enough. Until then . . .

At camp I checked things out, and everything seemed to be as I had left it. I settled down for a little more rest, heard that crazy laughter again, worried about it, stared up through the trees at the few stars, and grinned again when I thought of Mr. Doolin. Like I'd promised my pa, I'd been gentle as an elephant tromping through a herd of nasty-biting dogs. I hadn't hurt him at all. Nor did I feel truly evil for allowing him to think what he wanted concerning that same subject. Somehow it just didn't seem possible to go around correcting everybody's misconceptions. Still, I truly hoped that he'd had enough, for I knew that next time he might really get hurt. However, I fully believed that I would see him again, and then his lesson would come much more severely. His kind simply do not learn *anything* easily.

How still the night! How strange the sheen on the dark waters of the tiny lake! How bright the distant stars!

Down at the lake the water lapped quietly against the rocky shore, and beyond that, little moved, little stirred—only the water and the wind blowing down from the high peaks, and me as I wrapped my blanket more tightly about myself and waited.

Tired as I was, I was in no mood to sleep, and my ears began making a check on all the tiny sounds around me, sounds that had seemed nonexistent until I focused on them. They were sounds of birds, of insects, or of night-prowling animals, and all were familiar to me. But in every place some of the sounds were different. Dead branches make a rattle of their own; grass or leaves rustle in a certain way; yet in no two places are the sounds exactly the same. Always before I slept I checked the sounds in my mind. It was a trick I'd learned from Zene Hill and was something I'd do till the day I died.

I thought of that then and wondered again if I was going to die. Those fellers were still after me, the old man probably had me marked as well, my leg was not yet healed, and I was alone on the mountain with nowhere to go.

How much could a person endure? How long could a man con-

tinue? These things I asked myself, for speaking to myself is a habit
I developed when I was younger and lonely and so self-conscious
about my crippled leg. Yet even as I asked my questions, the answers
were there before me. If a man be a man indeed, he must always go
on, he must always endure.

I thought then of an account written by the Greek historian
Herodotus wherein he detailed the courage of a certain man taken
captive by the Spartans. This man had one foot locked in the stocks,
which were made of wood bound by iron. To escape, he measured
his foot against the size of the hole, cut off the offending front portion
of his foot with his own hand, withdrew his mutilated appendage,
and for three days eluded capture and made his way back to his own
lines. To me, that and not giving up to death is the way of a man.

Death seems to be an end to torture, to struggle, to suffering, but
of course I knew when I thought about it that such was not the case.

Still, death is very much an end to some things: to earthly
warmth, to the light of a morning sunrise, to the beauty of a running
horse, to the smell of damp earth after a rain, to a mother's smile, to
the walk of a woman when she knows someone watches, to the
savoring of a fine book—with death, these things would be in my
past, and I would have moved into the realm of spirits.

No, I would not die. I was not ready. There was too much I had
yet to do, to see, to feel, to learn. I yearned to serve a mission, to give
myself to a cause that was greater than anything I could ever of myself be. I yearned also to have a wife, to hold closely in my heart a
woman of my own, and to feel of her love while I gave her all of my
own. I yearned as well to sire a family of fine sons and lovely
daughters, to watch them grow, to ache with them in their sorrows
and rejoice with them in their triumphs. I yearned too to have them
feel toward me as I felt toward my own father, for such love and deep
respect was truly a powerful force.

I yearned to laugh, to see the humor that existed all around me.
Only the past winter I had read a copy of Mark Twain's new novel,
The Adventures of Huckleberry Finn, and I had enjoyed myself almost more than I could imagine. Laughter to me was a tonic easing
the common burdens of my life, and for some reason I did not feel
that I had laughed in my life anywhere near enough.

I yearned finally to strengthen my mind and my spirit, to increase
my testimony of the divinity and of the atoning sacrifice of Jesus
Christ, and to understand His Gospel of salvation. I would do this by
prayer and by reading the profoundest thoughts penned by the great-

est men and women of all ages. I yearned to read the Talmud and the Koran and the writings of Confucius, and especially to study our own scriptures ever more deeply, for in those works are the most inspiring thoughts ever written upon the face of this earth.

Having read them, I intended to make those thoughts mine, for by thinking them, by praying over them continuously, and by treasuring up in my heart such immense amounts of wisdom, I would be lifted so that I would become a better man than I otherwise might have been.

For all these things I yearned deeply, and so I would not give up. Not yet.

In the dimness of first dawn I broke camp and rode slowly toward the towering mountains before me. Once or twice I saw the tracks of the old man's horse, or traces of them. But I was not worried. The trail was difficult to follow, but the problem was not one to worry about. There was simply no other way for the old man to go but straight ahead, and so there I rode.

My leg throbbed with an endless pounding, and twice I stopped to bathe the festering wound in a cold stream, grimacing in pain as I attempted to squeeze out the vile fluids of infection that the yarrow compress seemed to be bringing out. Such efforts helped a little, I thought, but I knew that I needed medical help, and I needed it badly.

The trees around me were spruce and alpine fir. Occasionally when I rode out on some knoll, over the tops of the trees I could see the peaks and ridges above timberline, where I was certain I was going.

White streaks of snow showed on the bare rocks; above, on the peaks themselves, were the remnants of ancient glaciers, the ice and snow of many winters. Here and there a stunted fir or a lightning-struck tree would indicate an effort by the forest to advance beyond the limit set for it, an attempt to encroach upon the lonely domain of the lichen and the moss.

I circled another lake, one I was certain was called Fern, and then I climbed again, gradually moving southward toward a projecting arm of East Grandaddy Mountain. Grassy meadows opened and closed around me, tiny lakes were everywhere, and as I climbed, the forest grew thick and still. I was in the drainage of the East Fork of Rock Creek, and I knew that Zene Hill would be somewhere nearby, probably to the north, herding Old Man Aagard's sheep. He would also be alone, and I felt bad about that, for I was not where I had taken money to be.

I came suddenly upon the remains of another old campfire, and here again I saw what looked to be the suggestion of another track, scarcely to be made out. Yet it was fresh, and I was certain it had been made by the old man.

Carefully I studied the site, going from place to place with my eyes only, holding my horse still. On a limb hung a pothook made from a forked branch, such as Zene had taught me to use. It showed wear, and evidently it had been relied upon more than once. Here, I felt certain, was another of the old man's camps, one he had used while prospecting in the area.

A small lake was close by, and a spring ran a trickle of water into it. The shore was rocky, but trees came almost to the edge of the water.

I pulled up the horse inside the trees to consider. I was in a small basin, surrounded on three sides by steep mountains, except at the point where I had come through, and undoubtedly also at the point where the stream exited. Once outside, the stream cut more rapidly to join a larger stream, and that, I was certain, ran finally into Rock Creek.

I returned to the campfire and looked all about. So far as I could tell, the trail ended there, except for the walk to the edge of the lake. Might the old man have entered the lake and walked along it to hide the way of his passing?

Suddenly thunder rumbled, and I looked up, surprised. A thunder shower, one of the afternoon storms that frequent the Uintahs, was boiling my way, and I knew I was going to get wet. More thunder rumbled, lightning flashed rapidly, and yet there in that cove in the towering mountains I felt somehow secure.

I thought again of the laughter I had heard the night before. Had it been the old man laughing at me? Of course I didn't know, but deep-down I was certain it had been the old man, who had somehow known where Doolin and I were and what we had been doing.

I took another circle around the dead campfire, searching. But there was nothing, nothing at all. I tried again, still farther out, but the results were the same.

The storm was building, a slow, sullen storm that could burst with unbelievable fury at any moment. Moreover, somewhere about were Friendlessman and what was left of his gang. I knew of two who would be gone—Doolin and the one they called the Boss. I'd also noticed that Loose-lip Lundstrum was missing when I'd watched them eating my fish two nights before. But then, so had Friendlessman been missing, and I *knew* he was still around. So the gang had been cut by two, I hoped, and maybe by three. That still gave them three armed men, tough men as well. And who was I to fight alone and unarmed against such—

I felt the shock of the bullet before I heard the explosion, and the next thing I knew I was lying upon the hard earth of the mountain. There was a great pain in my stomach, and I was certain I had been gut-shot. Still, they would be coming, and I must not wait for them there.

Reaching out I gasped with pain and began to crawl, and strangely, I got stronger the farther I went. Looking down finally to my wound, I found that the slug had hit my belt buckle and had only grazed across my stomach. I later learned that it had hit the pommel of the saddle even before that. Once again I had been lucky. Or blessed, maybe, as Ma would say. Like I mentioned earlier, I'd had recent troubles with my prayers, somehow avoiding saying them. But now I'd become a real believer, and the past few days had brought me closer to the Lord than I'd ever been.

It's passing sad how it takes such heavy trials and nefarious tribulations to humble a man. Still, such difficulties do bring humility, and I reckon it is good that the Lord has *something* that can get the job done. Anyway, it seemed like maybe my tiny amount of faith was paying off.

I pushed myself to my feet, caught my breath with the pain, and looked about for the horse. Then I realized it had run off, and suddenly I knew I was alone now, truly alone. If I was to get out of this, I had only the Lord and my wits to rely upon. That meant that, happen the Lord chose not to get involved any further, I was in real trouble.

Still, us Soderbergs are doing folk, so I put my good leg forward, pulled my bad leg after it, held my hands to my throbbing stomach, and started out for the high-up cliffs that rose before me.

35

East Grandaddy Mountain Bench— Utah Territory

The thunder pounded upon its great drums, rolling cataracts of sound down off the wide reaching cliffs and exploding them against the quivering forests below. Lightning shot in vivid streaks across the sky, huge flashes of light that seemed not like the lightning seen in the lowlands but like a heaven of flame gaping open above me, giving me a view of the blazing heart of some other world.

Yet the rain did not come. The atmosphere was charged with electricity, and the streaks of flame seemed to bound and rebound from the peaks above me.

I looked down at the tiny lake below. A sullen sheet, it lay open to the sky, shining like a great bowl of mercury. I lay in a nest of boulders backed against the towering cliff, and I knew it would end there—from that point I had nowhere to go.

The clouds drifted about, now settling over me, now tearing themselves apart so that I could peer through and glimpse the dark trees, the great craggy rocks, the bleak grayness of the lake.

"Dear Lord," I whispered as I stared downward into the gloom, "this is surely one time when I could use a little help. If you could just temper a little with the elements . . ."

A bullet suddenly smashed into a nearby rock, and as I rolled away the clouds split open and the rain came, a hard driving rain that swept with sheets of fury down the cliffs and into the staggering trees. I stared up, amazed, and then, realizing that I was about to drown, I rolled over again, scrambled under a huge boulder that had fallen from the cliff above, saw a small hole or crack in the cliff, and instinctively dove into it.

For a second or two I slid downward; then I was brought up short against a fairly level rock or floor. For a moment I lay still, listening to the storm outside, and then gradually I became aware that I was in a cave, or at least a cavity, in the rock.

"So you found it," a voice suddenly declared from the darkness, and with my heart in my throat I spun about to stare into the blackness before me.

"Who—"

"Hyrum Soderberg, in spite of my warning, you've come to this place like a bee goes to honey. I even tried to frighten you and the others away last night in the dark, but no, you wouldn't frighten."

"The insane laughter was from you?"

"Of course. And it might very well have been insane, for I couldn't bear to think of you being destroyed like my . . . my . . . Oh, how I wish that I had never heard of this gold!"

There was the scratching of a match, a flicker of light as a lantern was lit, and suddenly I found myself gazing upon the old man who had abandoned me two days before.

And that wasn't all I was gazing upon, not by a long shot. Everywhere about me was the glitter of gold. The walls, the ceiling, even the floor, were laced with it. Moreover, there were mounds of bars, anciently smelted, stacked against one wall in three huge piles. Each of those bars was about a foot long, maybe four inches wide, and maybe two or two-and-a-half inches high. Roughly, I guessed there must be over a hundred of those bars in the three piles.

Near the piles of smelted gold were several pieces of old Spanish armor—breastplates, helmets, swords, and a single pike, and several smaller pieces of armor that must have covered arms and legs. What I really stared at, however, were the bones, the complete skeletons of at least four men, who lay just beyond the armor.

"Yes," the old man said, "you're looking at one of the sacred lost mines of the Utes. There are actually several of them, and this one is perhaps the least of them all."

"Who *are* you?" I suddenly asked.

The old man smiled. "I think you know, for you've suspected it all along. I am Caleb Rhoades, who sent my younger brother to his death. That's why I tried to escape you, my young friend. As I said, there's a curse upon this gold, or maybe it's a blessing. It depends on how you look at it. Nevertheless, this gold can be used only by the Indians, who do not use it selfishly, or by the Lord, for the building of his kingdom, and that's not selfish either. If it's sought for by others, no matter who they are, it always brings disaster.

"Until he died, this gold was Brother Brigham's, and he stewarded it for the Lord. But now they don't send for it any more, and I alone am trustee. I take a little now and then, bless lives here and there, and use a very little for my own needs. I suppose when I die it'll go back to the Indians until they and the Lord decide to bring it forth once more."

"Tell me about it," I asked, still awed by what was so brightly spread before me. "Tell me about this gold."

The old man smiled and shifted, and it was only then that I discovered he had hurt his leg again. "Yes," he said, noticing my gaze. "A rock fell on it, and I fear I'll be joining my Spanish brethren here, who were interlopers just as much as me. I don't sorrow over that, but over my wife, who hates so much to be alone."

Old Caleb Rhoades sighed and looked up at the roof of the mine, where myriads of strands of ore flickered and danced in the lantern light.

"Gold," he breathed. "Doesn't the very word itself create visions and dreams? And truly those visions are nothing when compared with the reality of this.

"Young man, this gold is part of a vast belt of quartz that runs in a gray vein across and through the entire width of these mountains. It is in such an unusual formation that for years prospectors have stumbled across it and haven't seen it at all. Yet the Indians did, and for untold generations they made use of it as ornamentation in their worship and their ceremonies.

"Then came the black-robes, the conquering padres. They enslaved the Indians and forced them to mine deeply and without thought to safety. They thought only of gold, of the wealth they were sending back to their homeland, and to them who had come so far in search of this wealth, no price was too great to pay in the taking of it.

"For years that went on, until the Indians could stand it no longer. Then came a rebellion, short and bloody, and the black-robes were slain where they stood. These four fell here; I've found the remains of two more outside. One group of them made a desperate stand further down on Rock Creek. I've found other remains over above Whiterocks, and who knows where else they fell?

"Some, of course, must have escaped, for there are stories that they returned and were again driven away. Following that, except for a few wandering parties, the Spanish came no more."

"So how did the gold become sacred?" I asked.

"By the blood of the Indians that was shed both in mining it and in driving the black-robes away. So it was told me by my friend Happy Jack, a Ute who knows as much about this gold as any man alive. According to him, the Utes call the mines Carre shin-ob, which means 'There, the Great Spirit,' or 'There dwells the Great Spirit.'

"According to Happy Jack, Old Chief Walker or, more correctly, Wakera, had a vision some time before the Mormons appeared here in the West. In the vision he was shown the yellow metal and was told that he was to guard it until the big hats came, and then was to give it to them.

"Wakera thought Bridger and the mountain men were the big hats, but they laughed at his tale of a vision and so got nothing. Then when Brother Brigham came, leading the Saints, he was also told of the vision. Brigham Young did not laugh, and Wakera gave the gold in the mines to him."

"So how did you learn of it?"

The old man smiled. "Brigham Young couldn't come to the mines personally, so he called my father, John Rhoades, who took an oath upon the Book of Mormon that he would never reveal the locations of the sacred mines to any other man. For several years he came alone into these mountains, taking out mule trains of gold for the Church. The Utes protected him in this, and things prospered. Then he became ill, and Brigham Young, needing gold again, agreed with him that I might come in his place. Old Wakera agreed as well, and I took the same oath as my father had taken.

"I continued taking gold from these mines until Brigham Young's death in 1877, and since then I've come here always by stealth and always alone. Yet I take little of the precious money rock and use it only for my own small needs and to help a few others. Truly I dare do nothing else, for I fear my oath and the curse."

"Yet you revealed this mine to your brother?"

"No, not this one. I told Enock only of a small mine I myself had prospected out and excavated. I did not think the Lord would think that mine was sacred, but obviously I was wrong, and my brother paid for my mistake with his life."

"You know the man who killed him." It was a statement, not a question, and old Caleb Rhoades looked quickly up at me.

"Yes," he said quietly, "I know. I just did not know where, and I did not understand exactly why."

"Who was it?"

"The Ute who rode into Tabby's camp after you, the tall man with the scar on his face. I think that scar was given him by my brother. He is a hard man, but I know his heart, and he is not a bad man. He simply did what he had been charged to do so that the honor and integrity of his people would be protected.

"You see, the Ute only watched until Enock went into that mine and removed the gold. Once he had done that his doom was sealed, for the Indians have sworn that no man will live who takes this gold selfishly."

"Well," I said finally, "I'm confuseder'n a blind buffalo bull in a bumbleberry bush. Why didn't you tell me who you were? And why didn't you tell me about who had killed your poor brother, instead of making me try to defend myself?"

Caleb Rhoades sighed. "I feared for you, Hyrum Soderberg. I truly did. I thought if you knew who I was, you would also try to force the secret of the gold from me. Many others have, you know, including Felix Friendlessman."

"I told you I didn't want the gold."

"Yes, you did. But at that time you had never seen such a sight as this—millions of dollars literally lying about for the taking. Now that you do see it, young man, do you not wish to take at least a little of it with you?"

I looked about me again at the glittering walls and ceiling, at the smelted and stacked bars, at the incredible, incalculable wealth. From the floor I lifted a fist-sized rock and hefted it, gazing at the gold that was laced through it. "Tell me about this gold," I said quietly. "What sort of gold is it, and how did it come to be here?"

"You've asked the right person," the old man said. "I've studied the subject for years. As you can see there is more gold here in this mine than there is rock. Most of it is wire shaped, extruded through small openings in the surrounding rock during some past era of great volcanic heat and pressure. And that, by the way, is when and how *all* gold is formed, in the pressured and fissured rock above huge and unbelievably hot volcanic batholiths.

"There is also leaf gold here, crystaline structures formed within pockets in the quartz vein. It's formed in the same way, only under slightly different circumstances.

"Near here I found a mound of tiny gold nuggets that were almost like kernels of corn. With those nuggets I also found the bones of a slain Spaniard, and so I left that entire fortune where it lay. I have no idea how those nuggets were formed, and I have never found them in their natural setting.

"Finally, the few actual geologists and mineralogists who have seen this gold call it five-niner gold, meaning that in its natural state it is .99999 pure. Truly there is more wealth here than any man on earth has ever imagined."

The old man took a deep breath, lifted a handful of golden detritus from the floor, held it up, and let it cascade down, sparkling in the lantern light as it fell.

"Are you not now tempted, my young Hyrum Soderberg? Can you not imagine the power and glory such wealth would bring you?"

Again I hefted the rock I held, tossed it into the air, caught it, and saw the gleam of the gold within it; then I tossed it toward the four whitened skeletons.

There was power indeed within that gold, and honor and glory as well. But power, riches, honor, and glory, those were transitory things, here and quickly gone. Riches were a claim to distinction for those who had no other right to it, just as the claiming of ancestry is most important to those who have done nothing themselves. Yet often the ancestor from whom such people claim descent would never be allowed in their homes.

Great families were often founded by pirates, freebooters, or energetic peasants and farmers who happened to be in the right place at the right time and took advantage of it. The founder would, in many instances, look with as great a disdain upon his descendants.

No, to me the goal of life could not be what Caleb Rhoades had described. To me it was to see, to know, to learn, to understand. Never could I see a far mountain peak or an unread book of good quality or the pure innocence of a tiny child's face but my heart would stumble and my throat grow tight.

Up to a point a man's life is shaped by environment, heredity, and movements and changes in the world about him. Then there comes a time when it lies within each individual's grasp to shape the clay of his life into the sort of thing he wishes it to be. Only the weak blame their parents, their race, their times, their lack of good fortune, quirks of fate, or, as in my case, accidents of birth for what they become in life. Everyone has it within his power to say, this I am today, that I shall be tomorrow. And then to succeed, the wish must be implemented with deeds.

"Any man would be a fool to claim that the sight of such wealth doesn't tempt him," I answered honestly. "Of course I'm tempted. Still, I'll take none of it with me, for I don't want the troubles that would accompany it."

"Is that your only reason?"

"No, not altogether. My father has cautioned me all my life never to seek gold, for so the prophets have counseled. Because I love my father and honor our prophets, I'll respect that. My father has also shown me, within our own small ward, the misery of those who have allowed themselves to love wealth. Laying aside the troubles that come with it, I don't want the misery and smallness of spirit that the love of gold seems to bring. And Mr. Rhoades, I fear that if I took even a little of this, I could learn to love it very quickly."

"And so, with hardly any thought, you choose a life of poverty?"

"There have been many thoughts, Caleb Rhoades, and of a truth I made this decision long ago when I decided who I truly was and who I wanted with all my heart to be. Nor will I be poor. You see, my gold is out there, in the morning sunrise on a mountain stream, in a V of geese winging north in the spring, in the trembling of an aspen leaf in the late fall, in the bugle of a bull elk on a frosty morning. It's in a noble passage of literature penned by a man who was grasping for the same almost unattainable heights of soul as I am; it's in an inspiring verse of scripture from the lips of God himself.

"It's also in the face of my mother and father, in the dignity and courage of their lives; it's in the love and pride I feel for my brothers and sisters, and in the trembling I once experienced when I felt the power of the Spirit of God. Finally, it's in the awesome glory of the temple of the Most High, where someday I will go.

"No, Brother Rhoades, I don't lust for this gold. Certainly I could use it, for my family is struggling terribly. Yet I'll get along without it, and one day I'll be the stronger for doing so."

I sat silently, and Caleb Rhoades stared at me, his eyes alive in the dancing of the light from the lantern. "Perhaps," he said finally as he lifted the gold-laced rock and tossed it back to me, and his voice was quivering as he spoke, "p-perhaps we *will* get out of here."

"We will," I declared strongly. "If there is a way, we will."

There was a sudden noise at the entrance to the old mine. I turned and heard a scuffling and sliding, and then with a cry of fear a form slid to the floor beside me. It looked up, and open-mouthed, I found myself staring into the bruised and muddy face of a bedraggled Ida Mae Sorenson!

"Oh, Hyrum," she cried out as she scrambled to her feet, and seconds later she was trembling within my arms.

"It's all right," I told her gently as I stroked her face, not even wondering how she had found us, and at that moment I was finally certain that it was all right.

36

East Grandaddy Mountain Bench—
Utah Territory—Again

The afternoon broke in a crimson flood upon the storm-shattered mountains, massive shoulders of granite thrown out from the fires of the earth's beginning.

Through the mists that were left from the rain I watched the men move slowly up the slope, small figures spread in a line, all moving toward me, all armed and ready. There were at least ten of them that I could see, and the magnitude of their numbers staggered me. Where had they recruited so many, and how had they come so quickly?

It wasn't happening the way it was supposed to happen. There were the cliffs behind me, and I needed more time, time to get away from the trap that the cliffs had become. But the men were driving me now, and I knew it; they were running me, making certain that I wasn't going to move around them.

It was late afternoon, three hours and a little more until sunset. The sun poured through the mists of the rain, creating a brilliant rainbow that arched up and away to the east. The light splashed golden on the rocks below, and I realized that there too was the gold I truly sought, and in fact already had.

"Ida Mae?" I said softly.

"Yes?"

Just hearing her voice did my heart good and made me believe that what I was planning might work. I hoped it would, for more than ever I wanted to live now, wanted to grow older with her, to share my life with her.

"Don't you forget. When I lead these fellers away, you help that old man down through the rocks. He'll find the horses; you help him onto one of them and then you climb on another and the both of you get away from here as fast as you can get."

"But Hyrum—"

"Ida Mae, I'd dearly love for you to stay, but don't you do it. It's hard enough worrying about my own hide. If I had to worry about protecting yours as well, especially since the only weapon I have is this old Spanish pike—well, you understand, don't you?"

"I do."

"Good. I'll meet you soon as I'm able."

There was silence on the mountain, and somewhere off to my left a marmot whistled shrilly. From farther along another answered, and then Ida Mae spoke again.

"Hyrum, I . . . I . . ." She paused, and I could tell that her voice was shaking with emotion. In my mind I tried to picture her, to see how she was looking at me. But I couldn't do it. All I could see were those outlaw fellers, coming forward—

"Hyrum, I love you!"

"I love you too," I said quietly, savoring the thrill that surged through me at her words. "Now go," I said, and then I moved. Hobbling forward, I staggered through the rocks, trying desperately to move away from Ida Mae and old Caleb Rhoades. A rifle shot rang out, a rock nearby shattered as the slug whined away, and then I was on my stomach and crawling. I could not go fast, yet I went steadily, and it is amazing how much ground a man can cover when he feels the urgency I felt. Nor did I feel fear, for there was no time for that, nor was this the place.

Another rifle boomed, a larger rifle, maybe a Sharps buffalo gun, and I cringed as the huge slug whapped past, sounding very close. Then suddenly I was there, where I had decided I must be. I squirmed through the boulders to see where the men were located and to decide what I must do to prepare.

Of the ten that I could count, only one was on a horse, and that would have to be Felix Friendlessman. He was much closer than the others, whom I could now see were some reinforcements I had never before seen, and the outlaws Silvertip and Blue John and—

Well, that dirty little sneak and liar! There was Doolin, big as life, after he'd promised he'd let me be, and it was him who was firing the big buffalo gun!

I grinned again, but it was more a gritting of my teeth than it was a smile. "Mr. Doolin," I muttered, "you come any closer, you'll run smack into a Soderberg with real fur on his brisket. I've come up mighty shy of patience in this last toss of the dice, and I'm ready to add up your points. Mr. Doolin, you can bank on that."

Yet still he came on, and so I looked away, at Friendlessman now, who was that much closer. I waited until he'd come through the dark green of the edge of the pines, and then I began to move back into a higher field of boulders. I picked my way carefully up the slope, glancing behind me, not wanting to stumble and lose time, yet not wanting to lose sight of Friendlessman either. Yet I caught only glimpses of the man, and I did not feel safe.

The slope was not steep where I climbed, and the boulders, huge monoliths of black stone, seemed almost uniformly placed, like an abandoned, petrified orchard. It was not a good place to stand with an ancient Spanish pike and face a man who had two Colts and all the time in the world in which to use them.

I moved back a little farther and came to an open place where no great rocks lay. It was spotted with patches of holly and cliffrose, but there was nothing to use for cover, not on the entire, gravelly, nearly one hundred feet of ground that stretched upward to the great stone cliffs above me.

Perhaps I could make it, but not straight up. It was now too steep, too open. I would have to angle across the slope and Friendlessman would have time to shoot me. Still, it was worth trying, and it was better than staying where I was. I would have to forget about Friendlessman and the others and concentrate on reaching the great bulging cliff. There I might escape—or I might not—but there I would most surely have led them away from Ida Mae and Caleb Rhoades.

I was in the open then, hobbling diagonally across the open space, my boots digging hard into the muddy talus of the slope. Almost at once I felt knotted pain in my wounded leg, that and the wetness of blood. But I kept going, not looking back and trying not to picture Felix Friendlessman closing in on me, or the others, farther back, taking aim with their rifles.

I cut through a patch of cliffrose, getting a better foothold and running as hard as I could with my club foot and wounded leg. But then I came suddenly onto a spine of smooth rock—it humped no more than two feet above the ground—and here I lost my footing and slipped to my hands and knees. I tried to get up and stumbled again, then I rolled over the side of the smooth rock surface and finally lunged to my feet.

I saw movement then, quick movement, off behind that smooth hump of rock, and instantly my breath caught. But it was only an animal, I was certain of it—probably a marmot. But I didn't have time to study it, for Friendlessman was coming still closer, and I needed desperately to hurry.

Anxiously my mind searched for a way out of the trap I was in, some great military strategy that Tacitus or Pliny or some other ancient had discovered and that would also serve me. But there was nothing in my mind, nothing but the growing understanding of what Friendlessman was going to do.

I was climbing again, less than twenty feet from the rubble at the foot of the cliff, when Friendlessman's voice finally reached me.

"Soderberg!"

I stopped, catching my breath and letting it out slowly before coming around. I knew I would never make the rubble, but perhaps now it wouldn't matter. Enough time had passed, and the old man and Ida Mae would surely be safe.

I watched Friendlessman walk out of the maze of boulders below; he had left his horse and now was afoot, facing me. His Colt pistols were holstered, but his hands hung close to them. He came on slowly, his face calm and his eyes not straying from my own.

"Why don't you show us where the gold is?" he asked as he advanced up the slope. "You've no chance against us, and if you'll cooperate, we will go easy on you."

He was not looking at the ground but was feeling his way along with each careful step, his dark eyes boring relentlessly into mine.

"You want to show us, don't you," he declared suddenly. "You want to, but you are stubborn as old man Rhoades, and you don't know how to change."

He was through the cliffrose now, still coming slowly along. "It will be easy, Soderberg," he called. "Drop that silly stick. Give me the word and I will call the men off. You perhaps noticed that we have added reinforcements? There will be many more, all of whom consider you to be their enemy. Your only hope of living is with me, and I will give the word as quickly as you agree to show me the mine."

I said nothing but stood silently, facing Felix Friendlessman and watching him move across the small field of muddy talus.

"Decide quickly, my young friend. Tell us of your own choice and easily, or refuse and tell us anyway as we slowly take your life." He seemed almost to be smiling. "Thinking of dying does tighten a man's nerves, doesn't it."

Friendlessman was ready, standing on his own ground, and for the first time I felt the fear of dying rise up within me. There was no way I could get to him, no way at all. Yet he could shoot and I would die a little at a time, and who knew what I would say as I suffered? How could I possibly keep from betraying the location of the sacred mine, especially when I was so powerless before him? Oh, if only I could stop him!

But no, I had no time, no chance.

Unless Friendlessman hesitated, or was thrown off guard.

My gaze went from the talus to the spine of slick stone where I had slipped. Again I thought I saw movement there, not much, but . . . pesky marmot. Didn't it understand there was great danger in this place?

Quickly I studied the spine of rock. If I could draw Friendlessman to that point, if I could startle him, jiggle him somehow, if I could throw him off balance only for an instant, then perhaps I could get to him with the pike. If I could do all that . . .

And the other men were into the orchard of boulders now, still climbing.

No—one thing at a time. Slowly I began again to back away.

Friendlessman shook his head. "Don't be foolish. You will never make it. Not ever."

I was still edging back, covering six, eight, almost ten feet before Friendlessman started forward again. I stopped, watched him come out of the talus and onto the spine of rock, watched him grope with one foot before stepping onto the smooth, rounded surface.

As Friendlessman's foot inched forward again, I stepped to the side, and with an underhanded fling I chucked the rock I still held, the rock that Caleb Rhoades had tossed back to me, the one that was so heavily laden with gold.

Friendlessman was with me, his right-hand Colt revolver out and swinging onto me, but the movement shifted his weight, and my rock, hitting him in the shoulder, threw him off balance. His boots slipped on the smooth stone, and even as he fired and fired again he was falling back, his free hand outstretched and clawing for stability.

Before me Friendlessman seemed suddenly suspended, and lifting the ancient pike I started forward, aware that he had caught his balance and that his Colt pistol was coming down once more upon me.

I saw that big gun dropping down in line with my body, and I

knew that there I would die. With the late afternoon sun on my face
and with the rocks of the mountain beneath me, I would die. It was
not fair, for I did not deserve such an end when a woman like Ida Mae
Sorenson waited for me. Yet Pa had told me that in this life there was
no such thing as fairness. There was only ultimate, and eternal, justice.

Was I feeling sorry for myself? Yes, I think so. Yet I was also
feeling sorry for Ida Mae and our children who would never be, who
would never feel my love or live to enjoy life as I had. I was also feeling sorry that unfairness had become so rampant and uncontrolled,
and suddenly that sorrowful feeling made me angry!

"Friendlessman," I shouted, "shoot! Do it now, but do it well, for
I will be coming for you, and there's no stopping a man who knows
he's in the right!"

Friendlessman hesitated, his dark eyes glaring into mine, and I
lifted the ancient pike to the ready and took another step toward him.
Surprised, he involuntarily took a step backward, and then his face
set and—

Suddenly there was a slight hiss, and from the air a rope settled
down around the body and poised arm of Felix Friendlessman. There
was a quick jerk and he was falling. The pistol went off into the air
and clattered away from his hand, and I found myself staring once
again into the grinning face of my younger brother Ernest.

"You did it again, Hy," he said easily while I stood gaping.
"You've just got to stop being so doggone predictable!"

I had started to grin myownself, for he had been the marmot I
thought I had seen. Suddenly there was another explosion, and rock
chips once more stung my face. I ducked down, heard the rattle of
more rifle shots, wiped a streak of blood away from my cheek, and
looked up in time to see one of the most amazing sights I had ever
seen.

Down the slope those men had seen Friendlessman go down and
had started to come to his aid. Suddenly there was rifle fire among
them, and they held up, bewildered, as a giant of a man with a missing front tooth and a star on his chest rose up from behind a boulder
directly before them.

Marshal Tinsdale, as he lived and breathed, direct from the Provo
jail! I could hardly believe it! What was *he* doing there?

Three men suddenly ducked down into the pines, and I hadn't
even had time to more than notice them when they hastily backed out

of the timber again, their hands in the air, followed by three men on horses. The men held rifles upon them.

Those three riders looked awfully familiar. Criminently, I thought. They were my brothers, Lyman, Jim, and Johnny! Now where had they—

I heard another scuffling, and from the boulders emerged the outlaws Blue John and Alpha Rachel "Silvertip" Garrett. Silvertip was striding up the hill, grinning like he always did, and putting up no struggle at all. Blue John, on the other hand, was dragging his feet somewhat but was being helped along pretty regular by the boots and stove-lid hands of my black-suited father, Jons Soderberg.

"Hyrum," Pa called out, "are you and Ernest all right?"

"Yeah, Pa. We're fine."

"I expected that you would be. I told your mother and Polly that both of you had a knowing way and that they needn't worry about either of you."

"Mr. Bishop, sir," Silvertip said then, his voice warm and cheerful enough to light a candle from, "what you say is sure true. That Hyrum and the little one up there with the rope sneak around quieter'n tumblebugs falling off a buffalo chip. Why, twice they slicked our horses right out from under us, and with Blue John around that ain't exactly an easy thing to do. Yes sir, Mr. Bishop Soderberg, sir, you've a right to be proud. Them're *my* kind of boys!"

"Silvertip," Blue John suddenly growled, "you ain't nothing but a chuckleheaded nincompoop. It's no wonder your mother named you—"

He never did finish his insult, however, for the huge hand of the outlaw Silvertip reached out, balled Blue John's shirt, and lifted him strangling into the air.

"Blue John," Sivertip said easily while I and everyone else around me stared in amazement, "in promulgating your esoteric cogitations or articulating your superficial sentimentalities and amicable, philosophical, or psychological observations, let your extemporaneous descantings and unpremeditated expatiations have intelligibility and veracious vivacity. Shun double entendres, prurient jocosity, and pestiferous profanity, obscure or apparent. And above all else, Blue John, be polite to your friends!"

Carefully then the big man set the bug-eyed outlaw Blue John back upon the earth and attempted to straighten his shirt. Blue John stared, gurgled, reached for his pistol and realized that it had been taken from him, and gurgled again, and suddenly he tightened his fist to come at his companion. Instantaneously, the meat-cleaver slash of Alpha Rachel "Silvertip" Garrett's huge fist neatly clipped Blue John's jaw, and without another word the thin and rangy outlaw dropped to the earth.

"He's my friend," Silvertip mumbled apologetically to my pa, "but I've enjoyed about all of his compliments I can stand. His manners are somewhat scant, and I reckon I'm tired of waiting for 'em to show up. Still, the poor misbeguided fool needs someone, so I'd best be loyal and stick with him. Maybe I can learn him a thing or two."

Pa clapped the big man on the shoulder. "You will. As Hyrum would say, you have more lip than a muley cow. Anyone who can speak as you have will have no trouble reforming a poor, unconscious outlaw."

Silvertip instantly turned red and was back to his old self. "Ah," he mumbled, "it wasn't nothing. Most folks think I ain't too smart, but my mother and pap were educated, and they learned me a few things, even if I don't always show it."

"They taught you well, my son's friend," Pa said quietly, and Silvertip beamed like he'd just been handed the winner's roses at the Irish Sweepstakes. And coming to that, maybe he had, for a compliment from Pa was a rare and meaningful thing, and not lightly given.

"Pa!" I called out, suddenly realizing that Marshal Tinsdale was headed directly toward him. "Look out! It's that marshal from Provo!"

But Pa only looked up at me, grinned, and waited for the marshal to reach him. The two men glared at each other; then they suddenly smiled and shook hands, and I was still staring in bewilderment when I felt a hand upon my shoulder.

"Hy," Ernest asked, "are you sure you're all right? There's a sight of blood on your leg. I thought that would've healed by now."

"Not hardly," I answered, noticing for the first time that my younger half-brother was suddenly growing. "But it will now. Golly, am I glad to see you, Ern. I was afraid you'd not get through."

Ernest smiled brightly. "No trouble at all. I had me a little up-scuddle with Loose-lip Lundstrum and his horse. Still, the horse was spirited, and last time I saw Loose-lip he was flying through the air with his legs flapping like a migrating bullfrog. Then, too, the telegraph operator at Soldier's Fort was some stubborn; he wouldn't send my message until I fetched old Chief Tabby along to encourage him. But finally he saw the light—"

"Chief Tabby? You saw him again?"

"Sure as lilacs smell sweet in spring I did. Me and Ingersol hunted his camp out. Fact is, he's the one who brought Pa and the rest of us here, showed us right where you'd be."

I stared at my little brother. He pointed behind me, I turned and looked, and there, standing quietly atop the rubble at the foot of the great cliff, were the ancient Chief Tabby and almost a dozen of his tribesmen.

"Ungh," the Chief grunted. "Hy-mum still strong, throwum money-rock far and well."

"Just luck," I declared modestly, knowing that it truly had been. "I don't—"

"Hy-mum have good heart. Tabby have good heart. Enn-nest have good heart. Tabby take Enn-nest as new son. Tabby giveum Hy-mum money-rock as gift. Takeum all the same takeum."

He stood still, in dignity, and the tall Ute brave with the scar down his face stepped forward and handed me the rock I had thrown at Felix Friendlessman. I looked closely into the man's eyes as he handed me the gold, for I knew who he was, but whatever I thought I'd see wasn't there. I saw only calmness—that, and a hard dignity that I knew I would never thoroughly understand.

"Thank you," I told the chief. "For as long as the sun shines upon these mountains, I and my family will treasure this great gift."

I don't know how much of what I said he understood, but old Chief Tabby bowed his head slightly. "It no considerable thing," he replied carefully. "Cover tracks over in your memory." Then he turned, was helped down from the rock, and was gone.

Suddenly there was a rattle of horses' hooves, and before I could hardly do more than turn around again, Ida Mae and Caleb Rhoades were there, and Ida Mae was once more in my arms.

"Ida Mae," Pa asked, and his voice was filled with surprise, "how did you get here?"

"I rode Pa's white mare up from Soldier's Fort."

"Alone?"

"Of course. I heard that Hyrum had been wounded, and I had to get here in a hurry."

"But—but—" I stuttered at Ida Mae, "I thought . . . Didn't you come here with my family?"

"I most certainly didn't. I didn't know anyone but your mother was coming, and I left her down at Soldier's Fort. You see, I knew *I* had to come, and so I did."

"Then who showed you the mi—"

Ida Mae quickly reached up and put her hand on my mouth. "Showed me what, Hyrum? Showed me you? That was easy. No one did, but somehow I was led right to where you'd be. I walked and climbed directly to your side. After all, that was my place, wasn't it?"

Well, what could a feller say to that? Nothing, for words at such a time aren't exactly needed. What is, however, is action, and a little of that I promptly initiated.

"Whew," Johnny said, grinning. "I'd admire, Hyrum, if you'd give me a few lessons, happen you ever take a break. I've been sparking Mattie Butts a little, and we *are* fixing to get married, but I can tell I am a babe in the woods when compared to your expertise."

"Me too," Jim grinned. "It's purely obvious that Hy's learned how honey draws more flies than vinegar when it comes to gathering women. I'll bet his verbal lather is some scented, too. Let's hear us a little of that sweet-talking syrup right now, little brother, and see how it increases what's already proceeding!"

"Now come on, fellers," Lyman put in, grinning from ear to ear, "can't you see how the poor boy is some busy. Kiss her a good one for me, Hy. That's the kind of lesson *I'd* like to see."

They all hooted. Pa and Marshal Tinsdale and his deputies and even the gentle outlaw Silvertip grinned, and both Ida Mae and I were getting redder'n maple leaves in October. This was going to have to stop, by thunder, or I—

"It plain to see boy knowum how," a deep voice grunted in agreement with my brothers, and I turned to find Zene Hill standing behind me. Good grief! I thought. What was this? A family reunion? Of course I knew it wasn't, but I can't hardly tell you how thrilled I was to see all of those folks there. Yes sir, friends and family are all the wealth a man ever needs in this life, and I surely had them in abundance.

"Yesum," Zene went on in his fake reservation talk, "it be plenty obvious. Lady, you be-um good squaw for boy. You tough likeum bottom of boot, tender likeum backfat of young steer." Zene rolled his eyes in obvious enjoyment of the fact that he was embarrassing poor Ida Mae and me plumb to death. "Yesum," he went on, "him heapum man, you heapum woman. Me betum in time make plenty heapum noisy kids."

I turned beet red and would maybe have slugged my sheep-herding partner had not other, more important things come to hand. Suddenly Felix Friendlessman stood there, glaring at Ida Mae and myself.

"Children," he snarled with derision. "Lucky, foolish children. Ida Mae, you and I had something fine between us, and with me you might have gone far. But now you choose to throw it all away on this . . . this *cripple!*"

Ida Mae turned white, but I stared straight at the man. "Don't you worry, Ida Mae," I said quietly, doing my best to control my temper. "Felix here thinks he's powerful evil, but that isn't so. Why, he isn't even a patch on a real bad man. He's just sort of petty, with a real mean streak in him."

"Bah," the man snorted, and then he spat. "Listen to my words, little girl, and remember. I will return when you have grown enough to become wise, and when I do, you will honor the promises you made me, promises sealed with the ring and with the kiss."

Well, I stared, thoroughly surprised. Friendlessman had fallen for Ida Mae, he truly had. Not that such an understanding thrilled me much, for it didn't. It only surprised me, is all.

I was about to come to Ida Mae's rescue, for I knew the man was trying to frighten her, to intimidate her, to punish her for turning against him. Therefore it can be clearly understood that I was just as surprised by Ida Mae's quick and ready response as I had been by Friendlessman's words, my family's timely appearance, and Silvertip's sudden verbosity. And believe you me, Ida Mae's response was quick and it was ready. That little woman needed help from no man alive. Right then I knew she was one to ride the river with, and again I determined one day to do it.

"Promises?" Ida Mae Sorenson snapped, drawing herself up stiffly and facing the tall man before her. "And kisses? Felix Ethelbert Friendlessman, I ought to have given you a kick instead of a kiss. And that ring of yours turned my finger green clear up to my elbow. I was lucky I didn't get the lockjaw from it! Promises indeed!"

"Why you rude and stubborn female jackass—"

"Female jackass? How could that be, you simpleton, you moron who claims to be educated? A female jackass is a jenny. A jackass is always a male. As well, some males are always jackasses. Especially you, Mr. Friendlessman, you misbegotten, half-baked excuse for a gentleman! Why, you . . . you're nothing but a festering pimple on the skin of time!"

Well, I grinned at Ida Mae's delightful way with words, but Felix Friendlessman fumed! "Miss Sorenson," he sputtered, "I've a mind to—"

"A mind?" Ida Mae snapped back, quicker'n scat. "Mr. Friendlessman, you've got no more mind than a mud coot. I've seen more brains in a lightning-struck sheep than you can claim. You have finally and truly lived up to your name, for you have no friends left in all the world. Why, I wouldn't look at you again if you were the last man in Sanpete Valley! And you might very well be, by the time you get out of jail.

"Hyrum," she then said as she spun to face me, "would you and your family be so good as to escort me off this mountain?"

I grinned and nodded, and as she and I turned away there was a loud cheer from my brothers—yes, and even from some of the others, if my ears hadn't mistaken me. Seemed like that little gal of mine was a real hand at winning friends.

Suddenly from down slope there was a flurry of movement, and I looked in time to see the little weasel Doolin scurrying down through the rocks, trying to escape. Without even thinking I shouted at him to stop, but of course he didn't.

Then without warning Silvertip reached out and took the old Spanish pike from my hand. Pulling back his arm, he heaved it quickly in Doolin's general direction. The pike arched through the air and slammed into a rock no closer than five feet from the fleeing little man, shattering itself to pieces. The throw was terrible, and poor Silvertip seemed embarrassed to have us see it. However, the results were what counted, and they were instantly evident.

It almost seemed as though poor Mr. Doolin had been shot. He screeched, grabbed his head with both arms, hollered and moaned, and finally dived headfirst into the rocks where he lay quivering and whining in fear.

I saw him do it, and so did the others. Virtually everyone sat up and took notice. The ability to act swiftly under fire never went unrecognized in a society of western men. That little thief could move! Such an instant sense of decision was an important asset in any frontier community, and I began to think maybe I had been wrong to order him away. His actions had to be saluted, and big Silvertip, who hated the name Alpha Rachel but manfully owned up to it anyway, supplied the verdict. "Feller's no ordinary coward," he said, and all of us there assembled, willing or otherwise, instantly agreed.

37

West Slope of Uintah Mountains—
Utah Territory

Ida Mae and I and my pa and brothers had a fine ride down from the mountain to Soldier's Fort and my mother and the railroad, and I wouldn't have stopped there except that Zene had reminded me that he still needed a camp tender, and Ma and Pa had reminded me as well that the family still needed money. In spite of the temporary truce between Pa and Marshal Tinsdale, Pa would still have to stay in hiding, and our family funds would be mighty limited for some time to come.

Somewhere behind us rode Deputy Tinsdale, his posse, and all their prisoners, and believe me, he had several. Ahead of us by about fifty feet rode my pa and my four brothers and Zenos Hill, side by side through the deepening twilight, and I'll have to admit that watching them choked me up so I could hardly talk. Just knowing they had risked their own lives to come and help me made me feel prouder'n a banty rooster in the first light of morning. Why, it was—

"They're wonderful!" Ida Mae suddenly declared, somehow sensing what I was feeling.

"They are," I agreed. "Good, strong men, all of them."

"Your mother is wonderful, too."

Well, I looked over at Ida Mae and grinned. Looked like a little peace had been made in other quarters while I'd been gone. "There is no finer thing," I said quietly, "than to have good friends like you and Zene and to be part of such a fine and wonderful family as is mine. I hope the Lord above knows how thankful I am to be a small part of all of you."

"He does, Hyrum. I'm sure He does. That's why He continues to bless you so."

"Well," I said sincerely, "you must be right, for I can't imagine a man having any greater blessings than I do."

"How's your leg feeling?" Ida Mae asked.

"Not bad. One of Tinsdale's posse was a doctor, and he cleaned it up good. He says all I need now is rest and time."

"Are you coming home?"

"No, I reckon not, at least for now. My job's here, and I'd better see it through. That way, happen Zene doesn't work me to death, I'll have plenty of time to heal."

Ida Mae giggled, and for a time we rode in silence while the darkness gathered quickly around us. "It is passing strange," I finally declared, "that I have been in the midst of more gold than a man can even imagine and yet have chosen to walk away and leave it behind, thus ensuring that my pa and my family will remain poor and so must struggle."

"Yes it is," Ida Mae responded quietly.

I reached down into my saddlebag and pulled out the heavy, gold-laden rock that Tabby had given me. "How much do you reckon this is worth?" I asked.

"Your word and your honor," Ida Mae answered instantly, and she looked steadily at me as she spoke.

Well, that set me back some, and so carefully I put the rock away again. "You're right," I finally admitted. "And you know something else, Ida Mae? That's what all the rest of the gold in that mine is worth too. My word and my honor. I gave ol' Caleb Rhoades my word that I didn't want none—I mean any—of that sacred money rock, and I meant what I said! That mine can sit there until doomsday, and I won't ever go back again."

"I know you won't, Hyrum. That was why I stopped you from mentioning that you had even seen it. You and I must make a promise that we will never mention, for so long as we both shall live, that we were there. It would be too difficult for others if we did. I now make that promise. Do you?"

"Yes," I said quietly, "I promise, though I feel badly to think that the children won't know of it."

"Children?"

"Uh . . . I . . . well . . . uh . . ."

"Perhaps we could write it down," Ida Mae said sweetly, rescuing me, "and keep it hidden until after we are gone."

"Yeah," I agreed. "We could do that."

"I'm proud of you," Ida Mae said sincerely as she reached over and took my hand in hers.

Well, I was waxing somewhat proud myownself, and my courage was growing more powerful by the minute. Still, it wouldn't do to show it, so very humbly I said thank you.

"But what about us, Hyrum?" Ida Mae suddenly asked.

"Us?"

"Yes, us. After your mission, of course. What if *we* need a little money as we begin our family?"

Well, I started to color up some, but it didn't matter because it was full dark and Ida Mae couldn't see my embarrassment. Still, such tongue oil as she was spreading out set my heart to pounding.

"No matter," I declared. "I'll find some other way. I took an oath about that gold, and need it or not, I'll never remove an ounce of it from that mine."

Ida Mae smiled sweetly. "I'm glad that you won't, Hyrum. I'm also glad that Mr. Rhoades told me I didn't have to take that oath."

"What? But—"

"Remember this, Hyrum. What I have is for you and for me, for the children you mentioned, and never for anything but good. And if you ever tell anyone about it, I'll deny it forever!"

Mystified, I stared at her. Then she smiled mischievously and drew back the hem of her long skirt, and I saw, glinting out of the top of her high boot, something that looked an awful lot like the tip of an anciently smelted gold bar.

"Ida Mae!" I said, and then she stopped me once again with a finger on my lips. Quickly then she started to sing; I gulped, grinned at this little lady who was so full of surprises, and joined in the singing with all my heart. Of course, I'm a singer from way back, having sung before crowds of several hundred—sheep, that is. Pa and the others up front heard us and joined in too, and it was a powerful chorus that we made coming down off that mountain.

A dozen or more songs we sang, Church songs and otherwise, and I was happier than I could ever remember being. That's what being with Ida Mae did to me. Made me happier'n a sheepdog with no wolves around. Finally, however, we all grew quiet. Ida Mae and I rode stirrup to stirrup with our arms about each other, and from then on we left the singing up to the coyotes that had joined up with us out in the dark.

Besides being a whole lot better looking than I was, Ida Mae Sorenson surely did have a better voice than me.

So did Pa, Lyman, Ernest, and maybe even Jim.

For that matter, so did the coyotes.

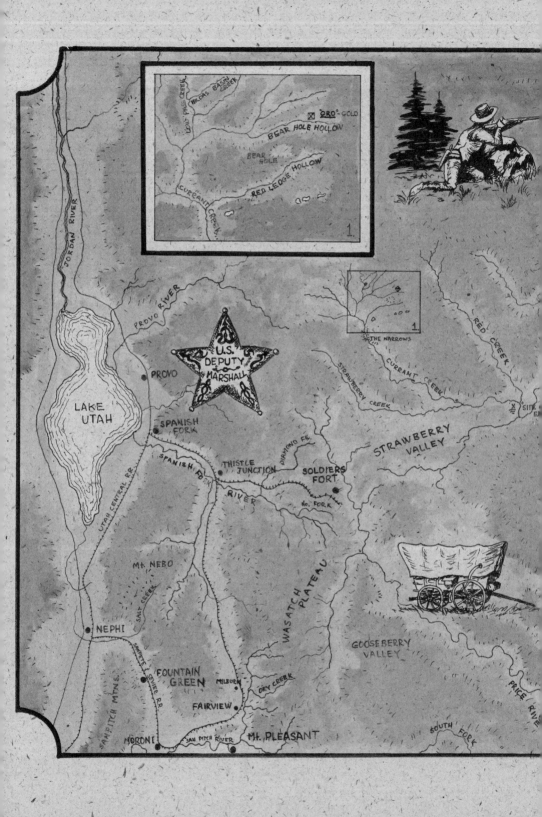